VICIOUS

A Truth or Lies World Collection VI

ELLA MILES

TRUTH OR LIES WORLD COLLECTION SERIES ORDER

ENZO & KAI'S STORY

Taken (Collection I)
Stolen (Collection II)

ZEKE & SIREN'S STORY

Sinful (Collection III)
Broken (Collection IV)

LANGSTON & LIESEL'S STORY

Vicious (Collection V)
Endless (Collection VI)

LIES WE SHARE: A PROLOGUE

LANGSTON

Five Years Old

"Langston!"

My name booms through the small house, rattling my tiny frame as I lie on the floor of the kitchen, staring up at empty cabinets. I wish these cabinets were filled with food, any food, to soothe my aching belly. I'd even take broccoli.

I don't know why my father has to yell so loudly. Our house is a tiny one-bedroom, one-bathroom, with a galley kitchen and a couch for a living room. My father could whisper in the house and I would still hear him.

I stop daydreaming about a stocked kitchen and pull myself up into a standing position. My bones pop and creak like an old man as I stand. It takes all of my willpower to walk into the living room where my father sits with a beer. He's staring up at the barely still working TV, watching some football game in between skipping channels.

I walk solemnly in front of him. There is only one reason my father calls my name. It's better to do what he says or my fate will be worse. Giving in means the pain will end faster.

My three foot nothing body stops in front of my father. I don't speak, I know better than to do something that idiotic.

"I told you to take out the trash," my father says.

"I did, but—" *Why did I open my mouth?*

It doesn't matter that the trash doesn't fit in the trashcan, and the trash company won't take any extra bags outside the designated can.

"It reeks in here! You didn't take out the trash like I said."

Smack.

My body is already prepared for the impact as his hand thumps across my cheek. I hold back the tears, knowing I just have to hold on until I'm no longer in his sight before I cry. Crying gets me beaten worse.

"Take out the trash now! Before I beat your ass until you can't sit for a week."

I run into the kitchen and yank the lid off the trashcan that is almost as tall as me, before using both of my hands to pull the bag out. It gets stuck—probably a liquor bottle my father jammed into the can.

I sweat and grit my teeth to keep from making a sound, to keep the tears inside. If I let them out, I'll end up with a broken bone. I do everything I can to get the trash bag out myself.

Finally, the bag comes free, knocking me off balance. I fall back to the ground, the bag landing on my lap. It smells like canned tuna and sour beer.

I wrinkle my nose.

I can feel my father's stare. I scramble to my feet, heave the bag up with my two tiny fists and carry it out the front door. Once outside, I can take a breath. Father won't care how long I take; he just wants me out of his sight and the smell gone.

I let the bag fall to the ground, dragging it down the front stairs and down the driveway until I reach the full trashcan.

I consider my options: leave the bag next to the trashcan and get in trouble when the trash company doesn't pick it up, or find another way to get rid of it.

I look at the house across the street that also has its trashcan out on the end of their driveway. It doesn't look like it's overflowing.

Maybe mine will fit?

It's worth a shot.

I drag my bag across the pothole-riddled street, hoping the bag doesn't rip. The bags we use aren't the durable kind; they're the kind that tears if you jostle the bag the wrong way. There is a high probability I'll leak trash all over the street—then I'll really get my ass whooped.

By some miracle, I make it to the neighbor's trashcan without a significant rip. I lift the lid off their can—*there's room!*

I heave my trash bag up...

"What are you doing?" a girl says.

I drop the bag at the sudden voice, and it lands in the trashcan. I snap the lid shut.

I look over at the girl crouched behind a bush, which must be the reason I didn't see her when I walked over. She's covered in dirt. I can't tell if those are freckles on her cheeks or just more dirt under her hazel eyes and shoulder-length blonde hair. The only thing girly about her is her pink shirt with a picture of a pony wearing a tiara on it.

"Disposing of a body," I say, wondering how she's going to respond. I figure if she calls her parents or the police and tells them there's a body in the bag, the relief when they discover no body will bode better for me than the truth.

I also expect my words will get rid of her faster than the truth.

I don't expect her to cock her head, her eyes to light up, and a smile to lift her lips.

"What are you doing?" I throw her words back at her as I cross my frail arms in front of my body.

"Hunting."

I raise my eyebrows. "Hunting what? I don't see a gun."

Her eyelashes flutter at that, but she's not afraid. You can't be scared to grow up on a street like ours.

"I don't think a gun would help me."

"What are you hunting?"

"A spider—I think its home is out here somewhere, but it keeps coming into my room at night."

I'm intrigued by this girl who hunts spiders.

I look back at my house. I should go back.

And do what?

I don't have any toys.

I don't have any food.

This girl will be a good distraction.

"I'll help you," I say.

"I don't need your help."

"Have you found the spider yet?"

"No."

"Then you need my help."

"Fine, but you have to do what I say. I'm the one in charge."

I smile. "Deal."

I walk over to where she is now crouched down again, examining the outside of a window where there are cobwebs scattered across the corner of the window.

"So, what does this spider look like?"

"He's big and black and has a red spot on it."

"And where did you see this spider?"

"It crawled on the floor by my bed last night. He scared the crap out of me. I'm going to find him. I think this is his web he uses to catch other bugs, and then he goes inside to sleep where it's warm." She points to a web along the windowsill.

"Uh-huh. What makes you think this web belongs to the same spider as the one you saw last night?"

That gets her thinking. "I don't know. Let's go inside and see if we can find a web there."

I nod and follow her into her house.

She starts crouching down in the living room.

"Where is your bedroom? Should we start there?"

She stops and looks at me with eyes that could kill. "This is my bedroom."

"Oh." She doesn't have a bedroom, either. She's just like me.

"Is that a problem? Can we not be friends because I don't have a bedroom? I'd like to see *your* bedroom then if you are too good for me."

I smile. I like how strong she is. She isn't embarrassed that she doesn't have a bedroom.

"Why are you smiling?"

"Because I sleep in the living room, too. I don't have my own bedroom either."

She smiles. "That's what I thought."

"Do you have any siblings?" I ask, sometimes kids have to share their couch with other kids.

"No, you?"

I shake my head.

That makes her smile more.

"Good, that means you need me to be your friend."

"I don't need you to be my anything. I don't need friends. I already have plenty of friends."

"Liar."

I frown. "I'm not lying!"

She takes my hand. "It's okay. I won't tell anyone that I'm your only friend."

I roll my eyes. *There is no winning with this girl.*

"Let's find this spider," I say.

She nods.

We both crouch down and search around the ten-foot by ten-foot square that is the living room.

"I found it!" she squeals.

I crawl over to where she's staring in the corner.

"You found the web and the spider, hunter."

She wrinkles her nose and sticks out her tongue. "Don't call me, hunter. My name is Liesel."

"Nope, your name is hunter."

"But that's a guy's name."

"Huntress?"

She nods, liking that better.

"What's your name?"

"Langston," I say my name out loud and shutter. My father calls me Langston. I only think of his beatings when I hear someone call me that name.

She notices; her eyes soft with sympathy as she looks at me more closely for the first time. She's probably noticing my swollen eye and bruise, but she doesn't say anything.

"Kill it before it gets away," I say, pointing to the spider that is now starting to crawl along the wall.

"I can't," her voice is quiet.

"Why not?"

"I just can't."

"You have to kill it. I think it's a black widow spider. It's poisonous. It could kill you if you don't kill it."

She thinks about my words for a second and lifts her pink sparkly flip flop to kill it, but then her foot slams back to her side. She can't kill the spider.

There is conflict in her hazel, gold speckled eyes. She needs the spider to be dead, but can't kill it herself.

I lift my worn, off-brand tennis shoes and slam it over the spider, killing it.

"Killer," she whispers.

"What?" I ask, terrified that she's going to be mad at me. I can't handle that. I really could use a friend.

"Your name. I'll call you killer. You'll call me huntress, and I'll call you killer."

I grin and nod, liking the nickname a lot better than her calling me Langston.

Just then, my stomach growls. I haven't eaten anything all day.

Hers growls louder a second later, making us both laugh.

"You got any food?" I ask.

She hesitates and bites her lip before she answers. "No."

She's lying—her first lie. I can tell. But when I look her over, I realize she needs whatever food she has a lot more than I do.

"It's okay. Enzo said he'd bike over later and bring me food."

"Enzo?"

"He's my friend."

"Sure, he is."

I laugh.

We both lay on the floor, leaning our heads against the foot of the couch.

Her smile drops as suddenly as it appeared. "How did you get that bruise on your eye?"

"That man I killed and put in your trashcan—he fought back. But don't worry, I won," I lie. Mine is an obvious lie, unlike hers. I'm five years old. I couldn't kill someone if I wanted to. The most I've ever killed is a spider. Although, I know my future. I suspect killing will become a means to survive.

She nods, pretending to accept my lie like I did hers, but she knows the truth. She knows my mother or father did this to me. It's the tale of too many kids in our neighborhood.

"I think we should make a pact," she says suddenly.

I sit up, looking at her. "Oh, yea? What kind of pact?"

"I'll hunt whatever needs hunting for you, and you'll kill for me." She holds out her pinky finger to me.

I'm not really sure why she thinks we need this deal. Maybe she needs me to kill her father for her like I need someone to do it for me. I'm not big enough to kill him now. But if she asks me to kill hers in a few years, I will gladly.

I link my pinky finger with hers. "And if either of us breaks our promise?"

"Then, the other gets whatever they want. They can take whatever they want of the other's. Demand anything. This is an unbreakable vow."

"Like in Harry Potter?"

"Yep."

"Fine, this is an unbreakable vow. I will always kill for you. And you will always hunt for me. Deal?"

We shake our pinkies together. "Deal."

CHAPTER 2

LIESEL

E ight Years Old

The sound of the police siren sends chills down my spine as I try to sleep on the couch in the living room. I only have a light blanket, but I'm still drenched in sweat from the summer heat and lack of air conditioning. I don't know what time it is, but I'd guess past midnight. I should be asleep—I have school in the morning—but even without the sirens blaring, I wouldn't be able to sleep between the heat and my empty belly.

I wait for the sirens to disappear again, but they grow louder, closer.

I hold my breath as I hear the sirens just outside my house.

When you live where I do, sirens are never a good thing. Sirens aren't coming to save someone. They are coming to lock someone up or to drag the body off after an overdose or gunshot. The police never make it here in time to stop the suffering. Not in a poor area like this.

I start running out of oxygen, and still, the sirens don't leave. Their lights continue whirling, reflecting into the living room that serves as my bedroom.

I lift my head to glance out the window and gasp.

The police are entering Langston's home.

I jump up and run to the window and peer through the broken shades at the scene before me.

My mind races with all the horrible things that could have happened to the boy who has quickly become my best and only friend. I call him killer, but the truth is I don't think he's killed much more than a spider. I still call him that because it beats seeing the torment in his eyes when I call him Langston like his father does. Someday, Langston will earn the nickname I give him. I know that. But for now, it's still an innocent nickname—one that doesn't haunt him, or me, yet.

What happened?

Did Langston's father finally take things too far? Did he hurt him, injure him, kill him?

Please, no.

Please let it be his father. Please let him have drunk too much alcohol. Let him have alcohol poisoning or, better yet, be dead.

Let it be Langston's mother.

Just don't let it be my killer—Langston has to live.

I should wait inside my house, where I at least have the illusion of being safe.

I can't.

Not when I don't know if Langston is alive, hurt, or dead.

I run out the front door, not giving a damn about my own safety.

My feet are bare; my frayed T-shirt hangs down below my knees, hiding my shorts beneath, and my hair hangs in frizzy blonde waves. None of that matters—only Langston.

"Langston!" I shout, using his name instead of killer.

I run across the street, slipping between the two police cars that have arrived so far. I hear more approaching sirens in the distance.

I make it across the street. The front door is open. I should wait outside, but I can't.

I run up the uneven stairs full of cracks. I know each crack by heart, which makes it easy to avoid hurting my bare feet as I run.

Then I'm inside the small house already filled with too many people.

Three police officers.

Langston's father.

I don't see Langston.

"Langston!" I shout even though I shouldn't. I should blend into the shadows for as long as I can before being noticed. As soon as the police officers notice me, they'll escort me outside, and then I won't know anything.

The female officer turns at the sound of my small voice. Her lips thin in disappointment as she walks over to me. She squats down so she is eye level with me.

"I'm so sorry," she starts.

"No," I whisper. "He can't be dead."

I look past her, searching for the boy—the only one in my life who matters, who will ever matter.

She shakes her head.

What does that shake mean?

"Your mother—she didn't make it. She's in heaven," the officer says, putting her hands on my shoulders to comfort me.

I exhale a breath.

I should cry, show some emotion. This woman thinks I'm Mrs. Pearce's daughter, that I just lost my mother. She'll let me stay with Langston if I cry.

So that's what I do. I cry like I just lost a caring mother, instead of being relieved that my best friend is still alive.

The woman pulls me into a hug. That's when I spot him, and my heartbeat settles.

Langston is standing in shorts and no shirt, revealing his too-thin frame. His hair is a shabby mess on top of his head, and he's staring down at something.

His mother.

My heart breaks for him. He wasn't that close to her, but his mom was the only source of affection or love he got at home.

Now it will be just him and his father.

I keep the crying up, and Langston eventually looks at me. He laughs quietly when he sees my dramatic acting.

Finally, the woman releases me.

"I want to go see my brother."

"Of course, sweetie. You two should be together."

I walk over to Langston with tears still dripping out of my eyes.

"You're a terrible actress," he says teasingly when I walk over.

I wipe my tears on the back of my T-shirt. "I fooled her, so I can't be that bad."

He grins.

And then we link our hands. "Thank you," he says.

"For what?" I frown, not understanding why he's thanking me.

"For crying, even though you hate it, so you can be here with me."

I squeeze his hand. I'm beginning to think I'd do anything for this boy. Fake crying so I can hold his hand while he mourns his mother barely touches the surface of what I'd do.

CHAPTER 3

LANGSTON

Today should be the worst day of my life.

I'm burying my mother today.

Today is the worst day of my life, but not because today is my mother's funeral.

Today is the worst day of my life because of what I'm going to have to tell Liesel.

I'm wearing an oversized suit my father got at Goodwill and sitting in the front pew of the church next to my father.

There are a dozen or so people sitting behind us as the preacher talks. I don't listen. All I can think about is what I'm going to say to Liesel.

How am I going to break the news?

I can't even believe it myself.

I'm thankful for the time in the church. At first, I thought I wanted Liesel sitting next to me. Right now, I couldn't be happier that my father didn't allow it and that she's sitting three pews back. As long as we aren't together, I don't have to tell her.

Too soon, the funeral ends. The preacher stops talking, and my father and I stand as we follow the casket out of the church. The cemetery is next to the church, so we don't have to drive anywhere.

We just walk to her grave with the small congregation of people behind us. I don't look back even though I can feel Liesel's stare, trying to reach out and comfort me.

I'm not the one who needs comfort, though.

Time moves too fast.

The preacher speaks more words.

My mother's casket is lowered into the ground.

And just like that—it's over.

My father gives me a stern look. "I expect you home in an hour."

I nod. He walks to the car and drives off.

A few people approach me, giving me their condolences.

I just stand, staring at my mother's gravestone like it's the most fascinating thing in the world. Reading my mother's name, dates of birth and death, and the words 'Beloved mother and wife' over and over to avoid what comes next.

Liesel doesn't speak. She just takes my hand like she did in the house three days ago when I woke to find my mother had overdosed on fentanyl.

I already know that isn't true. My father killed her. He slipped her the extra pills. He wanted her gone, so he got rid of her.

And then I feel something thorny being pushed in my other hand. I look down and see that Liesel has shoved a single rose-like flower into my hand.

"I'm sorry I couldn't afford more, but I think your mom would have liked it," she says.

I stare at the flower, similar to a rose but not. It's pretty—my mother would have liked it.

I look up at my mother's grave and then all the others around it. The surrounding graves have flowers. My mother's is bare.

The bastard didn't even spend money on flowers!

I feel the tear slipping down my cheek. I'll cry waterfalls later when I'm alone in the house. Right now, the single tear is enough.

I step forward, and Liesel steps right with me. Together we place the single flower at the base of my mother's grave.

"Goodbye, Mom," I whisper, keeping my tears and pain inside the best that I can.

Liesel pulls me into a hug. She isn't one for emotion. She's not a hugger, but in this moment, she is.

The embrace only makes me sob harder until there is snot running down my face and onto the shoulder of her black dress.

"I'm sorry." I let go of her as I suck the snot back in and try to compose myself. There are more important things to worry about than the loss of my mother right now.

Liesel's eyes flick right then left over my face. "What is it?"

How does she always know when something is wrong with me?

"We're moving," I spit out before I lose my nerve.

Her mouth falls, and tears spring into her eyes for the first time.

"But...your mom just died."

"Dad's remarrying some rich woman."

"Oh."

I don't have to tell Liesel what that means. I don't have to tell her that my father killed my mother. She can put the pieces together as easily as I did.

"He'll pay for this. Someday, he'll pay," Liesel says, her voice lower and grittier than before.

I nod, agreeing. One day my father will suffer for all of his sins—none worse than killing my mother.

Right now, I don't need to worry about my father though.

"Come on, we don't have much time." I grab Liesel's hand again and drag her over to the empty field behind the church.

"What are we doing?"

"I have a lot to teach you before I leave." Pain strikes my heart when I say the word—leave. I can't imagine leaving this girl. Not seeing her every day. Not talking. Not being in her life. It can't be true.

I let go of her hand and face her.

"Okay, first lesson, self-defense," I start.

"I know how to defend myself." She folds her arms and pouts, offended.

"Do you?"

She nods furiously.

We are relatively close in size. I have maybe an inch on her, but soon the boys at school will tower over her. They'll have more muscle and strength than she'll ever dream about. Not to mention all the creepy uncles and neighbors that Liesel will interact with in her life. She needs to be able to protect herself if I'm not here to do it.

I grab her, throwing my arms as tightly as I can around her, already knowing that I'm stronger than she is.

She wiggles in my arms. "Let me go, you asshole."

I hold her tighter.

"You can do this, huntress. Don't panic, think of a way to escape. Find my weakness and exploit it. Then run."

She stops struggling and thinks for a moment.

I search her eyes, trying to guess what she's going to do before she does it, preparing myself for her move.

Her knee pummels into my groin. I immediately release her, and she takes a step back, laughing lightly as I double over in pain.

"That's not funny," I say, my voice squeaking from the pain.

"It is to me."

"I told you to run after you got free."

"I know how to run. What's the next lesson you're worried about before you leave? Going to teach me how to kill too?"

We've never talked about it, but she knows what I'm capable of. I don't know how or why, but my future will involve killing people. It's not abnormal for our neighborhood; you either kill or be killed. My father tops the list of people that deserve to die. I'm too small to accomplish the task now, but soon...

I haven't killed yet, but I know how to hold a gun. I know how to use a knife; all I'm waiting for are my muscles to come in and the right opportunity.

But Liesel will never have to kill. I won't allow her soul to be in the torment to which mine is destined.

"No. We keep our promises. You'll hunt when I need you to."

"And you'll kill for me," she whispers back.

I nod. "I won't let you kill. I'll kill for you. No matter where I live. No matter where I go to school. I promise you."

She exhales a heavy breath.

"And you promise you'll never kill? You will call me and let me do it?"

"Yes," she says.

I'll hold her to that.

I don't have to worry about her killing to survive. I taught her the basics for protection, although, she'll need more lessons. What's more worrying is that she doesn't have any money or food. I've stolen food and money for us when we needed it. None of our parents can provide such simple things. At eight, we already have to feed ourselves.

I glance at my watch. Forty-five minutes until Dad said I needed to be home—it's not enough time.

"You need money," I say. I'm hoping that after my dad remarries his new wife will be gracious enough to give me money to help support Liesel. But until then, I need to ensure Liesel has money for food.

She opens her mouth to disagree but then snaps it shut. She knows she needs money.

"What do you suggest?"

"We are going to steal it from someone who doesn't need it. Okay, huntress?"

"And where are we going to find someone around here who doesn't need money?"

I frown. I honestly have no idea.

"You're the huntress. Do you have any ideas?" I ask, embarrassed that I don't have an idea of how to help her.

She smiles. "Maybe."

I grin along with her.

"Do you have money for bus fare?" she asks.

I reach into my pocket and pull the twenty-dollar bill out—the only money I have left.

"This enough?"

"It'll have to be."

We spend the next twenty minutes on the bus driving toward the beach. We've ridden the bus this way before, but usually to enjoy the beach, not to steal.

We stand on the crowded beach. I suggested we go to an area with shops and stores, but Liesel disagreed.

"Okay, we're here. Nothing but tourists for miles."

She grins. "Exactly. Tourists swimming in the ocean, leaving their belongings on the beach. And tourists always have cash."

I suck in a breath. "I hope you're right."

"I am. I hunted, it's your turn to go in for the kill."

I laugh. "Stay right here. I'll be back soon with plenty of moola."

She stands on the edge of the beach as I jog along the tourists' belongings, looking for an easy target.

Liesel was right—there are unattended bags everywhere. But if I start going through belongings, I'm going to draw attention to myself. So rather than going through every bag, I pick my targets carefully, only selecting bags where the wallets are already in plain sight.

I snatch a wallet and pull out the cash before dropping it back down before anyone notices.

I do this three more times, collecting almost two hundred dollars and then run back to Liesel. It should be enough for a while, but not enough to grow up on. She needs money for years. Money to feed her, clothe her, send her to dance classes or let her join the softball league. Money she'll never have. Money I'll never be able to give her.

"Here," I say, shoving the money into her hands.

"Wow, that's a lot of money. Um...maybe you should keep some of it."

"I won't need it where I'm going."

She nods slowly in understanding and fists the money.

I glance at my watch. I'm officially a half-hour late. I know the beating I'll have to endure for being late, but I don't care. Tomorrow, we leave. Tonight, I'm spending every second with this girl.

CHAPTER 4

LIESEL

We sit in comfortable silence on the bus ride home as I hold more money in my fist than I've ever held in my life because of this boy—this boy I'm about to lose.

It's more than him just moving away; there is something else happening. I don't understand what it is, but I can feel it in my bones. After tonight, everything changes.

The bus stops. We climb off and start walking the five blocks to our houses.

"You need to go home?" I ask.

Langston looks down, shuffling his feet with his hands in the pockets of his suit.

"No. I think we should camp under the stars tonight. One last epic night together."

"We don't have any camping equipment. How are we going to camp?" I really wish he'd stop insinuating that this is the end. We'll see each other again; it will just be different and less frequent.

"It's summer. I'll get us a thick comforter to lay on and some snacks. We can camp in the woods behind your house."

"Okay."

We separate at our houses.

I walk in the front door already knowing my mother has to work and isn't home. I glance out back as I enter and see Langston sneaking in the backyard a few minutes later.

He lied.

His father expects him home. I can feel it in my bones. But I'm too selfish to give up my last night with Langston so that his father doesn't beat him.

I quickly change into jean shorts and the T-shirt Langston gave me for my birthday that has a warrior princess on the front. The princess looks like she's about to go hunting. I pull my hair up in a ponytail and consider where I should hide the money we just stole.

I decide on the floorboard beneath my bed and shove the money deep inside, hoping my mother doesn't find it.

I walk back outside and find Langston already waiting. He too changed into more casual clothes—ripped jeans, a black T-shirt, and baseball cap. Years of sneaking around have made it easy for him to quickly step in and out of his house without his father noticing.

"Ready, killer?"

He smiles as I say his nickname. He swings a backpack over his shoulder, and then we head into the woods behind my house.

The sun is just beginning to set as Langston lays out the large blanket from his backpack.

We sit down on the blanket, surrounded by trees. For a moment, it feels like we are in our own little world. The real world no longer exists.

Langston pulls two Snickers bars out of his backpack and tosses one to me. I catch it with a smile.

Snickers are our favorite. They're cheap and filling and delicious.

"So, where are you moving to exactly?" I ask, biting into my candy bar.

Langston's eyes cut to me with a wary expression. "Palm Beach."

"Oh, wow. So this woman is really rich."

He nods and stops eating.

I do the same.

"I don't want you to worry, Liesel. This isn't the end. Our relationship won't change. We just won't see each other as often, but we can still count on each other. Always."

"I know."

"Maybe we shouldn't talk about this anymore tonight. Tomorrow is for goodbyes and tears; tonight is for making memories."

"Yea, we should enjoy our last night before you move."

"What should we talk about?" I take another bite of my Snickers bar, savoring each bite.

He lays back on the blanket.

I do as well.

We stare up at the sky, now shades of orange and red—the last moments before the sun sets.

"About a future that we can control. One where we aren't poor. One where we can live the life we want."

I frown as I look over at him. "But we never dream. What's the point?"

"The point is that the one benefit of my new life is that I just might be able to get us the life we want someday."

I take the last bite of my Snickers bar. He does the same.

Langston is so optimistic. His life might change for the better, but I'm destined to be stuck in this town forever.

I just smile at Langston. I don't care what we talk about tonight. I only want to spend it with him.

"You start. What do you want, killer?"

"First, I want everyone to call me killer. I want to be the strongest badass I know. I want to be in complete control and be able to take on any foe."

As he speaks, I know that will someday come true.

"What about you?" he asks.

I stretch my arms up and place them behind my head, thinking about a question I've never thought before. Most eight-year-olds have already thought about what they want to be when they grow up. They dream of becoming doctors, teachers, president, astronauts. I just dream of a day when I won't have to worry if the meal I just ate is going to have to last me days or hours.

"I just want to live in a world where I have enough money to buy as much food as I want and have a real bed in my own bedroom."

"That's not a dream. That's going to happen. Dream bigger. What job do you want?"

"Lawyer," I answer automatically. That seems like the kind of job where you can make a change in other people's lives.

"Where do you want to live? Beach, mountains, city?"

"Definitely the beach." I like Miami's warm weather. I can't imagine living anywhere else.

"Me too. The mountains are too cold, and the city is too busy. I want to live on my own private island."

My eyebrows raise. "We're really dreaming big."

"Absolutely. But I can't figure out what I want my house to look like."

"Ooh, I can help with that. It should be big and made of glass," I say as I relax my arms to my side again.

"Glass? Doesn't that mean it will be easier to break?"

I laugh. "No, it will be full of light. You'll have views of the ocean from every room."

"I like that. And it needs a big kitchen. One that can cook a meal for a dozen people."

"And an infinity pool!"

"And a huge balcony!"

"A bathroom outside!"

"A deck covered in vines and greenery that makes it feel like we are living in the jungle."

I look up at the stars.

"And the clearest view of the moon and stars," I say.

Langston's hand intertwines with mine. "That's the most important part."

"So that's your house. Where will I live?" I ask.

"In the house with me."

"You mean as your wife?"

He shrugs. "Maybe, or maybe we'd live there as friends. Would it be so bad, being married to me?"

"I don't know. We're eight. And all the marriages I've seen have failed. I don't want us to fail."

"Maybe we should kiss and see how we like it. That way, we'll know if we should be married or just live there as friends."

I've never thought of kissing a boy before. But I know Danica in my class kissed Ian last week.

"Okay, kiss me then." I sit up, leaning on one elbow.

Langston leans on his elbow, facing me. It's beginning to get dark outside, but I can tell he's nervous. He's hesitant. I don't understand why. It's only a kiss.

"Kiss me, killer."

Then his lips are pressed against mine. Our noses bump. Somehow, I end up biting his bottom lip.

"Ow," he says as we both pull away.

Then we laugh.

"Well, I guess that answers that," I say.

"Yep, friends it is," Langston says.

I smile, as we both lay back on the blanket and start trying to make images out of the stars.

For some reason, I can't get that kiss out of my head. Langston was my first kiss. It seemed terrible. I don't understand why anyone would want to kiss. But then again, I'm eight.

I snuggle up to Langston as we begin to drift off to sleep. I feel his steady heartbeat. I know what he's risking staying with me tonight. I won't let him get hurt for me. It may not be part of our pact, but I make a silent promise to myself to never let him get hurt. Tomorrow, I'll do what I can to keep that vow.

♡

I WAKE UP BEFORE DAWN, KNOWING THAT LANGSTON WILL WAKE AS soon as the sun touches his face. I have very little time to do this.

Carefully, I rise off Langston's arm.

He doesn't move.

I smile at my sleeping boy. Then I grab the T-shirt, hat, and jeans he took off when it got too hot last night. He's sleeping on the blanket only in his boxers.

I run off back to my house through the early morning hours. Once inside, I quickly throw on Langston's clothes.

His jeans and T-shirt fit pretty well since we are about the same size. Then I pull my hair up in a bun and shove it under my hat.

I look at myself in the mirror in the bathroom. Everything girly about me is gone. If I have to speak, this won't work. But I have to try. I have to try to protect the boy who always protects me.

I run across the street as the sun begins to climb.

I glance back and don't see Langston following me. He's going to be pissed, but I don't care. I have to do this for him, just like he would for me.

I take a deep breath when I reach the front door, trying to prepare myself. I've dealt with more pain than most eight-year-olds have. I know what it feels like to be hungry. To sleep alone. To fear someone will break in and hurt you at night.

But I've never been physically hurt before.

I push the hat down as low as I can over my eyes and push the door open loudly. I practically stomp inside, ensuring that anyone inside can hear me.

"I told you to be home an hour after the funeral," Langston's father says in a booming voice.

I don't look up, but I see his boot covered feet in front of me.

"I had to stay up all night to get your shit packed because you ran off."

He wasn't worried where Langston was. Missing free labor and not being able to sit back and drink beer all night were his only concerns.

"Look at me, boy!"

I don't.

That pushes him over the edge.

Slap.

I feel it hard across my cheek. My instinct is to run. Or, at the very least, try and fight back to protect myself.

I can't. I have to endure this for Langston. Spending his final night with me shouldn't get him beaten.

"You stupid fucking son of a bitch."

A punch to my chest knocks me to the ground. I land hard on my ass. I'm going to have a bruise in both places.

I focus my energy on keeping my face pointed at the ground to hide my true identity from Mr. Pearce. From the smell of alcohol oozing off his breath, I doubt he'd look close enough to notice, though.

Kick.

My body flings from his boot in my back. I'm not much of a crier, but that does it. I can't hold back my tears. For the first time, I realize why Langston is a crier. There is no other way to deal with this kind of pain except to cry.

I dissolve into my body as the pain wrecks me. My sensitive skin bruises while my ribs crunch as he kicks me over and over.

I've lost track of how many times he's kicked me.

His curse words have all muffled together.

Without warning, he grabs my arm and forces me into a standing position.

"Get out of my sight. I can't look at you. Clean yourself up and come back when you are presentable." He releases my arm, and I stumble, trying to remain on my feet.

The world is spinning; tears stream down my cheeks, everything in my body hurts. But somehow I stay upright.

"Cynthia will be here at five to pick us up and take us to our new home. If you are one minute late, I'll beat you until you're dead. Understand, Langston?"

I nod. Even if I wanted to speak, I couldn't.

"Get out!" he yells.

Finally, I run.

Every step I take requires all of my energy, to put one foot in front of the other, to keep from falling flat on my face.

This is Langston's life. This will always be his life until he's old enough to put a stop to it. He might be getting a fancier house to live in, but it won't stop his father.

At least I was able to prevent one more beating he had to endure. If I could, I'd take all the pain for him, but I can't.

As soon as I'm out of the house, I consider my options.

I thought I'd be able to go back to my house afterward. I could change clothes, put on a couple of bandaids and tell Langston I fell off my bike or something. But there is no hiding what I did—no hiding the bruises, the blood, the tears.

Langston will be pissed at me. He'll be angry and might even confront his dad, which would make everything I did moot. I'm not going to let that happen.

Yesterday was about making memories together.

Today was supposed to be about saying goodbye. About finding a way to connect in our new normal.

New tears spring.

We just lost our last day together because of me.

But I saved him from a beating. It was worth it. Even if I don't say goodbye.

I can't stay here.

Langston will eventually go home after he looks for me. I just have to make sure he shows up by five o'clock.

I run into my house and find a utility bill on the counter. I turn the envelope over and grab a marker before writing Langston a note.

KILLER,

I HAD TO GO WITH MY MOM TO WORK TODAY. I'LL TRY TO MAKE IT BACK before you leave at five. If I don't make it back in time, I'll see you soon.

—HUNTRESS

I GRAB SOME OF THE CASH LANGSTON AND I STOLE, AND THEN I leave. I'm not sure if I'll return in time to see Langston before he leaves, but I can't spend the entire day with him. He'd figure it out, and that would break me worse than Mr. Pearce's boot did.

The seconds, minutes, hours drag as I ride the bus to the mall and buy some new clothes that fit me, covering my arms and legs. I look at myself in the mirror in the public bathroom. The only visible mark now is where he grabbed my neck.

I brush my hair so it hangs down over my neck, making it that much harder for anyone to notice.

Finally, I take the four-thirty bus back home.

I don't know if I'll make it in time to see Langston before he leaves. I leave it up to fate.

I walk down our street at ten til five.

I'm not sure what to do. *Do I go over to Langston's? Or do I just go to my own house and try to forget about the boy?*

"I didn't think you'd show," Langston says from his house's doorstep, making my decision for me.

"I'm sorry, I did everything I could to get back. Mom needed me to help her clean houses—"

"Liar."

I frown.

"Your mother got home at noon. Want to try another lie, or do you want to tell me why you didn't spend my last day here with me?" He stands up and starts to approach me.

A vein is popping in his forehead, but he's wearing a T-shirt and shorts, and I don't spot any visible bruises.

I exhale a sigh of relief. I saved him from a beating. I would give up my last day with him over and over again if it meant I could spare him pain.

"I'm waiting. What lie are you going to tell me, Liesel?"

Liesel? He's pissed. He never calls me Liesel.

"Hugh, down the street, invited me over. I couldn't say no. He's going to be my only friend once you're gone."

"You're going to replace me, just like that? Like I mean nothing to you?"

I don't answer. How he can think that I lied about being with my mother but not about being with a friend is unbelievable. Why wouldn't I want to be here for my last hours with him?

He shakes his head. "I can't believe we were ever friends."

His words hurt worse than my cracked ribs.

I feel the burning of a tear in my eyes, but I don't let it out.

I swipe my hair to one side, revealing the bruise, revealing the truth.

But Langston won't even look at me. He's so irate.

"Langston! Time to go," Mr. Pearce says as a new Mercedes sedan pulls up.

Mr. Pearce walks to the front passenger side. A beautiful woman sits in the driver's seat—his new wife.

Langston still doesn't look at me. He just starts walking to the car.

"Langston," I whisper, hoping he'll look at me.

He'll give me a hug.

He'll say we are still best friends.

That he'll call.

Take care of me.

That this changes nothing.

Instead, he climbs into the back of the car without a word, without a glance back.

I watch in horror as the woman drives off with my best friend. I'm left stunned.

He left without a goodbye.

I hate him.

I shouldn't have taken the beating for him. It wasn't worth it.

I. Hate. Him.

I fall to the ground in a crumpled ball.

I hate him.

But that's a lie too. I can't hate him. Not yet. Soon though, I promise to hate him, to make it true. Because everything between us was a lie.

CHAPTER 5

LANGSTON

Fifteen Years Old

I've spent the last few years pretending that I didn't know who Liesel Dunn was. That when her mother took a job as a maid in my friend Enzo's house recently and they moved into his guest house, that I didn't know her. I pretend that at one point she wasn't the most important person in my life.

I pretend she was just a girl, just like all the rest.

A girl I would try to kiss, maybe even one day fuck before moving on to the next girl, and then the next and the next.

I pretend that Liesel means nothing to me. I pretend I don't ask Enzo about his new roommate because I care but just because I have a fascination with all girls. I'm a horny bastard, after all. That's all it is.

Zeke truly hates her. He thinks she's a snob. He doesn't know that she's broken. That she only has money because I give money to Enzo, who gives money to her.

Enzo, on the other hand, likes Liesel. *But what do I care?*

He can have the lying whore if he wants.

I don't hate her—I just don't care anymore.

Liesel has spent the last several years either ignoring me or hating me. She also pretends I was never a part of her life. Yet, she still hangs out with the three of us constantly.

So annoying.

"I'm going to need you tonight," Enzo says as he slams his locker shut.

I pull my algebra textbook out of my locker. "Just tell me the time and place."

Enzo nods.

I've been working for Enzo for the last year. I always knew I would. It was my destiny, as it was Zeke's. The three of us will conquer the world together. Threatening, stealing, killing to keep the empire that Enzo will one day inherit from his father.

We are the bad guys now.

"Do you need me?" Zeke asks.

Enzo turns to him.

"I could really use an outlet." Zeke pounds his fist into his other hand.

"Who are you guys taking down?" Liesel asks, wrapping her arms around Enzo's neck.

He kisses the back of her hand.

"Nothing you need to worry about, Liesel," Enzo says.

Liesel sighs and lets go of him as she makes her way to the middle of the group. She folds her arms as she looks into each of our eyes, trying to get answers. I don't think she wants to know because she wants to judge us. It's more because she's a nosy bitch who wants to be able to control my life like she did when we were little.

"Finally going to get this one his first kill?" Liesel asks, gesturing in my direction.

I seethe. She doesn't know that I've already earned her nickname for me. I've killed. I don't know if tonight's mission is to kill, but if Enzo requires it of me, I will.

My soul is already lost. I'm evil, and I like it. I won't let Liesel or anyone else change me.

Zeke laughs. "Langston isn't capable of killing a fly, sweetheart. If anyone does the killing, it will be me."

Liesel's eyes dart from Zeke to me. Zeke's words are true. He's killed the most of all of us so far. He's the biggest, the oldest, but Enzo and I will catch up soon. The only reason I don't have as big of a number as Zeke is because I do most of the behind the scenes work. I'm the most skilled with a computer. I've become both the hunter and the killer.

Liesel searches for the truth in my eyes, but she can no longer read me as easily as she once could.

When she doesn't find what she's looking for, she gives up and turns to Enzo.

"Walk me to class," Liesel says, shoving her textbook into Enzo's hands with a wink.

She tosses her blonde curled hair over her shoulder as she loops her hand into the crook of Enzo's arm, and he starts leading her away. I'm left to stare at her ass in a tight black dress with wedge heels, remembering her full face of makeup.

What the hell was that?

The only time I've ever seen her wear a dress was for my mother's funeral. I've never seen her wear a dress, or makeup, or style her hair like this. High school has changed her. Money has changed her.

Zeke makes a whipped sound at Enzo, who just flips him off as they round the corner.

My blood boils.

I'm not jealous, just pissed. I didn't think she'd become this fake just to get into Enzo's pants.

Not that he cares about her in that way. He might fuck her a couple of times, but he doesn't love her. He'll fuck her and then expect her to go right back to being friends like they are now.

Three hours later, I spot Liesel waiting for Enzo to walk her to lunch.

I can't take it anymore.

"If you're just looking for someone to break that sweet hymen of yours, look no further," I say as I approach her with a laugh.

Liesel folds her arms and stares at me like I'm a demon she wishes she could send to hell.

"Why would I want to fuck a puppet like you when I can have sex with the king?"

I laugh harder. "Enzo? Really? You think he wants to fuck you?"

"Yes. He does."

I shake my head as I put one hand on the wall behind her, leaning close but not too close.

"Enzo's like me. He's a fuck 'em and leave 'em type. I don't think your pretty little heart can take it."

I tug on her blonde curls—I can't resist.

She bats my hand away.

"I'm tougher than I look. And I know how to wrap a guy around my finger. If I want Enzo, I'll have Enzo."

I laugh. "Enzo Black will never be yours."

She pushes off the wall. "Don't worry, I'm not planning on stealing him away from you guys. You and Zeke wouldn't survive without your fearless leader telling you what to do all the time."

I growl.

She smirks victoriously.

"I'm calling in our pact," I say, preventing her from walking away.

"Our pact? Oh, you mean the pact we made when we were five? Before I knew you were a giant asshole?"

"Friday night. Meet me at Enzo's. We're going hunting."

She shakes her head and stomps off.

It's a test to see if she'll come—if deep down she still cares.

Now I just have to wait to see if she shows up or not.

CHAPTER 6

LIESEL

I finish the braid down the back of my head and then stare at myself in the mirror. I look like Katniss with my braid, all black clothes, and hunter mentality. All I need now is a bow and arrow and I'd be a true hunter.

Still, I feel ready. This day came a lot sooner than I expected it to. I expected I'd be older, about to leave this town for good. On the other hand, this day couldn't come fast enough.

I know without Langston telling me what today is about. There is only one reason he would call on our pact after years of ignoring and hating each other.

To kill his father.

I hate Langston.

I hate that he ignores me.

I hate that he is an obnoxious flirt in school.

I hate that he kills and has become Enzo's little henchman.

But most of all, I hate that he still knows me better than anyone. A part of me still wants to care, still yearns to return to the friendship we once shared.

I hate myself most of all for still caring.

That's not what killing Langston's father is about, though. I'm not doing this for Langston. I'm doing this for me. For the little girl who got beaten by this horrid man.

I will ensure that he dies, just like the part of me that died that day.

I step out of the small guest house on Enzo's property. I'm not sure if Langston invited Enzo and Zeke to take part in the hunting and killing of his father or not. Enzo and Zeke understand. They would want to help us kill him. They would be able to do the job as well as me, but that isn't what this is about.

Enzo and Zeke didn't experience the abuse. They didn't spend years with the monster. They have their own demons, but not like Langston and I do. For Langston and me, this is personal in an entirely different way.

I wait outside as the sun begins to set to see who is going to show up.

Langston appears from the side of Enzo's house. He must have come around back instead of through the house.

"Where are Enzo and Zeke?" I ask.

He shakes his head. "They aren't coming. This is just about the two of us."

I nod.

His hardened, cool eyes examine me from head to toe. I've never seen Langston so calm and cool. Usually, he has an air about him, a lightness. Not today.

"What happened to your dress?"

"I didn't think it was appropriate for hunting."

He chuckles. "We aren't literally going hunting. That's not how you catch a monster."

"How do you catch a monster, then?"

He shrugs. "You're the hunter. You come up with a plan. I'll just kill him once you lure him away."

What he's not saying is that he's too close to the man he plans on killing. If he comes up with the plan, he'll make a mistake because he's not thinking clearly. He needs me to help him.

"Where is he tonight?" I ask.

"There is some party that he and the stepmonster are having. We won't be able to kill him until after, maybe not even tonight. Tonight might just be about strategizing how to kill him. It—"

"No. He dies tonight."

Langston stares at me, really looking at me for the first time in years.

We may hate each other, but we know the depths of each other's pain. Killing Langston's father might be one of the few areas we still agree on.

"Tell me what your plan is," Langston says, his voice firm and yet hauntingly begging me to tell him how to end his pain and suffering.

My wheels start turning.

I know what we have to do, even though I sort of hate it.

"Go borrow Enzo's most expensive suit," I say.

Langston frowns. "I'm not wearing a suit. I'm not going to that asshole's party. I'm not—"

"Do you want to kill your father tonight or not?"

He sighs and runs his hand through his hair. "Yes, but—"

"This is the only way he dies tonight. We go to the party; we pretend that we are the perfect couple doing exactly what your step-monster wants, and then we kill him."

"There will be too many witnesses."

"No, there will be too many suspects."

Langston peers into my eyes. Neither of us blinks. His pain oozes off him, letting me know how desperately he needs this tonight. He can't wait. We can't fail.

"We won't fail," I say.

His lips thin into tight lines. He gives me a solemn nod and then heads back to Enzo's house.

I turn and head inside, already pulling the braid down. At least my hair will now turn into soft waves, so the braid wasn't a complete waste.

I dig through my closet until I find the perfect dress for tonight. A dress that Enzo bought me, just like every other piece of clothing in this closet. I'm so lucky my mother found this job and that Enzo helps me when he can.

I quickly change, apply makeup, fluff my hair and then run out the door just as Langston starts out the house.

He doesn't see me at first, so I get to watch him without feeling embarrassed that there is a little line of drool on the corner of my mouth.

The suit doesn't fit him perfectly. It's slightly too big in the shoulders and just a hair too short in the legs. But no one will notice because the boy wearing the suit demands to be seen. His tousled blonde hair, bright blue eyes, and toe-curling grin capture my gaze. Even with the look of complete determination on his face, he shines brighter than the sun.

I don't understand how he can pull off that look. And I have a feeling as he grows older, more and more women are going to fall for his charms. More and more women are going to want him.

Good thing I don't want him. I could turn into a jealous bitch if I have to watch years of girls parade themselves in front of Langston.

Langston finally looks up. He stops walking. The brightness is gone when he looks at me. That's who I am—I steal the life out of people.

He continues walking to me. He doesn't comment on my appearance, and I don't comment on his.

"Does your plan involve a way to get to my stepmonster's house? Because the bus doesn't stop anywhere near there."

Langston hardly ever stays at his house. Instead, he's almost always here at Enzo's.

"I thought we'd drive," I say with a smile.

"We aren't sixteen. Neither of us has a driver's license or has ever driven on our own before."

I roll my eyes. "You know how to use a gun. You know how to hack into any computer. You've most likely killed before. I don't think driving without a license even registers on the list of bad things you've done."

He frowns.

"Are you scared? Think you can't drive without wrecking us? I could always—"

"No, I'm driving. We'll take the Porsche."

I smile—my favorite of all Mr. Black's cars.

We head inside Enzo's house. Luckily, Enzo and his father are at the club working, so we don't have to ask permission to use the car. We just take it.

Enzo wouldn't care.

And if Mr. Black knew that we were killing Langston's father tonight, he'd probably approve. The only bigger monster than Langston's father is Enzo's father.

We both climb into the Porsche. Langston doesn't hesitate. He puts the car in reverse and backs out of the garage.

I flip on a pop song.

Langston growls and switches it to rap.

"Passenger gets to pick the music," I say, flipping it back.

"You're ridiculous."

He steps on the gas too hard, and we lurch forward.

"Easy, tiger. We don't want to get us killed before we even arrive."

He lightly taps the gas, and then we are driving like the grown-ups we were forced into being far too young.

Annoyed with my music choice, he turns off the radio. Then his eyes grace the hem of my mid-thigh angelic dress. It's covered in pretty white lace—the only part of it that hints that I'm still part girl. The rest of me is all woman. I developed early, already with plenty of curves at my hip and enough cleavage to draw in the most saintly of men.

"Why did you start wearing dresses, Liesel?"

There he goes calling me Liesel again.

I stare out the window. I started wearing dresses and acting girly when Enzo offered to pay for a new wardrobe for me, when I started a new school filled with rich snobs. The truth is I started wearing a dress because I liked the attention it gives me. I'm tired of blending in. Dresses make me feel like I'm more powerful than I really am.

"To drive you wild."

He grunts.

"Is it working?"

"What do you think?" he snaps.

Yes.

No.

I honestly can't read him well any more.

The conversation ends, though, as we pull up into the ridiculous circular drive in front of Langston's stepmom's house. Each of our doors is opened by a valet, and I take an offered hand helping me out of the car like we are about to attend a grand ball instead of a house party in Miami's richest area.

As soon as I get out of the car, I feel Langston brushing the valet's hand away from mine. He takes my arm carefully, like he's afraid that touching me is going to cause his hand to fall off.

I grab his arm more forcibly. "Holding my hand isn't going to kill you."

"Pretending that you're my girlfriend might."

I narrow my eyes. "If you don't want my help, then you can do this yourself."

"Fine, I'm sorry. Let's just get this over with."

I smile. "Follow my lead."

I spot our target and walk over to the stepmonster, who is talking excitedly with a group of chatty women. This will do perfectly to make our introduction.

"Introduce me to your stepmom with your charming smile," I say.

He frowns.

"Just trust me. Introduce me, I'll do the rest."

Langston leads me over and clears his throat as he approaches. "Ladies," he smiles at the women, laying on the charm. Then he looks to his stepmom. This part will be the hardest. "Mother, I'd like to introduce you to my girlfriend, Liesel Dunn."

He calls his stepmom 'mother' like she likes as he puts his hand on the small of my back with a bright, charming smile.

"It's a pleasure to meet you, Mrs. Pearce. I've heard so much about you."

Mrs. Pearce looks at me, hesitantly. She likes that Langston is here, that he called her mother, and that I look like a high-class girlfriend in my expensive dress. I just need to sell that I have money just like her, and then she'll approve of her stepson's choice in women.

"I'm sorry we were late. Langston had to pick me up on Fisher Island," I say, giving Enzo's house address. She doesn't have to know that the only reason my address is the same is because I live in the guest house while my mother works in the main house as a maid.

"Oh, it's a pleasure to meet you, my dear." Her eyes light up as she looks from Langston to me.

I gently lean into Langston's side, selling the appearance that we are boyfriend and girlfriend.

We pretend to be interested in what the women are saying for a while, before excusing ourselves.

"How did that help anything?" Langston asks.

I grab his tie and pull him into the nearest bedroom before I kick the door shut behind me.

"Your stepmom is happy. She'll think I'm good for you and start to trust you a little more. She'll tell your dad, who won't believe her and will come to us."

I sit on the edge of the bed. "And now, we are going to work on our alibi."

Langston raises an eyebrow. "I'm not fucking you, huntress."

I smile; he used my nickname.

"I'm not asking you to fuck me. Just pretend that having sex loud enough that other guests in the hallway will notice. Mess up our clothes enough so when we leave, everyone will know that we are just horny teenagers. Our entire focus was on each other, not on killing your father."

"I hate you." Langston's teeth grind together with each word.

"Make love to me, killer."

He walks over to me, stopping inches from me.

What is he doing? Is he going to kiss me? The only kiss we've had was the one when we were kids. That doesn't count. He's much more grown-up now. More experienced. This kiss could...

He puts his hands down on the bed on either side of me.

He's going to kiss me.

And then, his hands start bouncing up and down, making me and the bed shake.

I laugh.

"You aren't supposed to laugh when I fake fuck you."

I bite my lip, stifling another chuckle.

"Ooh, yea, just like that," I moan, my eyelashes fluttering as I gaze at Langston, who hasn't moved from his position.

"Louder, baby, I want the whole house to know you are mine."

"Baby? Really?" I whisper. "That's so cheesy."

He stops shaking the bed and gives me a stern look.

"Yes, Langston!" I yell a little too loudly.

He groans loudly.

Damn, it's sexier than I imagined.

And then he slams the bed hard, the headboard creaks, splitting one of the posts.

We both moan together, calling out each other's names.

Then I collapse back on the bed, exhausted like we really did fuck.

That was intense—too intense. I need to stay focused.

When I sit back up, Langston is leaning against the opposite wall, watching me.

I catch my breath and clear my throat. "Mess up your clothes a little."

He slowly starts loosening his tie.

I fuss up my hair; I let one shoulder of my dress hang down my arm and yank the front of the dress down, revealing more cleavage than before. Then I run my thumb over my lipstick, smearing it just slightly.

Langston lets out a strangled breath.

Do I affect him like he affects me?

Not possible.

It's just tension, knowing what we're about to do.

"Now, what's your plan?" Langston asks.

"To get your father to publicly kick us out to seal our alibi."

"When really...?"

"He's going to see us sneaking off to the lake behind the house."

"Where I'll kill him."

I nod slowly.

Langston walks over to me. His thumb brushes just below my lower lip.

"No one will need to see your smeared makeup to think I fucked you."

And then he takes my hand. I don't ask him what he means. I just let him lead me out of the bedroom.

"Out," his father's voice says the second we leave the bedroom.

I hide my smirk at how well my plan is working.

Langston glares at his father. "We were just leaving."

He pulls me past where his father stands in the doorway and out the front door. Our car is already waiting for us. We drive off silently, our alibi firmly in place.

Then we circle around to the back of the lake.

Langston glances at me one last time as if to thank me without actually saying the words. I completed my part of the pact, now Langston has to complete his part—killing his father.

CHAPTER 7

LANGSTON

"Wait here, I'll lure my father down to the lake. I'll come get you when it's done," I say to Liesel as I step out of the car.

When I exit, I hear her car door slam shut.

"I told you to stay, huntress."

"I'm not going to sit in the car and wait like some damsel in distress. I might not participate in killing him, but I deserve to be involved. To watch. To see with my own eyes that he's dead. I want him gone almost as desperately as you do."

I don't want Liesel anywhere near the danger, but more than that, I don't want her to watch me kill—even a monster like my father. It will change everything between us.

Like everything hasn't changed already.

I sigh.

"Fine. But don't let him see you. Stay hidden and don't try to help. Even if things go badly, promise me you won't interfere."

She bites her bottom lip as she thinks. "I promise to only interfere if he's killing you."

"No."

"You can't expect me to just sit by and watch you die!"

I start walking away from the car into the forest of trees behind the house. She chases after me.

"Langston!"

I stop abruptly, and she slams into my back.

"I won't watch you die."

"The fact that you think there is even a chance that he'll kill me tells me all I need to know."

She huffs. "That's not fair. I think you can handle him. I'm just saying if he brings bodyguards with him, then it won't be a fair fight, and I won't just sit by and let you die."

I should be thankful for her comments, that she cares enough to not let me die. In reality, my father could bring all the men in the house with him and I would still win. Liesel doesn't know the depths of my pain. She doesn't know how Enzo, Zeke, and I have trained for a day like this. My father and the men in the house are nothing but drunk fools. They don't know how to fire a gun or win in hand-to-hand combat.

I do.

There is no way I'll lose.

"Just stay hidden," I say, and then I storm off.

Liesel stops in the brush as I walk up the hill to the house where the party is still going strong.

I stand on the edge of the patio, just past the pool, and I wait. People don't pay me any attention, but I'm not here for their attention. I'm here for one man's—my father.

Finally, I spot him at the patio bar. *Surprise, surprise.*

I make my way over, ensuring that no one notices me. I need to keep my alibi alive.

If needed, Liesel will testify that I was with her all night, making out at her house.

I come up to my father from behind.

"We need to talk," I say.

He snaps at my words, turning around as he stumbles on his feet. I'd rather do this when he's sober. I want to be able to look him in the eye and know that he understands exactly what I'm about to do to him and why when I kill him. But if I waited until he was sober, I'd be waiting forever.

"My fists will be happy to talk to you," he turns, glaring down at me.

My eyes cut to the house filled with people. "Good luck kicking my ass here without one of these people hearing. Your wife wouldn't be happy if one of her guests saw or heard you beating your son."

"No one cares about trash like you."

Just then, a couple nearby notices the tension in my father's gaze.

My father realizes he can't give me the beating he's itching to give me here.

He grabs my bicep and starts yanking me down the hill behind the house, just like I knew he would when I goaded him. He continues to hold onto me even though I'm more than capable of getting free.

We are so close to the lake now.

Just a little further.

I pull against his hold, knowing it will only make him want to yank me further.

It does. He pulls me further until we are at the edge of the water, hidden from view of the party by the rows and rows of trees. Not even the moonlight will illuminate us.

Only then do I yank my arm free of his hold. He stumbles off balance at the sudden movement.

"Drunk bastard," I mumble under my breath.

"What did you say, boy?" He regains his footing. "I told you to leave. Your sorry ass didn't listen!" He pulls his hand back, preparing to hit me.

He won't be hitting me, not tonight. I'll never let him hit me again.

I easily duck as he takes a swing at me.

He huffs, his nostrils flare, and his eyes widen until I can see the whites of his bloodshot eyes.

I've dreamed about killing this man for so long—in so many different ways.

A gunshot to the head.

A knife to the throat.

A snap of the neck.

Right now, my mind is quickly rotating through all of my options, trying to decide which way this man deserves to die.

He tries to hit me again while I'm thinking. I take a step back and dodge his fist once again.

This time he stumbles and has to catch himself with his hand to keep from falling completely to the ground.

It's then that I realize how this monster deserves to die. He doesn't deserve anything special. It won't take much to kill him. Just one wrong step, one stumble because he's too drunk to stay upright. Then I can finish him off.

"Stop moving and take your beating like a man! You deserve it!" he shouts at me.

I step around him until I'm just in front of the water's edge.

"No son deserves to get beaten by their father."

"You're no son of mine! You're a bastard; your mother cheated on me so many times, I'm not even sure you are mine."

I wish his statement were true. I wish I wasn't his son, but we share the same eyes, the same lanky body, the same jawline—I'm his.

I stand firm as the lake sloshes at my heels, biding my time until he swings again.

On cue, he does. This time, I wait until the very last moment—until his fist almost brushes against my cheek before I move out of the way.

I watch his body fall face-first into the water. He can't catch himself; it's too late. His body hits the water hard. From the way his head bounces, he landed on a rock beneath the surface of the water.

Slowly, he tries to push himself up.

That won't be happening.

I press my foot down on top of his back, holding him down easily with my weight. He's too drunk, too weak to get me off, even though he's twice my size.

This is for everything he's done.

I watch wordlessly as he struggles beneath my foot. Every second he's one step closer to death. Each second he loses more and more oxygen. His lungs begin to fill with water. His arms stop flailing. His body stops moving.

He's dead.

I hold my foot on his back for another couple seconds—processing the moment. He's dead and I killed him.

My mind goes blank. I don't feel anything. I can't feel anything.

Then I feel her hand.

I glance down at Liesel's fingers intertwined with my own. She doesn't speak; she just guides me out of the water, away from my father's body. The whole time I was killing my father, I forgot completely about Liesel. I was so consumed by making sure my father paid for his sins.

I don't know where Liesel is leading me, and I don't care. I'd follow her anywhere.

It's not until this moment that I realize how much I needed her here with me tonight.

Finally, she stops on the edge of a hill that overlooks the lake.

We sit down.

"Thank you," I say suddenly.

She drops my hand then, as if the phrase makes her uncomfortable. Eventually she says, "You're welcome."

We sit in silence once more, both processing what happened.

"That wasn't my first kill, you know?" I say, needing her to understand what I've become—a monster.

"I know, and it doesn't matter," she whispers back.

Liesel reaches behind a nearby bush and pulls out a bottle.

"What's this?" I ask.

"Champagne I stole from the party. I thought we should celebrate."

She hands the open bottle to me. I hold it out like I'm about to make a toast.

"To one less monster walking this earth." Then I take a long swig before handing the bottle to Liesel.

"To being free and new beginnings. May that man rot in hell."

She takes a swig.

New beginnings—that's what she said.

Our eyes meet in the chill of the night. An unspoken connection we will always share rekindles between us.

I didn't realize how much I needed her here. How much I miss the girl who lived across the street from me when I had nothing. Now that I have everything money can buy, I'm still missing one thing—her.

I open my mouth to talk but then snap it shut.

Tonight isn't the night to talk to her about our future. To ask for forgiveness. To start over.

Tonight is about putting an end to this chapter of our lives. I won't start something new with Liesel so close to my father's death. I won't let this moment define us forever.

Someday soon, though, I'll tell Liesel how I feel—and it will change our lives forever.

Instead of acknowledging how I feel, I tell another lie. "This changes nothing."

CHAPTER 8

LIESEL

Eighteen Years Old

The night Langston's father died flashes in my mind. I don't know why that particular memory makes its way into my head. Maybe because I'm currently at my mother's funeral.

I thought that night was a turning point in my life. I thought things between Langston and I would change. I thought we would stop bickering and become friends again.

Instead, we continued the back and forth between liking and hating each other. Right now, all I feel toward Langston is hate.

I thought Langston's father was the biggest monster in my life. I was wrong. Mr. Pearce was barely a cockroach compared to the Godzilla I later faced.

I'm not going to think about that now. I have to focus on burying my mother. She died of an overdose on my birthday.

I release a fistful of dirt over my mother's coffin. The minster finishes speaking and starts walking back to the church, giving me some privacy.

I'm the only person who showed up to my mother's funeral.

Enzo and Zeke offered to come, but they're off training somewhere. I didn't want to bother them.

And Langston...I haven't spoken to him in a while. At first, I thought he might show up. But the short funeral came and went, and no Langston.

Stop thinking about him.

I force myself to think about my mother. About how I'll never see her again. I try to cry, really I do. But after the suffering I've been through in the last couple of years, I eventually stopped feeling pain at all. I couldn't cry even if I wanted to.

I stand another moment, trying to pay my mother her respects before I leave and never come back to this place. Too much torment has happened here. I'm about to turn when I feel his fingers brush against mine.

Chills race up my arm at his touch—that's new.

Then his fingers lock around mine.

I don't look at him. I refuse to be the first to speak.

Deep down, I'm grateful he's here, even if he is late. No one wants to bury their mother alone.

"Here," Langston says.

I glance up and see him holding a single flower—rose-like, but not quite a rose. It looks almost identical to the flower I gave him to place on his mother's grave when we buried her in this exact cemetery all those years ago.

I take the flower and place it on my mother's stone.

And then I look at Langston. I should say something—thank him, perhaps. But I don't need to use words to tell him how I'm feeling.

Langston, on the other hand, looks like he's about to spill everything inside him. He opens his mouth, "Liesel, I—"

"Hold onto that thought." I glance at my watch. "I'm supposed to meet my lawyer at the house to go over my mother's will and decide what to do with the house."

"What house? Enzo's guest house?"

"No, she never sold our old house here, even after we moved into Enzo's guest house. I'm meeting him there."

"Oh, okay." Langston rubs the back of his neck. He's wearing a dark shirt and jeans. Langston thinks he's the devil now after everything he's done. He's right, but I wish he would become my light, my laughter, the boy I used to care for.

"We could grab a bite after, though. Meet me at the house in thirty minutes?"

He smiles tightly. "Okay."

Langston walks to his car, while I walk to mine before driving the couple blocks to the house. I get out of the car, ignoring the feelings flooding me as I walk up to the house.

I stand on the single step and knock on the door, peering over at the dried-up bush under the window. There is a car in the driveway that I expect is the lawyer's.

The door opens.

I gasp.

"Dad?" I ask the man who has my hazel eyes, my blonde hair, my complexion. He looks almost exactly like the single picture I have of him. The only difference is his hair is now peppered with gray, and he seems to have a few more wrinkles around his eyes and mouth. He shouldn't be here. He left my mom and me when I was three. He has no right to be here.

"Yes," he says.

I turn to walk away.

"Wait, please, let me explain. Talk to me; then I'll be gone and out of your life forever."

"Why should I?" I snap at him.

"Because I'll keep hunting you, stalking you until you give in and talk to me. You might as well get it over with now."

I glare, my eyes narrow in defiance, but I eventually decide to stomp inside the house. "You couldn't have chosen a different day other than my mother's funeral to talk to me?"

He shuts the door behind me and stands facing me, like he's blocking off my escape route. He doesn't know that a man like him doesn't terrify me. Nothing scares me anymore, not after I've been through hell already.

"You have five minutes, start talking," I say, folding my arms over my chest. The ratty couch I used to sleep on is still in the living room, but I refuse to sit on it.

My father doesn't either.

"I didn't come here to apologize for leaving you. Although, I am sorry to hear about your mother."

"Good, because I wouldn't forgive you." I don't acknowledge his comment about my mother.

He nods.

"I came here to tell you about your inheritance, of sorts."

I frown. "Just take the house and whatever money Mom had. I'm not going to fight you. I have my own money now."

He looks me over, head to toe, taking in my appearance, my expensive clothes. I've come a long way in a short time thanks to the help of my friends.

"I can see that. Still, it's time I told you a story."

I huff. "Really? I don't have time for a story. My friend is picking me up any minute now."

He raises an eyebrow, calling my bluff.

"I still have four minutes remaining. I can tell you the story in that amount of time."

"Go on, then."

♡

ONCE UPON A TIME, I FELL IN LOVE.

She was feisty, radiant, and reckless. She had nothing. She came from nothing. And unless she found a rich husband—it would take everything she had to pull herself out of poverty.

I wasn't rich.

I had less money than her.

I had no college degree.

No job prospects.

All I had was five dollars in my pocket and the clothes on my back.

None of that mattered.

Our love was enough.

We vowed to love each other forever.

We got married.

A baby followed.

I thought our life together was so happy.

I thought we could make our marriage last.

I thought...

I thought it was enough.

Turns out, you can't live on love.

You can't eat love.

Breathe love.

Live under a roof made of love.

You need money.

We tried to make more of ourselves. I went to a community college.

It wasn't enough.

She worked three jobs.

It wasn't enough.

Our baby deserved more.

We deserved more.

So we started hunting for a way out.

Hunting.

Hunting.

Hunting...

Until finally, we found a way out.

We had more money than we could have ever imagined.

More money than the suits who used to look down on us as we cleaned their homes.

More money than the executives who those suits reported to.

More money than the queen of England.

We thought we had it all. We thought we knew what came next.

But all that came next was defending what we had stolen.

Our love wasn't enough.

Fighting our enemies wore us down until we had no energy left, no desire to fight. Until our love dissolved into ash, and our hearts were torn apart.

Sometimes fairy tales turn into nightmares.

Listen to my warning, child.

Don't search for it.

Don't seek the fairytale.

Don't seek the money like your mother and me.

Run, Liesel.

Hide.

Don't hunt.

Above everything else, don't ever tell anyone the truth—who you are or what you know.

♡

"I don't understand," I say. *All this time my parents had money? They had a treasure? The only reason I grew up poor was because they weren't strong enough to keep the money?*

"It's all in here." He hands me an envelope.

I stare at it with big eyes as I begin to remove the letter from the envelope. "What is it?"

He puts his hand over mine, stopping me.

"Later. Read it later, when you're alone. Then burn it. Forget about going after the money, the treasure. Lie to anyone who asks you about it."

"I have so many questions," I say, staring at the envelope cautiously.

"I know, and I wish we had more time."

"Is this goodbye?"

"It is, my sweet daughter. It is."

He leans forward and kisses me on the cheek before I realize what's happening. I'm in shock. This man is insane. There is no way any of this is true.

"Go," he says, breaking the trance I'm under.

I take a step out of the tiny house, knowing that I won't be back inside ever again. This part of my life is over. My mother is gone, and I won't search for my father. I doubt I even read this stupid letter.

I run out, and I don't hear him following me.

I head toward my car, planning on driving away before Langston appears. I just want out of here. I can't handle a dinner with Langston right now.

But Langston is already here, and he'll stop me. I feel him before I see him.

When I look up, I see the tension on his face, a vein bulging on his forehead. He's pissed, but I don't know why.

"Is it true?" he asks me, stopping me from entering my car.

"Is what true? You're going to have to be a little more specific. My mother just died, and my father decided to show up after fifteen years of running and dropped a bomb on me."

Langston's nostrils flare.

"Is. It. True?"

"I. Don't. Know. What. You're. Talking. About." I point my finger at him as I talk.

He doesn't back down, but I don't have the patience to deal with him. I grab my car door and climb in. He catches the door right before I slam it in his face.

One tense moment.

He slams the door.

I drive away.

I'll deal with Langston later.

I look at the envelope in my hand after a few miles, deciding I should just pull over at the nearest Starbucks to read it and blow off whatever ridiculous conspiracy theory my father stumbled on in a drugged up state.

I do a double-take—the letter is torn.

Right in half.

Langston. The asshole tore the envelope when he grabbed the car door.

Dammit—I pull over and slam my hands against the steering wheel.

I take a deep breath, composing myself, and then I open the letter and read.

I read every word on my half.

The words reverberate in my core; they're true. But I only have half of the secret. Langston has the other half.

My father was worried about the treasure staying hidden. He won't have to worry, though. There is no way Langston will give up his half of the secret, and there is no way I'll give up mine to him.

The treasure is safe.

Lie, Liesel—it's the only way to stay alive.

My father meant to warn me with his words. He didn't know that lying is all I do. Lying has kept me alive, even when I wish I had died.

I laugh, staring at the letter.

There is no way any of this is true. It's all a lie, yet another lie Langston and I share. A lie we will never reveal, just like all the other lies from our past.

VICIOUS LIES

PROLOGUE

Once upon a time, I fell in love.

She was feisty, radiant, and reckless. She had nothing. She came from nothing. And unless she found a rich husband—it would take everything she had to pull herself out of poverty.

I wasn't rich.

I had less money than her.

I had no college degree.

No job prospects.

All I had was five dollars in my pocket and the clothes on my back.

None of that mattered.

Our love was enough.

We vowed to love each other forever.

We got married.

A baby followed.

I thought our life together was so happy.

I thought we could make our marriage last.

I thought...

I sigh.

I thought it was enough.

Turns out, you can't live on love.

You can't eat love.

Breathe love.

Live under a roof made of love.

You need money.

We tried to make more of ourselves. I went to a community college.

It wasn't enough.

She worked three jobs.

It wasn't enough.

Our baby deserved more.

We deserved more.

So we started hunting for a way out.

Hunting.

Hunting.

Hunting...

Until finally, we found a way out.

We had more money than we could have ever imagined.

More money than the suits who used to look down on us as we cleaned their homes.

More money than the executives who those suits reported to.

More money than the queen of England.

We thought we had it all. We thought we knew what came next.

But all that came next was defending what we had stolen.

Our love wasn't enough.

Fighting our enemies wore us down until we had no energy left. Until we had no desire to fight. Until our love dissolved into ash, and our hearts were torn apart.

Sometimes fairytales turn into nightmares.

Listen to my warning, child.

Don't search for it.

Don't seek the fairytale.

Don't seek the money like your mother and me.

Run, Liesel.

Hide.

Don't hunt.

Above everything else, don't ever tell anyone the truth—who you are or what you know.

"I don't understand," Liesel says.

I wish I could explain everything to her. I wish I had more time. I wish I could ensure she didn't make the same mistakes her mother and I did.

But there is no time.

And I can't make her decisions for her. I've failed as a father in more ways than one. All I can give her now is my advice and hope she makes the better choice, becomes the better person.

"It's all in here." I hand her an envelope.

She stares at it with big eyes as she begins to remove the letter from the envelope. "What is it?"

I put my hand over hers, stopping her.

"Later. Read it later, when you're alone. Then burn it. Forget about going after the money, the treasure. Lie to anyone who asks you about it."

I want to ask her to promise me, but I don't. That's too much to ask of her. Someday, she may choose to go after the treasure. She may think it's worth it. My only hope is that it is—for her.

Just please, God, don't let it destroy her like it did me.

"I have so many questions," she says.

"I know, and I wish we had more time."

"Is this goodbye?"

"It is, my sweet daughter. It is."

I lean forward and kiss her on the cheek. I wish I could apologize for all the shit I've put her through. There is no apology big enough to earn her forgiveness.

"Go," I say.

She takes a step out of the tiny house that she and her mother lived in for years when she was little. A house I lived in with them when she was first born, before I made the worst mistake of my life.

It takes everything inside me not to chase after her.

But I pulled myself out of her life a long time ago. I don't get to come back into her life now that she's an adult.

Liesel runs down the porch without glancing back.

She heads toward her car, and just before she reaches it, a boy approaches her. No, he's all man. Tall, dressed in dark clothes, but his hair light as the sun. The tenseness on his face and vein bulging on his forehead says he's pissed.

He stops her.

I want to protect her, save her.

I can't.

This is the life she was born into. I have no way to save her.

But my Liesel is more than capable of handling her own with this man. She yells back, pointing her finger at him as she storms around him to the driver's side of the car.

There is more yelling I can't make out, before she climbs into the car. He catches the door right before she slams it in his face.

One tense moment.

He slams the door.

She drives away.

The man stands there a moment—watching her.

And then he turns and looks right at me.

I glare back.

I see what's in his hand—a ripped piece of paper.

He must have torn part of the envelope when they were arguing.

I told Liesel to keep it a secret, but it's too late now. Now someone knows.

Now she has no choice but to lie.

Lie, Liesel—it's the only way to stay alive.

CHAPTER 1

LIESEL

I will kill you.

I read the words on the piece of paper in my hand. *Who puts death threats in the mail anymore?* It seems archaic and old-timey. There are so many better ways to send a threat: a phone call, a text message, an email.

An in-person act of violence really sends a message too, if you really have the balls.

Why write a letter?

Because he's a coward.

I consider tossing the letter in the trash and not taking the issue any further, forgetting that it even happened. But I didn't survive this long by tossing away idle threats.

I will kill you.

This isn't the first time someone has made a threat like this against me.

I will kill everyone you love.

Again, not new. I just thought I was passed this part of my life. I thought I was done living in this dangerous, vicious world. One where there are no winners—at least, I never win. I just survive.

I thought, just like letter writing, this part of my life was buried in the past.

I tap my painted red nails against my desk as I read the letter over two more times. Nothing hints at who the author is. There is no name scrolled across the bottom. Like I thought—*wuss*.

But that doesn't mean there aren't hints of who my enemy is. The way the letter is scribed tells me it's a man who wrote it. It was scribbled quickly with a pen almost out of ink on a piece of computer paper. This note was written last minute; it wasn't thought through.

And it didn't arrive in an envelope in the mail. It was stuffed loosely into the mailbox. I wouldn't be surprised if I found fingerprints.

Whoever sent this is an amateur, or at least, wants me to think he's an amateur.

I'm not an amateur. As much as I never thought I would know how to hold a gun, fire a weapon, hunt down men, rescue myself, I've never had a choice in the matter. My entire life I've lived in a cruel underworld of men who controlled everything. Men who had no right to own anything. Men who ruled with guns and darkness in their hearts, taking no prisoners. Taking what they wanted without concern of whom they hurt.

I used to be a princess in a world filled with dangerous men. I used to have friends who would protect me above everything else.

But things started slowly changing when my best friend, Enzo Black, fell in love. And then Zeke, my other protector, fell in love next. It's only a matter of time until Langston, the playboy of the group, falls in love.

I could call any one of them to take care of the man who sent this threat. Enzo, Zeke, or Langston all have the power and abilities to handle this man without lifting a finger. That's what they do—kill dangerous men. They protect their family, which used to include me.

Until they failed me.

Until they fell in love.

Until I decided I didn't want to be a damsel in distress, waiting for a man to come and rescue me.

I saved myself.

I picked up every broken, shattered piece and put myself back together, painstakingly, piece by piece.

I'm whole now—even if the pieces don't fit together the same as they did before.

I'm a survivor—that's the term used to describe me. It's a term I hate, because I didn't just survive, I thrived. I fought back; I rescued myself. I'm a fucking knight in red high heels.

So while I could call my friends to save me and take care of this, I'm not going to. I haven't asked any one of them for help in years, and I'm not going to start now.

I lift my glass of scotch from my desk and swirl it around until the single ball of ice shifts in the glass, making a delicious rattling sound before I take a sip. I'm a woman in a man's world, but that doesn't mean I let the men rule me anymore. I won't give any man power over me—never again.

So that leaves me two choices. I can toss this letter in the trash and ignore it completely. There is a large chance whoever sent it will never grow enough balls to actually act on his threat. Or I go back into the world I never thought I would enter again.

A world of danger.

Cruelty.

Vows.

And lies.

A world that once consumed me. A world that turned me into the cold, heartless woman I've become. A world that took everything from me, yet gave me my power.

I thought I was done.

I thought this chapter of my life was over, buried.

I could leave it alone. For years, I've done everything I can to stay out of this life. To stay away from the evil that lurks in the night. Not because I'm afraid of the darkness hurting me. Not because I'm afraid that the man making the threat will actually succeed. Even if he did succeed, I'm not afraid of death.

No, I've stayed away from the darkness because I haven't wanted to become the villain I'm capable of being. Once the darkness surrounds me, I'll no longer be the princess. I'll become the evil queen.

Once I let it in, there is no way to get it out. That's why I've put up walls around my heart, to keep the vile out, the wickedness I can become.

But why?

Why can't I turn into the evil queen?

My friends and family are gone. The only man in my life is more than capable of taking care of himself.

I shouldn't go back to this life.

I should crumple the letter up and toss it into the fireplace to burn.

I should forget the threat until it comes true.

But I feel the walls lowering around my heart. All the men in my life are able to stay safe and protect those they love, because they don't fight the worst parts of themselves.

Enzo is a controlling bastard, who rules his world by loving Kai.

Zeke protects those he loves no matter the cost it inflicts on himself.

And Langston hurts others to protect himself.

All three men have done more than survived; they've become kings. They've languished and destroyed their enemies. They've gained enough power that no man dares to make threats like this.

It's time I try their tactics.

I toss the rest of the scotch back into my throat before slamming the glass down on my desk with a sinful grin across my red-painted lips.

The evil that I locked in my heart is free. I'm going to use every bit of its power to take care of this threat myself, so no man or woman will ever threaten me again.

LANGSTON

I sit in the darkness.

I love the darkness, but I hate waiting.

I'm not a patient man. I leave that to my friend, Zeke.

But my excited anticipation keeps me seated in this pine smelling office. I glance around the room as my eyes quickly adjust to the lack of light.

The office is just what you'd expect from a rich prick with no taste. A large mahogany desk with an oversized office chair in the center of the main wall with the large oval-shaped window behind the chair. *Why wouldn't you want to look out the window when you work?* It's all for show.

The same with the large bookshelf filled with self-help books, classics, and business books. None look like they've ever been read.

There is a piece of art by Picasso finishing the room. But I know how big the man's bank account is. At best, it's a print; at worst, it's a complete knock off. A fake—just like this room, just like the man.

And then I spot the one thing in the room that looks like it has been used—the liquor cart.

I get up from my chair and pick up the bottle of scotch sitting on the cart and read the label. Highland Park Orcadian—an expensive bottle that's been aged a long time.

My eyebrows shoot up in pleasant surprise as I pour myself a glass. I walk back to my chair, my wait greatly improved now that I have an excellent glass of scotch to keep me company.

I take a sip and then spew the liquid everywhere as I lift the glass to eye level to get a better look. I sniff the liquid, and it smells as retched as it tastes. There is no way this is what's listed on the label.

I shake my head in disbelief as I set the glass down on the desk, making sure not to use a coaster so a ring will form on the ridiculously ugly desk. That's what he gets for trying to trick people into thinking they are drinking expensive liquor when I doubt he paid more than fifty bucks for that shit.

My patience is waning when I finally hear the front door open.

"This condo is amazing," the woman with him says, shouting too loudly and giving this condo way too much credit. The condo is a mass-produced, overpriced box.

"Not as amazing as you are," he says back.

I roll my eyes at the ridiculous line. But it's not going to take much to impress this woman. She's drunk and clearly impressed with what she perceives as his wealth. She doesn't know real wealth. She doesn't know that real money is passed through generations and earned by spilling blood of others.

This man is barely a millionaire. He doesn't have the billions that flow through the Black empire, my employer.

My plan was to wait in the office for him to come to me. He works in security. He should easily realize that his security system was turned off already when he came in. I purposefully scuffed my shoes along his rug until the corner lifted, and turned the frame crooked on the wall in the office hallway.

He should know I'm here within minutes.

If this were my home, I would know the second the alarm was turned off.

So I try to remain patient and let him come to me. But, again, I'm not patient. From the moaning and groaning floating down the hallway, it doesn't seem like he is paying attention to any of the clues I left for him.

I open the office door and walk down the hallway, not hiding the sound of my footsteps. I walk toward the living room where I find them making out on the couch like horny teenagers. The kisses are sloppy, and from the way he's manhandling the poor woman, there is no way she's going to get off tonight from him.

I step into the light, but he still doesn't notice me. However, the woman's eyes shoot up to me. She shrieks out of surprise, but then her eyes are running up my body appreciatively. She'd rather I be fucking her than the schmuck she's straddling.

"Get up," I say calmly and firmly, keeping the anger I feel out of my voice.

The woman scampers off, listening obediently. The man only slowly turns his head.

"I said. Get. Up."

He swallows, and I know the options he's considering in his head. But he's an amateur, and I'm a skilled assassin.

He reaches for his gun, but I grab it, empty the magazine, and toss it to the floor.

His eyes grow big, his pupils dilate, his pulse beats rapidly in his throat as the fear spreads. He's defenseless. He has nothing to match my skill. Basically, he's my bitch, and he knows it.

His bottom lip trembles as he considers his next words, but none come out. I'm surprised the man hasn't pissed himself yet.

"Who are you?" the woman asks, licking her bottom lip. Apparently, I'm not scary enough to her. She thinks she can seduce me with her good looks. But she's as fake as this apartment—her curves don't come naturally. Neither does her bleach blonde hair or her pointed fingernails.

I turn my attention to her. My heated gaze ponders all the ways I could fuck her. She might be good in bed, but there are a million reasons I won't fuck her. The main one being that I'm in love with another woman.

"Go to the bedroom," I say to her.

Her smile curves up, revealing her wine-stained teeth and lips. Her breath catches as I stare at her before she obediently walks toward the bedroom.

With her gone, I can focus on my main task.

"What—what do you want?" the man asks, his voice trembling as he speaks. He knows exactly what I want.

I take my time strolling around the sofa between us as I casually sit in the single chair facing him, acting like I'm about to negotiate with him. There is no way that's going to happen, though. I'm in control, not him, and I know exactly how his story ends.

"I—I have money. You can have whatever you want."

"I don't want your money."

I adjust my watch, completely bored with this conversation, this task, this world.

I was hired to kill this man. For months now, I've been taking odd jobs like this to soothe my killer instinct. To get a little thrill, a little bit of danger in my life. Something I used to get working for Enzo Black, but the Black empire has grown so big, so powerful that no one dares to stand up to him. No one has threatened them in months. The job has become boring and unsatisfying.

But I'm finding that these jobs, hunting and killing killers, is even less exciting.

"Mr. Reynolds, thank you for helping me realize something," I say, standing like I'm about to end a business meeting.

His eyes fill with hope, and I can see the relief filled smile stretch over his lips.

"What's that?"

I crack my neck casually. His life means nothing to me. This is what I do. I hunt, I protect, I kill.

I pull out my gun and aim it at his heart.

"I've realized that you are going to be my last job." And then I squeeze the trigger, watching him drop to a puddle of blood on the floor as his heart squirts out blood.

I walk out the door before his date for the night comes out and realizes what happened. I'm not worried that she's going to report me to the police. I don't care that my prints are all over the condo. The police are no threat to me.

I take the elevator down, walk out to my motorcycle and start it up. This is definitely my last job. I don't need the money, I only do it for the thrill, and the thrill is gone.

My phone buzzes, most likely Adrian, the man who got me this job. I pull it out to answer him when I see the message come through. I'm already getting sent another job because I'm the best hitman. That's all this town sees me as.

They don't know that killing people doesn't even touch the depths of my capabilities.

They don't know exactly how evil my heart is.

They don't know what I've done, what I'm about to do.

I consider just deleting the message without reading it, but the way it starts catches my attention.

HITMAN NEEDED.

I DON'T NEED YOU TO FIND THE MAN WHO MADE A DEATH THREAT. I'LL find him.

I don't need you to kidnap him. I can do that too.

I don't even need you to actually kill him.

All I need you to do is say that you killed him if the need should arise. Just be there so I can say I didn't kill him.

You have to have a record. And you have to have killed before.

I'll pay one hundred thousand.

—HUNTRESS

I READ THE MESSAGE THREE TIMES BEFORE I ACCEPT THAT I'M NOT dreaming. This is my chance for payback, for redemption, for revenge.

Huntress.

It's been years since I've called her huntress. I don't think I've called her that since we were teenagers. And yet, she's using it here to hide her identity.

Or she's calling out to me? Hoping I'll be the one to answer her ad?

Not likely, since she hates my guts.

But this is too good an opportunity to pass up.

I kick my foot down, starting up my motorcycle as I text back: Accepted.

Then I slip the phone into my pocket, instead of deleting the message like I should. I keep it, knowing I'll want to reread the message over and over again as a plan forms in my head.

I shouldn't have accepted. I should stay far away from my huntress. She's destroyed me before, and there is a good chance she'll do it again.

But this time, things are different. This time, I won't give her my heart. This time, I plan on being the one who wins.

CHAPTER 3

LIESEL

Only one man responded to my message—*unusual*.

As shocking as it may seem to some people, this isn't my first time hiring a hitman. And only getting one response isn't typical, not in a town like this.

We are supposed to meet for coffee in SoHo. It's a trendy third-wave coffee shop that is almost always standing room only, so plenty of people to ensure neither of us is in any danger.

I'm not worried about being in any danger regardless. We could be meeting in a back alley alone, and I still wouldn't be afraid to meet him, whoever he is.

Fear is something that I no longer feel. My fear was taken from me years ago.

We are supposed to meet at ten o'clock.

I purposefully show up ten minutes late. I don't like to wait; I'm not a patient woman. And if he's not willing to wait ten minutes, then he's not the man for the job.

My heels click on the tile floor as I walk to order my drink—a coffee, black. I have no need for extra calories in the form of sugar or milk. Only once I have my coffee in hand do I turn to look for the man I'm meeting.

We didn't exchange any details about each other. And it's not like one of us is holding a single rose or something stupid like that from the movies.

I'm dressed in a slim navy blue dress and heels. I look like any other woman headed to work in the city. He's not going to be able to find me. I'm going to have to be the one to find him.

I walk confidently through the throng of people gathered around the too-small tables. Most people are chatting in a group—those I can rule out. There are a few on their laptops—I rule them out as well. I don't see a single person on their own.

I sigh as I sip my coffee. I'll walk through the room one more time, and if I don't find him, I'll have to put out a new call for a hitman. I'm not going to deal with a man being late.

Suddenly, goosebumps form down my arms, the hairs on the back of my neck stand up, and all of the air squeezes from my lungs. I don't have to turn around to know who is standing behind me.

This can't be a coincidence. *I haven't seen him in seven, or is it eight months?* He doesn't live here. He saw my call for a hitman, and he answered it. And I have no doubt he knew exactly who he was answering. I used the nickname that only he calls me.

"Huntress," Langston says, sending shivers racing through my body.

I try not to react. Only Langston has the ability to turn my body on end. To make me feel things I didn't know I was capable of feeling. And not all of those feelings are good.

"Killer," I say in a raspy voice, using the nickname I gave him when we were kids after I watched him kill a spider.

The flame that burns intensifies as we let it simmer between us. We both relish the feeling, even though we will never do a thing about it. An electric energy between two people doesn't mean that we belong together. In fact, I think it means we should stay as far away from each other as possible. If we light a match near our smoldering fire, we will burn the entire world to the ground.

I turn around, hoping that I'm in complete control. That I look confident, poised, and completely unaffected. But when I look at

Langston, it's not what I expect. He's wearing a suit. He never wears a suit.

It fits him well, which means he owns it and isn't renting it. It's a dark gray color with a white shirt opened at the collar, exposing his delicious sculpted chest. It also hides the muscles and scars underneath, which tell the story of the dangerous life Langston leads.

He doesn't look like a gangster, a devil, a killer. Instead, he looks like a businessman meeting a client for coffee.

"This is a new look for you," I say, my eyes purposefully trailing down his suit instead of staring at the harsh edges of his jaw and blue depths of his eyes that I'll get lost in if I stare too long.

"This is the same look for you," he says. His voice gives nothing away, but it's meant to be a compliment. He's always liked the way I look—neat, tidy, polished with just a hint of womanly curves.

"Shall we sit, or should we just agree this isn't going to work and go on with our separate lives?" I ask, lifting my cup to my lips, daring him to be the one to decide if he wants to take this meeting further. I don't want him to go, and I know he won't. He wouldn't have come all the way from Miami to meet me in New York City for coffee if he wasn't going to stay and talk to me.

The edge of his lip lifts, reminding me of the playful boy I used to know as a kid before the world darkened him and turned him into a monster that I barely even recognize. And then he walks past me. For a moment, I think he's leaving, but he walks to a small table in the corner where a couple of college-aged boys are laughing with two empty coffee cups.

"Time to leave, boys," Langston says, his voice low and deep, full of a harsh threat if they stay.

I don't have to be a fortune teller to know the boys will get up without protest. I know the look that Langston is giving them, I've heard the voice. No one denies him when he uses it. His voice alone holds that kind of power, which makes it all the more shocking that he doesn't use it to rule his own empire. Instead, he follows others' orders.

Langston pulls out a chair for me to sit.

I won't sit in it. He already knows this, which is why he gives me a smug knowing smile when I sit in the opposite chair. He takes his seat as well, and we both place our cups of coffee on the table.

"So, my little huntress is going to finally make a kill?" Langston asks.

"I guess that means we aren't going to small talk first." I cross my legs, purposefully pushing the hem on my dress higher up my thigh.

Langston's eyes flick down to my legs before meeting my gaze again. "I'd rather get right to the point than play games with you."

I smile. "We never play games with each other, killer. We just lie."

The disappointed frown Langston gives me affects me more than I want to admit.

"Yes, I plan on killing someone," I finally say.

"Who?"

"Does it matter?"

Langston shrugs. "Not really, but it's not like you to actually kill a man. You hunt them down, you track them, but you never do the killing. Never get your pretty little hands dirty."

"No, that's your job."

"So did you change your mind? Am I the one who is going to do the killing?"

I shake my head. "This one's mine."

His eyes narrow into tight slits as he stares deep into mine. There was a time where we could both read each other with one look. That time has long passed. He has no idea what's going on behind my hazel eyes. No idea what I'm hiding beneath the mask of makeup, curled blonde hair, and tight dress.

"Why?" he asks when he can't find the answer on his own.

I lift my coffee to my lips, avoiding giving him an answer.

"Tell me the truth. Why did you come when you knew it was me who sought a killer?" I ask.

"Now, why would I do that? We never tell each other the truth," Langston says, his voice angry and sultry as he throws my words back at me. It might be the only truth we ever tell each other.

I toss my hair over my shoulder. "This was a mistake. I'll find someone else."

Langston leans back in his chair. If I got up and ran out, I know he wouldn't chase me.

We never chase.

We don't play games.

We just lie. And lie and lie.

It's the only thing I can count on when it comes to us.

"No, you won't," Langston says.

I frown, my eyes flitting back and forth over his, trying to figure out the hidden meaning.

"I will. I don't need you."

"It's me or no one." His blue eyes shine brightly. He knows he has me cornered. And he's about to go in for the kill.

"I'll make sure that every man knows that you're mine. That you are tied to the Black name."

I grip my coffee cup tighter but don't show any other outward signs of my anger. "Always using the Black name instead of your own."

"The Black name is my own."

I run my tongue over my teeth, drawing his attention to my mouth. "Just another lie. You can pretend that it doesn't matter that you aren't Enzo's brother by blood, but it matters. He has a real brother now. He has another best friend. You are nothing but a disposable soldier to him."

I stand to get up. I don't need a hitman anyway. I can kill the man myself. And I can find a way to ensure that no one ties me to the crime.

Langston catches my wrist, though, before I'm even fully out of my chair. I'd forgotten how quick his reflexes are.

"When?" he asks, not letting me have any control. Just one of the many reasons why we will never work.

I inhale a deep breath, taking my time. I may not be able to deny him, but I can prolong my answer. It's a mistake, though, because all I smell is his husky scent. It fills my nostrils, and it's going to linger there all day. Every time I take a breath in, I'll breathe in him—a burning reminder of a man I wish I could get rid of forever.

"Saturday night." I don't give him any more specific details. I don't have to tell him what time or where. I know he'll find me. *He always finds me.*

He nods.

I think he's finally going to release me, but his hand is still wrapped around my wrist.

"We still need to discuss payment," he says.

"$100K. I told you how much in the ad."

He shakes his head. "I don't want your money."

"That's the only way I'll pay you."

His jaw tightens, and I chance a glance at his eyes. He doesn't have to tell me with words how I will pay him back. I know. I know what he wants from me. The same thing most men want from me.

But it's the one thing I'll never give him.

CHAPTER 4

LANGSTON

Liesel ran from the only family she's ever known. She did it years ago to start a new life. To get a fresh start. To stay away from what she deemed evil and brought up too many painful memories for her.

I understood at the time why she ran.

I know why she's disappointed in me.

I know why she's been gone all this time.

She's been running from her past. But it seems her past has caught up with her.

For a while, she lived in the middle of nowhere. She was hidden. *Safe*.

But that isn't the life for Liesel. She likes to be near people; she likes to matter. So she moved back to the city and started up her life again as a lawyer. She bought a high-rise condo. She became the powerful woman she once was. She thought she could hide in plain sight, but there is no hiding from our world.

I know—I've tried. Once you are in this world, you are in. There is no quitting. You can try to outrun it, but eventually, the darkness from your history catches up to you.

Liesel wants to hunt and kill a man.

She's always been a hunter, but never a killer. That was always where she drew the line. It's just another reason she hates me.

I don't only kill for self-protection; I kill because I enjoy it.

She left the coffee shop without telling me who or why. But I have time.

Saturday, she said. Today is Tuesday. I have four days until I see her again. Four days to figure out the truth she's hiding. The lies she spoke.

We never tell each other the truth. We can't.

It started as games when we were children. But then I stole half of a secret that I had no right to. She has half of the truth; I have the other half. Both of us will lie forever to keep our secrets.

My heart pounds in the cage that is my ribs as I think about seeing her again in person instead of watching her from the shadows or on a shitty security camera.

She's the same—exquisite beauty, full of all the confidence in the world. But that's her outward appearance. On the inside, she's a broken bird hiding beneath giant wings. She hasn't ever dealt with her past so she can never really live her future. She's living a half-life, one where she doesn't fully exist.

You could say the same thing about me.

For now, though, I have a new obsession. One I will enjoy immensely. I get to watch, study, and learn everything I can about Liesel.

She knows that's what I'm doing. It's why she didn't tell me all the details about where or even exactly when to meet her. She knows I can figure it out. And I haven't had such a thrill surge through me in months.

The next four days, I become mesmerized by her. I have an excuse to watch her more closely than I ever have before. She may think she was out of my life, but I've been keeping tabs on her. It's the most patient I've ever been, waiting for the moment she returned to my life. This wasn't the way I expected her to return, but I welcome it all the same.

I tapped into the security feed in her condo and spent most of my nights watching her. Unfortunately, there are only cameras in the main living portion, so the most I get to see of her is when she walks through the living room and then out the door in the morning. She doesn't even make a cup of coffee in her kitchen when she wakes up. She sticks to her bedroom. I don't know if it's her usual routine or if she knows I'm watching and is purposefully making it harder for me to see her.

But once outside her condo, she can't hide.

I follow her in her cab.

I watch her strut like a true New York woman in her high heels and tight dresses as she enters her office building every day with her name scrawled across the nameplate leading to the top floor of a sky-rise. She's the queen of her own domain.

The security in her office building has cameras everywhere. Watching her give orders in the boardroom to her team, give advice in a controlling yet flirtatious way to her clients, and then answer calls like a boss has me growing hard. Especially when she crosses her legs when she's alone in her office and lets her dress inch higher up her thigh until it's no longer professional. She holds a pen to her lips and sucks on the end, her long lashes fluttering up to the corner of her office every once in a while where the security camera sits.

My little huntress, drawing me in as she acts like a seductive minx, putting on a show just for me. And what a show it is. I could spend the rest of my life watching her.

But then I remember the truth. I remember who she is. What she's done.

You think you want to kill, my huntress? You have no idea how. You have no idea what killing will do to you. And what need do you have to kill when you can seduce and draw a man in with one flick of your tongue across your bottom lip, one bat of your eyelashes, one raspy word from your voice? Men spend their entire lives looking for a woman like you.

I've had you this entire time.

Men are stupid; they don't realize the thing they are drawn to is all a lie.

Liesel gets up from her desk and grabs her purse.

I frown as I look at the time. Four-thirty, way too early for her to be done with work for the day. Liesel is a workaholic. She usually isn't done for the day until seven or eight. And then even after work is over, she usually meets a client for dinner. And I suspect she still goes over files in her bedroom at night. She's never done working.

Where are you going, huntress?

It's Friday, my last day to figure out where to meet her and who she wants to kill. I haven't spent much time on the man she wants to hunt and kill. I've been much too focused on watching her.

Anyway, I could find the man in twenty minutes or less after I put some effort in, which I will tonight. For now, I need to know where she is going. I need to know everything about her.

Her cab stops in front of another shiny, high-rise building. My guess is that she's meeting another client at their office instead of her own.

I park my car illegally on the side of the road and watch her from the driver's seat. She doesn't go into the building immediately. Instead, she pulls out her phone and talks on it for a few minutes as she paces back and forth.

A man comes out in a suit—the client she's meeting.

I study him closer as he approaches her and then pulls her into an aggressively tight hug. He's at least a decade older than her, his hair has speckles of gray in it, and he has more wrinkles around the eyes than any man our age.

The hairs on my arms stand up, and in my gut, I know this man isn't a client.

Who is he?

His vile hand slips down from around her lower back, gripping her ass. His other hand tips her head back as his thumb strokes her carotid, like if she makes one wrong move, he'll apply just the right amount of pressure to kill her and make it look like an accident. It's a threatening move I've made too many times myself.

This is the man she is hunting.

This is the man she plans on killing tomorrow.

My gorgeous huntress, what trouble did you get into? What did he do to you to make you change your mind about killing men?

He had to have done more than just grope her inappropriately.

Unfortunately, that's something that she is used to. Men can't control themselves around her—they turn into disgusting, rotten pigs who touch without asking.

Liesel knows how to handle men like that. I taught her how to knee a man in the balls when we were eight.

So I watch with a smirk, waiting for the moment when she'll bring this asshole to his knees.

Her face tilts up with a smug smile. This is it—the moment she makes him pay for touching her without her permission.

She leans forward, closing the space between them as he plants a firm kiss on her lips.

I jump out of my car without thinking. My legs start moving toward them. *He has no right to touch her!* She didn't ask him to touch her. She didn't welcome his kiss. She didn't—

The kiss ends, and I stop in my tracks as I watch her smile up at the man with more brightness than I knew existed in Liesel.

This man made her smile with a kiss.

That's.

Not.

Possible.

Liesel doesn't smile, not like that. She prowls and smirks and flashes seductive grins. But she doesn't smile from true joy and happiness.

And yet, that's exactly what she's doing. She's smiling up at a man a decade older.

Her hand is slipping into his, their fingers intertwining like they've done this a million times.

Her purse falls down her shoulder, and he takes it off and loops it over his shoulder, making her laugh.

She's laughing.

I'm not close enough to hear it, but I'm close enough to see the sparks flying from her face.

Liesel is happy.

I never thought I'd see the day.

This isn't the man she plans on killing tomorrow.

But he's the man I want to kill for touching what's mine.

CHAPTER 5

LIESEL

I felt Langston all week.

He was watching me every second of every day. I doubt he slept a minute all week.

Langston hasn't changed at all. I know him better than anyone else.

I avoided the security cameras in my home that I know he tapped into. I avoided most of my usual evening routine.

The only time I put a show on for him was at the office. I drew him in like a hunter draws in prey. I just haven't decided when or how I'm going to strike against him. At least not yet.

For now, I have more important matters to attend to. I have to kill the man who threatened me and my family.

I have to stop thinking about Langston. It's impossible, though, since I feel him everywhere now. It's a strange, yet familiar feeling. One that sends goosebumps up my spine at the most inconvenient times.

But Langston will serve his purpose. He'll take the fall if or when the time comes for my blackmailer's death. And then he will get out of my life once again, gone in the night just like before. And I can go back to the life I've chosen.

I slip on my white gloves as Waylon enters my bathroom. He hasn't been sleeping over the last couple of nights since I've wanted to throw Langston off and not give him any information about my life.

But I know he saw us kiss yesterday afternoon. I felt Langston's heated, angry stare. He wasn't happy with that kiss.

Well, too bad. I haven't been happy with Langston my entire life.

"You ready, my love?" Waylon asks, as he leans against the doorframe, watching me. His eyes drag down my body, taking every inch of me in, sending butterflies fluttering through my stomach and up my chest.

Waylon's effect on me is different than any other man I've ever met. It's more intense. More passionate. Just more.

It took me months to decide if that was a good thing or a bad thing. I still haven't decided, and we've been together for over a year. I don't think I ever will.

But it's a feeling. There was once a time that I didn't think I could ever feel. So I welcome feeling anything at all, even if it isn't exactly pleasant.

I meet his eyes in the mirror. He's wearing a tux that makes him look rugged and sophisticated. It's black, like his hair, lightly peppered with gray. When we first met, he used to color it, but I find the fact that he's older, more mature, and understands the world more than I do, comforting. And I admit, a bit sexy. So he stopped—for me.

His jaw is clean-shaven, showing off its squareness. His eyes are dark with a few lines in the corner that show the depths of his knowledge and worldly experience.

Even though he's leaning against the wall, his posture is impeccable. He never falters on that. He always stands tall and proud—that's what I love most about him.

We are the same, him and I—we've been handed shitty cards, but we rose above it all. In our own way, we've found our power. And now together, we will rule this city—queen and king.

"Yes," I say, standing from my makeup chair and letting him see the full effect of my hair, makeup, and dress all at once.

Waylon's smile grows from ear to ear. "You're perfect, my beautiful one."

I force myself to smile. I hate compliments, but I should accept one from Waylon.

He holds out his arm, and I take it. He leads me to the waiting limo to take us to a ball where we will wine and dine all night, showing the city what true royalty looks like.

The ballroom is grand and sparkling as we enter. Tonight's facade is a fundraiser to feed the hungry in the city, but it's really an excuse for all the wealthy to dress up, network, and show off. They gain more power by making small threats and puffing out their chests to show that they should be the ones in control. That's what all these men and women are doing. They don't know that they've already lost. Waylon and I have already won.

Or maybe they do. Because all eyes in the room are on us from the second we enter. Everyone tries to jockey for our attention. Everyone murmurs, speaking in hushed tones about us.

I grin. Tomorrow my cheeks are going to hurt from all the smiling, but I'll keep doing it if it gains me more power.

"I hear you are running for governor," one of the men says.

"So word has gotten out already," Waylon laughs it off.

I flick Waylon a knowing look. We were the ones who leaked the news. Waylon is running for governor today. Tomorrow it could be the presidency.

He wants power, real power, legal power—unlike some people I know.

That's what draws me to him.

Langston Pearce.

He's hidden from my view among a group of men chatting together. All I can see is a single eye peeking out from between two people. An eye watching me with unsettling dominance.

I wobble on my heels as my knees weaken from the power of his gaze.

Waylon may make me feel things I've never felt before, but Langston is the only man who can turn my knees weak, my heart still, and my world on its head.

Both men have a strong effect on me. Both men make me wish I'd never met them, because being with them means giving up some of my absolute control.

Neither man will let me have complete control. They want it for themselves.

My life would have been the same with Langston as it is with Waylon—a constant battle of wills. The difference is Waylon makes me stronger, while Langston makes me weaker. And I won't accept weakness.

I draw my eyes away as I hold onto my champagne glass, blocking my face from Langston's view.

The group mingling with us laughs at something Waylon says, and I laugh along with them. I could play my role in my sleep—the role of a trophy wife, clinging to Waylon's arm. And yet, I won't cling. I'm not here because of Waylon. I'm here on my own. I made it on my own. I don't need any man, Waylon knows it. He can't control me. It's why he knows that if I touch his arm, it's not because I need him to lean on. It's because I'm playing the part.

Still, when I'm drawn back into the conversation, I'm no longer really here. Instead, I'm focused on the feeling of Langston's eyes lingering over me, heating me from head to toe with just his hungry gaze.

From the outside, I ignore his stare. But Langston's wreaking havoc on my insides—my gut is twisted, my heart is fluttering, my breath is shallow, practically panting to breathe him in.

But then I see Fitz—the other man I'm here for. The man I've hunted down and traced to the threatening letter I was sent—a man I plan on killing.

"Excuse me, gentlemen," I say with a seductive smile before I kiss Waylon on the cheek and whisper into his ear that I'll be back soon.

He nods solemnly before turning back to entertaining the group around us. He doesn't ask where I'm going. He lets me be as independent as I want, even if he disagrees with me.

I spot Fitz, my target, as I strut through the ballroom. I know I have several eyes on me, but I only feel Langston's. I don't let myself look at him. I know where I stand with Langston. I know that although we will never be together, never even be friends, he will follow me. So I focus on my target.

A waiter walks over to the group he's standing in, leaning in to offer more champagne. And I take my chance.

I step right into the center of the five man group. All eyes and voices fall, as they all concentrate on keeping their boners from making an appearance as they drool over my body covered in lace and black fabric. My ass and legs look great beneath the slit in the dress, but my boobs are the real show as the dress cuts down in a low V, showing off most of my breasts.

Men are so easy to manipulate when you have a body like mine.

I set my empty glass on the tray, leaning across Fitz's face as I do. I stand almost a foot taller than him in my heels. Then I take another glass of champagne from the tray.

"Meet me on the balcony," I whisper into his ear before I turn and walk away toward the balcony. I know that he's following me without having to turn and look. In fact, I know that two men are following me.

The air is warm as I stand on the balcony a dozen floors up, looking out at the twinkling lights of the city. Anywhere else, a balcony like this might seem romantic. But here in New York City, the city that never sleeps, all you hear is the honk of horns and the bustle of people. You breathe in the heavy haze in the air. This sight, the energy here, makes me never want to leave.

"You found me," I say when I hear Fitz's heavy footsteps. He would make a terrible assassin, which is one of the reasons I was able to find him so easily. He's used to dealing with much less skilled people. He didn't know he was dealing with a survivor. He doesn't know that I more than survive—I thrive. And I won't let a nameless suit like him threaten my life. I've survived much worse men. This man is nothing. Soon, he'll truly be a nothing.

"When a beautiful woman tells you to meet her, you meet her."

I hold my champagne glass up as I turn and lay eyes on him, reading him like a book. He knows exactly who I am. He knows that I know who he is. He has a bulge in the side of his pants, where I know he keeps his weapon. He thinks I'm weak, that he can just pull the gun out, and I'll be on my knees begging for my life, willing to do whatever he wants.

Not likely.

I'd rather die.

"Your first lie, Mr. Fitz Nash." I sip the too sweet champagne.

He puts his hands in his pockets, close to the gun, but not quite touching it as he takes a couple of steps toward me.

"I don't lie."

He stops and leans against the cement railing next to me.

I let my eyelashes bat down at him, drawing him in as I lick my bottom lip. He leans closer, thinking I'm going to kiss him. I'll do a lot to hunt a man. I'll play my part, but I'll never kiss or fuck a man I don't want to, just to get what I want. That's where I draw the line.

There will be no kiss.

"No, you're just a blackmailing bastard who thinks he can threaten me and my family for easy money."

His eyes blink in shock, and he reaches for his gun. But I'm faster.

I smash my champagne glass hard against his forehead. He palms the large gash while I take the moment to casually grab his gun.

It takes the bastard a few minutes to realize what's happening; he's so focused on the blood pouring down the front of his face, dripping into his eyes, spilling onto his lips and tux. He doesn't realize I'm aiming a gun at his heart.

Slowly, he raises his hands.

"You're not going to kill me."

I remove the safety. "Why do people keep saying that?"

"Because it's true. You don't have to kill me. I'll leave you and your family alone."

"Why? Why did you target us? Was it just about the money, or was it more?" *Please, don't say it was about the blasted letter my father gave me before he disappeared from my life.*

"I knew you two had money. I thought with your family's political ambitions that you would just pay and move on. I never intended to harm you."

He lowers his hands.

I don't know why I'm letting him talk. This is all information I can get on my own. And I suspect he isn't telling the truth. *Just shoot him.*

"Are you working alone?" I ask, instead.

He smirks, thinking I'm weak. It's exactly what I need to be able to pull the trigger.

I squeeze.

Unfortunately, he moves just in time, and I only graze his arm. His eyes grow wide, and the air changes as he realizes I truly do intend to kill him. And there is no one to save him.

The city is too loud for anyone to put a thought to the occasional gunshot. And everyone in the party is already occupied. They don't care about the outside world.

"Goodbye, Fitz." I squeeze the trigger, but a loud movement to my side makes me turn.

Langston.

I frown as I realize what he's done. The gun is battled out of my hand. Fitz holds the gun to my head.

I'm the hunter who never kills.

Because Langston is the killer.

That much will never change.

CHAPTER 6

LANGSTON

Liesel was actually going to kill this shithead.

She *would* have killed him.

I *couldn't* let her kill—not a low life like him. When she kills, it needs to be worth it. Her first kill will stay with her forever, as will each kill after that. I don't want her thinking about this bastard one second longer than she has to.

Liesel's fuming at me as Fitz grips her around the neck with one arm and holds the gun at her temple. She's not scared; she doesn't fear for her life. She knows that I won't let anyone hurt her, but her red cheeks, teeth biting down on her lip, and daggers for eyes let me know how pissed she is.

"You couldn't let me have him," she spits out as she pulls from Fitz's grasp, almost getting away on her own without my help.

I stand still as a statue, hoping that if I let her think about this a minute, she'll calm down. As long as she's in Fitz's hold, she has time to realize she shouldn't be fighting me. I already know how she'll feel in my arms.

As much as I yearn for that, and hate to see her in another man's, I can't have what I want. I never get what I want.

Yet, it won't stop me from demanding it, from eventually getting it. I'm tired of being patient when it comes to Liesel. Our story has lingered on for far too long. It's time to end it.

"You're the huntress," I say.

She shakes her head, her anger pulsing off her in waves. "You're the killer."

Fitz's eyes narrow as he takes me in, trying to understand who I am and what I'm doing here. Unlike Liesel, though, I won't be asking any questions.

"Don't take a step forward, or I'll kill her," Fitz says.

I smirk. *If he killed her, it would make my life a lot easier.*

Liesel notices my smirk, and her glare intensifies, as if to say, *I'll kill you and haunt you from the grave if you let me die.*

I give one look to Liesel, letting her read my thoughts like we used to be able to do as kids. She slams her elbow into Fitz's groin.

It's enough to get him to release her.

I take slow steps forward as Fitz hunches over in pain. I grab his gun that he so carelessly let Liesel take from him. He almost let her kill him. I pocket it from Liesel, and then I snap his neck. His body falls to the ground in one crumple.

Liesel gasps. Even though she's seen death hundreds of times. Even though she's seen me kill—it still takes her breath away every time.

After a moment, she composes herself and stares at me with such a harshness in her eyes as she folds her arms across her chest.

"I knew I should have found someone else," Liesel says.

I don't answer her. *She should have found someone else.* But she found me. She always finds me. That's why our lives keep intertwining.

I step closer to her. I expect her to slap me. To try and knee me in the balls. For her to try and steal my gun.

She does none of those things. She just lets me get close to her.

"If you need to kill someone, you call me. You don't do it yourself," I growl my command at her.

She scoffs. "Since when do I take orders from you?"

I grab her hips and jerk her to me until her chest is flush against mine.

"Never." *But you will soon, my huntress. You will soon. You won't have a choice.*

The music carries from the ballroom, making me want to dance now that Liesel is in my arms. So that's what I do. I sink my fingers into her lush hips, and we sway together.

It's wrong for so many reasons.

There is a dead man on the floor next to us.

We aren't together.

We will never be together.

She's with Waylon.

And I'm—well, my situation is complicated.

And yet, I can't not touch her. I can't not have her. It's always been this way with us. Even when she was in love with my best friend. Even when she finally set her eyes on me, we both knew that we could never be.

We just never speak the reasons out loud. The reasons would all be lies anyway. That's the one thing we share—lies.

We both grew up lying to survive, and it's stayed with us.

"What are you doing with Waylon Brown?" I ask.

She tilts her head as she looks up at me, her long throat revealed to me, and if I dip my head lower, I can see her glorious tits staring up at me. But it's her pulse in her neck that has my attention. I can see how fast her heart is racing.

Liesel wasn't scared of the man who held a gun to her head. She's scared of me. She knows I'm no longer on her side—and she knows I'm far more dangerous than Fitz was. I could harm her, kill her.

"He's rich and good looking, why wouldn't I be with him?" she answers back, tilting her head all the way back as I dip her over the ledge, knowing the danger makes her conflicted between desire and terrified. It also gives me the view of her elated face, and of course, I take the moment to run both my hand and eyes down the front of her dress. Her skin melts like hot silk beneath my fingers.

"Liar. You don't care about money. Or good looks."

I pull her back up, whipping her hard into my body. The movement takes her breath away.

"Power then?" she says it like a question.

I shake my head. *That's a lie too.* Everything the woman says is a lie. I haven't figured out what she's doing with that man yet, but I will.

I just have to read between the lines, do some investigating. There is always a reason with Liesel, and it's never the obvious. She would never let herself fall in love. Even though she doesn't supply love as an answer, I know that's not why she's with him.

"I didn't think you owned a tux," she says, her eyes suffocating my body with her stare.

"I don't."

She rolls her eyes, calling out my lie, before her eyes flick to the dead man on the floor, and suddenly she's sober.

"Why did you want him dead?" I ask, even though I already know the answer. I found the security video of her reading the blackmail, the threat against her family.

"Stop asking questions you already know the answer to."

She pushes away until she's no longer in my arms.

My arms hang at my side like dead weights, no longer having a purpose.

"I'll wire you the money I owe," she says, still staring at Fitz.

"I already told you, I don't want your money."

Liesel finally looks at me, her face unreadable. But I know she's scheming, trying to come up with a way to hurt me.

Just like I'm conniving ways to hurt her.

"You'll take care of the body?" she asks, already knowing I will. This isn't the first time I've killed a man. I work in security for the Black family, a crime family who rules the seas. I've disposed of plenty of bodies and killed more times than most people make new acquaintances.

I walk over to the body. There's a reason I didn't shoot him. I don't want to haul a body down the stairs.

"Stand back," I order.

For once, Liesel listens as I squat down to stare at the bastard. I should be thanking him. He gave me a reason to be in Liesel's life again.

Then I heave him up over the railing and watch as his body falls down the twelve stories and hits the sidewalk below.

There is a soft screech that reaches our ears from up here.

People will believe it was a suicide. I'll take care of the security cameras so no one knows we were up here with him.

Even if the police don't believe it, they won't trace his death to us. And if they found out someone in the Black family was involved, they wouldn't care. They know they have no power against us. We rule wherever we go.

I grab Liesel's arm—she trembles at my touch, and then I lead her back inside, off the balcony. Just because I can convince the police of anything doesn't mean I want to deal with them.

Liesel doesn't comment on how I decided to deal with the body. She may not have spent her life killing, but she's watched me kill. She's watched Enzo and Zeke. She's seen as much death as I have. She's felt as much loss.

She's just as broken and fucked up as I am.

I stop us in the hallway, and I cage her in, putting my arms on either side of her head. She doesn't act like she's trapped, though.

That's because she's not. My tricks don't work on her, just like hers don't work on me.

"We're done then. I won't see you again for six months or more. And when we both go to our friends' birthday parties for their kids, we won't speak to each other. Yes?" Her voice is sharp, full of authority.

She's my rival in every sense. Even if I was okay with her suggestion, I wouldn't let her win this easily.

I lean in, our faces inches apart until she can feel the power of every word I say to her.

"We aren't done, baby. I did you a favor. I killed for you. There was a time I would have done it for free, but not anymore. Now you owe me a debt."

Her nostrils flare, her pupils dilate, and her heartbeat jumps in her throat.

I drag my eyes down her body one last time—over her perfect blonde curls, down her sharp clavicles to her full breasts, over her lace-covered stomach, drooling as I continue down her hips to the slit revealing her toned legs. She's every man's dream—but she's my nightmare.

"I'll pay you whatever you want."

I shake my head. "I don't want your money."

She takes a shuttered breath. I have no doubt that her panties are soaked.

I let my eyes darken. I let my voice deepen. I let every bit of the menacing beast inside me roar to life. The part of me that scares most people, but will only turn Liesel on even more.

That will confuse her even more than she's already perplexed.

She thinks I came for her, and I did. She's terrified of what I could do to her. And she should be because I'll take more than she can ever imagine.

"You owe me a debt, Liesel Dunn. You've owed me a debt for a long time. And soon, I plan on collecting."

CHAPTER 7
LIESEL

I owe Langston a debt.

He thought those words would scare me. He thought he could just demand I give him whatever he wants because he killed for me.

I don't think so.

He calls me huntress, but I'm so much more—lawyer, badass woman, queen. I don't take orders from anyone. I don't owe anyone. Especially not an egotistical man on a power trip who negated our agreement when he killed Fitz instead of letting me do it like we agreed.

As far as I'm concerned, I owe him nothing for what he did. He didn't keep to our verbal contract.

I'd be willing to pay him for his time, nothing more.

And as for any past debts I owe him, he can suck it. Our past stays in the past.

There is no way he's going to start collecting on old debts. If he does, then it means I get to collect too, and he owes me as much or more than I owe him.

But I know what Langston really wants. The same thing he's always wanted.

Me.

My body.

My soul.

He wants to control me. He wants to boss me around in the bedroom.

No way in hell am I letting that happen.

Not just because I'd be cheating on Waylon if I did. Langston doesn't deserve that part of me—ever.

And the only person left on this earth who terrifies me is Langston.

"You're all worked up, my love," Waylon says, kissing my shoulder.

He's right. He can read me well when I get worked up like this. My body is hot and agitated and horny. *God, I'm so horny.*

Sure, Langston turned me on. He's a blonde god in a tux. He looked like a hotter James Bond. I've seen Langston a lot of ways—T-shirt and shorts, shirtless in swim trunks, even naked. But it's a rare occasion to see him in a tux or suit. He hates them.

Yet, he can wear a tux with the best of them. He fits into the world of powerful men, whether he wants to or not. All he has to do to belong is get a respectable job and wear a suit or tux with pride.

But that's something Langston will never do. He'd rather take orders from his best friend. Protect and serve—that's Langston.

I used to like it, especially when he was protecting me. But I lost that right a long time ago. And apparently, now I have to pay him back when he protects me.

Ugh, how annoying.

The elevator doors open to Waylon's penthouse. He has an early flight tomorrow, which is why we are staying here tonight instead of my place. People used to think it was weird that we both still have our own places, but both places are incredible; it would be a shame to give either of them up. We can easily afford both. And they are located across town from each other, which makes it convenient to stay at one or the other depending on our schedules.

"You think you can help me work off some steam?" I ask, running my tongue over my bottom lip.

His eyes light up with anticipation. He loses his stone, distinguished expression, and turns into a horny boy willing to please me—just the way I like it. Some women prefer a man who dominates them in the bedroom, one who ties them up, spanks them, bosses them around.

Not me—that all seems too degrading. I like the power. I like to be the boss.

Maybe it's because of my history.

Maybe it's because of who I am.

Either way, it's the only way I fuck—I'm the one who dominates.

Waylon unlocks the front door and holds it open for me.

I grab his tie as I walk past and yank him inside before slamming him against the wall, already feeling a tiny bit better now that I'm going to get a dozen orgasms tonight to make up for what Langston said and did.

"Yea, baby, use me. Hurt me. Take out your anger and pent up emotion on me. I want to know how badly you want me, because it can't be as much as I want you," Waylon says, kissing my neck sweetly.

I smirk. He has no idea about my past, but he does know that I'm fucked up.

And then I remember the cameras.

There are more in Waylon's place than in mine. Here there are even cameras in the bedroom.

Waylon is paranoid, and his one fetish is watching us fuck over and over. There is even a mirror on the ceiling so he can have a better view.

Where there are cameras, there is Langston. I know he's tapped into the security feed. I know he's watching, which makes this all the more fun.

Langston thinks he can demand I repay my debt to him by giving him my body. I'll show him exactly what he's missing, exactly what he'll never have.

"Kneel," I say.

Waylon looks up at me excitedly. He may like ordering people around in the boardroom, but here, he likes me bossing him.

I look up at the camera in the entryway corner.

I reach around my back and unzip my dress. Then I let the straps fall off my shoulders, before wiggling my hips as I push the dress to a pile on the floor.

I'm wearing nothing but heels and black lacy lingerie—bra, thong, and garter.

"Lick me. Make me come."

Waylon's eyes brighten. He loves making me come, but this isn't for him. This is for Langston, to show him what he will never taste. What he will never have.

Waylon's hands slide up the length of my long legs, and I focus on his touch instead of staring into the camera. Langston already knows that I know he's watching. Now to revel in the feeling of ecstasy as Waylon worships my body in a way that Langston never will.

His fingers hook into the bands of my thong, and he carefully slides it down my body, his brooding eyes locked on his prize as he drops my panties to the floor in a pile on top of my dress.

He licks his lips like he's about to devour his favorite food. Waylon is a lot of things; he has a lot of traits I like about him. But this might be what I like the most.

"Waylon, lick me," I command, my voice raspy in anticipation of him eating me out.

He grins at the desperation in my voice and then does as I order. His arms wrap around my hips as his tongue licks the length of my slit, tasting the sweetness of my arousal. He moans, sending vibrations through my body.

My body shudders, and I grab onto his head for support as he licks over me. Tasting, teasing until he's making me pant at a pace that rivals any exercise routine I've ever had.

"You taste so fucking good. I can't believe I'm the one who gets to taste you. The only one."

I grin as my hands sink deeper into his hair, gripping him so fucking hard that I should be afraid I'm going to rip his hair out. I'm not, though; Waylon can take it.

I do let my eyes roll up to the camera at Waylon's words. *You hear that, Langston? Waylon's the only one who gets to taste me like this.*

And then, he's pushing his fingers inside me. He's not gentle, but not rough enough to spark nightmares of my past. It's just enough to make my body explode in a rolling orgasm that is just the start of my night.

"Yes!" I scream, not using his name yet. After all, I'm the woman in control here. One orgasm isn't enough for him to earn hearing me call out his name. Not yet.

Waylon removes his fingers after I've come down from my orgasm. Then he licks his fingers, savoring every drop of my cum on his fingers.

"Stand and go to the bedroom. Undress and get ready to fuck my brains out."

Waylon stands and gives me the softest of kisses on the lips, reminding me, as if I could forget, how incredible his kisses are. Promising me that he's going to fuck me better than any fantasy I could ever imagine.

Waylon is breathtakingly sexy as he walks to our bedroom while still wearing a tux and my cum on his lips.

This is the life I always imagined but never thought I could get.

When Waylon is gone, I walk to the fridge, still wearing my heels, bra, and garter.

I grab a water bottle from the fridge and take a sip while I wait for Waylon to get undressed and ready for me.

It gives me a moment alone with Langston.

I take my time removing the bobby pins, holding my curls to one side until my hair is down. I run my hands through them to loosen the curls before taking one last sip of water.

"He's mine. And I'm no one's. You hear me, Langston? I belong to myself." I glare at the camera with the full force of warrior about to go into battle. I know that Langston won't back down easily.

But I just won the first battle. And I'm about to put an arrow through his heart with what I have planned the rest of the night. When I fuck—I fuck all night. I fuck until I can't move, can't think— until all I feel is the thousands of tiny nerve endings exploding from waves of pleasure beating through my body.

I fuck to forget.

I fuck to feel alive.

I fuck like it's what I was made to do.

"You will never have me," I whisper into the dark before I strut down the hallway to the bedroom where Waylon waits for me.

He's done what I asked. He's undressed. Condom is already on his hard dick. And he's lying face-up on the bed, the handcuffs ready for me to use on him.

He's ready to be dominated.

He's ready to give me what I need, and take what he needs.

I'm not sure if this is love or something like it—but I never feel happier than I do in moments like this where I can take complete control. I love that I don't have to fight him, that he just follows my orders.

I walk over to the bed silently. His eyes follow me. I'm sure Langston's eyes follow too.

I never thought I was one to enjoy having another watch me fuck, but the heat spreading through my body is like nothing I've ever felt before. So maybe I like being watched. It's something I'll have to explore after I deal with my Langston problem.

I grab Waylon's wrist and pull it up until I can lock the first handcuff around it, tying him to the poster bed. And then I kiss the palm of his hand as he lets me tie him up.

"Good boy," I say.

His eyes roll back at my soothing words. I may dominate, but it's not about pain. It's not about hurting Waylon. I just want the control —no, I need it. I can't fuck without it. I can't be in a relationship without complete control.

I have trust issues.

But it's also my greatest strength. I don't need a man to make me feel wanted or powerful. All I need is me.

I repeat the same binding to his other wrist and both of his ankles. He's tied up and ready for me to fuck him. He can't hurt me. He can't touch me. And unlike me, Waylon trusts me completely.

I climb up onto the bed as I kiss up his body. His thick, muscled thighs from all the weight lifting he does. His hard condom covered cock. He's hard and ready for me, but I lick up and down his shaft to feel as turned on as possible, as wet as I can get before I fuck him.

I vowed to myself a long time ago that I wouldn't let sex ever be painful—not ever again. He knows I won't fuck him until I'm completely drenched and have already come at least twice.

I continue my teasing up his rippled abs, his strong chest, and chiseled jaw.

"Make me come," I say as I straddle his face, my pussy hovering over him.

"My pleasure, my love."

He lifts his head to feast between my legs while I grab the headboard for support with one hand while my other plays with my breasts, freeing them from the lace bra and then rolling my thumb over one of my nipples. I shift my hips back and forth over his face to increase the friction as I get riled up again.

My mind flickers to Langston, watching me come apart. I shouldn't even let him see this part of me. He shouldn't get to see me orgasm.

But it's not about him. This is about me. About taking control of my own body. I want to show him this incredible experience he'll never get.

Finally, my body is coaxed into another orgasm.

As soon as I come down enough to move, I slide down Walon's body, grab his cock, and push him inside my slick walls.

He curses as he fills me tightly with his long, thick rod.

My nails dig into his chest as the pleasure fills me, and I lock my eyes with Waylon.

I won't think about Langston again, not until I'm finished with Waylon, which won't be until he has to leave for his flight in the morning.

Waylon reads my mind, knowing exactly how intense sex can get with me, how long it can last. He's on board and has the stamina to keep up with me. I'm going to need release after release to get me through an entire week without sex.

Langston may get to watch, but he doesn't get me. He doesn't get my attention, my thoughts, and definitely not my body—my orgasms. Those are all for Waylon and me.

I start off slow, getting my rhythm, and then Waylon's hips start thrusting with me. My body glides over his, my clit hitting the point of his hard, sculpted V, and soon I'm convulsing around him as he pours his cum into the condom within me.

"Waylon!" I finally scream, making it clear that he's the only man for me.

I climb off of him and remove the condom as I walk to the bathroom, still wearing my power, 'fuck me' heels.

I am a goddess; three orgasms is nowhere near enough to satisfy me.

I grab the box of condoms in the bathroom and bring them to the bed before I untie Waylon. I want to be fucked in every position. Now that I've established my authority, my need, my control, Waylon will respect my power.

"Fuck me from behind. I want to be fucked in every position, in every way, until the sun comes up. Think you can handle that, baby?"

He smirks. "For you, I'd do anything."

He rolls a condom on, then grabs my hips, and carefully slides between my legs as he fills me and reaches around to stroke my clit.

My eyes roll back at the feeling. This is the life. This is my life. This is what I chose. And I won't ever let a man take anything from me ever again.

CHAPTER 8

LANGSTON

*F*uck, Liesel.

She knew I was watching.

That was complete torture for me.

Fuck.

Fuck.

FUCK!

My blood pressure soared to a thousand over a million watching her get fucked by that cocksucker.

The message was clear, though—she's his, not mine.

I laugh at that.

She thinks she won.

Sure, she pissed me off to no end. No amount of jacking off has brought me down from my pent up frustration.

She has no idea what I want from her, but I'm going to enjoy showing her.

Soon, my huntress, I'll be coming to collect my debt. And your little show just made collecting my debt that much sweeter.

CHAPTER 9

LIESEL

Not many men have the stamina to go all night.

Waylon does.

Sure, his cock needed a few minutes to rest between each round, which was when he put his lips and tongue to good use. He knows how to pleasure me all night.

Just staying awake all night is a feat. Waylon never let my brain go anywhere except the intense pleasure I was feeling.

Then he was sweet enough to pour me a heaping cup of coffee and set it on the nightstand in one of those self-heating cups so it would be warm and ready for me when I woke up—which was about an hour after I fell asleep.

I don't need much sleep after a night like that. Nights like last night are what I live for.

I stretch, feeling how sore my muscles are.

I smile at the comforting ache. I don't have a need to workout. Sex with Waylon like this a couple of times a week gives me more stamina than running or biking or pilates ever could.

I take my time finishing my coffee before heading to the shower.

I walk naked into the en-suite bathroom that is larger than most people's bedrooms, especially in New York City.

I flip the shower on and immediately step in, the cold water soothing my aching muscles.

Most people prefer warm showers. Not me; cold showers wake me up and keep my skin youthful far more than warm showers. I grew up taking cold showers; we rarely had enough heat for warm ones, and it's a habit that's stuck.

It's one of the reasons Waylon and I hardly ever shower together.

My mind starts to wander as I close my eyes and wash my hair.

I think about the dozens of orgasms I received last night. I think about how high I feel, the happy hormones pulsing through my veins. I think about Waylon, about how he looked, sounded, and felt as he drove inside me.

But I don't let my mind go free. I don't let it wander to who I really want to be thinking about.

I get a sudden chill down my spine, but I don't turn the water warmer. Eventually, the feeling fades.

I know a lot of time has passed when I finally step out of the shower with a towel wrapped around my body onto the heated bathroom floors. It always shocks me every time when I step out. Somehow I always forget about that feature when I look at the marble floor.

And then I look up, and my heart skips.

The mirror has fogged over, and there are three words written in the fog.

Five More Days.

I quickly glance around the bathroom, but there is nowhere for someone to hide.

Did Waylon come back?

Did he leave a message on the mirror before he left?

No, that can't be. Waylon is only going to be gone for three days.

I dart out of the bathroom and into the bedroom. I still don't find anyone.

In fact, I run through the entire condo and find no one.

I could call our security team, but I don't.

I don't need to.

I know who left the message.

The only man who could have snuck in and out without security spotting him.

A man I thought I had made perfectly clear to last night that I was not his. That I don't owe him anything.

Langston Pearce.

I know how our security team didn't catch Langston, but I don't know how I didn't notice myself.

Even with my eyes closed, I always know when Langston is nearby.

The chills—that was Langston.

I did know. I just didn't let myself acknowledge it.

I walk back to the bedroom just as I hear my cell phone buzzing on the nightstand.

I jump at the sudden sound, and slowly walk over, assuming it's Langston who's calling and he can wait.

But when I pick the phone up, it's Kai on the caller ID.

I sigh and almost decide not to answer the call, but she'll keep calling the rest of the day, especially if Langston put her up to it.

"Kai, now really isn't a good time. I have to meet with a client in an hour, and I'm already running late," I answer, not giving her a chance to speak first. Kai is the only one who continues to keep in touch even when I insist I no longer want to be part of that life, that family.

There was once a time when I loved being the only woman among three dangerous men—Enzo, Zeke, and Langston. I was their entire focus. I thought I would end up with Enzo, the leader, but I realized too late that that was never meant to be. Enzo ended up with Kai.

I'm not bitter. They belong together, but my life changed after that. Everyone pushed me to Langston like they thought we needed our own happily ever after. None of them know our true history. None of them know our past.

And then Zeke found Siren, and the pressure increased for Langston and me.

But I don't want a happily ever after.

I don't want to live in their dangerous world.

And I don't need friends, especially girlfriends—I'm a lone wolf.

"Then I'll keep it short. Siren and I are going on a pampered girls vacation to Santorini for a week, and we'd love for you to come with us. We are leaving in two weeks, I know it's short notice, but hopefully, you can get someone to cover your clients for you."

"I—" I start.

"You are not giving me some excuse why you can't come right now. I have two weeks to convince you to go, and I want to spend every day of that persuading you. We haven't seen you in six months, and we miss you."

I sigh. "I'll think about it."

I have no idea how to get out of this. A girl's trip sounds like my nightmare. Kai and Siren are nice enough, but to be trapped on an island with them for an entire week of gossiping, drinking, and sunshine?

No, thanks.

I wouldn't survive a week with them.

Kai squeals excitedly like I just said yes, instead of blowing her off like I did.

"I have to go," I say.

"Of course, will talk to you tomorrow!"

I end the call. Kai is going to keep to her word and call me every day this week. And then again the next week. There is no stopping her once she gets going. She's the boss for a reason. Her orders are followed, no exception.

I don't have a clue how to get out of this.

I walk back into the bathroom and look at the words again—*five more days.*

The words have started to fade, and soon they won't exist at all. Then I'll be second-guessing myself, thinking I made it up.

Five.

More.

Days.

What will Langston demand of me then?

I have an idea—and I suspect I just found out my excuse for why I can't go on the girl's trip. I'm with Langston—that would shut Kai up. She wouldn't dare interfere if she thought there was a chance that

Langston and I could get together. She knows nothing about my life here. She doesn't know about Waylon.

Langston has a plan to extract a debt from me in five days.

I smirk as I drop the towel, knowing that Langston is watching.

I'm not going to wait five days. I'm done waiting, and I'm done playing by his rules. This is going to end much sooner than five days.

LANGSTON

Liesel thinks she's going to win.

Not this time.

We've been fighting since we were kids. Fighting an invisible war with each other—one that was never spoken about. One that neither of us knew the terms, rules, or even what we would win. We just knew that we had to win.

Since we were five, we've been fighting, hurting, deceiving one another.

Why?

Because hurt people, hurt people. And we've been damaged more in our youth than any of our friends could imagine.

Our battles didn't always involve hurting one another. Although, that was the majority of what happened.

We were enemies—usually fighting and angry at each other. Liesel was chasing my best friend, Enzo, and I thought she was annoying. So I would tease her, piss her off.

As horny teenagers the lust and attraction grew, but I was beneath her. She was after Enzo, the man with power, not me—his side-kick.

The lust turned to sexual frustration and then serious feelings we both had no right to feel, which just pissed us both off more. We both knew from a very young age that we could never ever be together.

If we could have escaped each other, if we could have never met, we would have. As much as we needed to stay apart, the world kept pushing us back together over and over again.

Things have changed.

We can't keep living our lives like this. We can't keep battling forever. This war has to end. This is the start of our end.

It's not going to be easy for either of us, but it's necessary.

We've both been holding onto secrets for too long, since I ripped half of that envelope out of her hand—it's time.

Neither of us will give up our truths easily. We will fight with our lies until the bitter end. Until one of us finally breaks down, until one of us loses.

But as soon as either of us speaks the truth—that will be the end of us.

We will no longer be friends.

We will never have a shot at being lovers.

We won't even be enemies anymore.

We will be out of each other's lives for good.

Which is why I'll drag out this final game as long as I can. I'm not ready to let go of Liesel yet.

I smirk when I see Liesel on the security camera in the lobby of the hotel I'm staying at. It seems that Liesel is ready for this to be over faster than I am.

She doesn't get to be in control of this.

She doesn't get to win.

She's an excellent hunter. She can seek whatever and whoever she wants. There is nothing that can be hidden from her.

She found me—four days earlier than I'm ready to be found.

So I won't let her find me.

She is a great hunter, but she's rusty. She's been away from danger for far too long.

I, on the other hand, never left the darkness. Over the last year, I've only let it deeper into my soul until I've become as evil as the world I was born into.

She can hunt all she wants, but she'll only find me when I'm ready to be found. She should have learned that by now.

I watch on my computer as Liesel walks to the elevator in a tight red dress and heels. She came straight from the office. In the last month that I've been following her, I've never seen her out of her dress or heels outside of her condo, and she makes no exception today.

She likes the dresses and heels so much because it's her suit of armor. It protects her and makes her more powerful. It's not because she's a girlie girl. She doesn't love always being so dressed up. She just likes the power she's able to wield while dolled up.

I take a quick glance around the hotel room as she rides up in the elevator to see if there is anything lying out that I don't want her to see, but there isn't. I already know that without looking. I travel light. All of my stuff is already in my backpack.

I close my laptop and stick it into my backpack before zipping it up.

I pull out my cell and switch the feed to my phone. I watch her exit the elevator with complete confidence like she belongs here.

I have thirty seconds until she makes it to my room. I spot a pen and paper on the desk and scribble on it before I move to the bed. I lift the ceiling tile, and pull myself up just as I hear her scan the hotel keycard she flirted her way into getting.

The tile pops back in place before she opens the door, and I switch the feed on my phone until I'm tapped into the security in my own room.

This is what I do for a living—security. I design security systems for the wealthy. Usually, on yachts or mansions, but it gives me the skills to tap into the best-designed systems.

Liesel's eyes flitter around the room.

"You couldn't stay in a nicer place, huh, Langston?" she asks to the room as she wanders around, looking under the bed and then in the bathroom to see if I'm hiding anywhere.

I smile at her words, though. She knows even if I'm not here that I'm watching. I'm always watching. It's the only way to protect everyone I love.

Not that she falls into that category anymore.

After a half-hearted attempt to find me in the room, Liesel walks over to the piece of paper I left for her.

"Four more days," Liesel reads out loud.

She balls the piece of paper up and tosses it into the wastebasket under the desk before her eyes scan the room one last time for any clues as to where I am or where I could have gone.

Her eyes flit up to the ceiling, and I almost think she might have found me. She starts talking, and I realize she's found the security camera in the corner so she can look into my eyes as she speaks.

"I don't owe you anything, Langston Pearce. And you won't be demanding anything of me in four days. You won't be taking me. You don't own me. You will take nothing from me."

She licks her red lips, knowing that her lips are my favorite thing about her.

How I've wanted to kiss her lips. There have been so many opportunities throughout my life where I could have kissed her, but something always held me back. I've never tasted them—never tasted the poisonous, tempting red apple lips.

She knows her seduction won't work on me. And yet, she still does it, driving me mad.

"I gave you a chance to end this war, to talk face to face. You ran, hid. I'm usually the hunter, the seeker. And you follow me in order to kill. But not this time. This time, I'm going to hide, and you'll have to do the hunting.

"And if all these years of hunting have taught me one thing, it's that I know how to hide better than anyone. You'll never find me unless I want to be found. You aren't going to win, Langston. So surrender, and maybe I'll let you live."

With that, she walks out. Her fighting words hit me in the chest as hard as a bullet.

Liesel thinks she can hide.

She thinks she has power.

She has no idea of the truth.

It's impossible to hide from someone whose heart you stole when we were five. That piece of me she stole calls out to me no matter where she goes. I won't have to hunt her to find her; I just have to follow the beacon, the signal that she involuntarily sends to me.

She can't hide any more than I can. And in four days she'll be mine. I just don't know what I'm going to do with her when I claim her.

CHAPTER 11

LIESEL

My plan didn't work. Of course, Langston, king of security, saw me coming on the cameras. I knew he would see me the second I walked into the hotel. Hotels are full of cameras, which makes it impossible to sneak up on Langston. He can hack into any system. He sees everything.

I shiver at that thought, of all the things he's seen. Things he's seen and done nothing about.

Four days.

That's how long I have until he comes after me to extract a debt he thinks I owe him. I still don't know why he thinks I owe him for killing one man for me. He's killed dozens of men for me when we were younger. *Before...*

Before he tore my secrets from my grip.

He won't let me find him before the four days are up.

But I'm not going to let him take me in four days. I'd rather hide the rest of my life than let Langston win.

I'm not going to have to hide the rest of my life, though—just for four more days.

If I can stay hidden, away from Langston's reach for four days, then I win. He may still come for me. He still may come to collect his debt after four days, but he will have lost. He will lose his power, his upper hand.

He knows that, that's why the timing is so important to him. He wants complete control over me, he always has. He's been trying to boss me around since we were kids.

I start my Porsche and head back to my apartment to think in the comfort of my own home. I blast the radio as I drive, trying not to think about Langston, the best way for my ideas to flow.

The problem with Langston being able to see everything is that I can't write anything down. I can't look anything up on my computer. I can't make plans except in my head.

When I get to my condo, I pour myself a glass of scotch while avoiding looking up at the security camera. I refuse to talk to Langston anymore if he's too much of a coward to show his face. I won't let him into my mind either. From now on, he only gets to see what I want him to see. And he sure as hell won't be getting another glimpse of my body.

I swirl the liquid in my glass as I contemplate my choices. I can hide in plain sight or hide at the ends of the earth. Anything less means he will win—he'll find me.

An idea forms.

It may not work, but at least I'll go out fighting. I won't make Langston's job easy.

It wouldn't shock me at all if Enzo and Kai put Langston up to this thinking they could drag me kicking and screaming back to their world, back into that life. I won't do it. I'd rather die than go back.

I pick up my phone and dial Waylon's number.

"Hey, sweetheart, miss me already?"

I smile at his response. "I always miss you."

I hear the clinking of ice. "You enjoying a glass of scotch?"

"Yes, same as you."

I can feel his grin through the phone. We always drink scotch together. It's one of the many things Waylon and I have in common.

"Unfortunately, you're going to have to miss me for a while longer."

"And why's that?"

"Some old girlfriends invited me on a girl's trip to Santorini, and I had to push up a business trip before I meet them, so it will be three weeks until I'm home."

"A girl's trip, huh? I thought I was your only friend?" he teases.

"You are, you know that."

"I think a girl's trip would be good for you. You work too hard; it's time you got a little vacation. Where is your business trip? I might be able to meet up with you before you go, but my schedule is crazy these next couple of weeks as well."

"Sacramento and then Chicago."

He sighs. "I'm in Houston and then Hong Kong."

"It will just make our reunion in three weeks all that more enjoyable," I let my voice drop into a raspiness that turns him on.

"You're going to need to take off another week when you get back. I'm going to need that long to show you how much I'll miss you."

My panties soak, and my nipples peak up at that thought.

"Deal."

I end the call, and then I call my assistant Gerald.

"What can I do for you, Miss Dunn?"

"Can you book me a flight to Tokyo and then a private jet in Tokyo to take me wherever I might need to go next?"

"Of course. When would you like to go?"

"Tomorrow afternoon, please."

"I'll book you a first-class flight to Tokyo and arrange the usual private jet for you to be ready at your beck and call after you arrive. I'll email you the details as usual."

"Thank you, Gerald."

"You're welcome, Miss Dunn."

I end the call. I just gave Langston two separate leads to follow, and I'm about to give him a dozen more. He'll have no idea where I'm going when I'm through with him.

I book more commercial and private flights on my own.

I book bus tickets.

I rent cars.

I rent yachts.

I spend more money in a single hour than most people do in a lifetime, arranging dozens of leads that Langston will be forced to check up on.

And then I call Tiffany.

"Liesel! I'm so glad you called, it's been too long."

I love her enthusiasm. She's a struggling actress I met at the beauty salon years ago, and she's always looking to pick up extra money. Plus, she has a very particular skillset that has come in handy a handful of times before.

She's not a great actress, but she's good enough to play me when she needs to. It helps, that with the right makeup, she looks exactly like me. That's her real skillset—doing makeup. I've tried to convince her to become a makeup artist, but she's always resisted.

"Can you meet me at the salon tomorrow? I need someone to help me with my makeup," I ask, providing our shared clue that I will be needing her services as discreetly as possible.

"Absolutely."

I PULL TIFFANY INTO THE BATHROOM OF THE SALON BEFORE WE have our hair done.

"You have a job for me?" Tiffany asks with hope.

I look her up and down. She's skinnier than the last time I saw her. Her hair is a disheveled mess.

"Yes, I do."

She lights up with a bright smile.

"I need you to take a one week trip as me; I'll pay for everything."

"Where to?"

"Where would you like to go?"

"Paris!"

I laugh. "Paris it is then. If you want to check out London, Rome, Barcelona, or any other city while you're in Europe, go for it. I'll pay you a hundred grand in addition to the trip expenses."

"Oh my god, that's too much to just take a vacation."

"No, it's not."

"Will I be in danger?"

I shake my head. "The man who is after me won't hurt me. And he will have no reason to harm you either." *At least, I don't think Langston will hurt me.*

"But we have to make the switch right now. We have to change clothes, you have to drive my car with my cell phone and credit cards to the airport right now, and I'll have to go back to your place."

She frowns. "Um...you don't want to go back to my place."

"Why?"

"Because my place is a closet with a door that doesn't lock, cockroaches, and no hot water."

I smile. "That's perfect."

A place like that won't have any working security cameras. There will be no way for Langston to follow me. And hopefully, he'll be chasing Tiffany halfway around the world anyway.

We quickly swap clothes, and I tie my hair up in a messy bun. I start tying her broken tennis shoes that are two sizes too big on me, while she fastens on the straps of my heels.

But even dressed in jeans and a T-shirt and her in a dress and heels, I still look like I come from Beverly Hills, and she looks like she hasn't gotten a decent night's sleep in months.

I pull a wet wipe from my purse and wipe the makeup from my face before I hand my purse to her. She digs through and starts applying makeup that makes her freakishly look exactly like me. When she's done, she turns and looks at me.

"How do I look?" she asks with big eyes.

I let my eyes drag up and down her body, looking for any tiny details that will tip-off Langston right away.

"You look perfect," I say with a tight smile. "Now remember how I said you should act when you're playing me?"

"Like a bad bitch who isn't afraid of anyone and looks up to no one.'

"Exactly."

I feel around in my pockets. All I have is a twenty-dollar bill, her ID, and a pay-as-you-go phone to get me through the next part.

"I'm going to go. But you stay and get your hair done however you like before you leave. What's your address?"

She gives me directions to her place, which will either cost the entire twenty dollars I have in bus fares to get there, or I'm going to be taking the subway—something I haven't done in years. But now isn't the time to get grossed out by how half of New Yorkers live.

I thank Tiffany one last time, and then I sneak out the back door of the hair salon while Tiffany struts out into the front.

I look around for any way that Langston could be following me, but I don't see any cameras or any people.

This will work.

Three subway trains later, I finally make it to my stop, which is still a good ten-block walk away from the apartment. Thankfully, I have tennis shoes instead of heels. For the first time that I can remember, I let my head fall a little. I let my shoulders slump. I feel less than I actually am. And for once, it feels good to not have to worry about anything. To not have to worry about power or control. To just be.

When I make it to Tiffany's apartment building, the sight of a crumbling building and cockroaches does nothing to deter me. I head inside to the third floor and then collapse onto her stained mattress on the floor. She doesn't have a pillow, just a ratty old blanket.

Regardless, I will rest well, because tomorrow I have to do something much worse than sleep in an unsafe apartment with no air conditioning or pillow. Tomorrow I have to go back to where my life began, to where the nightmares started. That is the one place Langston thinks I'd never go.

♡

THE NEXT DAY, I WAKE UP EARLY. THE SOUNDS OF PEOPLE YELLING and alarms blasting fills my room even though I'm in the apartment alone.

I don't know how Tiffany lives like this. I hope the money I gave her is enough to start a new life.

I rinse off in her cold, broken shower. I change into sweatpants and a sweatshirt I find in her closet but keep the same tennis shoes. Lastly, I start the long subway journey to the pier.

After several train switches, I make it to my boat rental.

My heart freezes at the sight of the boat. It's modest, nothing like the yachts of the family I grew up next to but never truly in. My mother worked for a dangerous man as a maid. I grew up with that dangerous man's son, Enzo, and his friends Zeke and Langston. I know how to operate a boat. I know the benefits and dangers.

I just never thought I'd willingly step onto one.

"Do you know how to operate this thing, miss?" the man in overalls and a bandana asks.

I smile as I take the keys from him. "Better than you do."

His eyes widen, and then he chuckles like there is no way a woman like me knows how to operate a boat better than him—*misogynist*.

I start untying the boat before he's even stepped off, and then I start the engines, forcing the man to jump back onto the pier.

I wave at him with my adorable, shameless smile, letting him know how much of a catch I truly am beneath the ratty clothes, but he'll never get me. Then I peel out in the boat, taking off hard and fast and letting the breeze run through my hair.

Langston used to be a knight in the sea. He used to monitor every boat, every passenger in the ocean. But he won't be looking for me here. The boat I rented isn't under my name, and I didn't use any money tied to me to pay for it. It will take a lot of digging on Langston's part to find me.

Three days.

I have three days until Langston comes for me.

It will take two to make it to Miami, where I grew up. Where I met the boy who shone brighter than the sun. I'm tired of living in his shadow. In three days, we end this.

I DRIVE THE BOAT STRAIGHT THROUGH DAY AND NIGHT. I DON'T sleep. *Thank God I've learned to operate without that basic need.*

I'd forgotten how thrilling it is to be driving a boat by myself with nothing but the lights of shore and the stars overhead. I'd forgotten how bumpy the waves feel when you're alone in a boat. They feel ten times as intense as they really are. I'd forgotten how eery the calm quietness of the ocean seems with only the waves knocking against my boat, reminding me of how quickly the sea can turn dangerous.

But even being here, I'm still not called back to this life. I'd rather be anywhere but here. The ocean hasn't been kind to me.

I get to Miami as the sun rises on the third day, the day that Langston says he's coming for me. But if I succeeded, today will come and go without a word from Langston.

I dock the boat, and then I walk down the pier, the sun already heating me as I walk, making me want to strip out my clothes and into a bikini, but I won't. Not today. Today is about hiding, not being seen.

I rent a car from the car rental down the street; then, I drive to the house I grew up in.

No, that's not true. The house I grew up in was Enzo's guest house, and that house burned to the ground.

No, I drive to the house my mother lived in when she wasn't working. The house I lived in until I was ten but barely remember.

The house we fought in.

The house I begged her to take me away from, to move anywhere but here. She did as I asked. We moved, and my life turned upside down in one night. Forever changed, all because of where we moved to and who my mother worked for.

She couldn't be a teacher or a hairstylist or a maid in a hotel. No, she had to be a maid for a man who took whatever he wanted with no regard for life. No regard for consequences.

I never thought I'd be back in Miami, let alone the tiny one-bedroom home that I once shared with my mother. That was when I wasn't sleeping at Enzo's or even Langston's. I did anything I could to avoid coming here when I lived here. I never thought I'd visit now that I'm an adult with options.

Still, it's the place I feel my mom the most. I should have visited before, but I just couldn't.

"Hey, Mom. You've been taking care of the old place?" I ask to the sky as I walk inside. My mom died from an overdose the same night I learned that my jackass father was still alive on my eighteenth birthday.

The house is empty. There is no furniture. No sign any human has stepped foot in here since the time my mom lived here.

I sigh and look at Tiffany's phone. It's nine o'clock in the morning. I have a long time to wait.

Thankfully, I have my nightmares to keep me company.

I sit on the floor in the corner of the living room, and I wait, hoping my hiding spot is good enough to hide from the devil.

♡

Two minutes left until midnight.

Two minutes left until I win.

That's when I hear the car. The slamming of a door shut. The honk of the horn as he locks the car. The heavy footsteps as he approaches the house.

Langston's here.

I know it without looking up as the front door opens.

He found me.

"You've gotten better at hide and seek, I see," Langston frowns at me.

"And you've become more of a monster," I shoot back.

CHAPTER 12

LANGSTON

I almost lost.

I almost didn't find her in time.

Liesel almost won.

Almost...

It wouldn't have really mattered if I didn't find her the day I said I would. The game we play is invisible, with invisible rules, and invisible rewards. We are playing a game without all the pieces, without knowing how close the other is to winning, without even knowing if we are playing the same game or different games.

But we do know one thing—we both share lies. Lies that keep us from freedom, from living the life we want.

It's time to end this.

Time to finally finish our game.

To have a winner.

Our game is nothing like Enzo and Kai's game was with official rules and an empire to gain at the end.

Our game is nothing like Zeke and Siren's game, spilling sinful truths that harm more than they help.

Our game is simple: lie until you can't lie anymore. Try to get the upper hand. Try to get the other to fold first.

That's what having control of this meeting was about. We were always going to eventually meet. But on whose terms—*mine or hers?*

I got here just in the nick of time. I won this round.

But Liesel has gotten more skilled than I give her credit for. She may live a cushy life now, yet that doesn't mean she hasn't been honing her skills on the side.

She put out fake leads, trying to throw me off her trail, so I had no choice but to consider every lead. There was no way for her to hide once she decided to board a plane, car, or boat. She couldn't hide from me; she never could.

I thought I had found her when she boarded a plane to Paris. Of course, she would choose the most extravagant, beautiful place to try and hide. She wouldn't take one of the dozens of flights she booked to the middle of nowhere.

I boarded my own flight and followed her to Paris. To my surprise, I found a woman who looks strikingly like Liesel and yet isn't. They could be twins if I didn't know that Liesel has no siblings, no family. She gave up her family.

Once I arrived and realized my mistake, I only had hours left to find Liesel before my time was up. I had followed all the leads she left for me. I searched all the surveillance at every airport, bridge out of the city, bus stop, harbor and found no sight of her.

I wasn't going to find her via my usual routes. She slipped by undetected. My only choice was to choose one last place to search for her. She could have been anywhere, but that's when I realized where she had chosen. The one place I knew she'd never go. My own backyard.

Miami.

Her mother's house specifically.

Now, I'm standing in the small, broken-down room face to face with Liesel.

I say room, because this has never been a house, definitely never a home. It's barely big enough for two people to breathe in comfortably. A strong wind would knock the whole building down.

Liesel hardly stepped a foot inside her mother's home growing up, and it surprises me the strength it took her to come back here to Miami—the place that ruined both of our lives.

"You win, okay? You win," Liesel finally says, the pain etched around the edges of her voice. She hates losing as much as I do.

I take a closer look at her. She looks like she's been on the run for months instead of days. This is the first time in decades that I've seen her in anything less than designer clothes. She's usually radiating confidence and beauty. Right now, the oversized rags that cling to her body scream homeless.

She did everything she could to avoid me. To escape, hide, and prevent me from winning. I should compliment her on her hard work, but I won't. I like watching her squirm.

I glare down at her as I step further into the small room, forcing her to stand and step back to avoid me touching her. She hates showing defeat, but she hates me touching her more.

"What do you want, Langston? I'm tired of our game." Her eyes drag up my body in my dark jeans and a fitted gray shirt.

"Really? Then why did you run? You know the only way to end our game is to finish it. Declare a winner once and for all. But we can't finish the game if we keep avoiding each other."

She shakes her head as the corner of her lip rises into a smirk. "You have no idea what finishing the game means."

"Maybe. Or maybe I know more than you could imagine." We talk in circles, neither of us speaking the truth. Neither of us showing the other our cards. Neither of us showing the other the final move we need to make to win.

"You owe me a debt, my huntress."

"I already offered to pay you for that debt, even though you don't deserve it. The arrangement was that I would kill the man, you would just be present to give me plausible deniability." She pauses for effect. "Instead, you murdered him."

I pet my chin, staring at her, as she continues to pout and throw a mini tantrum, reneging on our agreement. She's forgotten our deal. One we made a long time ago.

"Are you finished?" I ask.

She folds her arms over her chest in a huff. "No, but I'm sure you're going to interrupt me to spew your lies."

"No, I'm going to interrupt you to remind you of an agreement we made a long time ago."

Her wheels start turning as I speak. "We were five when we made that deal! You can't hold me to that now."

"We've kept every other promise we've made. We lie, but we keep our promises."

She rolls her eyes. "I promised to hunt. You promised to kill for me. And if either of us failed, then—"

"Then, we owed the other anything we wanted—and I want you."

You might think the promise was something silly little kids promise each other—like play getting married or promising to never give each other cooties.

That might be what it was for Liesel. She hunted down a spider in her room, but couldn't go through with killing it. So she called me. I promised to always kill for her. She promised to hunt down any creature.

It may have started as innocent kids making silly promises. But for me, it was so much more. We promised each other a life if we failed. And we've both failed more times than we can count.

I'm ready for my life.

I'm ready to end this.

I'm ready to learn her truths while keeping my lies.

I'm ready to win and take the truth of that moment, along with hundreds of others to my grave.

Liesel will never know my truth, but before the end of this year, I'll learn hers.

I watch Liesel closely as she realizes what's happening.

"You're really going to use a promise that we made when we were kids to get me to go with you? To take me as your prisoner? To convince me to follow you? To become your slave? To let you own me?" Her voice gets louder with each question.

I'm silent.

She knows I'll use whatever I can against her to get her to come with me. She can either come willingly, or I'll take her. She can't keep running and hiding.

Her chest rises and falls quickly under her stained sweatshirt. She's considering her options and realizes she has none. She needs answers as much as I do.

We both need answers.

We both need truths.

We need to continue to hide behind our lies until the bitter end.

What happened that day when we were five changed the course of both of our lives and led us here.

"What will it be, Liesel? Will you come with me willingly, or will I take what is owed to me?"

She shakes her head slowly. "You evil bastard. You have no right to take me. I'm not yours. I'm not your property!"

"I'll take that as a no, you won't come willingly."

"I will fight tooth and nail. And I will never stop fighting. You know my past. You know the pain I've endured. You will never break me. You will never get any truths from me."

"I know."

"Then what do you want with me? My body? To fuck me every night like your whore?"

I'm silent.

"You want my money? My power? My name?"

I don't answer her. I let her throw her theories out. I let her spill her lies. I let her expel her anger out. Better to get it out now than later.

"What do you want with me?" she yells.

I step closer, and to my surprise, this time, she doesn't back away. She's done running. She's ready to fight. I'm prepared for her to draw a knife, a gun, even blow up the entire house with both of us in it if she has to. I knew she would fight when she was done running. It's exactly what I want.

I grab her wrist and yank her to me until my breath is just above her mouth. I pause, lingering for my words to make the most impact.

"I want the same thing I've always wanted—I want to know what was on your half of the paper. I want to know the truth, not the lies. I want the treasure that secret leads to. I want to take everything from you. I want the truth, Liesel, and I don't care what I have to do to get it."

"Why do you want the treasure? You have more money than you could possibly ever need."

"To ruin you." *Like you ruined me.*

"You won't kill me," she says, her voice shaking, not sure if her words are true or more lies.

"If killing you gets me the secret, I will."

Then I shove a sleeping pill into her parted lips and cover her nose and mouth with my hand.

She struggles for a moment as she backs into the corner of the wall. Her eyes go big, and the veins in her eyes turn bright red as she struggles for breath but still refuses to swallow the pill.

"I'm crueler than you'll ever be, Liesel. You don't know how far I'll go. You may think what I did to Siren was savage, but it is nothing compared to what I will do to you."

She stops fighting as more oxygen leaves her body. Soon she won't have a choice but to surrender.

She closes her eyes hard and then opens them defiantly before finally swallowing. I may win this round, but she thinks she's only allowing me so she can fight another day. So tomorrow she can slice my balls clean from my body.

I kiss her neck, thanking her for swallowing the pill that will soon knock her unconscious.

"I can't wait for you to fight back, Liesel. I'm going to enjoy every second of it. But for now—sleep. Tomorrow you can fight."

I remove my hand, and she gets one solid breath in before she collapses. I catch her in my arms, finally having a moment to really study her. To hold her close. To revel in the fact that she's finally mine.

Mine—if only that were true.

CHAPTER 13

LIESEL

*L*ife or death.

How much does Langston know?

Does he know my truth or only part of it?

Does he know the missing piece of the puzzle I've been desperately trying to put together for years?

No, there is no way he knows the truth, but he does have the missing piece of information. There is no way to know its significance without the rest, which is why he needs me.

I hear the roar of the plane engine near my head, giving me a pounding headache.

I want to open my eyes, but I won't, not until I've figured out every clue I can while Langston still thinks I'm asleep.

I'm surprised I'm on a plane. I thought he would take me back to Enzo and Kai's compound to be tortured until I told the truth. Or at the very least back to Langston's house, which is also in Miami.

I'm a monster with plenty of dark savageness in my heart, but it doesn't mean that I deserve to be taken like property.

So why am I on a plane?

Is the plane flying around in circles to confuse me before he inevitably takes me to the dungeons in the Black house? He thinks if I don't know where I am, I'll be more scared. He doesn't know there is only one thing I fear.

One thing in the entire world—and Langston can't use that fear against me.

No one can.

Not anymore.

I smell coffee brewing nearby, and I'm desperate for a drink. It would help my splitting headache from Langston's sedative.

But I doubt Langston will serve me coffee now that I'm his slave. *Dammit.*

I'll survive whatever he has planned for me. I'm more than strong enough. I'm a survivor.

But that doesn't mean I'm happy about it.

In the end, Langston will pay with his life for what he's about to do to me.

He thinks fucking me against my will will bring back all the horrible memories from that night. It will make me talk. That he won't even have to actually fuck me to get me talking, just threaten me with rape.

I smirk. He doesn't know me at all—not anymore.

"You can open your eyes. I already know you're awake," Langston says.

"Why? So I can look at your ugly face? No, thank you."

Langston sighs. "Get up, Liesel. Don't make this difficult."

"I'm not going to listen to a word you say. I'm going to make this as difficult for you as possible."

Then the bastard puts the cup of coffee right under my nose. It's a heavenly smell and my parched mouth waters. I'm desperate for a taste. My body betrays me and opens my eyes, showing how desperate I am for the cup of coffee.

I reach for the cup—he jerks it away just out of reach.

I grit my teeth together to keep my steaming anger inside. I feel the burning anger in the pit of my stomach shoot up my chest like lava, but I won't let it gush all over him until the right moment. As much as I want to tell him off right now, I don't have any power on a private jet miles over the ocean.

I sit up on the couch and lean my head back against the wall.

Only then does Langston hold the cup out to me again.

I don't immediately reach for it this time. I just watch him, trying to figure out the thoughts churning in his head. There was a time when I knew exactly what he was thinking before he spoke it.

"Take it, Liesel."

That only makes me want to disobey more. But damn do I want that coffee. *No, I need it!* It may seem ridiculous, but I know that I need that coffee to survive. I'm going to need every bit of my strength, every drop of caffeine to fuel me.

I snatch the cup out of Langston's hand and drink it before I feel any self-pity that makes me want to throw the cup of coffee in Langston's face.

The coffee tastes like heaven to my dusty mouth. It's warm and rich with a hint of cherry and chocolate—my favorite.

I look up at Langston, expecting him to gloat. To say 'good girl' or something condescending, showing that he's in control instead of me.

Instead, Langston stares at me like he's seeing me for the first time. His eyes have narrowed, his jaw clenched, his mind closed off. I can't tell if he's angry, or happy, or confused, or annoyed, or pissed, or turned on. All I know is there is a lot of emotion brewing beneath the surface of that half scowl, half awe expression.

We sit silently as I drink my coffee. I don't know what's about to happen next; this might be my only moment of happiness for the day, week, month, year...

So I savor every sip.

Down to the last drop.

Langston stands up just as I'm about to finish my cup and walks to the front of the private plane and disappears through a door, leaving me alone in the back. Some people might try to take this chance to snoop, to find a weapon, something to help me escape.

But that would be a waste of time. Langston is better at wielding a gun than I am. Even if I had a gun or knife, he'd stop me long before I was able to wound him. And there is no escaping on a private jet.

Langston returns a minute later with a pot of coffee and a plate of scones. He snatches the cup from my hand, refills it, then hands it back, before putting two scones on a plate next to me.

He doesn't give me an order, but it's clear in his gaze that he wants me to eat or he'll force-feed me.

My queasy stomach makes my decision easy. Whatever he drugged me with has made my head dizzy and my stomach upset. I need food. I pick up one of the scones and nibble on it.

"Where are we going?"

Langston leans back in his single chair across from me on the couch. He's wearing his usual outfit of jeans, boots, and a plain black T-shirt. He blends in and is ready to fight at a moment's notice.

He looks like Langston, but there is a heaviness to his stare. Something has changed about him; I just can't put my finger on it.

Not that I care. I don't care about Langston. I need to get him out of my life, once and for all.

"You'll find out soon enough."

I sigh. *Same old Langston—it's either no answer or a lie.*

"What are you going to do to me?"

He peers out the window next to him as if he didn't even hear my question. *Or maybe he's considering how to answer me?*

Finally, his heavy gaze returns to me, and I wish he'd kept staring out the window. As much as Langston tries to hide it, there is only one stare he gives me when he looks at me. And as much as I try to hide it, there is only one reaction my body returns when he stares.

Lust.

No matter how we hate each other, we missed our opportunity for one night in the bed, and our bodies resent us both for that.

That's probably why I'm here? For Langston to have his way with me. That way, he gets control of his lust without giving up any power to me.

I'm not naive enough to think I could truly fight him. If he wants to torture me, rape me, kill me, he can. But I can make the memory one that haunts him for the rest of his life.

"If I answer you, you won't believe me," Langston says in a deep octave that vibrates through my chest cavity and hits me in the heart, making it beat rapidly in response.

"That's right, you're a liar."

He smirks. "Same as you."

"How long will you keep me?" He'll hurt me to get whatever he wants—my pain may, in fact, be what he wants. He's a sadistic bastard, after all.

I know what he did to Siren—all in the name of helping her. They are besties now, but she doesn't know him like I do. She doesn't know the true depths of his danger.

"Seatbelt," Langston says suddenly out of nowhere.

I glance out the window and realize we are low to the ground. It looks like we are about to land in the ocean, not on land, but I know that isn't true.

I buckle my seatbelt and stare out the window for clues as to where Langston will hold me captive until he gets whatever he wants from me.

I spot the small island we are about to land on. The water is crystal blue.

Caribbean?

Hawaii?

Maldives?

There are so many places we could be landing. I don't know how long I was unconscious. For all I know, we could just be over in Key West, or we could be thousands of miles from Miami, like the coast of Australia.

Langston won't be telling me the truth, but hopefully, the airport will have signs once we land to tell me where we are.

We approach the rough-looking runway, and I'm glad I put my seatbelt on. The runway looks more dirt than concrete.

I brace myself, and I notice Langston do the same as we make a rough, bumpy landing.

I stare out the window, waiting for a building or other planes to come into view. None do.

The plane slowly creeps to a stop, but no cars drive up to greet us. No security comes to check our passports.

It seems we've landed on an island in the middle of nowhere.

I look over to Langston, who is looking at me curiously with a small grin lifting up his sharp cheeks, like he knows it will piss me off that he took me to a place I'll have trouble escaping.

If there were men here on the island, I could escape. Use my powers of flirtation to get one to help me, but I can't use that power if there are no people.

"Would you like to change, or are you going with the castaway look for our entire trip?" Langston says, his eyes dragging up and down the dirty rags I'm wearing.

I want to change, but he's won enough for one day.

"How long?" I say, my voice tighter.

"Long enough that your boyfriend will get worried. Long enough that he will give up looking for you and find someone else to become the future Mrs. Waylon Brown."

I shake my head. "Waylon will never stop looking for me."

Langston laughs. "I give him six months tops before he moves on. He's planning on running for office, and he knows that having a beautiful woman on his arm will serve him well."

Beautiful—that's the only characteristic that Langston uses, like beauty is all that matters.

"Don't underestimate him. He has money—more than you do. And we both know that men with money usually get what they want."

Langston unbuckles his seatbelt.

I do the same.

I stand to follow him off the plane.

"How long?" I repeat again. He won't give me any other answers, but I need to know how long I have to endure whatever he has planned. It will give me something to focus on.

Langston mentions six months, but that was just a random number he threw out to frighten me. I doubt Langston has six months to give up with me on this island. He works for Kai and Enzo Black. He's part of their family—basically, a brother to Enzo and Zeke. They won't let him hideaway on an island with me for long. They will say I'm a lost cause, and he should give up whatever he thinks he's going to accomplish with me.

Langston whips around at my words. "I told you I wouldn't answer you. No matter what my answer is, you won't believe it anyway."

"One month? Two? Three? How long?" I ask, watching the vein on his forehead balloon as he becomes more impatient with my annoying question.

Then he turns and walks toward the plane's door to exit.

I realize there is no one on the plane except the pilot.

"If you're going to rape me, just get it over with tonight. Rape me all week, and then we can both go home next weekend," I mumble under my breath.

That does it.

Langston snaps.

Turning on a dime, he has my arms pinned above my head, my body pressed against one of the windows, and my pelvis pinned with his.

He's breathing hard and fast—out of control. His eyes shine red, his nostrils flare, and the demon within him comes out to play.

He might rape me right here, right now.

Good—get it over with.

"Why would I give you what you want? Why rape you today when I can take my time? When I can make you wait and fill your head with all the torturous things I will do to you?"

"Because then you would have to wait too. You're the most impatient man I've ever met. You *can't* wait."

He grips my wrist with one hand as he strokes the side of my face with his knuckles so gently. The combination of his rough grip combined with his soft touch sends delicious sinful desire through my body.

I hate men being rough with me. *So why does his grip turn me on, even a little bit?*

"I've waited a long time for this, Liesel. I think I can wait a bit more."

"How long?" I breathe, my voice giving away my neediness.

"As long as it takes."

Langston releases me and undoes the door of the plane, leaving me with his parting words.

As long as it takes.

As long as it takes for what?

Langston stops just before he exits the plane and pulls out his gun. He aims it into the cockpit. "But this only ends one way—"

He fires.

I scream.

I don't have to look to know that he shot the pilot.

"Death."

CHAPTER 14

LANGSTON

iesel is going to kill me.

I don't mean she's going to stab me in the heart with a knife or shoot me in the head with a gun—no, I mean she's going to kill me slowly with her luscious lips, her sparkling eyes, her deadly curves. She's going to break me down by throwing her alluring body at me and her smart mouth until I give in and spill everything I know.

We both share a secret.

One from when we were children.

I have half of the secret. She has the other.

Neither of us can do anything with the information we have without the other.

But neither of us is willing to share the truth because we don't want the other to have any power over the other. Once the secret is shared, it will be a battle to solve the puzzle that will lead to the changing of our lives forever.

I used to think that we would never solve the puzzle, never share the secrets. But things have changed, and we no longer have a choice. Time is no longer on our sides.

Liesel doesn't realize this yet, but she will. She may want to hide the truth, but she doesn't know that time is running out every day.

I hear Liesel climbing down the stairs of the plane behind me as I walk across the dirt runway. I'm not worried about her running off; there is nowhere for her to run off to. That's why I chose this island.

I throw a glance over my shoulder anyway, to see what she will do once her feet hit the ground. She thinks I'll rape her, torture her—she's not wrong. I'll do anything it takes to get the truth.

Anything.

That's how badly I need her to share her secret.

Liesel is right to think I'll hurt her. She's only ever seen the worst of me. The worst of me is harsher than the devil himself. I've killed more men than Enzo or Zeke combined.

Tortured more people.

Ruined more lives.

You could blame my rough childhood on why I am the way I am, but I don't. I blame no one. I chose this life. I wanted this life.

Liesel thinks she's seen the worst of me, but I'm capable of so much more.

Most women would run in a situation like this. Run, flee, hide somewhere on the island to avoid being hurt. Others might search the island for any civilization to help her.

Not Liesel.

She knows the truth of her options. She knows she can run, but she'll only end up dead from dehydration. She knows that anyone she finds on the island works for me.

She's right on all accounts.

The only way off this island is death or me.

For now, I'm the lesser of two evils.

Her last option is to fight.

That's the option she'll choose, but she will take her time—planning, scouting her options until she knows everything there is to know about the island. Until she thinks I've lowered my defenses. Then she'll strike.

I'll be ready, though.

Liesel will follow me wherever I go for the time being. She will want to learn everything she can. So I don't have to worry about giving her orders or tying her up. Not yet.

The island is split in two. One half holds a small native population of maybe a hundred people. The other half is vast jungle forest, almost completely uninhabited, except for one house—the house I own.

I could call a car and we would be at the house in ten minutes, *but where's the fun in that?*

So instead, I throw my backpack over my shoulder, carrying the essentials—water, food, a change of clothes. And then I take off into the jungle.

"Really, Langston? You don't have a car, a four-wheeler, something, to take us to wherever we are staying?" Liesel shouts.

I smirk. Liesel pretends she's a girly girl—one who is afraid to chip her nails or mess her hair or makeup up, but that's not who she really is. At least, that's not who she used to be.

"I would call for one if there was a car to call on the island," I lie.

Her feet stop moving. I no longer hear the crunch of leaves under her feet. "There isn't anyone else on the island?"

"Just the two of us."

Her mouth falls open as she stares back at the plane—the only chance she had to escape is now gone after I shot into the cockpit.

"We're really alone?" she asks, recomposing herself.

"Yes."

She grips her oversized sweatshirt around the neck, tightening the garment against her body like she's hugging herself. She's going to sweat to death in that sweatshirt. The only benefit is that she might get fewer bug bites this way.

I want her to take it off so I can get a better view of her body; it would make the hike more enjoyable. But I'm not sure my cock would survive if that were the case.

The one thing I know is that I won't be fucking Liesel tonight, not even if she begged. And she won't beg. If I touched her, she'd scream rape. She would survive and keep her secrets locked away.

She's suffered a lot in her past, more than any woman ever should.

My throat closes up, and my eyes water just thinking about what she's endured. It's going to take a lot more than violating her to break her. *A lot more.*

Pain and fear are only one way to get her to the edge of breaking. Something much harder is the only way to get her to fully break. Something so dark and dangerous that I'm not even sure if I can endure it—but we must.

A trek through the woods is going to do little to wear her down. It will irritate her, but it'll be worth it to sleep under the stars with her tonight.

Tomorrow we can sleep in the mansion. Tonight is about getting reacquainted with each other.

She stomps over to me, and the next thing I know, she's pulled her sweatshirt off and tied it around her head to shield her head from the sun. Her sports bra shows off her flat belly just above her sweatpants. She's wearing tennis shoes, so this trek isn't too hard for her. It's not like she's wearing six-inch heels.

"Did you come prepared with any water or gear, if you expect me to hike through the jungle and risk catching malaria? Or are you hoping I'll die of dehydration or become delirious to make it easier for you to rape me?"

I roll my eyes at her rape joke. She thinks that's all this is about—a sexual tension and itch I need to scratch, that I've brought her here to fuck and nothing more. She has no idea of the truth.

I reach into my backpack and pull out a water bottle and sling it at her. She catches it and sips on the water.

"Now, stop complaining and get moving. We have a couple of miles to hike before dark."

"Are we building a house too tonight? Or is there somewhere we are making it to? I'm guessing not since there are no cars on the island."

"I thought we'd sleep under the stars like we did when we were children."

"You better have two tents and two sleeping bags in that small backpack of yours."

I grin. "Nope, just water and some food."

She puts her hands on her hips like she just can't believe she's stuck with my incompetence. "Really? You didn't even pack a tent? I'm not staying out here on this island for days or weeks without at least basic shelter. We are both going to die."

"Stop being dramatic. We aren't going to die. I was a Boy Scout, remember? I know how to survive in the woods for years without anything but a knife. And I have a lot more than a knife on me."

"I don't think your handgun is going to help much with hunting, Langston."

"Maybe you can bore the poor creatures to death with your incessant whining."

"I wouldn't have to whine if you didn't kidnap me and leave us stranded on an uninhabited island!"

I walk through a bush, pushing a branch back hard and then releasing it just as Liesel walks through. She catches it with one hand to avoid it hitting her face.

"Real mature," she says, pushing it back to walk through behind me. When she releases it, though, her hand is bloodied from the thorns on the branch.

"Your hand," I say, holding mine out.

She shakes her head.

"You need to clean it out and bandage it; you wouldn't want to get an infection in the middle of nowhere, would you?"

She glances around, and then a smug smile trickles over her lips. She hikes off the trail I've made and yanks a couple leaves off a nearby bush, then stomps back. She takes her water bottle, pours water over her wounds and applies the leaf to her hand.

"There. This is an aloe vera leaf; it has medicinal powers. No infection."

I study the leaf closer. "Looks like poison ivy to me."

Her eyebrows jump up, and she goes to remove the leaves, but my heavy chuckle stops her.

"I hate you."

I snicker. "Right back at you."

She stomps past me deciding to take the lead, which is fine by me. I can enjoy her ass so much better from this angle. But I do end up having to duck a lot to avoid branches hitting me.

"And as for your kidnapping comment—I didn't kidnap you, just held you to an arrangement we had."

She huffs, jumping over a fallen tree trunk. "One we made when we were five. I don't think that counts. This is kidnapping, and as soon as I get back to the mainland, I'll make sure you are punished for everything you do to me."

I look at her with a dark expression. "I didn't think you were patient enough to wait to punish me until we get back."

"You're right, I should punish you sooner."

"It's getting dark; we should find a spot to sleep for the night."

Liesel wipes the sweat from her brow, and I know she's relieved to not have to walk any further tonight.

We are maybe twenty minutes or less from the house with air conditioning, a nice bed, a shower—all the things Liesel craves.

But I'm the cruel bastard who is going to make her sleep in the dirt, in the heat, with mosquitos swarming.

"Start collecting firewood, I'll work on the fire," she says.

I like it when she's bossy, but it doesn't mean I'm going to let her be in control. "Do you remember how to start a fire? I'm guessing you haven't been camping since we were kids?"

"I can start a fire—just get the wood."

I hold back a smile as I collect wood and underbrush to start a fire. As warm as it is now, the first rule of camping under the stars is having a fire. Nights can get cold, and it will keep any wild animals from coming too close.

I pull out another water bottle to drink and sit on a fallen tree as I watch Liesel struggle with the fire. She tries over and over again, getting more and more frustrated.

She's covered in dirt, sweat, and mosquito bites. Finally, she falls back to the ground, exhausted.

"You win, again."

I stand and flick a lighter into the woodpile. It starts up immediately.

"That's cheating," she looks at the fire, still lying on her back, her breasts pushed up in her bra, revealing more of her stomach.

I could stare at her all night. She's beautiful even though she's covered in mud and dirt. Her body calls to me—begging me to show her how to truly fuck. That little show she put on for me with her boyfriend wasn't fucking. She doesn't know the meaning of the word.

I could show her.

My mind spins with thoughts of how I could take her here on the dirt, against the tree, or in the ocean.

"Are you okay? You look like you're about to go murder an innocent rabbit for our food," she says.

I reach into my backpack, pull out two Snickers bars. I toss her one and keep the other for myself.

"I won't be hunting for rabbits tonight. I'd rather hunt for something else."

She's halfway opening the wrapper, when my words catch her by surprise. She freezes and looks at me, searching for answers behind my words. I'm not going to make this easy for her.

I had to kidnap her. And I'll have to go much further to get the info I need from her.

"You have no need to hunt me, you already got me. Or do you think I'll run off in the night?"

I take a bite of my bar. "You can run, but we both know no matter where you go on this island, I'll find you. You can't hide from me. And if I don't find you, dehydration or exhaustion will."

She continues to lie on her back as she nibbles on the corner of her bar, savoring every bite. She doesn't know I have a dozen more in my backpack. She thinks this might be her only meal I give her.

Torturing her by withholding food or water isn't really the best method to get her to talk to me. No, what I have planned is more sinister and won't require me to watch her wither away into bones.

I like her curves. I want her curves. I'm a selfish asshole in that way. I won't mark her body in any permanent way. I can't say the same about her soul.

I wait until she's finished with her bar before I speak again.

And wait.

And wait.

And wait.

I'm not a patient man, but I'm becoming one with her. The more patient I am, the more I mess with her head, the higher the chance she will start talking.

The sky has turned to dusk. The moon has started peeking out behind the trees, shining down on us. The fire illuminates her silhouette casting shadows over her face.

"Why did Fitz write you a threatening letter? Why did he want to kill you?" I ask.

I already know the answer.

Liesel knows the answer too.

This is a test of trust and truth. *Will she answer me honestly? Or will she lie?*

"I don't know. I'm as bewildered as you are. I would guess Waylon's first political run put a target on us. Fitz wanted our money, and he thought we'd pay to avoid a scandal," Liesel says, pulling her sweatshirt over her chest as she shivers. The wind has picked up, and the fire alone won't be enough to keep her warm tonight. She stares up at the scattered stars through the trees, not looking at me.

Lies it is.

She didn't tell me the truth. She knows why Fitz came after her. It's the same reason I came after her—to figure out her secret and find the treasure she's hiding.

My heart thumps hard like the beat of a war drum picking up steam. I used to like the lies we shared. Not anymore. There is too much at stake.

Liesel looks over at me, either because she can hear the heavy beat of my heart or because she wants to see my reaction to her lie.

Her lips thin as she tries to hide her emotions, but I can tell I've lit a spark of fear in her. I look like a deranged madman and the possibilities of what I will do scare her.

"No more lies, Liesel."

She sits up, tucking her knees to her chest as she tries to stay warm on the opposite side of the fire from me.

"We don't know how to do anything else, Langston. Don't pretend like you've told me the truth either. I'm not here because of some silly promise when we were five. I'm not here because I owe you for killing Fitz. I'm here because of that damn letter you ripped in two.

"Nothing has changed, though. I won't tell you what my half said, and you won't tell me what your half said. So why try to get answers now? Why am I here?"

She hasn't earned the truth. She hasn't earned an answer. But I'm about to give her more truth than she'll get from me the rest of her time here.

"I want the truth. And I will get the truth—no matter what it takes. The sooner you tell me everything you know, the better for you.

"Let's start with one. One truth you've never told another soul. One piece of yourself that has only ever belonged to you."

The wind stops. The leaves stop rustling. It's eerily quiet as my words are the only sound on the island.

"I tell you a truth, and I go free?" she asks, her voice pained. She'd rather be raped, tortured; her body pulled apart limb by limb than offer me a truth. She will never admit that to me, but it's true.

I shake my head. "One truth buys you more time on this planet. A lie shortens my patience, resulting in less time."

"That gives me no incentive to tell you anything!"

I gave her a path to freedom. *Death is freedom, right?*

For most people, one honest truth would be easy. Not for Liesel. Not for me. Not when your whole life has been a lie.

She takes a deep, exhausting breath—one that consumes her whole body, and then as she exhales a breath so strong it persuades the winds to pick up again. And then she looks to me like a scared little girl.

I try to squeeze out the thoughts of the girl I used to know. The one wearing pigtails and pretty pink dresses, who would run through the forest and chase after me and our boy crew. She was the princess we all protected. We all failed.

She was the one that got away.

Not anymore.

Now, she's mine. I have her trapped physically, but I need more.

"So what will it be? Ready to tell the truth and earn more time? Or lie and be punished?" My voice is deep and haunting. She has no idea why I'm pissed—what she did that makes me so willing to hurt her, kill her. She never will. But she knows that I'm serious when I say that I will hurt her if she doesn't tell the truth.

She nods as she shakes out her hands, but I can see them trembling. She's trying to psych herself up to speak—to tell the truth.

"I'll tell you a truth, and for every truth I tell you, I'll be the one hurting you. I'll kill you with truths."

Liesel means every word she says. I have no doubt that she will choose whatever vicious truths she can come up with to hurt me. To cut me down until I beg her to stop.

However, the only things that could hurt me are her lies.

CHAPTER 15

LIESEL

Langston wants a truth.

There are so many truths to choose from. So many from my past that frighten me, including one that I'm afraid will change the course of my life forever.

I'd rather him rape or torture me than make me tell the truth. I'd do anything to avoid my past.

Langston knows that better than anyone.

As much as I'm all talk, telling him to rape me and get it over with, I don't want him to hurt me. I'll do anything to avoid being hurt by Langston, because I remember the boy I used to care about, buried beneath his brawny exterior. Knowing that boy grew up to be a true killer is more than I can stand.

So I'll try to tell the truth. I'll try to gain more time. I'll try to hunt for my freedom and hope that Langston doesn't kill me.

An idea forms as I sit across the fire. I tremble from a combination of the cold and my fear. If it keeps me safe from Langston, then I'll do almost anything to make that happen.

Langston is being relatively nice at the moment, but there is nothing he isn't capable of. The darkness in his heart rivals my own. Everyone may think I got out, that I'm no longer mixed up in the underworld, but they don't know all the horrible things I've done since.

Langston is the same. And right now, I'm his prey.

I won't let him hurt me.

He's sitting on a log across from me. He thinks he's more powerful sitting higher than me, but he just gave me the ammunition to fire back and win.

"The first night I was raped..." I start.

"Telling me about your rapes won't earn you your freedom, but if you want a free counseling session, be my guest. I'll enjoy listening to all the ways you were abused. It will give me lots of ideas on how to break you."

His words are harsh and villainous. I just wish I knew if they were true or not. His words are meant to strike fear into me, but there is nothing physical he could do to me that would make me tremble quite as much as I am now.

"Will you shut up? You want a truth, then let me tell the story."

"One more thing," he says.

"You don't get to add addendums to our deal now."

He leans forward, closer to the fire, and the flames reflect in his eyes as if the fire is coming from his eyes, not the pit.

I gasp at the evil I see reflected back at me.

"You aren't in control, huntress. You never were. You are lucky I'm giving you a way out at all. I could just torture the truth out of you and then kill you. That would be easier."

"You would never kill me," I call out his lie.

"Things have changed. You aren't someone I care about anymore. The Liesel I once knew is gone."

"That she is," I agree, my voice stronger than I feel.

"If you lie, instead of telling me the truth, if you tell a truth you've already told before, I will punish you."

"You'll punish me if I'm silent."

His eyes disappear back into the darkness, but I know my words are true. It doesn't matter. He'll hurt me, drive fear into me, all so that he can get power over me. He may say he's only hurting me to get info, but he'll enjoy every second of it.

"Continue with your story if you dare, but know what awaits you if you lie."

I want to move closer before I open my mouth. I want to be able to read all of his expressions. But I dare not move closer. If I move at all, I'll lose my resolve and won't tell my story.

No, I won't let the fear win. I haven't been afraid of anything in years. I won't start now.

I stand up. I won't move closer to Langston, but I'll stand taller as I speak. I have power. I have strength. And this story is the start of that.

"The night I was raped should have been the worst night of my life," I start again, wishing the wind would pick up again to drown out my voice. Instead, it's stopped, ushering in an eerie silence, as if the entire forest is listening to my story, ready to call me a liar if I slip one time.

The quiet pushes my thoughts back to the beginning, back to the moment fear became normal in my life—the moment when I learned how evil men could truly be.

It's not the story I intended to tell. This part of the story Langston already knows, but it's what spills. I become consumed, and I can't do anything but speak what happened...

I FINALLY BOUGHT MY FIRST BIKINI, EVEN THOUGH I'D ASKED MY mother for one every year for the last three years. I finally saved up enough money to buy one from hours working at the ice cream shop.

I could have just asked Enzo for the money, and he would have gladly given it to me. Enzo doesn't need to worry about something as simple as money. He doesn't have to save and scrap. He just has it, an overabundance of it.

He's not in the pool yet, but I know he normally swims around this time, so I start doing laps myself. I hear a splash and look up to find Enzo swimming towards me.

I watch Enzo's arms stretch over his head and dip into the water. His muscles lengthen and contract as his legs propel him forward.

He could swim laps for hours without stopping to rest. He's a machine.

Soon, he'll be mine.

"Enzo," I shout, excited to see him.

He stops mid-stroke and turns in my direction.

It takes everything in me to not drool or let my mouth hang open at the sight of him shirtless. I've watched him swim countless times, and each time I'm shocked by how sculpted he is. How his muscles look like they've been chiseled by an artist into his chest—they are too perfect to have been gained from just regular working out. And that happy trail that leads down into his black swim trunks—yummy.

"Do you need something, Liesel?"

I walk up the shallow stairs, so he can see my body, and put my hand on my hip. When I shift my weight, he notices. His eyes heat, wanting to touch my hip.

I'm elated, but I try to keep my face sultry and indifferent.

"Want to join me for a swim?" I try to let my voice drop, to show how mature I am.

I've been infatuated with Enzo since my mom got a job here when I was ten. My interest in him has only grown as we've both grown older. Enzo is the boy for me. He's the strongest boy I know. He would never hurt me. He is powerful enough to protect me. Someday he'll own the Black empire—the money, the houses, the yachts—all his. And he's smoking hot. I could fall in love with him.

I want him to be my first.

I've already given away my first kiss, but he could be the one to take my virginity.

Enzo grins smugly as he swims closer to me. I think for a moment that he might be getting out.

I don't really want to swim—I just want an excuse to be half-naked with Enzo.

He walks into the shallow end, towards me. Then I feel him grab my hips.

"Enzo!" I squeal as he pulls me deeper into the pool. I fall headfirst on top of him. He doesn't let go once we are in the water. His grip on my body tightens as if promising to protect me no matter what happens.

We both surface at the same time—gasping for air and laughing as I splash Enzo for pulling me under like that.

"Hold still," Enzo suddenly says as he looks at my face with concern.

I still, except for my heart—it thumps and thumps and thumps, beating in anticipation of what Enzo is going to do.

He's holding me by the waist to keep me afloat in the water, where he's just tall enough to stand.

Enzo's face turns serious. His lips part. He's going to kiss me.

His hands inch up my body painfully slowly. I want him to take his time. I want this moment to last forever, but I'm not sure my heart can survive this slow pace. I need his lips on me like I need air.

His lips against mine might send my heart pounding at the speed of light. I'm not sure I'd survive his kiss, but I'll gladly chance it to taste him.

Finally, his hands are gripping my face.

This is it.

The moment he's finally going to kiss me.

Then, his thumb brushes across my cheek.

"There, you had mascara under your eye." He smiles down at me.

I bite my lip in frustration. *How could he not kiss me?* We are so close.

He's still gripping my face even though my mascara is fixed. We are still inches from each other. My hands are gripping his biceps to keep myself afloat.

I'm not going to miss my shot.

Without thinking, I pull Enzo to me and steal a kiss.

This could ruin everything if Enzo doesn't feel the same way as I do. He could turn me down. He could stay away from me for fear that I will kiss him again.

The second our lips touch, though, I know I have nothing to worry about. A burning desire sparks deep in my belly. Enzo pulls me tighter to him, deepening the kiss instead of pushing me away. I feel how hard he is as his tongue explores my mouth. He's a good kisser, real good.

I feel myself flying high on adrenaline and lust, the longer the kiss lasts.

I want Enzo.

I want his kisses.

I want his body.

I want his heart.

I want him to be mine.

Suddenly, Enzo pulls away. His ears perk up, and he presses a finger to my lips to keep me from talking.

I listen carefully, not sure what we are listening to. Even through my blissful haze, I can make out the car horn as Mr. Black's Bentley locks.

Enzo's father is a horrible man. I know to stay clear of him. He's cruel and vicious and rules every room he enters. I don't fully understand Enzo and his father's relationship, but I do know that Enzo has no choice but to follow his father's orders.

"Run," Enzo says with intensity in his voice, along with what must be fear.

I don't know why he wants me to run. My only guess is that he doesn't want us to get caught together. His father wouldn't approve of his son, who is about to gain an evil empire, ruling it with a poor maid's daughter.

He boosts me out of the pool and then jumps out next. I start running toward the guest house I share with my mother at the back of the property, even though it kills me to be running from Enzo. But before I take two steps in that direction, Enzo grabs me and yanks me to him, stealing one last hungry kiss.

A kiss that will be my downfall.

"Enzo!" Mr. Black yells from the deck above us.

Goosebumps form and the hairs on my arms rise at the single word.

"Coming, Father." Enzo grabs my arms around my biceps and motions to the basement door nearby.

"Go hide in my bedroom. I'll come find you when I'm done with my father," he whispers.

I nod, speechless. Enzo isn't done with me. He wants more. A tiny thrill shoots through me.

He winks at me before he runs up the stairs to meet his father.

I wait until they've both headed inside before I slip through the sliding glass door. I've done this hundreds of times before, but usually to hang out with Enzo, Zeke, and Langston. Never just Enzo alone.

A grin stretches through my entire body as I race up the back staircase to Enzo's bedroom. I run so hard that I don't notice someone is watching me. Someone is standing in the hallway just outside Enzo's bedroom.

I run smack into his chest.

Only when I look up does my smile vanish.

Enzo isn't the chest I ran into. It's his father.

"Hi, Mr. Black. I, uh…, I was looking for Enzo. We have a school project that we have to work on together. I was just looking for him to see what time we should meet. Is he in his bedroom? Or is he upstairs?"

Mr. Black looks at me with a stern expression. His eyes are thin slits, his nostrils spread, and his mouth tightens.

"Don't lie to me, girl." His eyes run down the length of my body. "You aren't studying looking like that."

I instinctively move my hands over my body to hide it from his gaze. But I'm wearing a tiny red bikini, and I don't have a towel. I've been dripping water all over the hardwood in the hallway.

"I'm sorry. I'll just go." I turn to head back out, hoping like hell he doesn't take my indiscretion out on my mother. I hope he doesn't fire her, thinking that it's the best way to keep me from Enzo.

As I turn, I hear him speak a low command. "Stop."

I don't know why I stop. I just do. My feet seem to stop midair like I just ran into a wall.

"Good girl." He steps closer until I feel his hot breath on my neck. "You're a very obedient girl, aren't you?"

My mouth runs dry. The mouth that was just kissed by a boy I've dreamt about for years, that thought my life couldn't get any better, is now dry and speechless.

I nod, it feels like the right thing to do.

"Liesel?" Enzo asks quietly from up the stairs.

I open my mouth to answer, but Mr. Black grabs my neck. "Don't speak."

There is no threat at the end. Just a command. But with his hand on my neck, I don't have to know what he will do if I speak.

Mr. Black drags me by the neck into his son's bedroom, still gripping my neck so hard that I'm not sure I'm going to be able to breathe much longer. He leaves the door cracked.

"Liese—" Enzo stops dead in his tracks when he sees his father through the crack in the door. The room is dark, so I have no idea if he can see me or not.

"I told you to go to the club and handle business," Mr. Black says demandingly.

"I'm headed there right now."

"See that you do."

Enzo turns. His eyes leave the room. He looks straight at me, and my heart freezes again.

Enzo sees me. He has to.

Do something.

Stop this.

Save me.

I beg Enzo to do something, anything. Just don't leave me here alone.

The seconds creep by in extremely slow motion. But a second later, Enzo turns, and he's gone.

Enzo's gone.

I'm alone.

With his father.

In Enzo's bedroom.

"Good girl," Mr. Black says, loosening his grip on my neck.

I still don't speak, though. I've grown up poor. I know what my mother does to earn extra money, and I know how evil this man is who is holding my neck.

I can see in his eyes what he wants to do with me.

Enzo is gone.

The house is empty.

There is no one to save me.

He'll rape me. Torture me. Kill me if he wants to.

For a split second, I think about fighting back, *but what can I do really?* I have no muscles. I can't get free. If I yell, no one will come.

So I do nothing.

I surrender, hoping it will be over faster, that it will hurt less if I give in.

"Good girl," he says again, watching me silently crumble before him.

I must blackout.

Or maybe my brain blocks it out.

The rest comes in flashes.

My bikini being ripped apart.

Him palming my breasts.

Shoving fingers inside me.

Grabbing my throat so hard it left marks.

Beating me so hard I can still feel the bruises.

Forcing my mouth open to suck him.

Being tied up so hard it left marks on my wrists.

And the violation.

Over.

And over.

And over.

That day was both the longest and the shortest of my life.

In the moment, it seemed to last forever, but huge chunks of the night have been taken from my memory that it makes the day feel too short.

♡

SLOWLY, I START COMING BACK TO REALITY, REALIZING THAT I'M not in Enzo's room. I'm in the woods with Langston.

The part of the story I've spoken so far is known. I could keep going; I could get to the part that he still knows, but if I take it far enough, I could speak a truth he doesn't know.

But I can't.

I'm drained from telling that much of the story.

The pain that comes after is too much. It's not something I speak about.

I won't be able to gain myself more time. I'll be sleeping in the dirt on an uninhabited island with my enemy, who will punish me for lying.

At least I can lash out at him with the end of my story.

I glance over at Langston. He's still sitting on the log; his eyes focused on me through the flames of the fire. He's motionless, expressionless—almost like a statue.

He doesn't speak. He doesn't rush me. He doesn't call out any part as a lie. He doesn't tell me that I've already told this story before.

My eyes meet his for the first time since I've been talking. Actually, I have no idea if my eyes have met his or not. When I was telling the story, it was like I was reliving it.

Now, though, is about delivering a blow to Langston.

"I was angry at Enzo when I thought he knew what happened to me and didn't stop it. When he didn't help me. Didn't save me. But I still wanted him. Still thought I could fall in love with him. He was still the better man, the better choice."

I pause.

And I notice Langston's shoulders tense—disagreeing with me.

"You know why? Because Enzo didn't know what his father did. I just thought he did. He should have known, but he didn't. But there was someone who did know. Someone who watched it all happen from the security camera."

I glare at Langston.

"You. You watched me get raped by that sadistic devil. You watched my life be torn apart. You saw what happened next, and you did nothing."

My voice shakes as I speak. This isn't new. I've told this story to our friend group. Langston was there. But I've never screamed it in his face. Never confronted him with what could be the truth.

Langston is always watching. He's the best at security. He knew what happened to me. He was either watching in real-time, or he watched a recording.

He knew, and he did nothing.

My body shakes, but tears never come. I don't feel sadness, pain, or fear. Not after that night. Not after my worst night, still yet to come.

Langston watches me through the fire.

And for a moment, I think he's going to say nothing.

"I was just doing my job," he says.

"You're a heartless monster."

He stands up. "And you're a liar."

LANGSTON

Liesel is a liar.

A schemer.

She knows how to draw men in with her words. She knows exactly what she's doing. She chose her story well and spun the web of lies so tightly that it's hard to make out which parts are the truths and which parts are the lies.

It pisses me off. I should be able to tell. I know practically everything there is to know about this woman—except for one missing piece. A piece she will eventually tell me, but not without a fight.

She won't fight with her fists. She'll fight with lies. Cruel, merciless lies that will be carved into my heart forever. There is no way to verify which parts are true and which parts aren't.

But I know she lied.

I can verify at least one part of her story that isn't true. And the fact that she didn't fight me when I called her a liar tells me she did indeed lie.

But how much of it was a lie?

I march through the darkness away from the fire, away from her. If I stay, I'll do something I'll regret.

I start jogging as my eyes adjust to the darkness. Working for Enzo and Kai has trained me to see through the jet black night, but it's still careless. I shouldn't leave Liesel alone. I shouldn't run when one wrong step could mean I fall off a cliff or get attacked by a wild animal.

I run from Liesel, but it's more like I'm running from her words. *God, how her words cut me deep.*

It hurts.

It all hurts.

Liesel blames me for the rape, just like she blames Enzo.

I should have been there for her. I should have saved her just like Enzo should have.

But I wasn't watching her on the security cameras. I didn't know. At the time, I was in charge of security at the clubs, not at the house. I was good at hacking back then, but the cameras at the house were the most sophisticated we had. I'm not even sure if I was capable of hacking the system to watch out for her then.

Liesel knows that.

But her words cut me nonetheless. They hurt because despite what she says, I do have a heart—one I've tried to eliminate every chance I've gotten. My life would be much easier if I could. But as hard as I've tried, it's still there.

It just doesn't feel the same way about Liesel as it once did.

All her words rip through me, shredding me to pieces.

The rape.

God, she's told the story before, but hearing it tonight with no one else but us, it hit me harder.

She was just a girl.

We should have protected her.

We failed.

As hard as it was to hear the details again, it was harder to hear of her and Enzo.

How they kissed.

How she wanted him.

Could have loved him.

Maybe even would have ended up with Enzo if it wasn't for his dad.

And I have no idea if it was all a lie or a truth.

She said she forgave him, but could never forgive me.

She shouldn't forgive either of us.

Just like I could never forgive her.

That's what I have to remember when my feelings spike again, being so close with Liesel. I once thought she was the only woman for me. Now, I can't think of a worse human being on the planet.

I stop running, my lungs finally burning, finally reminding me of pain instead of the ache I feel for Liesel after her bearing her story.

"She's a liar, Langston. Don't believe a word out of her mouth," I tell myself as I try to catch my breath.

I put my hands over my head as I walk through the forest.

She's a liar.

Never forget.

As I walk back, the story replays in my head, and I realize that I don't think that was the story she intended to tell, it just spilled out. She didn't have a choice but to speak the words, which makes me think the beginning was true. Everything with Enzo—true. It was the second part she changed to try and hurt me.

I won't let her see my hurt.

My pain.

When I approach the fire where she still sits, I'm stone —emotionless.

"Ready to punish me?" she asks into the darkness. She can't see me, but she can feel me, just like I can feel the icy daggers she willingly flings in my direction.

I'm silent as I walk back over to my backpack and pull another bottle of water out. I drink it as I sit on the ground, leaning against the log. I stare across the fire at her.

"Rape me just like he did. Ruin me. Make me hate you," she says.

"You already hate me."

She bites her lip. "Do it. Prove to me once and for all—you're the monster I always thought you were."

Provoking me isn't going to work. We both know I'm a monster, but the only way I gain control is if this happens on my terms and not hers.

"Come here," I say.

Her lip slips from her teeth. She thinks I'm calling her bluff, but there is no fear. Liesel isn't afraid of anything. She's lived through hell —there is nothing worse that could happen to her.

Liesel stands and walks to me. She won't fight me, just like she didn't fight Mr. Black. She thinks this is the best way to survive. Get me to rape her, and then she doesn't have to have nightmares about what might happen, she'll already know.

"Sit."

Liesel sits face to face, her eyes turning yellow as the flames reflect off her pupils.

"I didn't bring a blanket. Keep me warm tonight."

She blinks rapidly, her ears straining like she thinks I misspoke.

"What?"

"You heard me."

I lie down on the dirt. I'm not the least bit cold, not after I ran a mile. The fire alone would keep me plenty warm.

But I want her to have to touch me all night. I want her to feel me. To lose control. To wonder if, at any moment, I might change my mind and have my way with her.

I must break her.

This will drive the first nail in harder than fucking her against the dirt ever would.

"Keep yourself warm," Liesel spits at me.

I shake my head. "You lied. There are consequences. Keep me warm."

"Or?" she asks, wanting to know what I'll do to her if she disobeys.

"There is no 'or.' You will use your body to keep me warm."

We stare at each other—a silent standoff.

The wind howls.

Liesel shudders.

I don't know if she decides to follow my orders or if she's looking to warm herself. Either way, she finally lies down on the dirt next to me.

"Liesel," I warn when she doesn't touch me.

She lifts an arm over my body. It floats in the air, refusing to touch me. It hovers there until her arm trembles, and she can't hold it up any longer. Only then does she let it wrap around my shoulders.

The touch sends a million emotions through us both. It reminds me of when we were kids. Long before she knew Enzo, she knew me. It was my bed she snuck into, not his. It was me she longed for, not him.

"My legs are cold too."

Her eyes shoot up to me, and she practically pouts.

I smirk, but I'm not sure she can see it, which is a shame, because I look irresistible when I smirk.

Her leg moves in a hard lump as she drapes it harshly over my legs.

I close my eyes with a smile. I've formed a tiny, almost unnoticeable crack in her shell. Tomorrow I'll form another and another. I'll torture her with tiny little cracks until she finally bursts.

I need her truth.

I need her answers.

I need her apology for what she's done.

But I refuse to need her.

CHAPTER 17

LIESEL

Snuggling with Langston is torture.

It's worse than anything Mr. Black did to me.

It's worse than…okay, it's not really as terrible as the worst thing that's ever happened to me, but I imagine this is how it feels to be shot and slowly bleed out to death. Every drop is painful, and you just want to get to the end so it can be over.

Holding Langston feels like that.

I can smell the sweat from his pores that he worked up after he stormed off. It overpowers even the smell of the fire.

I can hear his gentle, controlled breath in and out, louder than the chirp of the bugs and hum of the wind.

I can feel his warmth—there is no way he needs my body to stay warm.

Why do I stay draped over his body, then?

Because as soon as I touch him—I'm his. I can't turn away. Some part of me I thought I had long ago buried likes his smell, how he sounds, his touch. I like it more than I should. I like a man I hate—a man who wants to kill me.

I've always wanted Langston. He was the first boy I ever wanted. I wanted him before I wanted Enzo. I just don't think about that time

175

and wanting Langston was something I never spoke out loud. I never let anyone know, even him.

That could be the truth that frees me, but I will never admit it to Langston.

It was just lust, not want for the man beneath the muscles, the smug smirk, the light-colored hair boy who taught me how to hunt, to search for secrets. He was the boy who taught me to lie.

If I could separate Langston the man from Langston's body, maybe I'd finally give in to my desires, and we'd fuck willingly. Unfortunately, the only way to separate the two is to kill him and then fuck him, and I'm not into necrophilia.

Langston starts snoring. He's asleep. Now's my chance—to break free of his arms, to run.

I don't want to run, but I shouldn't stay snuggled up against him.

I force my head to lift and my arm to slink off his chest.

But his hand grips my arm, gently pulling it back over his chest. He's still snoring; I'm not even sure if he woke up or not.

I huff out a deep breath.

There is no way I'm sleeping tonight.

THE SUN IS WHAT WAKES ME. IT'S BRIGHT AND HOT AND MAKES ME squint as I open my eyes.

I slept.

I didn't think I could.

And I'm still lying on Langston's chest.

I jump up.

"Easy," he says. "Wouldn't want you breaking a nail. There are no salons around here."

I frown as I regain my composure and remember what happened and where I am.

Birds are chirping happily nearby, and I swear I hear monkeys in the distance. We are in the wild, and I just slept on dirt. Well, technically, I slept *on* Langston. I should be grateful, but I'm not.

I fold my arms over my sweatshirt that is once again heating me up. I really should have taken Langston up on his offer for me to wear new clothes. These sweatpants and sweatshirt really aren't made for the jungle.

"What now?" I ask. *Please tell me this was all a joke. That we are in Santorini and he dragged me here to meet Kai and Siren.*

"Breakfast."

He snuffs out the fire and then stretches.

"You have more bars?"

"Nope, you are going hunting for our breakfast."

I laugh. "When you call me huntress, you know it's a nickname, right? I don't actually hunt animals." *I hunt men. I hunt secrets. I hunt truths. Not poor, furry animals.*

"There's a first time for everything."

My stomach growls right on cue, but I refuse.

"I'm not going to hunt and kill an animal. I'd rather starve. I—"

Langston starts walking away even though I haven't finished my sentence.

"Really?" I huff after him, annoyed that he won't even listen to me.

I stop dead in my tracks as Langston pulls something out from behind a tree and holds it out to me.

I blink several times—Langston holds out a bow and arrow.

I scrape my teeth over my bottom lip to hold back my excitement. I haven't held a bow and arrow in my hands since I was seven, when Langston took me "hunting." All we did was target practice since I couldn't kill anything.

I was a perfect shot.

I cautiously reach out for the weapon.

My fingers brush his as I take the bow and arrows in my hands.

I have a weapon.

Something I can use against Langston.

He looks at me wearily. "Don't even think about it."

My eyes light up. "What? I'm not thinking about shooting this arrow into your heart."

He grins. "I'll give you one shot."

"What?"

"One shot to shoot me."

"And what happens when I hit you in the heart and you drop dead? How do I survive?"

He reaches into his back pocket and pulls out his phone. "I unlocked it. When I drop dead, you can call for help."

I lean forward. He unlocked the phone, and it has service.

Langston takes his time walking ten strides away from me. Then he turns and looks me in the eyes.

"I'm waiting."

I hold his gaze as I reach into the bag and pull out a single arrow. It feels familiar in my hand.

I could do this.

I could kill him.

I could...

I take a deep breath as I position the arrow against the bow and pull back on the string, aiming at the ground as I get used to the feel of the bow in my hands again.

And then I look up at Langston—his light blonde hair, his gleaming blue eyes, his tense smirk. He knows that I might shoot him, kill him, but it doesn't matter. Death has never scared him, just like it doesn't scare me. We've seen too much, he and I.

Can I really kill him?

I aim the arrow at his heart.

He doesn't flinch—I doubt even a hurricane sized wind would move him. Langston is testing me, seeing how badly I want to kill him.

I do—I want to be free.

But can Langston really be the first man I kill?

Without another moment to think about it, I let the arrow fly.

The moment the arrow leaves my grasp, I know I've made a mistake.

Was the mistake aiming too high?

Or letting the arrow go in the first place?

My eyes have squeezed shut out of instinct. My heart rattles quickly in my chest as my breath whooshes out of my body at the release of the arrow.

The jungle is still and quiet.

I force my eyes open, terrified to see Langston standing but equally afraid to see him lying on the ground.

Langston.

He's still standing.

The arrow didn't hit him.

I sigh.

"Is that a sigh of relief or a sigh of anguish?" Langston says with a wide grin like we were just playing a game he won—not one that could end in death.

I ignore his snark.

He pulls the arrow from the tree I hit, just over his left shoulder.

"You're rusty," he says as he begins to stride back to me.

I pull another arrow out and aim it at his heart. He's much closer this time. I wouldn't miss a second time.

"Or maybe I missed on purpose, realizing that you were lying, and cell service doesn't work on this barren island."

He takes another step closer until the arrow is touching his chest. Then he grabs it slowly, his eyes begging to be let into a window of my soul.

"Liar."

"Scoundrel."

He grins at that.

"Are you ready to hunt for breakfast now?"

"No." My hands shake at the thought of killing something on this island with my own hands.

He takes the bow from me. "But so sure you would be able to live with killing me."

"You deserve death," I snap back.

He puts the bow and bag of arrows over his shoulder. He looks rugged and woodsman-like, like he could kill any animal that crosses our path. Any human too.

That's Langston—he fits into any situation. The city, countryside, woods, castles. He can belong anywhere.

"Maybe I would have," Langston answers. "But I won't be dying today."

He turns, leaving me no choice but to follow.

I yank my sweatshirt back off and tie it around my waist as I follow Langston pushing through the brush.

"You aren't really going to kill something for our breakfast, are you?"

He looks back at me with an amused expression. "You eat meat, don't you?"

"Actually, I don't," I lie.

"Liar."

I shake my head. "Well, I would be a vegetarian if I had to actually kill the animal before I ate it."

"That I believe." Langston stops, putting his backpack, bow, and arrows down.

"What are you doing?"

"Getting you breakfast without killing anything."

Langston grabs the base of a palm tree and begins to scale it. It takes him five seconds to reach the top. He slices off two coconuts before sliding back down. He cracks them both open and hands me one.

"You're welcome," he says before sucking the juices out.

"Thanks for providing me with food, oh great one. You forget you wouldn't have to feed me if you'd just set me free."

"I could stop providing you with food, then, if you don't appreciate it."

I roll my eyes. "Then I would die from starvation instead of at your hand, before you've had your way with me. Now, who's a liar?"

After that, we finish eating our coconuts without any more smart remarks.

"Let's go," Langston says soon after I've finished my last bite.

"Where? Back to camp?"

He raises a brow with a large smirk as he holds his hand out to me. I reluctantly let him help me off the ground. "No, to my house."

I gasp.

"You're lying."

"Follow me, and you'll find out." He takes off at a quick speed, almost like he's running as he carries his backpack, bow, and arrows.

I run after, still not sure if I believe him or not.

Suddenly, Langston stops at a clearing.

I follow his gaze out to see a large house—the kind you see celebrities renting when they take vacations to private islands. I would guess the house has at least ten bedrooms and as many bathrooms. I can see a large infinity pool, and the landscaping is immaculate. There are people living on this island.

"You son of a bitch! You had us sleep on the ground last night. You made me think that we were on a deserted island, just the two of us. You bastard!"

I hit him squarely in the shoulder. More pissed that he lied to me, tricked me, and I fell for it than I am that he made me sleep on the dirt when there was a mansion with big fluffy beds not ten minutes from where we slept.

He catches my fist before I hit him again.

"We lie to each other, Liesel. Don't expect anything less from me. I will lie, cheat, trick you, hurt you, go as far as it takes. You think what I did last night was cruel? You have no idea what I have planned for you. End this now and tell me the truth."

"I'll decide if I tell a truth or a lie. I'll decide what happens to me."

He stands tall, looking down at me, making hot desire shoot through my body.

Damn him and his commanding expression turning me on.

"You'll tell me every truth you have. You won't be able to survive without spilling your secrets."

I'll survive, alright. He won't get the truth, only lies. I just hope I can keep to my own words. I hope I'm not lying to myself.

CHAPTER 18

LANGSTON

I let Liesel aim an arrow at me, knowing how good of a shot she is. She could have killed me if, deep down, she truly wanted to.

But she didn't. She's not a killer like I am.

She's done some horrible things in her life, but she doesn't kill. Even her worst enemies. *Even me.*

It was a gamble.

I didn't know how Liesel truly felt—now I do. She hasn't changed. She's a monster, done some horrible things. Things she deserves to pay for, die for, but I don't have to worry about her slitting my throat in the middle of the night.

That's where she draws the line—murder.

There are two types of people in this world: the kind who kill and those who can't, no matter the circumstances. You could say there is a third group of people: ones who kill in self-defense, only when their own life is threatened. But those types of people don't exist. It's a lie.

You can either kill or you can't.

It makes no difference the reason why. And once you cross that line, you can never go back.

Liesel hasn't crossed that line. If she can't cross that line to save her own neck now, then she never will.

Still, letting her shoot at me was incredibly reckless.

I shouldn't have been so careless. There was a time when it wouldn't have mattered if I died. Now, it's important to stay alive.

Liesel may not have meant to offer a truth, but she did. It may be the only truth I get from her for a while, but it's a start.

"Stay close," I say to Liesel as we start walking down the hillside toward my home.

She laughs. "I'm not following any of your orders."

She takes off at a full sprint toward the house.

She's not running away. I should just let her throw her tantrum, let her think she's won and punish her for her mistakes later.

But I'm not going to let her gain an inch.

I run after her.

She's quick and has a head start, but I'm faster.

She drops her sweatshirt, trying to sprint faster, but running won't save her.

Two more leaps, and I tackle her to the grass. Liesel tries to fight back, but she doesn't have a chance. I overpower her easily, pinning her arms above her head as my weight holds her waist and legs down. She pants heavily with more anger than fear flickering in her hazel eyes.

She's covered in dirt, sand, and grass. There is nothing sexy about our appearances, and yet my erection pushes against her stomach. There is no hiding it.

I growl instead of claiming her mouth like I want to.

"When I give you an order, you follow it."

She grins. "No. I'm not afraid of you."

"Liar," I breathe against her neck. "I can smell the terror in your sweat, feel the speed of your pulse—you're petrified."

"I'm out of breath from running. Of course, I'm sweating, and my pulse is racing."

I shake my head as I see my staff approaching to greet me. They pause, but Liesel glances up, realizing we have an audience.

"Do you see them?" I say, grabbing her chin and tilting her head up so I know she does.

Her eyes cut back to me.

"They work for me. They know exactly who I am, the evil I've done, and they still choose me. Their loyalty is with me. Every single one would die for me. *Try to turn them. Try to run from them. Try, huntress.*

"Heed my warning…don't trust anyone here. Don't think you are safe. Everyone here has done fucked up things—stolen, tortured, killed. That's the only way they end up working for me. And I won't stop them from hurting you…"

Liesel's eyes widen.

"You are only safe by my side, following my orders. If you do as I say, if you tell the truth, then your life here will be easy."

"I'll still end up dead. What incentive is there to follow your orders?"

I stroke her face, and she turns her head, trying to get away from me.

"Your body might enjoy my touch, but would you enjoy theirs?"

She gasps.

Finally, I got through to her. She's in danger when she's not with me, not following me. It won't keep her from fighting, but it might prevent her from seeking help from someone she shouldn't.

Slowly, I inch off her, despite my body screaming to crush her. To have my way with her right here, right now in the grass in front of everyone. To show everyone that she's mine.

She's not mine. She never will be. Not truly.

I stand, but don't offer her a hand. I watch her closely, waiting to see if she will follow my orders this time or not. When she stands close and doesn't run, she's agreed to be obedient—for now, at least.

I nod my approval at her change in attitude.

It's fake. I'm not naive enough to think this will last, but it will for now.

"Stay close," I say again.

She grabs my hand and squeezes, pressing her vivacious body against mine. "Close enough?" she purrs.

"Don't test me, Liesel."

She lifts our joined hands up to her lips and plants a kiss on the back of my hand. "I'm just doing as you asked."

"Sir, would you like me to take your bag?" Shawn asks.

"Yes, thanks." I realize I dropped my backpack when I was chasing Liesel down the hill.

"Aren't you going to introduce me to your employee?" Liesel asks, batting her eyes like a shy little girl at Shawn.

Liesel isn't shy. This is all an act.

"No, you don't need to know anyone. And they already know who you are."

"Oh? What did you tell them about me?"

"You're a lying bitch, and they shouldn't trust you." I drop her hand.

"At least I'm not a murdering asshole."

I grab her hand again and pull her toward the house. I'm tired of dealing with her smart mouth.

"I'll show you around." The sooner I give her a tour, the sooner I can be done with her. I'll lock her up in a room and run the hell away.

If I spend too much time with her, I'll lose my mind.

"Pool," I say, pointing out the infinity pool that rivals any view in the world. It shoots out over the cliff and looks down at the beach. The sun sets every night over the ocean, and my house has a perfect view.

"Are you just going to state the obvious during this tour or actually point out the things that matter?"

I frown and ignore her, jerking her hand, pulling her along as I walk.

Several of my employees scatter at the sight of us walking in through the back door. *Good, they got the message I made clear to Shawn. Don't talk to us.*

"Kitchen," I point to my left.

"Dinning room," I nod to my right.

Liesel stops, and my arm jerks back. I think she's afraid I'm going to lock her in a dungeon, but when I look at her, I realize she stopped because she's in awe.

She's taking in all the finishings—the bamboo floors, the giant glass doors that open up the entire house, the handcrafted cabinets.

I take a moment to glance around and really take in the house, trying to see it for the first time through her eyes.

Her mouth falls open when she spots the porch swing that looks like it's in the house, when really it sits just outside the living room. When the glass walls close, the swing is outside, but the doors are almost never closed.

Slowly, her head turns to me. "This house..." she whispers.

She can't finish.

"I didn't build it for you. I built it for me. This was my dream."

One of her eyebrows raises—she's skeptical. She should be. When I built this house, it was built with our childhood dream house in mind. This was the house we both dreamed up when we were eight. This house. Whether I meant to build it for her or for us, it makes no difference. It's our dream house to a T.

"It's incredible," Liesel says, and she really means it.

"I know. I built it. Of course, it's amazing."

That earns me the tiniest smile. For a moment, it feels like we are kids again, teasing each other, instead of foes locked in a battle to the end.

"Let's finish the tour," I say. I don't take her hand this time. I don't want to be connected to her as I realize that sharing this house with her is as personal as if I were to cut my chest open and reveal the depths of my heart.

"This floor is the staff bedrooms," I say, walking her through the house.

The number of bedrooms is the only thing that differs from the house we imagined and this one. In our dream house, we only needed two bedrooms.

One for each of us.

We didn't need bedrooms for staff.

We didn't need bedrooms for kids.

We didn't need guest bedrooms.

In our world, this house was meant to be just ours.

Ours.

Of course, there was never an 'ours,' never an 'us.'

Just her.

And me.

Locked in a bitter war.

I lead her up the stairs.

"More bedrooms," I say, showing her a couple. And then we walk past a door.

"And this room?"

"Is mine, not yours. This half of the house is off-limits to you," I say, pointing down the hallway.

Before she asks more questions, I pull her into my bedroom.

It wasn't my intention to bring her here. I had other plans for Liesel, but the second I drag her into my bedroom and shut the door, I realize this is where I need her.

Liesel's eyes bulge as she looks around the room, another combination of my and Liesel's dreams. It can turn into a dark cave, like I wanted, at a push of a button—the curtains close, the lights dim, and a dark duvet gets thrown over the bed. But it's also what Liesel envisioned—light, bright, and airy with a picturesque view of the ocean, a balcony for two, and a mostly outdoor bathroom ensuite.

Liesel smiles, really smiles. "You did it. You built our dream. It's beautiful."

I'm silent for a moment.

"It's not yours."

Her smile falters. "I never thought it was."

"You're not going to get free, Liesel. There is no way off this island. You'll live the rest of your life here. You'll die here."

"Then, lucky for me, I'll die in my dream house."

I nod.

She glances out the window, her smile returning. "That is if Waylon doesn't come for me."

"Waylon has money, but no skills. He will never find you. And I doubt he loves you enough to devote his life to searching for you, which is what it would take to find you."

She tucks her mud and leaf-stricken hair behind her ear. "Waylon loves me more than you know. He asked me to marry him."

My throat tightens, and my eyes flatten into slits. I grab her left hand, not believing I missed anything. I hold it up.

"I don't see a ring."

She pulls her hand free. "I don't need a ring for Waylon to prove his love for me. For us to promise to spend our life together forever."

"I don't believe you."

She shrugs. "You don't have to. I'm just trying to warn you. Waylon will come after me. He's not just a fling. He's the only man I've ever loved. And somehow, he feels the same way about me. He loves me. He'd die for me. He won't give up searching for me once he realizes I'm taken."

Liesel is an excellent liar, but it doesn't feel like she's lying now. She has to be. She can't be engaged. She can't want another man. She can't...

"As I recall, you told him you'd be gone for three weeks. So we have at least that long before he suspects anything."

She shakes her head. "He'll expect me to call, to text. We've never gone three weeks without a healthy round of phone sex. You saw how we fucked on the cameras, don't deny it. He'll come looking for me before three weeks."

"That display of sex wasn't love!" I yell in her face.

"How the hell would you know? You haven't ever been in love!"

I open my mouth to scream a truth and stop myself at the last second. I will never admit the truth.

Instead, I grab her arm and pull her into the bathroom.

"Clean yourself off. I'll be back tonight, and you and I will have a little chat about your lying. Until then."

I step back and slam the bathroom door shut, locking her inside.

My blood is boiling. The only person in the world who can drive me this mad is now locked in my bathroom. Those walls won't hold her. If she decides she wants to escape, she can.

The only way to prevent her from running is being with her, but I can't stay here another moment. I need a break. I need to remember why I'm doing this.

Fuck, I need Liesel out of my life for good.

CHAPTER 19

LIESEL

It may look like Langston just got the upper hand. I'm locked in his bathroom, after all.

But I won.

I pushed enough buttons that Langston can no longer stand the sight of me. He's losing control already.

He said he's going to kill me, and I believe him.

He said he's learned patience—that I don't believe. If I can get him to lose control, maybe he'll slip, say some hint of his truth or give me a clue of how I can escape.

He ran off instead of laying down the law like he wanted to.

I grin wide.

I'm not going to worry about Langston. Right now, I'm going to enjoy this glorious bathroom—a bathroom I dreamed about when we were kids.

This house only confuses me more. *Why did Langston build the house we dreamed of as kids? Why, if he's hated me this entire time? Wanted me dead?*

So he could torture me with it, that's why.

I won't let him win. I'll enjoy every second of my time in this house, and I won't let him control me.

The entire house is built to enjoy the elements. The bathroom is no different. The shower and tub sit just outside of the main house amongst exotic plants, providing some privacy but allowing you to shower outside while looking at the ocean. There is a freestanding sink attached to the house, and a door that leads to what I assume is the toilet room.

I have my eyes on the shower and tub, trying to choose which one I'm going to use. I suspect Langston will have me locked in here all day, so I decide to shower first to get the muck off, then bathe to soothe my sore muscles.

I step into the glass shower filled with more buttons than a computer after stripping out of my dirty clothes and leaving them in a pile on the bamboo floor.

When I press one of the buttons, the walls slink away into the floor, and then I'm truly showering outside.

I take my time washing, then spend an hour soaking in the tub, letting all thoughts of Langston slip away. Only once an hour has passed of enjoying the ocean, the sun, and the warm, relaxing tub do I let myself think about where I am and what's going to happen next.

I climb out of the bath and look for clothes, but I find none except for the filthy rags that I wore here. I won't be putting those clothes back on.

I find a white robe hanging on the back of the bathroom door and put that on.

Langston wants me to stay locked up like Rapunzel in a tower.

I glance over the edge of the balcony and smile.

Well, he shouldn't have made it so easy for me to escape then.

I'm on the second floor, but jungle vines have grown up most of the balcony.

Without thinking too hard about what I might break if I fall, I hook a leg over the edge and then the other. I hold onto the railing as I try to find my footing.

The sun beats down, making the task harder, as does the robe that I keep stepping on unintentionally.

"Here goes nothing," I say, letting my weight down onto one of the vines.

It holds.

I exhale a deep breath as I start scaling down the vines.

My vine breaks.

I fall, holding onto the vine for dear life, hoping I'll stop.

I do, inches from the ground.

"Holy hell." I laugh, *because what else are you supposed to do when you almost fall to your death?*

I untangle myself from the vine and land on my feet. I retie the robe around me and glance at the house, expecting to see Langston or one of his men chasing after me. This wasn't about escaping; it was about letting Langston know that he loses once again.

I spot the security camera, and I flip it off.

When I glance back through the glass of the house, I don't see anyone coming to chase after me.

Not Langston.

Not his guards.

No one.

I squint at the camera. Langston is watching, surely, but he's allowing me to be free.

Huh.

Still, I don't want to push my luck. I'd prefer to be free as long as I can.

Langston said this island was uninhabited. Obviously, that isn't true, so we must be somewhat close to other houses, businesses, people.

I climb down the cliffside to the beach. There is nothing but beautiful white sand for as far as I can see in either direction.

My feet are already burning in the sand. I wish I had shoes, clothes, something other than this damn robe, but I'll take what I can get. The robe is better than the muddied clothes I had.

So I walk and walk and walk.

I find nothing.

No houses.

No buildings.

No people.

There are obviously people on the island, but they don't live close to Langston. It would take a very long journey to reach another house from here.

And the fact that Langston didn't send anyone after me tells me he's not worried about me running into anyone.

I sludge back to the house as the sun begins to dip toward the water.

Several of Langston's employees are going in and out of the house —cleaning, bringing in supplies, cooking.

"Miss Dunn, I have dinner ready for you. Where would you like to eat it?" a man in jeans and a dark shirt asks me.

I'm surprised he talked to me after Langston made it clear earlier in the day that no one was to talk to me.

"And you are?"

He shakes his head. "I can bring your dinner out to eat on the terrace."

I sigh but nod.

He disappears inside.

I look more carefully at the employees going in and out. They are all muscled, have guns, could be killers themselves. That's why Langston hired them.

"Here you are, Miss Dunn." The man returns with a plate of food and sets it on the round table at the edge of the terrace.

"Thanks," I say, unsure of myself as he pulls out the chair for me like I'm dining at a five-star restaurant instead of being fed while captive on an island.

He nods, as I sit, and then disappears back inside.

I'm alone again.

I eat my food quickly, realizing I'm hungrier than I thought. I don't taste the food, I inhale it.

I don't know when to expect Langston, but I do know that he's been watching me. He knew the second I would return and had food prepared for me.

So it doesn't surprise me that the second I finish eating, Langston appears.

He doesn't speak or walk loud enough to make his presence known, but my heart recognizes the second he's near.

I look up at him standing in the shadows, just outside the house.

I stare back.

"Did you enjoy your walk?" he asks.

"It was just great, especially knowing there were men watching my every step."

He chuckles. "Up for another walk?"

I tilt my head. "I thought you gave commands, not asked questions."

"I'll be giving orders soon enough. I'll let you decide where we talk tonight."

I stand. "Where do you want to walk?"

"Down to the beach."

I nod.

He picks up a small bag I didn't notice on the floor and slings it over his shoulder, before taking off down the cliffside.

I follow after, still barefoot in my robe.

Langston walks to the edge of the water then plops his bag down. He pulls out a towel and lays it out before sitting down on it. Langston turns and looks at me.

All I see is the glistening water reflecting off the blueness in his eyes. He looks warm and welcoming, not like the killer he is.

He pats a spot on the towel next to him.

I take a deep inhale before sitting down beside him. I'll reserve my strength to fight him later when I'm really going to need it.

Langston gives me a slight nod of approval and then pulls out two lowball glasses.

"Hold," he says, handing them to me.

I take them and hold while he pours two fingers of scotch into each glass. He remembers my favorite drink.

I frown as my eyes slant up to meet his.

"What is this? Why are you being nice?"

He takes his glass and takes a long sip.

"I'm not being nice. This conversation could go long, and I want to be able to enjoy myself while we talk."

I roll my eyes. "Liar. Then why do I get a glass?"

"The drunker you are, the more likely you are to spill the truth and put us both out of our misery."

I down my drink and hold it out with a smug expression.

He shakes his head.

"You don't get more until I say so. We are going for tipsy, not passed out throwing up everywhere drunk."

I pout and continue to hold my glass out to him.

"You look ridiculous," Langston says.

I sigh and set my glass down. "You used to like it."

"Never."

A wave splashes hard against the sand, distracting us both for a moment. The sun has almost completely set, and we simply enjoy the view, waiting for the colors to fade and darkness to settle in before we talk about the darkness we both share.

When the last of the light leaves the sky, Langston finally talks.

"One year."

My head whips to him.

"You will stay on the island for one year. That's the timeline I'm giving you. One year to tell the truth. One year until you die."

My mouth dries. Now I wish I hadn't downed the scotch so quickly.

Langston notices, or it's a strange coincidence, because he picks up my glass and pours me more scotch. He then takes my hand and places the glass in it.

"Thanks," I whisper, my throat burning from the single word. I take a small sip, savoring it this time.

"Every night I will give you the opportunity to extend your time or reduce it. If you lie, your time shrinks, and I will punish you. If you tell the truth, you gain time, and your time here will be more enjoyable."

One year.

I'm still caught on that part.

I can't stay on this island for a whole year.

Langston said I would die in one year. Death doesn't scare me, but the thought of being trapped this long, even in this beautiful of a place, sends icy blades jolting down my spine.

"During the day, you can spend your time however you want.

Check out the island, swim, read a book, plan your escape, I don't care. But you will spend it away from me."

My eyes narrow, and my forehead wrinkles. "Why?"

"Why do you think?" he breathes, his breath full of warm alcohol. He's had more than the single scotch to drink tonight.

I don't answer. I honestly don't know why he hates me so much.

"At night, you can sleep in my bed or be locked up."

"Locked up. There is no way I'd be able to sleep with you in my bed," I retort without a thought.

His fist tightens around his glass, but he doesn't say anything.

"This is where you'll meet me every night after the sun sets. You'll make your choice—tell me a truth to gain more time alive, or lie and lose time. Depending on what you tell me, I'll decide how much time to add or take away. Or..." He stops and takes another swig of his scotch.

"Or you tell me every truth on your half of that piece of paper right now and I'll let you live."

I purposefully don't look at him as he speaks. Langston is a good liar when he wants to be. His sparkling ocean eyes, his bright smile, his sun-kissed hair all make him look like a handsome lifeguard about to save me.

But he's like medusa, one look at him and he's deadly. His look can kill.

I know his tricks, though, so I don't look. I don't listen to the timbre of his voice or the shift of his weight in the sand. I definitely don't listen to my own heart, because that sucker just wants to get laid.

No, I take my cues from the wind, the ocean, the stars. I listen to the truth that only the world holds. There is no listening to Langston.

He knows there is no way I'm telling him what's on my half of the letter, a letter he ripped and stole. A letter he should have never even known about.

"What did I do to deserve death?" I continue to look at the ocean instead of him.

Our relationship is complicated; it always has been. We've saved each other as much as we've tormented each other. Protected each other as often as we've thrown the other to the wolves. And yet, we've never threatened to kill each other.

I'm missing something—something vital.

"You know what you've done. You may not realize that I know, but I do. Just think about the worst thing you've ever done and start there. That's why you deserve to die."

He pauses.

"I'm giving you a way out. You can live if you tell me everything tonight—right here, right now. This is your only chance to tell the full truth. Tell me the truth tonight, and I'll save you. Tell me a lie, and you've sealed your fate. This is a one time offer. Take it or leave it. Life or death."

I chuckle. "God, you are such an impatient man." Finally, I look at him and take in his big frustrated eyes, his ruffled blonde hair, and his stern lips. I'm used to smiling Langston. As a kid, he would always rather be playing than stewing in his anger.

"Impatient or not, I'd take my offer. Save yourself."

"You mean, tell you the truth so you will have no use for me and will kill me faster?"

He growls.

I growl back, but it's the truth. No matter what I choose, I'll end up dead at Langston's hand if I don't figure out a way to stop him. The only way I live is to be more valuable to him alive than dead. As long as I have my secrets, I'll stay alive.

But I'll be trapped.

"What will it be, Liesel?"

I fold my knees up and rest my arm against my knee, holding my glass. I stare at it, wishing we could both just tell the truth.

I'm not afraid of death—I just don't want to die at Langston's hands.

I spot the tattoo I got on the inside of my wrist.

I smile, knowing the story I'm going to tell tonight.

♡

IT'S BEEN ONE MONTH SINCE I WAS RAPED.

My life is spiraling.

And no one has noticed.

One. Whole. Month.

I walk into high school on the first day of my senior year expecting everyone to notice that I'm different, that everything has changed.

My locker is next to Enzo's.

I walk up to my shiny red locker where Enzo, Langston, and Zeke are gathered.

"Really? You couldn't let his best friends have the locker right next to him? Now, we have to deal with your overpowered perfume smell, glitter, and bobby pins every time we want to come to our lockers," Zeke complains like a bitch.

"Trust me, I'd rather not be stuck between Enzo and Zeke—the Sasquatch. Now I'll have to deal with your sweaty odor, hair ties, and hair that escapes your stupid man bun."

Langston snickers at my zing.

Enzo smiles.

Zeke looks ready to kill.

And I've never welcomed that look from Zeke more.

If no one is going to save me, the least they could do is kill me.

"What class you got first period, Liesel?" Enzo asks.

"Calculus."

Langston starts rolling in laughter.

"What's so funny?" I ask, thinking I have something stuck in my ponytail. I hardly bothered to get dressed for school today. The boys should notice that I'm not wearing my usual skintight dress, heels, curls, and makeup. Instead, I'm wearing ripped jeans, flats, a plain black v-neck, and my hair in a ponytail. I look like most girls around me, except, I'm not most girls.

I'm Liesel Dunn—glamorous, spirited, take no prisoners with my curvy hips and sassy words. I rule this school with my good looks even though I have exactly five dresses—one for each day of the week that I scrapped to save enough money to buy. No one cares that you don't have money when you walk with confidence like I do.

"There is no way you are going to pass calculus; you can barely do basic addition."

I flip him off, which makes the immature asshole laugh even more.

I have no hope that Langston or Zeke will notice, but Enzo should. Unfortunately, he hasn't noticed me hiding out all summer.

He hasn't noticed that I haven't swum in the pool since that day. Or that I haven't worn anything except bags for clothes to cover my body.

I haven't hung out with Enzo or the guys for weeks.

I haven't asked for a second kiss.

I haven't asked for more.

Instead, I'm hiding and trying to move on.

"Nah, Liesel is smarter than you two idiots," Enzo says, defending me to his friends.

I smile—it's fake, but when Enzo smiles back at me, it turns genuine. Butterflies swarm in my belly as the familiar aches of being around Enzo return. After everything that happened, I still want him. His father didn't take those feelings away.

He took more.

"Enzo! Walk me to class?" Bridget says, pushing her way into the group and grabbing Enzo's hand.

My smile vanishes, gone from my face in one swipe.

Langston and Zeke give each other mischievous smirks.

Enzo throws his arm around her shoulder and walks her to class with Langston and Zeke strutting behind them.

They ignore me.

They forget about me.

They don't see my pain.

I'm nobody to them.

I never make it to class.

Instead, I walk out of the building.

I walk to the beach.

And then I sit on the sand watching the world go by. I watch the sun rise high in the sky. I watch it fall below the edge of the water.

I'm alone. I have no one.

I pick up my glass water bottle and slam it on the ground, wishing I had something stronger than water.

Soon, I won't need anything.

The glass breaks into several pieces.

I pick up one of the pieces under the darkness of night. The piece has a sharp edge—it will do.

Looking up at the sky with tears in my eyes, I slice through my wrist until it's deep enough to hit a vein.

The second I do, a calmness passes through me.

I've taken back control. My life is mine again. This is where it ends.

Pain creeps through my veins slowly, but I feel it. I feel all of it.

It makes me cry—not from the pain, but from the existing. From feeling something when I haven't felt anything in weeks.

I can still feel.

One last time.

My head starts spinning. I feel weak and tired, so tired.

I fall back onto the sand.

Finally, I managed to kill someone—me.

I look up at Langston sitting on the sand, listening to my story.

That was the last time I remember crying.

The last time tears fell down my face.

I hold out my wrist where the scar remains but is now covered with a tattoo of the word 'beautifully.'

"I killed myself that day."

Langston shakes his head. "No, you survived."

"No, the girl I was before that day flowed out from my veins. I killed her. I used to be kind, sweet, forgiving. After that, I became cynical, angry, bitchy. I became evil."

Langston narrows his eyes, not sure what I'm going to say next or why I'm telling this story.

"How did you survive?" Langston asks with a heavy breath.

I stare at him, unblinking.

We both know the truth, but I won't give him any credit.

"The devil saved me. He thought he was doing me a favor. He didn't know he was only saving a monster."

He looks away from me back out at the ocean. "Then, you got the tattoo so you wouldn't have to walk around with the reminder every day."

I look back at my wrist. "No, I got the tattoo to remind myself that I died beautifully, and that the beauty within me is now gone. All that remains is the wicked."

"At least that's the truth," he mutters under his breath.

Our eyes meet again, cutting through each other.

We both know who found me that night.

I still don't know why Langston saved me. I don't know how he found me. I don't know what happened. I just woke up in his arms.

"You won't kill me, Langston. I'll kill myself before you ever get the chance."

CHAPTER 20

LANGSTON

The truth is going to kill me.

I realize that after listening to Liesel's second story. I didn't think she'd get this deep with her stories this quickly, but she dove in head first. She flirted so closely with telling the complete truth, but twisted one tiny detail to make the story dig in like a knife to my heart.

It wasn't so much a lie as an omission.

She didn't include me in her story.

I noticed her when she showed up at school. I had been waiting for weeks to get to see her in one of her slinky school dresses.

My mouth almost fell open when I saw her in jeans. She still looked hotter than sin, and her muscled legs looked fantastic in her skinny jeans, but I knew something was wrong.

I thought she was pissed at Enzo.

I thought they were together.

I thought he had moved on and dumped her for Bridgett like I knew he would.

Then Liesel disappeared.

She didn't show up in any of our classes.

She didn't come to her locker.

She didn't sit with us at lunch.

She was gone.

I had to find her, clearly something terrible had happened.

I ran back to the club where I worked for Enzo's father. I pulled up all the security cameras I could find. But I didn't find her at the house, the club, or any of the properties Enzo's family owns.

She wasn't at the guest house or the house she grew up in either.

She was gone.

There was only one place she could have gone—the ocean.

It took me all day to find her.

When I did, she was passed out. Blood spilled from her wrist onto the sand.

I had killed before but never saved.

Until then.

That night I saved her.

"I regret it," I say.

"What?"

"I. Regret. It."

We stare into each other's eyes, and we both know what I'm talking about without saying it—I regret saving her. I wouldn't be in this mess if I had just let her die. If I hadn't searched for her that day. If I hadn't found her.

"Me too," she snaps back.

I nod.

She lets out a deep breath as she pulls her knees to her chest.

"I lied," Liesel says.

I let a beat go by before I answer her.

"I know."

Just like I know that she didn't want to die that day. She wanted the pain to end. She didn't want to be alone.

Liesel opens her mouth to speak, but I beat her to it.

"Come on—bedtime," I say.

I snatch her glass and put it back in the bag along with mine. Then, I pick up the towel we were sitting on and pack it in the bag before I start walking toward the house.

Liesel keeps step with me, walking by my side instead of behind me, almost like we shared a connection, instead of more lies.

I drop the bag off in the kitchen, and then head up the stairs.

Liesel follows silently, but I can feel the apprehension flowing off her.

We reach the top floor before I stop.

"Last chance, my bed or locked up?"

"Locked up," she says fiercely.

It pisses me off.

I may not be able to handle her near me during the day, but at night, I want her with me. Her words feed the monster inside me.

An idea forms to persuade her.

"Follow me," I say.

Liesel does. She chooses her moments, and it seems she's going to fight me with her lies, not her fists.

I lead her into my bedroom.

She stops abruptly in the doorway. "I said I wouldn't sleep in your bed."

"I'm not asking you to sleep in my bed." I walk over to the closet door and open it.

"This is the only room in the house that doesn't have a window or door for you to climb out of."

She smirks. "Why did you let me roam around the beach when you knew I escaped?"

"Because I don't care how you spend your days. I just care about your nights."

She tugs on her robe, closing it tighter around her waist.

She hasn't asked for clothes.

And if I know her, her stubborn ass won't.

She can pull it as tightly around her as possible, but it can't hide her body from me. The robe is too big for her, which somehow makes it easier to see the swell of her breasts and the muscles of her legs. The rest of her, though, is left up to my imagination, at least for tonight.

"Don't test my patience, Liesel. Get in the closet or get in my bed."

I won't chase her if she runs; I won't have to. She wants to act strong and tough, as if I don't affect her. Her body tells the real story though—the storm brewing in her eyes, the way she's biting her plump lip, the way she's twisting her body away.

Her eyes run down my body, and she notices that my cock is straining in my pants for her.

Before I can say anything, she runs into the closet like that's going to save her.

I move to close the door.

"You lost a week of time for lying."

"What about my punishment?"

My jaw ticks. "Goodnight, Liesel."

Then I close the door, locking her in my dark closet.

I pull out my phone and text Joel.

Liesel is in my closet. Do your worst.

I grab my tennis shoes by my bedroom door and slip them on. I pull my shirt off and head out into the night for a run.

This time, I won't be here to save her.

CHAPTER 21

LIESEL

Langston won't forget about my punishment.

The door closes shut with a hard thud, followed by a clink of the lock.

I grip the handle, feeling Langston still standing on the other side of the door. I press my other hand to the door, and I feel his hot desire.

Why didn't he rape me?

Why didn't he kiss me? Touch me? Force himself on me?

I know he'll punish me. He won't forget.

I made sure the lies I've told stung. I may not be able to escape, I may not be able to fight back physically, but I can inflict pain with my words.

I hear footsteps and then nothing.

He's gone.

It's still early. *Maybe he headed back downstairs for another drink before bed?* I wish I had drunk more, then maybe I'd be able to sleep in this dark closet.

He put me in a fucking closet—*the bastard.*

I feel around the walls, hoping for a big pile of clothes to sleep on. All I feel is drywall.

He removed all the fucking clothes!

My back hits the wall in the farthest corner of the dark closet before I slump down to the floor.

I can't see an inch in front of me in the darkness.

Langston left me alone in a pitch-black, box of a room. *Maybe my punishment is sleeping in the darkness with my nightmares?* He doesn't know that it's not the darkness or the nightmares that I'm afraid of.

The pain I feel comes from somewhere else—something Langston will never understand.

I squeeze my eyes shut, hoping the pain and torment won't come for me tonight. There are only two ways to keep the pain out: sleep and sex.

Sleep isn't going to happen for hours. I'm used to living on very little sleep. And there is no way I'll be able to fall asleep on this cold, hard floor.

I can do something about the other option.

The one good thing about being locked in a dark closet is that there are no cameras in here.

When I fucked Waylon all night, I did it as much for the cameras, for Langston, as I did it for me. I put on a show for Langston, showed him what he can never have.

Tonight is all about me. I need this. I need the distraction. Langston doesn't get to watch me pleasure myself.

I grab the strap of the robe, untie it, and let the robe fall open.

Instinctively, I look up into the corner to double-check there isn't a camera. If there is one, I can't see it. And if Langston is watching, an uneasy feeling will take hold of me.

None does.

There is no camera.

I purse my lips as I let out a breath, trying to relax. This is my happy place—fucking.

I can't fuck Waylon, but I can fuck myself.

I close my eyes, tuning out the world.

It helps that the room is silent. I can't hear Langston.

So why do I keep thinking about him?

He's holding me captive and has threatened to kill me—that's why. *Stop thinking about Langston!*

I open my eyes, staring out at the darkness.

Focus.

I bring my knees toward me, placing my feet flat on the floor and letting my legs fall apart, wide and open.

My hands take their time exploring my own body. It's been a long time since I've needed to get myself off. Waylon keeps me more than satisfied.

And before that, it was Jason, Andrew, Carter...

The men in my life have been endless.

My hands start sensually exploring with a light touch down my neck. My skin is soft and hot beneath my fingers. My breasts feel large in my hands. Down I trail my hand over the softness of my stomach, purposefully avoiding any scars that remind me of my old life, before I feel between my legs.

I'm dry, not wet.

I haven't done nearly enough to turn myself on yet.

My hand rises back up, and I suck slowly on my fingers, providing moisture to turn myself on.

I use one hand to spread my pussy lips and the other to find my clit. I rub my saliva over my clit, warming myself up. I move slowly; I have all night after all. There is no pressure to come quickly.

It's been so long since I've touched myself like this that I've forgotten what I like—*slow, light pressure or fast, hard pressure. Do I like a circular motion or the flick of my fingers over my sensitive bud?*

Soon, I find my rhythm. I'm breathy, warm, and my heartbeat is pounding.

That's when I slip a finger inside.

I'm wet—but barely.

"Jesus Christ."

I think of Waylon—of his tanned skin, his thick rippling muscles, his perfectly plump cock.

I pump two fingers in and out, concentrating on Waylon.

I get minimally wetter.

Dammit.

I remove my fingers in frustration.

I know what will turn me on—a stubborn asshole who locked me in a closet but not before giving me a panty-melting, hungry glare. One that tore through my robe and told me he knows exactly what to do with my body.

With Waylon, I had to teach him how to turn me on. I have a feeling Langston would just know. There would be no need for instructions. He'd sense what I needed; understand me more than I do myself.

I won't let my mind think about Langston.

I can make myself come without a man's help.

My fingers return to my pussy as I focus on my breathing. I pump in and out of myself while my thumb circles my swollen clit.

A low moan hums through my belly, bringing me closer to the beautiful explosion my body is capable of making.

Footsteps creep outside the floor, startling me.

"Fuck," I curse under my breath.

I was so close to coming.

Who am I kidding? I wasn't anywhere close.

I remove my fingers and fumble with the robe, tying it around my waist.

I'm sure it's just Langston returning to go to sleep, but the heaviness of the footsteps concern me. Langston can move silently if he wants. All of Enzo's men can. Enzo taught them how to move like ninjas before they turned ten.

The fact that I can hear the creak of each step tells me he wants me to hear him.

Maybe he saw what I was doing and thought he'd interrupt? Make me sexually frustrated all night? Maybe that's my punishment?

The footsteps stop.

I hold my breath, listening carefully for Langston in the bathroom or climbing into bed.

Will it be easier or harder to touch myself knowing he's so near?

I guess I'm about to find out.

Clank.

I hear scratching at the door. The sound of the lock turns, followed by the door. A sliver of moonlight creeps in behind him, illuminating his outline, but hiding his face.

"Langston?" I breathe out. He's returned to punish me, I have no doubt.

He doesn't answer me. He walks silently toward me, his feet sounding loud and heavy.

He's trying to scare me, prepare me, for what he's about to do to me.

But I'm one step ahead of him.

He squats down in front of me and takes my hand in his.

"You smell that?" I ask, my voice is raspy.

He lifts my fingers to his face and takes a deep inhale. There is no mistaking what my fingers smell like: sex.

He growls low and deep. The sound vibrates through my body— the missing piece to my arousal.

He grips me hard on the biceps, pinning me against the wall with his legs between my knees and thighs.

I don't know what he has planned as punishment for me, and I don't care.

Right now, I need to come. I need to chase the demons inside my head away.

I grab Langston's hand and tear it from my bicep. He thinks I'm going to fight him, that I can't handle his touch. Just the opposite. My body is begging for a man's touch.

I spread my legs wider. And although I can't see Langston's face, I know he's shocked.

His heart rate is about to double in speed.

Carefully, I pull his fingers to my mouth and suck viciously. I let my teeth scrape harder than I should, but I want his fingers nice and wet before he touches me. Then, I glide his fingers to my entrance.

"Fuck me," I whisper.

His fingers don't move from my slit, but they don't push inside me either.

I'm impatient and needy. I won't wait.

I grab his hand and push his fingers inside me.

I gasp as I grip onto his shirt with one hand, and keep my other around his wrist.

"Fuck me, Langston."

I guide his hand in and out. Eventually, he starts moving his fingers in and out on his own accord.

My head falls back against the wall, and I spread open wider for him so he can get deeper inside me.

Langston takes full advantage.

"Yes," I moan as he pounds his fingers inside me.

I bite my lip, and he pushes again and again.

"More," I breathe. "I need more."

It takes him a moment to catch my meaning, but he pushes a second, then a third finger, inside.

"Oh, god, yes!" I moan, no longer forming coherent thoughts in my head.

It feels incredible, but he has yet to touch my clit. Probably because he thinks if he doesn't touch me there, then I won't gain pleasure. Then this is still a form of punishment.

Ha.

There is nothing punishing about this.

I grab his other hand and slide his fingers over my clit.

"Rub," I order.

He growls again but complies.

He starts rubbing, but his fingers only manage a couple of rubs before he slips off my clit.

Damn, Langston!

There is a loud sound.

Langston stills.

"I'm so close," I exhale.

He ignores me.

Then, suddenly, his fingers are gone.

And then, so is he.

No!

He doesn't get to get me all worked up and then not finish me.

I jump off the ground and run to the door.

It's open.

I run out and chase Langston down the hallway. I don't care if an army is attacking us, he better come finish what he started right now.

I don't make it far until I run into a brick wall of a chest.

I stop abruptly.

His fingers hold me back at the waist.

A light flickers on.

Langston's angry glare leaves me timid and weak at the knees.

His eyes roam up and down my body, like he's taking inventory of it.

A soft breeze blows through the window. It's then I realize I'm naked. My robe must have fallen off as I was chasing after him.

His eyes heat on the scar on my stomach.

I move my hands to cover it, but he gently and firmly removes my hand so he can inspect my scar.

"Are you ready to sleep in my bed?" he asks sternly.

"No."

"Then what are you doing out of the closet?"

"I—I, uh, just wanted to know why you stopped. What you were chasing?"

"Go back to bed, Liesel."

"What about—"

"Now!" His booming voice demands compliance.

I have no choice but to walk back to the closet.

I find my robe on the floor and cover my body. Once again, I find myself slumping in the corner of the closet.

He walks to the door, and this time, I see his eyes before he closes the door. They brand into me, hiding his thoughts but making it clear he's angry with me.

Then the door is shut and locked.

I'm left alone once again.

Once again with my demons.

Once again to finish myself.

I huff, knowing there is no way I'm going to come now. Tonight, I'm going to have to deal with my monsters.

To make things worse, I've shown Langston how weak I am for his body. Now he has an even bigger advantage. I need to figure out how to get the upper hand. I need to get ahold of a phone and call Waylon, Siren, or Kai. Anyone who might search and find me.

Or I could strike my own deal with Langston. One that keeps him from touching me during the day, but at night...

CHAPTER 22

LANGSTON

I wake before the sun—not that I slept. I couldn't after what happened with Liesel last night.

The woman is the most irritating, confounding, frustrating woman on the planet. She's also the most intriguing, alluring, beautiful woman.

And that means I'm fucked.

I should stay away, except when I'm pushing her to spill her secrets, but I can't. I want to fuck her so badly. My balls are blue just thinking about it.

I can't.

I can do many things to Liesel—torture her, demand truths, even kill her. I just can't fuck her.

Dammit, do my balls ache. My cock is stiff as a board, and after thirty minutes of trying to jack myself off, I'm more sexually frustrated than I was when I started. Finally, I just give up and decide to start my day.

I flick the lock on the door and wait, but Liesel doesn't move inside the closet.

I listen carefully and hear her soft snoring—she's asleep.

She'll figure out soon enough that the door is unlocked.

I head downstairs and find Amelia in the kitchen.

"Oh, Langston, I don't have coffee made yet. I wasn't expecting you to wake up for another hour like you usually do," Amelia says.

I grunt and make my way to the coffee machine. I don't usually operate it, but I'm too tired for words. I take the bag of coffee beans and put them into the hand grinder. I begin grinding when the handle pops off.

"Son of a bitch." I slam the grinder down on the counter—beans and broken metal fly everywhere.

I breathe heavily, realizing I need a release, any release. I need to get far away from the blonde upstairs.

"Let me work on your coffee for you," Amelia says, taking what remains of the grinder from my hands.

I nod and place my hands on my head as I storm out of the kitchen.

I should go for a run. Or meditate. Or swim. Something healthy to get my pent up frustration out.

Instead, I go see Joel.

I'm not sure if it will help or make things worse, but I need to see him. I need answers to what happened last night.

Joel is one of my trusted men who lives in the house with me, so I don't have to go far.

I walk to his door, letting my feet hit the floor roughly so he can hear me coming. When I knock, the sound is loud enough to wake the entire house up.

I can hear him moving in his bed, and then his feet hit the floor as he runs to answer the door. He knows it's me. He knows I have questions for him.

He opens the door without a shirt on. His hair is a disheveled mess, and a five o'clock shadow covers his face.

"Yes?" he asks as he grips the doorframe.

"What happened last night?"

He frowns. "Nothing. Nothing happened."

My eyes scan his face, looking for the truth.

For the first time, I wish I had cameras in my bedroom so I could know for sure if he's telling the truth.

"Did you do what I asked?"

Joel's eyes linger behind me, and I realize that Liesel has woken up. Probably my knocking or the blunder with the coffee grinder jolted her into the morning.

I glare at Joel.

I don't care that Liesel is standing behind us watching the exchange. I want to know what happened from his mouth because Lord knows I don't trust a word out of Liesel's.

"Yes," he answers before closing the door.

I turn and glance at Liesel but don't speak to her. She's still wearing that damn robe, even though she can't seem to keep it on her body all the time. She won't ask for clothes, but I won't survive her staying here a year without her completely covered in layers.

Liesel's eyes follow me while I walk back to the kitchen.

"Amelia, get Liesel some clothes and make sure she's wearing them by the time I get back."

Amelia blushes with a knowing smile as Liesel enters the kitchen.

"Langston, can we—" Liesel starts.

"I'm taking the helicopter to the other side of the island. Don't worry about lunch or dinner for me today, Amelia."

Liesel's mouth snaps shut. Finally, she understands I won't be talking to her during the day. My only use for her is at night.

I walk away from Liesel before she has a chance to open her sassy mouth.

I'm grumpy, annoyed, and sex-deprived. And based on how Liesel is telling her stories, I know what story she's going to tell next.

I'm terrified of her lying about the next part of her story.

I'm more terrified if she finally decides to tell the truth.

One of us might end up dead tonight.

Or worse—I'll lose control and fuck her. Although, from the way her body responded to me last night, she just might enjoy that.

♡

I'M NOT SURPRISED TO FIND LIESEL ALREADY SITTING ON THE BEACH as the sun begins to set.

She's wearing a red bikini top and jean shorts. Her skin is more tanned than it was this morning. She must have spent the day in the sun.

Meanwhile, I spent the day in torment.

I readjust the bag on my shoulder as I walk down to the beach to meet her. I'm glad she's wearing clothes; I just wish she was wearing more clothes.

The waves crash against the shore as I take a seat next to her. I don't bother with a towel this time. We sit directly on the sand tonight.

Once again, I pull out two lowball glasses and pour them with Liesel's favorite scotch. Luckily, it's my favorite scotch too.

She takes her glass, and we drink, watching the waves and the setting sun.

Clouds are covering most of the sun. Instead of the vibrant yellows, oranges, and reds that usually paint the sky, tonight's sunset is muted. It's gray and pale yellow. It's fitting for the conversation we are about to have.

"Care to skip ahead to the part about what your half of the letter says? Or just skip the next couple of years of our past? Maybe tell a happy story. I'm in a foul mood."

She smirks. "Why? Didn't get good sleep last night?"

I lift my glass to my lips. *I'm going to need a lot of alcohol to get through tonight.* "Something like that."

"Try sleeping on the hard floor of a closet. Then you can complain."

"You are welcome in my bed anytime."

She bites her lip but doesn't take me up on my offer.

"That's what I thought." We both finish our drinks. I take the bottle and pour more scotch into our glasses.

"You're terrified of what I'm going to say, aren't you?"

I roll my shoulders back. "No."

"We can always tell when we are lying to each other. You're grumpy, sleep-deprived, and antsy. And you're a shot away from being drunk. You only get like this when I get under your skin."

"Start talking before I decide to take away a month of your life."

Her eyes narrow at me.

"I'm going to enjoy this," she says.

That makes one of us.

"I had three protectors. Three men who cared about me in very different ways. One claimed I drove him mad. That I was a spoiled little princess even though I didn't have a penny to my name. That I took more than I gave," she starts her story.

Zeke—she's talking about our friend Zeke who always found Liesel annoying. But he never took the time to get to know her like Enzo and I did.

"One claimed to love me. He stole kisses, fucked me senseless, gave me everything—money, clothes, college tuition."

Enzo. Her words burn through me like a raging fire. She's trying to get me irritated before she gets to the hard part. But it's all difficult. Hearing that she fucked him, even though I already knew it, hurts.

"And one claimed to be my best friend. He claimed to protect me, to kill for me. He couldn't offer me money, or love, or kindness, but he could offer me his protection."

Me—she's talking about me.

"All three failed. I could have forgiven them the first time. I did forgive them. I moved on with my life. I went back to school and started flirting with Enzo again. But when they failed twice, I was well beyond forgiveness."

I squeeze my eyes shut to block out the pain.

I should blame myself for how Liesel turned out. I failed her. Sure, Enzo and Zeke should have known as well. We all should have protected her. But this is my biggest failure, and she's about to rub it in my face.

I deserve every bit of pain I'm about to endure.

I should apologize for my failure.

I should beg for her forgiveness.

But I'll do neither.

I don't deserve compassion.

And there are no words to apologize for what I've done.

Liesel has stopped talking.

"Keep going. I deserve to know the pain I caused."

"Why? So you can get off on it?" her head whips to me.

"No, so I can do penance."

"Like you care at all. You're going to kill me! You don't care about my pain."

"Then do it for the boy who once did."

She blinks rapidly, looking at me.

"Enzo's father raped me a second time. I won't go into the gory details, but he would have raped me again and again..." her voice falters as she speaks.

"The first time, I was able to survive it. Somehow I went back to my normal life. After getting raped again, everything changed."

She finishes her glass.

I pick up the bottle to pour her more, but she shakes her head.

Uneasily, I put the bottle back down in the sand.

"Six weeks later, I found out I was pregnant."

Her words squeeze around my heart. I already knew she was pregnant, but it still hurts that she went through that alone.

"Did you tell anyone?" I ask, wondering if Enzo knew. Her mother, anyone? I clearly wasn't worthy of the news. She didn't think I would help her, protect her.

"No. The first person I told was a nurse at an abortion clinic."

There is so much agony in her voice. So much outrage at what she had to endure in solitude.

She was raped—twice.

And everyone in her life who was supposed to protect her failed.

I failed.

And then worst of all, none of us realized anything was wrong.

I saw something was different and still didn't protect her. I didn't hold her hand when she went to the clinic. I did nothing.

Liesel purses her lips and blows through them. She's trying not to cry.

Her and me both.

"What stopped you from going through with it?"

She bites her bottom lip, rolling it around between her teeth.

"The child's father did."

"Jesus," I curse. Enzo's father stopped her.

I didn't know that part of the story. It's bad enough the bastard raped her, but then he forced her to have his child.

She shakes her head. "He told me if I aborted our child, he'd just rape me again and again until I got pregnant.

"I never wanted to have children. Especially not as a teenager, but I had no choice," she says.

I should have been there. I should have helped her.

"After graduation, I ran. I told everyone I was taking a gap year before I went to college. Enzo had given me some money, and he'd already paid for my college. No one questioned why I wanted to take a break before school.

"I ran. I hid. And I had the baby—alone. Then I made the choice to give him up—alone. That was the hardest thing I've ever done," she whimpers.

Sharp pain shoots through my body at her words. I tracked her every day of her trip. I watched her from afar. I knew the truth, and I did nothing. I let her be by herself.

I pound my fists into the ground, trying to hold back the tears.

Liesel was my best friend growing up.

Until everything changed.

Until she started chasing Enzo instead of hanging with me.

Until I fucked it all up by not keeping my word.

Until I made a promise that ensured I would stay away from her forever.

I put my hand on the ground behind me as I lean back.

Somehow, my hand finds hers.

Our fingers intertwine.

We sit on the beach, holding hands like lovers.

"Did you know? Did you know that I was pregnant? That I was raped?"

I squeeze her hand as my tears finally fall.

She doesn't cry, though.

She never cries.

"No," I lie.

Her teeth grind together as she nods.

She's the strong one. She's the one who doesn't cry.

If things were different, if I had the power to forgive her, I probably would, but I don't have that power.

And what I did to her is just as unforgivable.

I let go of her hand and stand up, wading into the water until the waves crash against my feet.

Liesel was raped, had a baby, and let him go. And all I did was watch from the sidelines, thinking I was doing the right thing.

No, I did do the right thing, even though it killed me.

Liesel did one decent thing—give up her baby for adoption. Still, it doesn't forgive her for what she did after.

"I hate you, Liesel, but not because of this. You saving that baby, getting him away from Enzo's father, that was the bravest thing you've ever done. I hate myself for not being there for you."

"I hate you for not being there that night. But I hate you more for trapping me here and threatening to kill me. What did I do to make you hate me like this?"

I ignore her question. "Thank you for the truth. You gained back the week you lost yesterday."

Then I walk back into the house—a broken, weak man. I'm afraid of what I'm going to do next. Weak men only make mistakes.

CHAPTER 23

LIESEL

Langston thinks I told the truth, maybe because he wants it to be the truth.

I hate children.

I wanted to be childless.

I was forced to have the baby.

I wanted to give my baby up.

I'm not sure which parts of the story are truths and which are lies. That's not true. I know, I just can't admit the truth. It's too painful.

But there is one big part that I lied about.

Giving my child up was the hardest thing I've ever done. It was torment. That was the last time I remember crying. The last time I remember feeling anything. After that, I became numb. I became a bitch a hundred percent of the time instead of most of the time.

It doesn't shock me to think that Langston thinks everything I said was the truth. He wants to believe what I said was as awful as it gets. That I have a child out there somewhere, and I gave him up rather than have his rapist father hunt and search for him.

After my child was adopted, I was shocked that Enzo's father never came to claim him. I thought he was just biding his time.

Thank God, he's dead now. I'd do it myself if he wasn't.

My heart bleeds on the inside. For once, I wish I could cry, could show real emotion. But if I ever started, I would never stop.

Langston cried, though.

He can still feel pain.

And I can still tell when he's lying.

Langston knew I was pregnant.

He knew I was raped.

He knew I was alone when I gave the baby up.

He was always watching me.

Langston could have been there with me.

He could have held my hand as I gave birth.

He could have wiped my tears when my baby was taken from my arms.

I hate him.

Whatever I did to make him hate me now was warranted. He left me all alone. He made me like this.

Langston starts the climb up the cliffside back to the house.

He stirred emotions deep inside me, forcing me to re-evaluate my needs. Usually, I just fight with my words. And my words hurt Langston. But I want more than his tears; I want his blood.

I run at Langston.

I know he hears me, but he doesn't stop me.

He lets me tackle him hard into the side of the cliff. I jump on his back as my fists pound into his head over and over, hoping to bludgeon him to death.

Only after I've gotten a few good punches in does he grab my wrist to stop me and twist me around to his front. I wrap my legs around his waist and continue beating his chest with my free hand.

"You're a fucking liar! You knew! You fucking knew!"

I hit him so hard that he falls back onto the sand with me strad-dling him. I hit his chest over and over.

My frustration is building, brick by brick, as I pummel him repeatedly.

He lets me.

He lets me hurt him.

I need a release.

I try so hard to cry, to let out the emotions I'm keeping inside, but none come.

I scream—it's a high pitched, glass shattering kind of scream. But it's not a release, not a real display of emotions.

Finally, Langston grabs my wrists, forcing me to stop.

"I'm going to kill you. You say that I can't kill, but that's only because I've been saving my first kill for you."

"Are you finished?"

"No, you fucking liar."

"Yes, I lied."

My breath catches. *I can't believe he admitted that.*

"I knew you were raped. I knew you were pregnant. I knew you gave the baby up."

Heart. Beating. So. Fast.

"You knew?" My voice is soft, still not fully believing it until this moment.

He nods. "I knew."

"Why didn't you tell me? Why didn't you approach me? Help me?"

He shakes his head. "Sorry, huntress. You can know that I lied, but you don't get to know the rest."

I hit him as hard as I can muster in his chest.

"I can't believe you. I—I don't understand how you are mad at me. Why do you want to kill me? You were the one who knew and did nothing. You betrayed me!"

"Think really hard. Your only chance at redemption is to tell me what's on your half of the letter. And even that won't earn my forgiveness. I won't be merciful."

"Then we will both die hating each other," I vow.

My entire body is pain. I need a release. I need to forget.

Langston notices.

"Can't cry, can you?"

I shake my head slowly.

He smirks. "And you haven't orgasmed since you came here either?"

I shake my head and look away.

He turns my head back until I'm looking at him.

"At least when I die, I'll die after coming."

"Fuck you."

"You wish."

I growl.

"Now, which will it be? My bed or the closet?"

I roll off of him and stomp all the way to the fucking closet.

$\heartsuit$

I ROLL OVER ON THE HARD, COOL GROUND IN THE CLOSET.

Then I turn the other way.

Back and forth. Tossing and turning.

The floor is uncomfortable, and I don't have a blanket, but that's not why I can't sleep.

I stand up and begin pacing back and forth. I take five steps in one direction, then turn around and return my five steps.

It's pitch-black, but you would think my eyes would have adjusted to the darkness by now. They haven't. I still can't see, and if I miscount or take an extra-large step, I bump into the wall.

The pacing won't help me sleep, but I hope it will address my flooding urges. I feel my control slipping.

I rub the back of my neck—it's soaked in sweat, along with my forehead and neck. I'm sweating everywhere.

I'm hot, burning hot.

I need a release, but I don't know how to get one without a man.

Jesus, I'm fucked up.

If I could just cry, feel something, maybe I wouldn't feel this way. I don't know how to cry anymore.

And I don't know how to come alone.

I need help.

I storm to the door and grab the handle, knowing it's time I talked to Langston. I won't survive the year like this. If Langston wants a chance to get answers, then he needs to help me live long enough to be able to tell him the truth.

I rattle the doorknob, but it doesn't open.

"Fuck!"

I slam my hand on the door, pounding on it.

"Langston!"

Knock.

Knock.

Knock.

"Open the door! We need to talk!"

I press my ear up against the door, but I don't hear anything. If Langston is in his bed, he would have heard me. He's either ignoring me or not here.

He's never here for me when I need him.

My nails dig into the back of the door and then scrape down. I hope I'm destroying the perfect finish on this pretty door, but I doubt I am.

I collapse to my knees as I cry out, begging my body to surrender, to give in.

Cry, dammit.

Shed one fucking tear.

Make this easier.

I feel under my eyes, but all I sense is the sticky sweat clinging to my cheeks.

I'm broken.

As much as I don't want to admit it, I need Langston.

"Liesel?"

Langston's voice.

I exhale sharply.

"Yes," I croak back.

"What's wrong?"

Do it. Say it and get it over with.

"I need you."

There's a pause.

He's not going to answer. He's not going to talk to me. He's not going to help me.

The door opens.

No light shines in—the room remains dark as he steps inside the closet and then shuts the door behind him.

"I never got my reward for telling you the truth," I say.

I hear him swallow, but he still doesn't speak.

I stand up and shimmy my jean shorts down until they are a heap on the floor. He must have heard the flop my jeans made, but he doesn't react. At least, he doesn't react in a way I can see.

I reach up and untie my swimsuit top and let it fall to the floor. Lastly, I shove my bikini bottoms to the floor.

"I need a release, Langton. Fuck me. Make me come. I need it if you want me to survive long enough to spill my secrets."

He doesn't move.

I hate how desperate I am. I hate that I'll be cheating on Waylon, but I literally won't make it without this.

"I'm sorry, Waylon. Please forgive me."

I grab for Langston.

He doesn't move as I grip onto his bare chest. *He sleeps shirtless, does he sleep naked?*

My claws dig into his chest, sliding down his muscles until I find out.

He's wearing boxer briefs.

So sexy.

I can't see him, but I imagine him in my head.

No.

I don't need to imagine Langston. I just need his body.

"Sit down," I say, pushing his shoulders down.

I'm not sure if he will obey me. I'm not sure if he will take control and rape me.

As long as I'm in control of this, then it's my decision. Unfortunately, Langston has never been very good at letting me have control.

Surprisingly, he sits on the floor.

"Don't kiss me," I say, as I climb on top of him.

I find his cock hard as stone, lift it out of his shorts and let it push at my entrance.

I'm frustrated, worked up and horny as hell. I'm not sure if I'm wet, if I'm ready for him, but I'm too impatient to wait.

I slide down hard on top of his cock, my fingers digging into his shoulders as he tears through me. I wasn't wet enough, but I don't care.

I feel the pain.

I feel—that's enough.

"Now, I'm going to fuck you until you make me come."

I slide up and down his cock—hard and furiously fast.

I don't feel myself getting wetter, just hotter.

I thought fucking Langston would be explosive. I thought he'd know how to work my body, make me come in seconds.

He does, but I'm not letting him have control. That's why I'm not coming yet.

If I gave up control to him, then he'd have me panting and screaming his name in minutes.

I'm not going to give Langston control yet. That's one step too far. I need to come, but I need to control myself.

"Fuck," I moan as I ride him harder, rubbing my clit up against the deep V of his sculpted abs.

Faster.

Faster.

Faster.

Maybe if I kiss him? Just once?

Nope. That's too far.

I won't betray Waylon like that.

This isn't about cheating. It's about taking what I need to survive.

I rub myself against him, creating more friction.

I'm so hot, soaked in sweat, this is the moment...

"Liesel?" Langston's voice is so soft, full of pain and sadness. He knows I can't come. This won't work.

"I hate you. I hate you. I hate you. I hate you!" I pump over him, begging my body to give in.

I try one more time, but it doesn't happen.

I don't come.

It was all for nothing.

I shove him hard, and I climb off him.

I scream.

I pound my fists into the walls and consider pounding them into his head.

Before I can decide what to punch next, I collapse from exhaustion.

CHAPTER 24

LANGSTON

What the hell happened last night?

I yawn.

I'm going to need an IV of coffee to keep me going today. I didn't sleep more than five minutes all last night, not after what Liesel did.

How do I deal with her?

What the hell do I do?

Coffee. Coffee first, then I deal with Liesel.

I get dressed, flip the lock of the closet door, and race down the stairs. I know she didn't sleep a second last night, either. She'll be chasing me down the stairs, wanting answers.

I'm on a mission.

Coffee.

Liesel won't get in my way.

The damn grinder won't get in my way.

Not today.

I march down the stairs and over to the kitchen.

"Morning, boss," Amelia says with an annoying smile as she holds out a cup of coffee for me.

"Thanks," I grumble, grabbing the cup of coffee from her hands.

She smirks. "I figured you'd be up early again and need this."

"You're a lifesaver." I guzzle down the first cup and then help myself to a second.

"Didn't get much sleep last night?" She blushes, tossing her auburn hair over her shoulder. Amelia is a fantastic cook, but she's equally as capable equipped with a gun in her hand as she is a chef's knife.

"Don't ask."

I carry my cup of coffee outside onto the patio just as Liesel comes downstairs in her jean shorts and red bikini top again.

Jesus.

She's going to kill me.

And she's going to succeed long before I can kill her.

Less than a minute later, Liesel is opening the glass door and walking toward me carrying her own cup of coffee.

I frown.

I need to tell Amelia that the first pot of coffee in the morning is mine and to not share it with Liesel.

Liesel, unlike me, looks ready to go. Her blonde hair hangs in waves over her right shoulder. Her face looks bright with just a hint of freckles over her nose instead of the painted face I'm used to seeing on her. She looks young and carefree in her red bikini top that I want to rip from her body.

"I know you won't talk to me until the sun sets, but you should make an exception today," Liesel puts one hand on her hip while the other lifts her oversized mug to her lips, as she stands in front of me.

I shake my head and then press my fingers against my forehead, trying to relieve the pressure from my pounding headache.

"You know what would fix your migraine? Talking to me," Liesel says.

Ignore her.

I keep my eyes closed, hoping she'll go away if I don't give her any attention.

"Really? You think ignoring me is going to work? We aren't kids anymore, Langston! This isn't a game. You can't just ignore me. You can't just do what you did last night and not talk to me."

Fuck.

I run my hand through my hair.

I don't want to talk about last night.

I don't want to think about last night.

Last night was one giant mistake.

Liesel steps closer to me, and I finally look at her.

She's right.

I should talk to her.

A buzz in my pocket brings me out from under her spell. I pull out my cell phone.

"Yes?" I answer without looking at who's calling me. I'm just thankful that someone is before I made another mistake.

"Siren's missing," Zeke says.

My heart stops. "What do you mean she's missing?"

Zeke has been my best friend for years. Siren, his wife, has a connection to my soul.

"I mean she was supposed to pick up Cayden from daycare, and she never showed up. I think someone kidnapped her."

Rage consumes me, and I welcome it. As much as I hate to admit it, I'd rather be dealing with Zeke's crisis than my own.

"I'll be there soon. We'll find her."

"Hurry," Zeke says.

I hang up and start marching inside, my shoulder brushes Liesel's as I pass, but I can't think about anything except getting back to Miami and finding Siren.

"Langston!" Liesel yells, following me inside.

I keep walking. *Ren, I'm coming.*

"Langston Pearce! Talk to me right now!"

I stop. I turn and look at her. "I don't have time for you to throw a tantrum right now, Liesel."

"I'm not throwing a tantrum. Just talk to me."

"Fine. Someone I love is in danger. And as you've pointed out, I have a habit of not being there for people when they need it. I'm not going to let her down."

Liesel's shoulders drop. Her lips curve into an O. Her breathing slows.

"Joel!" I yell.

He pops his head out of his room.

"You're on security, Joel. Make sure everyone is safe."

He nods.

"Amelia, you're in charge of the house."

She salutes me. "Yes, Captain."

I shake my head. Usually, I like her teasing. Not right now.

Amelia steps back, noticing my change in mood.

I jog over to the locked part of the house. I unlock and open the dividing door. "Phoenix," I holler.

She steps forward out of her bedroom, still wearing a robe. "Yes?"

I glance back to Liesel.

"Phoenix, you're in charge of Liesel."

Liesel's eyebrows draw up.

I glance to Phoenix, and she nods solemnly.

Then I lock the door again and pull my phone out. I start making calls to arrange for a flight, walking around the house with Liesel on my heels.

"How are you going to fly somewhere when you killed the pilot?" Liesel hollers.

"You killed Ken?" Joel asks.

I growl at him.

Joel moves out of my way and doesn't ask any other dumb questions.

Liesel, on the other hand, continues to run after me as I head to my car.

I unlock my Range Rover and open the door.

Liesel is there to grab the door before I climb inside.

"You didn't kill the pilot, did you?"

I don't answer her.

"You're a piece of work. You just did that to scare me."

She takes a step back.

"When will you be back?" she asks.

"When I save my girl."

My words cut her. She doesn't know who I'm talking about. All she hears is the *my girl* part. I'm talking about a woman I seem to care about more than her. I see the jealousy in her eyes.

When I return, Liesel will make me pay for that.

But just as quickly as it came, the jealousy is gone.

She wasn't able to do that before. I'm guessing it has to do with her having trouble feeling anything anymore.

"Whoever *she* is, save her like you didn't save me."

"I won't fail." I slam the door and drive away, while Liesel watches me leave her, like so many times before.

CHAPTER 25

LIESEL

*W*ho is she?

Who is the woman Langston dropped everything for? At a moment's notice no less, scrapping all of his plans for the day.

She's a lucky woman, whoever she is. Even when we were best friends, Langston never looked at me with that much worry or concern in his eyes. He never ran the second I called.

Who is she?

Who is he running to save?

Who does he love?

All those questions burn through my head as I watch Langston drive off.

Is she a girlfriend?

A woman he wishes was his?

Is it Kai or Siren?

Who?

It's like a punch to the gut. My world spins. My eyes slant into slits of anger.

I'm jealous.

For a split second, I wish I was the lucky girl to whom Langston is running.

"Snap out of it. Langston is a cruel, sadistic killer. Nobody wants to be loved by a man like that," I coach myself.

I walk back inside the house just as Joel heads back into his bedroom and slams the door shut. He doesn't care about protecting us. He's useless. I doubt I see him out of his room again.

I head into the kitchen, where Amelia is making breakfast. She's holding a plate of food, which I assume is for me.

"Thanks, I'll just eat it out—"

Amelia takes a bite of the toast on the plate. "There are groceries in the fridge. I hope you know how to cook."

She flashes me an annoying, sarcastic grin before she takes her breakfast out on the patio, where I usually eat it.

"Bitch," I mutter under my breath.

I'm alone.

And I'm not hungry.

I stare at the door Langston had to unlock to relay an instruction. There is a woman who lives in the other half of the house.

Who is she?

I walk to the solid wood door. I put my hand on the door handle and twist.

It's locked.

I jiggle the door handle a couple more times just to be sure, but the door is definitely locked.

I consider spending all my time trying to break in, but I have more important things to do today. I need to find a way off this island before Langston returns.

I run upstairs to Langston's bedroom.

I search for his phone, his laptop, any electronic device that I can use to contact Waylon.

God, Waylon, I miss him.

Langston is a bit of a minimalist. He has a nightstand with no drawers. His dresser only has clothes in the top two drawers and the bottom drawers are empty. His bathroom only holds the absolute basics—toothbrush, soap, towels. I find nothing useful.

I search all the guest bedrooms.

I search the library.

I search the kitchen, the dining room, the living room. I search the entire house but find no phone, no computer, no tablet. Nothing that can help me contact Waylon.

I grab a banana from the counter for energy, not bothering to cook anything while I think about what to do next.

My eyes linger on the door again.

The door that has remained locked the entire time I've been here.

It has to be locked for a reason.

My guess is a computer and phone sit on the other side of that door, maybe in Langston's office.

I shove the last bite of banana in my mouth while I listen carefully, trying to determine if anyone else is in the house.

I don't hear Amelia or Joel. I don't hear maids cleaning. The house is eerily quiet.

I grin and pull a bobby pin from my hair while I walk to the locked door. Hopefully, it will lead to a phone, computer, or some way to contact the outside world on the other side.

There are security cameras watching me, but Langston is on a plane right now to God knows where, and Joel is probably passed out drunk on his bed, ignoring me.

I hated growing up with a group of monsters who knew how to hold a gun before they hit puberty. They also knew how to hack security cameras and break into any room.

I jostle the door handle and then insert the bobby pin, easily popping the lock.

I smile slyly when I open the door. I can't believe that Langston didn't use more than a simple lock to keep me out.

My smile is quickly wiped away at my realization. If he was truly hiding something important, something he didn't want me to have, he'd have made it harder.

There is a long hallway before the second half opens up.

I gasp when I see the living space.

It's big and grand—made of marble, quartz, and all the shiny things of a modern fairytale castle. The ceiling on this half of the house is double the height of the other side. The decor is 11th-century castle with a modern touch, not beachy, warm, and full of nature like the rest of the house.

But the biggest difference of all is how dark it is. There are windows, but they are all covered with heavy, black-out curtains. You wouldn't even know you are on the beach in this half of the house.

A woman suddenly appears from deep down the hallway. I didn't hear her because I was too entranced by the house. It's like two houses in one. Two separate lives.

Why did Langston create a house that was half my dream and half this? Whose dream house is this?

The woman folds her arms as she stares at me wordlessly. She has short, choppy hair dyed bright red, so I have no idea what her natural color is. Her skin is toned and unmarked with scars or tattoos. She's wearing a long-sleeved black shirt and dark jeans, not clothes one might wear while living in a beach mansion.

"Phoenix?" I ask, using the name I overheard Langston say.

She stares at me, sizing me up.

"I'm Liesel. I'm wondering if I can borrow your phone?"

On my last syllable, I'm tackled to the ground as if I was aiming a gun at Phoenix's head or something.

"Get off me," I yell as I try to break free of whoever tackled me. It's not Phoenix, she's still standing wordlessly a few feet in front of me.

"Don't move," Joel says. Suddenly, I feel the barrel of a gun against my temple.

I immediately stop moving, stop resisting, and let him pin me to the ground.

"Good girl," Amelia says.

"Amelia?" I glance out of the corner of my eye and see Amelia holding the gun to my head, while Joel applies his full weight to my back.

She smirks at me.

"So, you really aren't a chef?"

"Oh, I can cook. I just also know how to use a weapon."

"Get up," Joel says, yanking me to my feet.

"Is it really necessary to keep pointing that gun at my head?" I snark at Amelia.

She tilts her head. "We were told to keep you out of here at all costs."

I roll my eyes. "You were also told to cook for me, and you were told to keep me safe. You've both already failed."

I look between the two. "And I'm pretty sure if you killed me, Langston wouldn't be too happy. Am I right?"

Joel grabs my hair and sniffs along my neck.

I freeze at his touch, my mind going back to all the times I've been tortured like this.

"Kill me, and Langston will kill you. I'm not afraid of you," I say, keeping my voice calm and steady. They can try to intimidate me all they want, but they can't kill me without dealing with Langston's retaliation.

Joel twists my arm, hard. "We might not be able to kill you, but we sure as hell can punish you for breaking one of Langston's rules."

"Sweet dreams, princess." Amelia hits me hard on the head. It's the last thing I remember.

⟡

I LIFT MY HEAD AND REGRET IT IMMEDIATELY.

My head feels like a knife was jabbed into my forehead and then twisted around.

"Son of a bitch," I groan.

I try to sit up more carefully this time, when I feel the tug of a rope around my wrists.

"Really?"

I glance around the room. I'm in Langston's bed, tied by the wrists to one of the bedposts. Otherwise, the room is empty.

I doubt Langston is back from his expedition, so Joel and Amelia had to be the ones to tie me up.

I take careful inventory of my body as my breathing speeds.

What did they do to me?

I start at my toes and work my way up my body.

No broken bones.

No bruises.

My clothes are still on.

I exhale a heavy breath.

That doesn't mean that they won't do something to me—torture me, rape me.

I have to get out of here.

As much as Langston thinks he has his employees under control, I doubt he told them to knock me out or tie me up. Langston may like to threaten my life, he may torture me, but he's a control freak. He won't like his employees taking matters into their own hands.

I test the rope tying my hands together. It's a good knot—the person who tied it clearly knows how to tie a knot. But they don't know how to keep a woman like me tied up.

A woman who Langston tied up in the third grade after I stole his favorite Hot Wheels car and threw it in the river. I had rope burn for a week after that. Langston got in so much trouble from his dad. His apology involved teaching me how to get myself out of any binding. We practiced all summer until he could never use that power over me again without me being able to escape.

So untying a sailor's knot is no problem for me. Joel could have made it more difficult if he hadn't used a traditional knot and just tied me up any which way. That would have thrown me for a loop, made it more difficult to undo.

I'm out of the simple knot in three seconds.

I take a second to consider my options. Glancing out the window, the sun is just beginning to set.

I could barricade myself in the bedroom and hope Joel or Amelia don't come check on me, *but how long can I last? How long until Langston comes home?*

No, I don't want to be in this house.

I don't know what Joel and Amelia planned after they tied me up, but I'm not going to wait around to find out. I head to the bathroom balcony and climb over. I scale down the vines, this time with more agility now that I know the easiest path down.

I land on my feet and stare back at the house. Neither Joel nor

Amelia come running for me immediately, which gives me time to get away.

I head straight for the ocean. I figure if I run toward the beach, then I can head into the jungle and live off of coconuts until Langston returns and finds me.

I run as fast as I can down the cliffside, so fast that I don't notice her until I'm right on top of her.

Phoenix.

She's sitting in the spot where Langston and I have met every night at sunset.

It's sunset.

There is a bottle of alcohol and two shot glasses sitting next to her.

"Care to join me?" Phoenix asks without glancing back at me.

I raise an eyebrow as I cautiously near her. I wish I had a gun, a weapon, something. She wasn't the one who knocked me out, but she did stand by and watch Joel and Amelia drag me off.

"Who are you?" I ask, standing a few feet away from her instead of sitting down.

"I'm Phoenix; I work for Langston."

"Why do you live in a locked and walled off part of the house?"

Phoenix smiles and looks out to the ocean. "It's part of my job. If I told you, I'd have to kill you."

I shake my head. "That I don't believe. Langston wouldn't allow any of you to kill me. He wants to do that himself."

Phoenix laughs and finally turns to look at me. "That he does, so I think it's best we don't talk about me. That way, neither of us has to kill the other."

"What are you doing?" I nod toward her two glasses of drinks.

"I was instructed to meet you out here every night at sunset, drink a bottle of scotch with you, and try to get you to spill your secrets."

I glance down. "That's a bottle of tequila, not scotch."

She scrunches up her face. "I'm not really a scotch fan, and I don't really plan on getting any secrets out of you. But I figured I should at least attempt to do the job Langston gave me so I don't get fired, unlike those idiots back at the house."

I smirk as I rub the spot where the rope started to dig into my wrists. "Yea, I'm going to enjoy watching those assholes burn when Langston gets back."

Phoenix grabs the tequila bottle and pours us both a shot.

Then she holds out a glass to me, waiting patiently for me to sit.

"Can you just sit and drink the tequila, so Langston can see that I tried on the security footage?"

"Fine, but only because I want the tequila." I sit down on the sand next to Phoenix, who is still wearing jeans and a long-sleeved T-shirt despite the heat.

I want to be nosy and ask her about it. I want to ask a lot of questions, but based on her appearance, the Langston employee uniform, she must really work for him. My guess is she's a hacker who controls the security cameras. She's probably been watching me this entire time.

Instead of talking, I throw my tequila shot down my throat, enjoying the fiery burn.

"How long have you known Langston?" Phoenix asks me.

I raise an eyebrow as I hold out my glass. She pours me another shot.

Apparently, she doesn't know Langston and I's story. Or if she does, she's playing dumb.

"We met in high school," I lie.

I take the second shot.

"What about you?"

"We've known each other since we were kids," she replies.

I blink rapidly. There is no way Langston has known this woman since they were kids. I knew Langston back then. We used to hang out every day. I would have known this woman, too, if that were true. She's lying just like I am.

"So you go way back. When did you start working for him?"

"Really? We are going to talk about boring topics when we could be trading dirt on Langston?" Phoenix smiles.

"Fine, tell me an embarrassing story from his childhood."

Phoenix's smile falters for just a moment before she starts talking. "We were eight. Langston crashed his bike racing me down a hill. He broke his arm and cried like a baby. I nicknamed him crybaby after that, and I've called him that ever since."

I nod, she's a good liar. She hardly hesitated before launching into the story. It had just enough detail but not too much.

"There's only one little problem with your story," I say.

Phoenix frowns.

"Langston didn't get his first bike until he was twelve. I was there the first day he learned to ride it. He made me hold on to it while he rode it, and when I let go, he fell and skinned both of his knees. And yes, he did cry, but he didn't break an arm. That didn't happen until he was fifteen, was drunk, and fell out of a tree."

Phoenix bites her bottom lip, caught in her lie.

I hold out my drink.

She refills both mine and hers.

I hold out my shot glass. "To being good liars."

She clinks her glass to mine, and we both do the shot together.

"Sorry I lied."

"I'm not. And I'm glad I'm not the only one who thinks Langston is a crybaby."

We both start laughing.

"He's also a control freak," she says.

"A sadistic bastard."

"Fucking secretive asshole."

"An obnoxious liar."

We give each other a knowing look.

"But hot as hell," we both say at the same time before cracking up laughing again. It's probably the tequila warming me to Phoenix. I don't have girlfriends; I don't even have girls that I like. My only friends have been boys. *So why do I feel an instant connection to Phoenix? Like in a different life, we could have been best friends?*

"You ever slept with him?" I ask, jealousy hanging in the air.

"You think I'm going to answer that question honestly?"

I sigh. "Nope. I wouldn't either."

We both sit silently after that.

I don't gain any answers about who Phoenix is. I don't know if she's on my side or not. I don't know anything about her, but I feel a strange connection to my soul. The fact that we can sit silently under the stars, having just met and it not be awkward, tells me all I need to know.

Phoenix isn't being honest. She's a pretty good liar. And yet, she might be the one person in this house who could save me. She might be the key to me getting off this island alive.

I just have to figure out how.

"Liesel, I think—"

"Move, and I'll shoot you," Joel says, interrupting Phoenix.

I freeze, assuming a gun is pointed at the back of my head.

"I'm here talking with Phoenix under Langston's orders. I'm not going anywhere. The gun isn't necessary. I'll lock myself up in my closet for the night, so leave me alone."

"I don't think so. You're a conniving bitch. Langston put me in charge of security. You broke in where you weren't supposed to go. I think I'll use extra rope this time," Joel says.

"Is that really necessary?" Phoenix says, standing and turning around to face Joel.

I, carefully, stand too with hands raised in surrender.

"Yes. You don't know who Liesel is, what she's done. If you did, you'd agree with me, Phoenix."

Phoenix looks at me with new eyes, seeing the monster that I am.

"Shoot me, Joel. If you think I'm so awful, just shoot me. There is no way I'm going to let you tie me up," I say. And then I run.

I run until I feel the sting of a bullet in my shoulder.

CHAPTER 26

LANGSTON

"What's the plan to get Siren?" I ask as I walk into Zeke's house without saying hello.

"We don't have a plan yet. We don't have any leads. There has been no ransom, no security feed. We don't have any current known enemies," Zeke says.

I could kill Zeke for letting Siren get kidnapped like this. They've been married, what—less than a year, and he's already failed at protecting her.

"You have one job as her husband," I say through gritted teeth.

"Don't lecture me, asshole. Why do you think I called you and Enzo?"

I look past Zeke and see Enzo using a laptop on the kitchen counter, already searching for a clue as to where Siren might have been kidnapped.

"Where's Kai?" I ask.

"She has all the kids in a safehouse with Beckett," Enzo answers.

"Good, now move and let the master work," I say, pushing Enzo off the barstool so I can sit behind the computer.

Enzo doesn't complain. He knows I'm the best behind a computer. I can hack any system, find any missing person.

"Where was Siren last seen?" I ask Zeke.

Zeke runs his hand through his ridiculously long hair while he paces back and forth.

"Zeke!" I growl.

His head snaps to me.

"Focus. Where was Siren last seen?"

"I, uh, I don't know. She told me she had some errands to run. She told me she would pick up Cayden from the nanny and meet me for dinner."

"What errands?"

Zeke shrugs. "I don't know. She didn't tell me. I didn't think to ask."

My eyes flick to Enzo, and we exchange annoyed looks.

I start typing into the computer, searching for Siren's cell phone.

"Her cell phone is turned off," I say a second later.

"Where is the nanny's house?"

"South Beach," Zeke says.

I start there and then expand my search, but as Zeke said, there is no sign of her at the nanny's.

I start searching through the main streets of Miami, searching for a sign of her or her car.

"Wait—her car was last seen at the corner of 15th and Drexel," I say.

Zeke and Enzo both crowd around the computer. We have hope. We are going to be able to find her.

The crank of the garage door fills the silence.

I look from Zeke to Enzo. "Are we expecting anyone else?"

Both men draw their guns in response.

I take a step back from the computer and draw mine as well.

We all aim our guns at the back door as footsteps approach.

The doorknob turns.

And then the door opens.

"Siren," Zeke exhales, dropping his gun and running to her. He grabs her and takes her in his arms. He squeezes her tightly then quickly looks her over for any injuries. He finds none.

"What's going on, guys?" Siren asks, stepping further into the room.

Enzo offers her a quick hug. "I need to go tell Kai you're okay." And then he walks out the door. He's a bit rattled, but he doesn't let anyone see that.

Siren looks to me, and then she runs into my arms. I squeeze her as tightly as Zeke did.

"Don't do that to me, Ren," I whisper into her ear, tears threatening at the fear of losing her.

"Do what? Get a flat tire while I was out shopping for my husband and let my phone die? That?"

"Yea, don't do that. Don't make me install a tracker in you so I never lose you again."

She smiles. "You'll never lose me."

I nod.

"Can I talk to my wife alone now?" Zeke asks, giving me a grumpy stare.

I roll my eyes. "She might be your wife, but she's my friend."

Zeke grabs Siren's hand, and she winks at me. "Be back soon," she whispers as Zeke pulls her upstairs to most likely fuck her brains out and remind her she's his.

I find the liquor cabinet and pour myself a drink before walking outside to the deck that overlooks the beach.

I sit outside, alone for a while with my thoughts. None of them are about Siren, only Liesel.

"Care to tell your best friend what's on your mind?" Siren asks as she steps outside.

"Worried about you," I say.

"Liar." She leans back against the railing, facing me in my chair. "Are you going to tell me the truth, or do I have to beat it out of you?"

I chuckle at that.

"Liesel," I surrender.

"Oh. What's new with Liesel? Did Kai tell you that she's thinking about going on our girl's trip with us in a week?"

"Liesel's not going."

Siren frowns. "Why not?"

"Because I kidnapped her, and I say she's not going."

"You what?" Siren exclaims.

"I kidnapped Liesel. I'm holding her hostage. I threatened to kill her."

"Please tell me this is a joke? That I'm not hearing you correctly?"

"It's not a joke."

"What? Why...? I don't understand."

"It's a long story that I'm not going to get into, but she left me no choice."

"Langston Finn Pearce, you do too have a choice. What the hell? Let her go right now!"

"No."

"Langston? What is your plan?"

"I'm going to get Liesel to talk, and then I'm going to kill her."

Siren gasps. "You're lying. You're not going to kill Liesel. Aren't you, like, in love with her?"

I shake my head. "I was never in love with her."

"Let her go, Langston."

"No."

She shoves me hard. "Let. Her. Go."

"You're not the boss of me." I shove her back.

"What the hell is going on out here?" Zeke sticks his head out.

"My best friend is being an ass. Do something about it for me." Siren throws her hands up.

"What did you do?" Zeke asks.

"I kidnapped Liesel. No big deal. I have everything under control."

Zeke's fist comes flying at my face.

I try to deflect, but my reflexes are slow after all the alcohol, and he hits me in the eye.

"Should I punch him again or is once enough?" Zeke asks Siren.

"I don't know. Do you think kidnapping Liesel and threatening her with death only deserves one punch?" Siren puts her hands on her hips, looking stern.

Zeke punches me again.

"Stop," I say. "You've made your point. And who are you to punch me when you did the same thing to Siren?"

Zeke looks to Siren. "He has a point."

"It's still doesn't make it okay," Siren says.

"Come on, let's go to sleep. We can try to talk some sense into him in the morning," Zeke says, walking back to the door.

Siren nods but stops before going back inside. She looks at me with concern.

"Be careful with Liesel, she's dangerous."

I chuckle. "Liesel is no you, Siren. She's a terrible shot. She's never killed a man. All she knows how to do is hunt and lie. I think I can handle her just fine."

I rush past her to go sleep off my hangover in one of their guest bedrooms.

"That's not what I mean. She has the ability to hurt you in other ways."

"How?"

"Like stealing your heart," Siren smirks and then leaves me all alone.

Siren is wrong, but she is right about one thing—Liesel is dangerous.

CHAPTER 27

LIESEL

When I wake up this time, I already know where I am, and that I'm tied up.

Joel and Amelia are predictable in that way.

This time instead of just my arms, they've tied my legs together too. Thankfully they've tied them together instead of spread apart. I can hope that means that they don't plan on violating me.

I wiggle my wrists, testing my bindings.

"Don't even think about it," Amelia says from the corner of Langston's bedroom.

She stands from the chair she must have brought up and looks down at me with a bored expression. "We tied them with extra rope, and I'm under specific instruction to shoot you again if you move."

Again?

I shift my shoulder slightly, and I feel the burning pang of the bullet lodged in my scapula. I don't let her know how much pain I'm in, though. I'm too stubborn to show any weakness to this woman.

"Under whose instruction?" I ask.

"Langston's. I called him and told him you were trying to run. He told me to do whatever it takes to hold you until he returned."

"When is he returning?" I ask.

"He didn't say. But you and I are going to enjoy our time together until he does."

I try to relax. I try to fall back asleep. There is nothing I can do right now but wait until Langston comes back, or at least until Amelia makes a mistake and gives me a chance to escape. All I can do is live with the pain in my shoulder.

There is a knock on the door. My eyes fill with hope for a split second that Langston has returned. I know the bastard wants me dead, but not yet—not for an entire year. Not until he's bled me dry of my secrets. This bitch, Amelia, will kill me without thinking twice about it.

Langston wouldn't knock, though. My hope quickly floats away.

"Yes?" Amelia answers, sounding irritated to be interrupted.

"It's time for a shift change," Phoenix says, walking into the room. Her eyes hold no emotion as she looks at Amelia, acting like I'm not even in the room.

Amelia glances at her watch. "I still have thirty minutes left. And Joel is up next, not you."

"Joel told me he needs you to fix the coffee machine before he goes on shift. He's hungover and showering," Phoenix says.

God, she's a good liar.

"Fine. Do you have a weapon? This one needs it to make her obey. We tied her up with extra rope this time, but somehow the bitch figured out how to untangle herself last time."

Phoenix eyes the gun in Amelia's hand. "I'm good."

Amelia nods. "Call me if you have any trouble."

And then Amelia leaves.

Phoenix stands quietly in place. I'm not sure what she's doing, but then I notice that her eyes are closed. She's listening.

I close my eyes too, and hear Amelia's footsteps downstairs.

"We don't have much time," Phoenix says, running to me and going to work on my wrists.

"No, start with my ankles, I can do my wrists."

"There are too many ropes; there is no way you can untie yourself. If I can get your arms free, then you can help with your ankles."

"Trust me, work on my ankles."

Phoenix hesitates for a second, but I nod my encouragement.

"Okay," she relents and moves to my ankles.

I start working on my wrists.

"The coffee machine needs fixing, huh? That's probably because you were the one who broke it," Joel says from the doorway.

We both freeze.

"Shit," Phoenix mutters under her breath.

She turns and looks at him. "I was just making sure you tied these ropes tight enough so she doesn't get away this time."

"Uh, huh. Sure, you were. Get back to your half to the house and leave this to us."

"But—" Phoenix starts.

"Now," Joel grows.

Phoenix flashes me a look of apology. There is a guilty sadness in her eyes. She knows what happens next, and there is nothing she can do about it.

I smile. "It's okay, go," I whisper so only she can hear. My voice is full of strength.

Phoenix bites her lip, clearly concerned, but her staying won't stop this. She doesn't have a weapon; she's not like Amelia, who has clearly had combat training. I don't know what role Phoenix plays yet, but my guess is some kind of IT role that helps manage the computers and security systems. An important role, but useless right now. If she stays, she'll just end up beaten as well.

"Go," I nod.

Phoenix gives me a stubborn look, and I think she might stay, but at the last second, she turns and leaves without a word.

As soon as Phoenix walks out the door, Joel slams it shut and flicks the lock.

He looks at me with a sadistic grin. His eyes turn fiery, and he cracks his knuckles, preparing to hurt me.

"If you touch me, Langston is going to kill you," I say, warning him.

He laughs. "You still think after everything Langston has done to you that he cares about you?"

No, Langston doesn't care about me. Not anymore. But he wants information from me. And he doesn't like sharing me while he waits for me to spill my guts.

"Yes," I lie.

That makes Joel laugh harder as he walks toward my prison bed.

My wrists are tied together and then to the headboard just like before. My ankles are bound, but not to anything else. I can move my legs, just as one unit.

Joel eyes my legs.

"Kick me, and I'll shoot you again," Joel says, pulling his gun out and aiming at me.

I force my legs to remain still.

"I thought Amelia was the one who shot me?"

"Nope, I did. Amelia doesn't have the guts I do."

I'm sure.

Slowly, with his gun pointed at my chest, Joel climbs onto the bed and then eventually straddles me until he's crushing my stomach with his weight. My legs are now basically useless. I could kick him in the back, but not hard enough to force him off me.

He grabs my chin and holds me still, lowering his head toward mine.

"Langston is going to kill you," I say again.

"Keep dreaming." Joel forces a slobbery kiss onto my lips.

I try to squirm away, but he's stronger.

He chuckles. "What? You don't like that? You didn't seem to mind before."

Wait...before?

I search my mind. *Did he rape me last time I was tied up?*

He laughs at my quizzical expression and then holds up a finger to my lips.

"That's right. You enjoyed my fingers in your cunt. This time, you're going to enjoy my cock."

Oh.

My.

God.

It was Joel whose fingers I rode, not Langston. *Was it Joel's cock that I fucked too?*

I squirm hard, my fingers going to work to untie myself. The pain in my shoulder is exploding with every move, but I won't let this man touch me.

"Langston's going to kill you!" I yell.

Joel slaps me hard across the cheek, the sting making me stop squirming long enough for his words to land.

"Langston was the one who told me to do my worst that night. He doesn't care what I do to you. He's just using you, and as soon as you are no longer useful to him, he'll dispose of you."

Joel's words impact me more forcefully than the bullet in my shoulder. I thought I was safe with Langston. I thought he would protect me. I thought...

Everything I thought was wrong.

I'm on my own.

Langston won't protect me.

The epiphany makes me fight like hell.

Joel leans in to kiss me again, and this time, I open my mouth, enticing his tongue deep into my orifice. Then, I enjoy biting down as wickedly as I can on his tongue.

I feel the iron taste of blood in my mouth and hear the high pitched squeal of pain leaving Joel's throat. In response, I bite down harder.

Joel is smarter than I give him credit for, though. He punches me hard in the stomach, making me gasp for air, releasing his tongue.

I'm rewarded with the sight of blood covering the bastard's mouth. I got him good.

His face turns sinister, his eyes swirl in evil circles, a vein bulges in his forehead, and his mouth growls like a bear.

I injured him, and that pissed him off. He's going to try and take his fury out on me, but it still won't stop me from fighting.

"You fucking cunt! You bit me!" he roars.

He grabs my shoulders, one hand digging into the back of my shoulder on my gunshot wound.

The pain bolts down my arm excruciatingly, races down my back, and crashes in my head. My body is firing off a million nerve endings all at once, telling me to run, to get away from this man. He will destroy me if I don't stop him.

I refuse to scream, to cry out.

He smirks. "You think you're a tough woman? Don't worry, I can do this all day. Eventually, I will get your screams."

He grabs for my jeans shorts and starts shoving them down my body.

I know what comes next.

And I can't take it.

I try to headbutt him, but I miss.

I frantically try to untangle my wrists, but he notices and holds onto my hands with one of his large, dirty mitts while the other shoves unwanted into my panties.

I cringe and turn my face away, so he can't see the suffering he's causing me. I won't let him have my pain, my fear, my agony. That I will keep to myself. If I can't beat him, I at least won't give him what he wants. That's how I survived Enzo's father. That's how I'll survive this scumbag too.

A throat clears, and my head snaps in the direction of the door.

Joel hears it too. His fingers stop fumbling in my bikini bottoms. Slowly and carefully, he removes his hand, trying to hide his actions from the voice at the door.

"You're back early, sir. I was just teaching Miss Dunn a lesson in what happens to thieves on this island," Joel says, his head looking over his shoulder at Langston, while continuing to straddle my body.

Liar. I didn't steal anything.

"I can see that," Langston answers, his voice low and orderly. He doesn't seem upset at all to find Joel groping me.

Joel was right, Langston doesn't care about me.

Langston doesn't look at me; he only looks at Joel.

"I can handle Miss Dunn from here. Thank you, Joel."

"Yes, sir." Joel smirks at me and then rolls off me before exiting the room.

Then it's just Langston and me.

I'm still tied up. My face is covered in Joel's blood. Surprisingly, my shoulder has little blood on it. I doubt he even realizes I'm bleeding from a gunshot wound.

Langston doesn't say anything. He just studies me a second, taking in the scene. I take the moment to study him.

He's wearing jeans and a grey V-neck. He looks the same, but I see the bruises around his eye. Whatever he went and did, he got at least one punch for it. There are probably more beneath his shirt.

"Can you untie yourself?" he asks.

My eyes narrow. "Yes."

"Good."

And then Langston turns and walks out of the room.

That's it? That's all Langston is going to say or do?

Now, I'm pissed. He didn't even ask what happened or check if I'm injured, check to see what Joel did to me.

Langston really does hate me.

His hate motivates me to untie myself faster.

I had already made progress on my wrists, so I finish them quickly and start on my ankles. I fumble once or twice before finally freeing myself.

I pull my jean shorts back up and then head to the bathroom. I wipe the blood from my face on Langston's white towels, happy to be ruining them. I can't reach my wound, and I don't want to look at how violently my shoulder is fucked up.

I rummage for some painkillers and find none.

Dammit.

I run my hand through my blonde wavy hair. I'm strong. I'm going to go kick Langston's ass and demand painkillers and a doctor. Then I'm going to find a way off this motherfucking island.

I consider my options: walk down the stairs or climb down the vines.

I choose vines.

It takes everything in me to climb down the wall, basically one-handed. My left shoulder is useless with the bullet lodged in it, but finally, my feet hit the ground.

I sneak around the house, keeping my head low to avoid being seen out the windows as I look for Langston.

I make it to the front of the house before I hear voices.

"I told you not to touch her," Langston says, he has a gun pointed at Joel's head, and Joel is kneeling in front of him.

My eyes widen. *I was right, not Joel.*

Amelia is standing off to the side with tears in her eyes.

"You didn't listen. You touched her that first night when I told you not to. I told you to just scare her a bit. And what the hell was that I just walked in on?"

"She broke into the half of the house that was off-limits, sir. She was trying to run. She—" Joel says.

"No, I pay you to prevent that. She shouldn't have been able to escape in the first place if you were doing your job. And you sure as hell aren't allowed to touch her."

"I'm sorry. I—" Joel says.

Langston doesn't let him finish his sentence. He shoots Joel square in the forehead. His body drops lifelessly to the ground.

I gasp but snap my hands quickly over my mouth so Langston doesn't know that I'm watching him.

Amelia holds her hands up as Langston aims the gun at her. "Please, I'm so sorry. It will never happen again."

"I'm only letting you live because I don't want to deal with the body. Get rid of him and then get off my fucking island. If I ever see your face again, Amelia, I'll kill you, too."

Amelia nods, tears streaming down her face now.

I slink away from the window and along the house.

I can't believe what I just saw. Maybe I wasn't so wrong about Langston after all.

I stop to dart into the kitchen and find a bottle of scotch and a towel, quickly running back outside. I don't know what to make of everything that just happened. I need some space to decompress everything. The scotch will help with the pain until I'm ready to face Langston again.

What are you up to, Langston?

I always thought I was the only one with secrets. I thought his only secrets were the contents of the half of my letter he stole. Now, I'm beginning to think he has secrets of his own.

CHAPTER 28

LANGSTON

It's been a long time since I've felt this level of anger.

I thought shooting Joel would dissipate some of it, but I'm more pissed off than I was when I first caught them.

I can't trust any of my employees.

I've always known that. The only way you gain the kind of trust required to do this job is by working side by side, battling for your lives and growing up together. The kind of trust that I have with Enzo and Zeke. That's not possible with any of my employees.

I have money, but I'm not filthy rich like Enzo. I can pay my employees well, but not well enough to ensure they are loyal. And the threat of death only goes so far. I'm guessing now that I've killed one of them, the rest will be more likely to stay in line.

God, I can't get the images out of my head.

I was still in the air, about an hour out, when the security feed came through. I just wanted to see Liesel, see what she was up to. That's when I found her tied to my bed.

She looked dead, but I couldn't see any bullet or stab wounds, no blood.

I implored my pilot to fly faster, but we weren't fast enough.

As soon as I landed, I drove like a maniac to get here. I didn't trust

261

anyone to stop what was happening. And then I saw Joel enter the room.

Up to that point, Liesel was just tied up. I could think of a million ways my huntress could have gotten herself into that position. A billion tricks she could have pulled on my staff that made them think she was a vicious creature needing to be tied up.

Joel climbed on top of her.

He kissed what is mine!

And he said he had violated her before.

I became a bull about to ram through everyone in my way at that point.

I couldn't watch the rest, and yet I couldn't drag my eyes away.

I watched as she drew blood.

I watched as she struggled to free herself.

I watched her stronger than I've ever seen her, not making a single sound of pain, fear, or defeat. It's then that I realized my entire strategy had been wrong. There is no way I'm breaking Liesel. She's too durable, impenetrable.

But if anyone is going to break her, it's going to be me.

When I finally got here, it took all of my control not to show her how I felt. I was the one breaking for her. I've always been breaking for her.

I ordered Joel away.

Even then, it took everything in me to walk away from her. We both needed space. She deserved space to hate me for failing her again.

After shooting Joel, I probably should have killed Amelia too, but I didn't want to spend the day getting rid of two dead bodies.

Instead, I spent the day giving Liesel space. I spent it trying to put the fear of God into the rest of my team, laying down rules and making it perfectly clear what will happen if they lay a finger on Liesel without my permission.

I pick out a new man as my head of security to replace Joel. Unfortunately, no one else on the team is a good cook, so we will be chefless for the time being.

All I know is that I don't trust a damn soul on this island—not even Phoenix, who has decided to give me the silent treatment today.

As for Liesel, she's been at the beach all day.

I gave her her space. I needed it as much as she did.

But the sun is setting—it's time to talk.

I grab the most expensive bottle of scotch I own. One I don't think Liesel has tried, but she'll love. I carry it and two glasses down the sandy cove to the beach.

Liesel is sitting in our spot in the sand already. I'm pretty sure she's sat here all day. She has a towel wrapped around her like she's cold, but the sun's heat is still beating on us. I'm sweating as I walk, so there is no way she's cold.

Then I spot the bottle she's lifting to her lips. It only has a fourth of the liquid left in it. She's probably drunk off her ass if that bottle was full when she started this morning. She's trying to chase her demons away with alcohol, trying to chase away Joel. She doesn't know that he's already paid for what he did to her.

I sit down next to her in the sand.

She doesn't look over at me, just brings the bottle back to her lips.

"Where's Joel?" she asks with surprising clarity for a woman who spent the day drinking.

"He quit."

"Uh-huh," she says, not believing me.

"You don't have to worry about Joel anymore."

"I know."

I frown, not sure what she means. She's drunk, so I'm not going to get any clear answers from her tonight. Tonight is just about getting back into our routine.

"I told you not to trust anyone but me," I say.

"Oh, so this is my fault?" Her head snaps to me with the venom of a cobra as she looks at me.

Her towel drops away as she snarls at me, and my world freezes.

Blood.

Dried blood covers her shoulder.

I think back to Joel. I don't remember him having any wound

except for his tongue, where she bit him. And of course, the giant hole I put in his head.

I reach out to examine her shoulder, but Liesel pulls away, recovering herself with the towel.

That's why she has the towel: to hide her pain.

"Liesel, let me see your shoulder," I say calmly and firmly. I won't give her a choice in the matter. I need to see her injuries, but I won't physically force her.

Her eyes tear into me, and once again, she looks ready to strike.

"Please," I force my voice to soften.

She blinks rapidly, trying to find a way out of showing me her shoulder. Eventually, something she sees in my eyes forces her to let me.

She nods and relinquishes her hold on the towel, but doesn't remove it herself.

I reach out, and she doesn't pull away this time.

I grab the towel, preparing myself not to react to whatever I see.

When I lower the towel, I see the dried blood once again, and then I see the gaping hole blasted into the back of her shoulder.

A bullet hole.

In the back.

The fucking bastard shot her running away. He didn't even have the decency to shoot her face to face.

"Shit," I curse, grinding my teeth together.

Liesel's hazel eyes water, but she doesn't cry.

Once again, I failed her. I should have been here instead of searching for Siren. I should have known Joel was a bastard. I should have known she'd been shot.

And I shouldn't be showing her any damn emotion, but there is no hiding how I feel.

I pull the rest of the towel from her back, examining every inch of her with my own eyes, but I only see the single bullet hole.

"Joel did this?"

Liesel nods.

"Did he hurt you anywhere else?"

Please, don't tell me he raped you and I didn't realize.

"No, you got here before he could do worse."

I narrow my gaze; my heart roars in my chest full of a thousand exploding angry cannons. I didn't get here in time. He should have never touched her. Never tied her up. Never shot her.

I regret killing the bastard now—he deserved worse than death.

"Hold this," I say, handing Liesel the expensive bottle of scotch.

She leaves her bottle in the sand and takes mine in her arms, cradling it against her chest.

Then, I scoop her up in my arms, lifting her as gently as I can. She hisses when I first touch her, but something in my eyes must convince her to not fight me.

I carry her back into the house and up to my bedroom before realizing that putting her back in the bed where she was tied up and almost raped probably isn't the best idea.

"It's okay," Liesel says when I start to turn back.

"You sure?"

She nods.

I set her gently on the edge of the bed, and then I run to the bathroom, popping open a panel in the wall where I keep my emergency supplies. I grab the first aid kit. It's more like a wound healer kit, though. The only thing the kit is good for is dealing with bullet or knife wounds.

I carry the bag out and set it on the bed. Then I take the scotch bottle from her and set it on the nightstand. My eyes don't leave her now. I can't stop looking at her.

"Do you want me to call a doctor or do you want—"

"You—I want you to do it."

I nod.

"Painkillers or more scotch?"

The corner of her mouth lifts at that. "What do you think?"

I smile lightly and grab the bottle of scotch from the nightstand. It's the most expensive bottle in the house, over $30K. This isn't exactly the situation I imagined using it on. She's not going to take the time to savor the thick peat and sherry cask finish.

But right now, I'd give Liesel the world if I could.

I pop the bottle open and take a quick sip myself to steady my nerves before I hand it to her. She takes it, but I realize now it's a mistake. The bottle is heavy and hard to lift with her injured shoulder.

I hold the base and help lift it to her lips. I keep holding it until she gets enough down to ease her pain.

When I remove the bottle and set it back on the nightstand, she lifts an eyebrow. "I may already be drunk, but that was the best damn scotch I've ever tasted."

I smirk. "Don't get used to it. That's a thirty thousand dollar bottle."

Her eyebrows shoot up. "If you're paying, I could definitely get used to it."

I shake my head and then move closer to the bed.

"I'm going to sit behind you so I can get the bullet out, okay?"

She nods.

I've removed plenty of bullets before—out of my buddies, my coworkers, my employees, but never out of Liesel.

I gather my supplies, trying to think of her like any other person, but as I hold the tweezers up to her back, I hesitate.

"Oh, don't puss out on me now. If you can't pull a bullet out of my back, how am I supposed to believe that you're going to kill me?" Liesel teases.

But I hear the underlying fear. She knows there is a difference between hurting and killing her. When you kill someone, you don't have to deal with their pain and agony. Pulling this out is going to hurt like a motherfucker. I know, I have scars all over my body to prove it.

"Hold still. Scream, yell, cry if you have to, just don't move, understand?"

"Yes," she hisses.

I wish I could hold her hand as I do this. Not that that really helps, but at least I'd feel like I was doing something for her.

I push the tweezers in, digging for the bullet.

She doesn't move.

She doesn't hiss.

Scream.

Cry.

Did she pass out from the pain? Die of a sudden heart attack?

No, she's still breathing.

"Will you hurry up? This isn't exactly enjoyable for me, you know?"

I laugh. "Deep breath, Liesel."

And then I yank the bullet out on her exhale.

I plop the bullet and tweezers into a plastic bag and then apply gauze to her shoulder to stop the bleeding.

"Hard part's over."

"Really? I imagine the stitches aren't a cakewalk."

"Staples are faster."

"Let's go with the staples then," Liesel says, flashing me a grin over her shoulder.

I grab the bottle of scotch and hold it up to her lips. "Take one more sip."

She grips the bottle with her good arm and starts drinking while I apply the three quick staples into her back. Then I secure a gauze bandage to the wound and wipe the blood from her back and arm.

"All done," I say.

She nods and rests the bottle between her legs on the bed.

I gather up the supplies, put them back in the bag, and carry them into the bathroom, where I catch a glance of myself in the mirror.

I'm a monster.

She deserves better.

When I walk back into the bedroom, I lock eyes with her.

Liesel—the badass motherfucker.

My huntress.

My liar.

Mine.

I won't fail you again.

And to prove it, I say two little words I never thought I'd say to her.

"I'm sorry."

CHAPTER 29

LIESEL

Langston apologized.

I don't know what to do with that.

"Need anything else? Can I get you more painkillers? Food? Anything?" Langston asks.

I'm still sitting on the edge of the bed, and he's standing just inside the room looking like someone stole his puppy, and he got into a fistfight.

"Ice," I answer.

He nods and then jogs out of the room.

It gives me a moment, but there is too much to process.

My shoulder throbs, although not as painfully as before. The alcohol is numbing the most intense suffering.

It did hurt like hell when he dug the bullet out, though. I refused to show weakness, especially in front of Langston, my killer.

Is he still going to kill me?

He hesitated to pull the bullet out. It was as difficult for him as it was for me.

A lot can change in a year which, give or take a few weeks, is what I have left. That's the timeline he gave me.

One year.

I can get him to change his mind in a year. Get him to warm to me again like when we were kids. Get him to feel things so he can't fathom killing me.

Langston is back.

"Do you want to move to another bedroom?" he asks. It's clear he's worried that I'll have nightmares about being tied up and almost raped if we stay in here.

I shake my head. "That's not how my nightmares work."

He enters, carrying a bag of ice and a bowl of something with two spoons sticking out.

"Climb under the covers and sit back in the bed," he orders.

I do.

He plops the bowl down in my lap and then puts the bag of ice on my shoulder. Finally, he climbs into the bed next to me. He sits on top of the covers, while I sit under.

He brought me a bowl of buttered pecan ice cream—my favorite.

"You should have more than just scotch in your belly."

I smile lightly; I can't help it.

"What's the second spoon for?"

"Me." He takes a bite of my ice cream before I can jerk the bowl out of his reach.

That makes us both laugh. We both need a laugh, even if it doesn't make sense.

"Here," I say, reaching behind my shoulder to grab the bag of ice and toss it at him.

"What's this for?"

"Your eye—it looks terrible. And if I know you, you didn't ice it at all today. You might need your eye to be able to see and shit."

"I think your shoulder needs it more."

"Nope." I grab the bottle of scotch. "This is all my shoulder needs."

He doesn't argue with me, probably because he feels guilty. He just puts the ice to his swollen eye.

Progress.

I smile to myself as I take a bite of the heavenly ice cream.

"I haven't told you my story for the night," I say after taking a few more bites.

"I'll give you a pass for tonight, since you were shot and all."

"You're not getting out of story time with me that easily."

"Story time with you? I thought I was the one torturing you by making you tell me stories."

I put the spoon in my mouth and scrape the ice cream off with my teeth.

Langston stares at me like he's entranced with my mouth, wishing he was my spoon right now.

"Nope, story time is about putting tiny little cuts into your heart every single night. I can't kill you with one big blow, but I can kill you if I inflict enough scratches."

"Okay, what story are you going to tell me tonight?" He leans back, resting his head on the headboard. He holds the ice to his eye, and I hold my spoon of ice cream up to his lips.

He hesitantly takes a bite. Now I'm the one who can't stop staring at his lips.

"Liesel? Are you going to tell me a story or not? It's been a long day, and I'd like to sleep at some point." He says it like he's irritated with me, but we both know it's out of concern for me. He's just looking out for me, making sure that I get sleep, which is the best thing for my shoulder.

Rest and time are the only things that will heal it now.

I lean back too, trying not to wince when my shoulder hits the headboard.

"I think we were twelve or thirteen; I can't remember the exact year. That doesn't really matter, anyway. You had just kissed Ruby."

"Thirteen. I was thirteen."

I hit his shoulder playfully. "Of course, you would remember how old you were when you kissed Ruby."

"Wouldn't you?"

I hem and haw. "Yea, probably. No more interrupting my story."

He gestures to zipper his mouth shut.

I smile and get distracted by his adorable dimple.

No—focus.

"You and I rode our bikes together on the way home from school. I saw you kissing her earlier that day, and I teased you the whole way home."

Langston's face drops as he realizes the story I'm going to tell, but he's not sure why I chose it.

"We got to your house, and I kept teasing you, even though I saw your father drinking beer in his chair. Even though I knew not to be loud. Even though I knew not to tease you about something your father wouldn't approve."

"Liesel," Langston says in a warning tone.

I keep going.

"I knew what was going to happen, and I kept pushing, teasing. I was jealous that you kissed that girl. And I wanted to make you pay."

Langston's eyes close, as if remembering.

"Your father beat you, and it was my fault. I provoked him. I knew you got beat every time he was triggered, and I did nothing."

I reach up and touch his face.

He opens his eyes.

When he looks at me, he knows why I told this story. Every time he gets hit, it reminds him of his father. And I'm still sorry for not saving him when we were kids.

"I'll go sleep in the closet," I say, moving to get up.

Langston grabs my wrist, stopping me.

"Liar."

"What?"

"You're a liar."

I frown. "What part of that story was a lie? You lived that story with me. Every word was the truth."

He removes the ice from his face and looks at me with both eyes.

"You did do something to stop him, Liesel."

How does he know?

"You did something every time you could. You told my mother. You tried to calm him down or get him extra drunk so that he wouldn't be able to hit me."

He's right. I did. I just never realized that Langston knew that.

"But that night—"

He puts a finger to my lips, getting me to stop.

"You took a beating for me."

I freeze, and my eyes widen. *How did he know?*

He nods as if my reaction confirms it. He didn't know for sure until this very moment.

Langston gets up out of bed and turns off the lights.

I feel him return a moment later.

He climbs into the bed, this time under the covers.

"Go to sleep, Liesel."

This time he doesn't give me a choice between the closet or his bed; he demands I sleep in his bed. For the first time since I slept next to him when we were kids, I want to share a bed with him.

LANGSTON

"**P**lease."

The single word stirs me awake.

I'm a light sleeper. It's one of the many reasons why I excel at security and protecting people—well, protecting everyone other than Liesel.

My eyes fly open and look to the woman lying on my shoulder.

Liesel Dunn.

Her head is snuggled up against my bare chest.

"Please," she whimpers again.

"Shh, I got you," I whisper into her ear, but I don't think she's actually awake. She's just having a dream or, most likely, a nightmare.

I feel her forehead—it's covered in sweat. Her body trembles in my arms. She feels like an addict in need of her next fix.

I've had my suspicions of what her demons actually are ever since she arrived. Holding her while she sleeps seems to confirm them.

"I need you, please," Liesel whispers again, her hands start clawing at my chest.

"Liesel," I say, freezing.

Her thigh drapes over mine, and she starts humping my leg, moving her body over mine like she's desperate.

"Liesel, wake up." I stroke her hair.

"Please, make me come. I need it."

She tries again to rub herself against me. To feel something. To let go. But she can't.

Suddenly, the dream shifts.

"Get off of me!"

She's no longer begging for my body but begging me to let her go.

Her fists slam against my chest, over and over. Her body somehow heats to an even higher temperature. She has to be running a fever. She has to be having a nightmare.

"Let me go!" she yells.

Now I'm not sure if she's awake or asleep, but I can't let her go. If I let her go, she'll run. She'll hurt herself—her shoulder.

"Liesel, wake up."

"Let me go!" Her legs start kicking. She's terrified.

I don't know what to do.

I don't know how to help her.

"Please," her mood shifts again, and this time she's begging.

I don't know what to do.

I don't know where my brain goes or why I think this is a good idea.

I roll her onto her back and hover an inch over her.

I kiss her.

The second our lips touch, her eyes open.

I should stop the kiss.

I should pull away.

I don't.

And she doesn't push me away.

So I savor the moment. This kiss won't be repeated. This kiss tastes just like I always thought it would. Sure, I kissed her when we were kids, but that was before I knew how to actually kiss.

This kiss, I take everything I can.

I feel the soft warmth of her lips.

I plunge my tongue into her depths, finding hers and dancing with it, already knowing her next move. Her tongue is going to battle mine for control. I expect to feel frustrated that she doesn't just resign to me.

Instead, I feel like she woke a hurricane of emotions inside me. I feel the sparks, the electricity, the waves crashing between us.

I would say I didn't expect this—but that would be a lie. It's one of the reasons I haven't kissed her until now. Until I felt like I didn't have a choice.

Liesel grabs the back of my head when I start to pull away.

There's a pause, and then I attack her with my kisses. I can't control myself. I can't think. I want to drown in her kisses.

I shouldn't. This is wrong for so many reasons.

I'm destroying everything I've worked for with one stupid kiss.

But damn, this kiss is worth it.

Suddenly, the intensity of it all becomes too much. Like two spark plugs forced together, the zap eventually pushes us apart as much as it pulled us together at first.

We both pant heavily.

"That was our first kiss?" she says like it's a question.

"Yes, if you don't count that kiss when we were eight."

"I don't."

I nod in agreement. That was nothing like this kiss.

"You've never fucked me?" she asks. She's just now figuring out the truth.

I shake my head.

"You've never fingered me?"

I shake my head.

"Never done anything sexual with me?"

I shake my head.

"Oh my god, then who did?"

"Mostly hallucinations in your nightmares."

She holds onto her shirt, gripping for reality, for truth.

"Joel?" she asks, her voice terrified of my answer.

"No," I lie. I failed to protect her before, but dammit, I'll protect her now. She never has to know about Joel.

But the rest?

The rest of the truth, I'll take to my grave.

LIESEL

That kiss.

That kiss was terrifying, breathtaking.

It also brought me back to life.

It changed how I felt about Langston. Or maybe it brought me back to how I once felt?

I want to kiss him again.

And yet, if I kiss him again, I'll ruin everything.

But did he ruin everything already?

Is he lying?

He said we never fucked, he never touched me, and that Joel didn't touch me. *Is it true? Or is it all a lie?*

I trust him.

It doesn't matter if it's the truth or a lie. It's what I need to hear.

I'm a sex addict. I use sex to deal with the pain of my past.

But god, that kiss—do I wish I could have more than one.

That's what I think about as I drift back to sleep. It's what I think about all night. That kiss is still playing on my lips in the morning when I wake up.

"Langston?" I ask to an empty room as the sun rises.

I get no answer.

The room is bright. Maybe I slept in too long, and that's why he's not here.

Or maybe I scared him off last night.

Maybe he's changed his mind and wants to end my life sooner than planned.

I sit up, my body aching with pain. I need more painkillers or more scotch.

I reach for the scotch bottle next to the bed and see that it's been replaced with a bottle of painkillers and a glass of water.

"Fine," I say, resigning myself to meds instead of alcohol to deal today.

I pop two pills and drink the water.

Then I get out of bed. I consider showering or soaking in the tub, but I want to find Langston.

So I just head downstairs, feeling much happier and lighter than I should.

The house is quiet as I hit the bottom step.

I decide to grab a coffee before I continue my search. The pot is still on, and there is enough for one cup left. I pour myself a cup, happily humming a song in my head when my world stops.

I look out the big glass doors that are usually open to the outside by now, but I'm guessing that was Amelia's job. No one else has gotten into a routine to open the house up yet.

It's not the closed doors causing my heart to skip—it's what I see just beyond them.

Langston kissing Phoenix.

Not a chicken peck either, a full-on slam me against the wall and take my breath away kind of kiss. The kind that you get swept up in and don't notice the world around you. I know what kissing Langston like that feels like. I experienced it last night.

And now he's kissing Phoenix.

They don't notice me. *How could they, locked in a lip battle like that?*

I have two choices—go back to Langston's room and pretend I didn't see them, biding my time until I bring the subject up, or make it clear that I see them and I'm pissed.

I'm usually pretty good with self-control. Not today.

Coffee still in hand, I storm through the glass doors, making my presence as obvious as possible. They can't hide what I saw.

They both stop at the sound of the door swinging open. Or maybe it's my stomping and the fire shooting from my body that drew their attention my way, but they don't separate. Phoenix still clings to Langston's arm.

"So you're not only a liar; you're also a cheater," I say, glaring at Langston. Phoenix, I can't really be mad at. I thought she was my friend, but then I've only known her for a couple of days. I can't be upset with her. Langston, on the other hand, I want to bury with the fires of hell.

I want to fight. I want to knee Langston in the groin. I want to run him off a cliff.

But I know that not doing any of those things is more powerful. He knows I'm pissed, and now he has to wait to see what my next move will be and when I'll make it.

I walk past them and head to the beach, wishing I had something stronger than coffee in my hand. I plop down on the sandy beach with the sun beating down on me. My hot coffee isn't going to do much to help with the sweltering sun. Soon, I'll have to go back and get water, or at least find a shady spot to sit.

"I'm not a cheater," Langston says from behind me.

I snap my head. "Oh, really? What would you call kissing me while you're dating her? I'm pretty sure most people would classify that as cheating."

"I only kissed you to get you to stop having your nightmares." Langston's hands are in the pockets of his swim trunks, and he's wearing a plain white T-shirt. He looks like the boy I used to know before Enzo sunk his claws into him. He looks light and carefree, but I can see the turmoil in his eyes.

I nod and glance away. He's right. He only kissed me to help me. All the rest was just my imagination. Langston didn't touch me; he didn't fuck me—it's true.

I can't be mad at Langston, at least not for this. *But why does it hurt worse than him threatening to kill me?*

Probably because deep down, I always thought we had a future together. At least as friends. As one time lovers.

But that was always just a dream.

Still, I want to hurt Langston more than I've wanted to torture anyone. I want to strike a hot branding iron into his heart like he did to me with that kiss.

"I'm ready to tell you one truth from the letter in the envelope."

Langston's eyebrows shoot up, and his blue eyes widen.

"Yea?"

I nod and pat the sand next to me, trying to act like I've forgotten all about that kiss. I could fight him, but that wouldn't help. I'd lose. This is the only way to win—with vicious words.

Langston sits down, resting his wrists against the top of his bent knees.

"I want a month for telling you a truth."

"A month seems fair," his words seem pained, hesitant.

"The letter said the first requirement for going after the treasure is to be married. I have to be married. Only that person and I will have the keys to be able to open the treasure. Whoever I choose, I have to choose wisely, because I can only be married once. One love to go after the treasure with."

He looks out at the ocean, his thumbs circling each other, fidgeting. He knows I'm not done.

"Liesel, will—"

"And you can't ask me to marry you to get the treasure. You can't even force me to marry you in exchange for giving me back my life."

"Why not?"

"Because I'm already married to Waylon."

His eyes flash to my hand to see if he somehow missed a wedding ring. He didn't.

"Liesel Dunn wouldn't get married without a gaudy engagement ring."

"Oh, I have a ring. I have everything. We were going to announce it at the next fundraiser event when he announced his candidacy, make a big splash."

"You're lying."

"Am I?"

Langston studies me, but he has no clue. The only way to know for sure is to go look it up in the wedding registry back in New York.

"Yes," he hisses, his pain oozing off of him.

"You can get me to spill all of the information on my half of that letter, but it won't matter. You can't go after the treasure for yourself. This whole exercise in kidnapping me and threatening my life was all for nothing."

Boom.

An explosion rings through my ears.

Langston tackles me to the ground, shielding me with his body.

"What was that?"

"We're under attack," Langston says, but he's not worried. His voice is calm. Fighting a battle is his happy place.

"You have to do exactly what I say if you want to survive, you hear me?"

I nod, my body trembling from his weight pressed against mine.

"I wasn't going to ask you to marry me, that was never the plan."

"Wasn't it?" I breathe, not sure why we are still talking about this when bombs are going off in the distance, growing closer with each moment.

"I couldn't even if I wanted to. I'm married, too."

No.

My mouth falls, my eyes swell with threatening tears, and my heart slows.

"I'm married. I have two kids."

More burning words. He just lit me on fire and left me to burn.

"Your marriage won't help you. You have to be married to a Dunn to be able to go after the fortune, and last I checked you didn't marry me. I'm the only Dunn left."

Langston is quiet a minute.

Another explosion goes off, and somehow his body presses harder against mine until I swear I feel his erection at my stomach. I must be dreaming, though.

"I married a Dunn."

I frown, completely confused.

"You cheated on your wife with me and Phoenix?'

"Phoenix is my wife—Phoenix Dunn."

I search my brain, trying to figure out how she's related to me.

"My cousin," I say, remembering long ago when my father once mentioned I had a cousin. He told me she's the only family I have left if I wanted to search for her. I never did. I didn't want family.

Another explosion, this one close to the house.

"You promise to do what I say?" Langston asks.

I know he won't let me up unless I do.

I nod.

He frowns, knowing I'm lying.

"Run, Liesel. Run until you can't run anymore. Tomorrow, come find me, huntress. Come find me, and I'll tell you a piece from my half of the letter. I'll give you another piece of the puzzle."

Langston removes his body from mine.

I run.

And run.

I run from the pain.

I run from Langston.

I run for my life.

He wants me to hunt for him tomorrow, to find him.

The only thing I plan on hunting for is a way off this island. There was once a time when I thought Langston was the one. The man I would marry—the love of my life.

But this isn't a love story. This is the story of all the reasons Langston and I can't be together.

Reason number one: we lie.

DESPERATE LIES

PROLOGUE
LIESEL

I want to kill Langston, but I'd also die for him.

He ruined my life.

He made me so desperate to get my life back that I'm about to murder in cold blood.

Langston took every-fucking-thing from me.

He took my money.

My career.

My heart.

My soul.

My life.

He took the one person I care about above all.

Langston couldn't just be happy taking me, controlling me, demanding I give up my life to pay for my sins—he wanted more.

And he won't stop until he has everything.

I'm pretty sure he already does.

But at least I'll take the one thing from him he truly loves. I'm desperate to find out the truth, to find out if he really took everything. This is the only way to separate the truth from the lies.

I've always been the huntress, but I'm about to become the killer...

CHAPTER 1

LIESEL

I lied—those words flood me as I run down the beach.

Should I run on the sand where it's easier to run, but I'm an open target? Or should I dart into the jungle where I'll have to fight through thick brush, but I won't be spotted?

I decide speed is better than cover and keep running down the beach, away from Langston's house, and toward the airport.

I lied.

I'm not really married to Waylon.

Langston lied, too, right?

We lie—that's what we do. All we've done is lie to each other since we were kids. That's what we were doing—lying. Not letting the other person see our cards.

He definitely lied. There is no way Langston is married to my cousin, Phoenix, and already has two kids. Siren or Kai would have said something to me.

Right?

RIGHT?

Yes.

Langston is just as single as ever.

He may be dating Phoenix, hedging his bets so if I don't marry him, he can still marry a Dunn and go after my inheritance.

Boom.

I duck at the sound, covering my head like somehow my hands are going to be able to stop a bomb.

I shield my eyes as I glance up at the sun, trying to see if we are being attacked from above. I don't see any planes.

It's a ground attack; probably someone who wants Enzo and Kai's empire like usual. There is a reason I don't really hang out with them anymore—this is why. I'd rather not be ambushed and spend my time running from guns, bombs, and dangerous people every second of every day.

I prefer to be able to go to an excluded beach island to actually relax and not worry about bombs being dropped on my head—call me high-maintenance.

I hear gunfire behind me.

Jesus.

How did I end up in this world? When will it end?

I decide that I should take the jungle route after all. I slip between some bushes, scratching my arms and causing some nasty red bumps to pop up.

Another loud bomb goes off.

I stop and turn my head in the direction of the house.

"You better not destroy the house!" I yell into the jungle. I plan on taking the house from Langston someday. I may not like Langston anymore, but I dreamt up that fucking house when I was eight—it's mine.

I turn back in the opposite direction of the house, hoping to eventually find the runway we landed on.

I take a step, and a green leaf with tiny razor-sharp teeth digs into my thigh. I take another step and almost trip over a branch. One more step, and then I stop.

There is no clear path. I realize now that when I followed Langston to the house, he was clearing the path for me, stomping down leaves and branches. He was making it easier for me, even if he was teasing me by letting his branches hit me.

Now, I'm all alone to make my own path. I like being an independent woman carving my own path.

I sigh, covered in sweat dripping down my forehead and pooling around the base of my neck. Getting off this island is going to take forever.

I curse to hell whoever it is attacking. I'd rather be stuck talking to Langston than running for my life through the hot jungle.

Why am I running?

Does Langston think I'm not strong enough to stay and fight with him?

Will he be too worried about me if I'm nearby while he's fighting?

Or is he hiding something?

My money is on Langston hiding something. He doesn't want me to know who's attacking. Or he doesn't want them to know that I'm here.

Either way, he's hiding.

That alone should make me turn my ass around and demand answers from Langston.

My leg is straddling a fallen tree; my hair is stuck to my face. I would do anything for some water to fix my bone-dry mouth, too.

I look left then right.

What do I do?

Do I run back to Langston, into the danger, and demand answers?

Do I do as Langston said and run? And run? And run?

I'm already running; I'm not turning back now.

He said to run as far as I could tonight, and then to come find him tomorrow.

He's crazy if he thinks I'll return to him—back to being his captive and back to the place where he said he'd end my life.

There is no way I'm going back now.

Langston promised me answers. He promised to give me one clue from his half of the torn paper.

I look left—toward Langston—man, do I want to know what his half of the paper says. I want to know what my dad's last message to me was. I want to know because I'm curious—not because I give a damn about the treasure.

I make my own money—I don't need any inheritance or treasure.

I may have had some help from Enzo, giving me enough money to go to college and feed myself, but after college I got a job. I worked hard. I've even offered many times to pay Enzo back. He just never accepts my money.

Good riddance, I huff, pulling myself over the log.

A mistake—I come crashing down into a pile of mud on the other side.

Can this day get any worse?

My shoulder throbs, reminding me of my bullet wound. Memories flash, reminding me of the rape, the abuse, the child I gave up.

Yes, this day can get a lot worse.

I sit up as I hear more gunfire.

Langston said to run.

No one can move very quickly through this thick brush, but I should start moving faster in case anyone starts following me—mainly Langston.

So I force myself to get up.

I force my legs to run.

And run, and run, and run.

I stop thinking about Langston.

I stop wondering and analyzing his words—trying to determine if he lied or not.

I stop worrying that a stray bullet or misplaced bomb is going to blow me into a million tiny pieces.

I focus on putting one step in front of the other.

Again.

And again.

And again.

Until the sun has set.

Until it's pitch-black outside.

And even then I keep going.

I refuse to be killed.

I refuse to be anyone's captive.

I refuse to let any man control me.

I take another step.

This step makes all the difference.

I may not be able to see very well, but I don't hear the crunch of leaves. I don't have to dodge low hanging limbs. I don't feel the brush of branches scratching my mud and sweat covered skin.

My feet sink into sand.

Did I take a wrong step toward the beach instead of walking in a straight line to the airport?

Or did I make it?

I take another and another.

The concrete of the runway greets my feet.

I smile for the first time all day. I bite my bottom lip as the grin spreads.

My lip—Langston's kiss.

No, stop thinking about him, brain.

Focus.

I made it to the runway. There are no airplanes stored here, but I've spotted a handful of planes landing on this island while I've spent my time here. There are planes that fly here that don't belong to Langston Pearce.

There will be a plane if I wait here long enough for one to land.

Tomorrow, come find me, huntress.

Langston's words ring in my ear.

I don't have time to wait—to get lucky.

I make my own luck.

There is a small building near the runway. It looks more like an outhouse than an actual building, but I have to try something.

When I get to the entrance, I realize there isn't even a door.

I exhale loudly.

I'm not counting on there being anyone inside, or any electronics to call for help.

I step inside anyway.

The room is dark. I search the wall with my hand, but I don't find a light switch.

I should just leave, but it's the middle of the night.

The explosions and gunfire stopped—not that that's comforting. It means Langston is probably looking for me now. If I head into the jungle again, I have to deal with jaguars, venomous snakes, poisonous spiders.

I need sleep if I'm going to have any energy to face tomorrow. This tiny building is better than sleeping on the jungle floor.

There isn't a door, but there are at least three walls to protect me.

I lie down on the floor and curl up in a ball as I hear rain starting overhead.

Please, let the roof be waterproof.

I cross my fingers, squinting my eyes up at the dark roof.

After five minutes pass and I'm not wet, I realize my luck might have changed. At least the roof is holding.

A soft smile spreads as I close my eyes and begin to drift off to sleep from exhaustion with the help of the lightly tapping rain. The rain will make it harder for Langston to find me. And he won't think I made it all the way to the runway in one night.

Tonight, I'll sleep soundly. Tomorrow...

♡

A BUZZING WAKES ME UP.

I blink rapidly, trying to make sense of my surroundings. I've been sleeping in a closet, and this room isn't much bigger than that, but it's not Langston's closet.

I moan, wishing a buzzing noise would stop and let me sleep. It's still dark outside. I have no idea how long I've been asleep, but it can't be more than a couple of hours at best.

More buzzing.

Wait—buzzing!

There is something electronic in this room. It's probably just a battery-powered alarm clock, but I can hope.

I move onto all fours as I pat around the floor, searching for the source of the buzzing.

I feel a strap.

A bag!

It's sitting on a small chair in the corner.

I pick up the bag and put it on my lap, as I furiously search inside.

My heart races. *Could I really find a phone? A way to make contact with the outside world and escape?*

I touch a piece of glass.

My heart thumps to a stop.

It's too big to be a phone.

I pull out the device—an iPad.

My heart flutters, not knowing if I should be elated or crushed.

I click the home button to get the screen to light up—praying that the iPad has a cellular connection. I doubt there is wifi.

Please, please, please.

I stare at the screen after the split second it takes to light up. I silence the alarm buzzing the device.

My eyes dart to the upper right corner.

It has cellular reception.

Thank god.

I pull up the phone app and am about to call Waylon when my fingers suddenly stop.

I don't know what island I'm on. I care about Waylon. He's a smart man, but he's never had to worry about money, never gotten scrappy or creative, never dealt with dangerous people. The most he'll be able to do is call the police or FBI to search for me.

By then, Langston will have found me and moved me to another island.

But who else do I have on my side?

Enzo?

No, he'd take Langston's side.

Kai?

She's sweet, but becoming a leader has made her tougher. She will do whatever is in the best interest of the empire she controls, which means not pissing off one of her best employees—Langston. She would help me and then rat me out to him.

Zeke?

He's always hated me. He wouldn't help.

Siren...?

Siren! She's my answer. Yes, she and Langston have a weird relationship that I will never understand. They say they are just friends, but

I've always wondered if Zeke and Siren have an open relationship. There is no way she and Langston got so close without fucking each other's brains out.

That might seem to make her the last person on earth I should call to help me, but because Siren is so close to Langston, she will call him out on his bullshit. There is no way any of them: Enzo, Kai, Zeke, or Siren would be okay with Langston kidnapping me and threatening to kill me.

But three out of the four will stand by Langston because he's one of them. Sure, they've been nice to me over the years, but I've never been one of them—not truly.

Siren is the only one who will put a stop to this.

I dial Siren's number from memory. Most people in this day and age don't have many numbers memorized. Call it a skill I learned from being poor, but you never know when you are going to not have a phone, or when you're going to be in a dangerous situation and need someone's help.

Like right now.

I don't expect Siren to answer—I'm calling from an unknown number. And it's the middle of the night, or at least, it's the middle of the night in whatever time zone I'm in.

"Hello?" Siren answers on the second ring.

I let out a long, steadying breath, putting all of my trust into this woman.

"I need your help."

CHAPTER 2

LANGSTON

I watch Liesel run away from me.

Somehow, I keep my feet firmly planted in the sand.

I try to ignore all of her features—her toned legs, tight ass, feminine curve of her hips, long untamed hair. It's like all of her features were specially designed just for me. She's my ultimate tempta-tion; one I will never succumb to.

I kissed her to wake her up from her nightmare. That's it. That's all that kiss was. It wasn't weakness. It wasn't losing control. It wasn't a slip.

At least that's what I keep telling myself.

Liesel keeps running down the beach, around the edge of the island, until the jungle brush blocks my view. I don't know if she stays on the beach or bolts into the forest. She's gone, and I have no idea if she's coming back.

My throat dries, turning into ash at that thought. She has to come back. I don't have all the information I need from her.

Married.

That's what she said. She's married to that old fucker.

Liesel just said that because of what was on her half of the letter. I suspected that marriage was the first step in searching for Liesel's inheritance based on what my half of the letter said.

But Liesel married—it doesn't make sense to me. She would never get married just to go after some treasure, and I don't think the woman is capable of falling in love.

No, there is no way Liesel Dunn is married.

My skin begins to boil in jealousy just thinking about Waylon touching her. Proposing to her. Her saying yes. Planning a wedding. Saying I do. And then fucking as husband and wife.

I'm lying to myself. It was all too easy to imagine her married.

I hear gunshots, and I know I can't focus on Liesel anymore. She's safe. No one knows she's here. It's for the best until I can figure out who's attacking us and why.

If Liesel were here, I wouldn't be able to focus. And if she's the target, then she really can't be here. She'd do something stupid like get herself kidnapped.

I don't have my gun on me, which is idiotic. But having a gun on me around Liesel is dangerous—for both of us.

If she smacks off, I might kill her. And if she tricked me and I let my guard down for a single second, she'd find it and kill me. I figured it was for the best to not put either of us in that situation.

I run up the hillside, staying as low as I can to avoid any stray bullets. Our assailants don't seem to have made it past the front of the house. At least my security measures are working.

I make it to the open glass door at the back of the house and peer inside. My team of about a dozen is assembled in the middle of the living room.

I step inside.

"What are you doing standing around? Get to your positions, now!"

"Yes, sir," they all mumble at different times and take off.

I sigh. I really should have found a better number two to train and prepare them for these scenarios better. Especially since I've been spending too much of my free time with Liesel.

Phoenix looks at me with concern in her eyes. "Liesel?"

"She's safe."

She nods.

"I need you to go to the bunker."

"But I can help! I know how to shoot a gun as well as half of these yahoos."

"I know, but you are way more important to me than those yahoos. I pay them to protect us. Your job is to stay safe."

"What about you? Are you going to hide out in the bunker with me?"

I crack my neck back and forth, my face morphing into one of terror, preparing myself for what I'm about to face.

"Don't worry about me, Dunn. No one can touch me if they can't find me."

She frowns. "You're not invincible. You know that, right, Langston?"

I narrow my eyes and grab her hips, pulling her tightly against my body. "I've let these bastards get a ten-minute head start, and they haven't so much as broken the exterior perimeter. Have a little faith in me."

"I do, but I just worry."

I kiss her forehead. "Don't. Go to the bunker. I'll come to you soon."

I step away from her, putting an arm's length of space between us. "Go."

I don't have time to make sure Phoenix gets to the bunker. She'll either listen to me or she won't. If she doesn't, she'll have to deal with the consequences.

I start to walk away, but Phoenix grabs my hand at the last moment.

"Dunn, I really don't have time—"

She yanks my arm as hard as she can, closing the space between us. Her hands come up to my cheeks, grabbing me hard. She plants a hard, wet, all-out kiss on my lips.

I kiss her back, savoring how her tongue feels in my mouth.

Liesel.

Of course, my dumb-ass brain thinks of my kiss with Liesel instead of enjoying this moment.

When Phoenix kissed me earlier, it was greatly appreciated. I needed something to distract me from my kiss with Liesel. But this kiss now—all it makes me think about is Liesel. She's the last person I want to be thinking about right now.

I want to end the kiss. I need to deal with whatever jackasses are trying to kill us all right now. But if I stop the kiss early, it will only make her desperate to kiss me more.

So I let Phoenix end the kiss.

"Get your ass to the bunker, now. I don't want to have to worry about your safety."

She touches her swollen lip with her finger. She's going to spend her entire time in the bunker thinking about our kiss.

"Dunn," I warn.

"I'm as safe as you are standing here, but fine, I'll go."

I watch as Phoenix walks away toward the more secure half of the house that sits on top of a bunker.

I stare at her legs tightly covered in jeans. I watch the sway of her hips as she walks away. My eyes drift up to her black long-sleeved T-shirt and her short red hair. Phoenix is the complete opposite of Liesel.

I like Phoenix's body, but I don't crave it like an addict craves heroin. With Liesel, if I get the tiniest taste, I'm going to lose myself. I'm going to become so addicted that I won't be able to do anything but think about her.

A loud explosion grabs my attention again.

Jesus, I barely even kissed Liesel, and I'm already going down the rabbit hole. What would happen to me if I did more than kiss her?

That's just one of the many reasons why I can't.

I grab one of my many stashed guns by pressing my finger to the scanner under the kitchen counter. A compartment opens, and I grab the two guns inside, along with plenty of ammunition. Then I take off toward the garage.

The garage is dark when I get there. No one has entered yet.

I run to the Range Rover, pop the door open and then climb in.

This car is bulletproof, and the large tablet inside is hooked up to my entire security system. I'm a great fighter, but the best place for me to help my team is here, being their eyes in the field. My first task is finding the man who ordered this attack so I can put an end to this and save as many lives on my side as possible.

All of his team will end up dead, no matter how many surrender.

I turn on my radio, instantly connecting my voice to my team. "They are only attacking from the front. They're trying to get past the minefield."

"They won't get past it, boss," Seth says.

"Don't get cocky. Be prepared and alert. I'll let you know if any of them get through the perimeter."

I need to find their leader and figure out why they are attacking. Whoever it is, they aren't very skilled. Or at least, they didn't bring very many men.

I dial Enzo's number. Kai is technically in charge, and I love her to death, but Enzo and I go back since forever. And I don't like to bother Kai and unless it's important.

"What do you need?" Enzo says matter of factly, knowing that I never call him just to chat about how our lives are. I only call when I need something from him.

"The island is under attack. I don't know who it is or if they're after you or me." I leave out the chance that they're attacking to get to Liesel.

"I'm not aware of any threats against us, but let me do a security check and speak with Kai. I'll get back to you in one." He ends the call.

Enzo will call me back in literally one minute. Moments like this are all about speed. I need to know who, where, when, why, and I need to know it all right now.

I zoom in on the men shooting at us. There is nothing special about their clothes, their equipment, nothing that tells me who they work for.

My phone buzzes.

"And?" I answer.

"We don't think they're after us. I'll keep finding out any info I can and leave a message for you. Do you need backup?" Enzo says with a bit of teasing in his voice. He knows I'm more than capable of handling this myself, and it would take him hours to get here. Even if I did need his help, we'd all be dead by then.

Unfortunately, these men are most likely after us because of Liesel's money. Any leak of a treasure and it brings out all sorts of crazies to try and find it. I don't know how anyone knows when we have taken zero steps to go after the inheritance, but that's a question for a different day.

"Nope, I'm good, brother." I end the call and then look back at the screen. It's going to take these guys hours to get through the perimeter. I don't have hours. I want this over with now.

Then I can go back to Phoenix and show her I'm still alive.

Then I can go hunt Liesel.

I cock my gun and climb out of the car, ready to put an end to this bullshit they call an attack.

I walk down my driveway.

"What are you doing, boss?" Seth says.

"Ending this. Everyone, hold your positions. Don't interfere unless I tell you to."

I click a button on my phone that stops the minefield from going off so I can meet the men head-on. As I scan the area, I realize they didn't even bring any heavy artillery. The only bombs going off are our own.

I aim my gun through the haze and shoot five men dead.

Then I step through the fog.

I'm an easy target. Any one of the remaining seven men could kill me, but I need a moment to look them all in the eyes to figure out who is most likely to rat out their boss. That man gets to live.

I only need a second to scan. They are all terrified. Any one of them would spill the truth.

I roll my eyes.

Why do men try to attack me like this?

They are so unprepared there is no way they are going to be able to defeat me. It's like they don't care about their men at all.

I don't have a choice but to kill them all. There is no way I'll let any of these men hurt my team or the others I'm protecting. Plus, I don't really need any of them alive to find answers.

Almost bored, I shoot them all one by one. A few get a couple of bullets off, but the closest to hitting me barely grazes my arm. It's not even close enough to break skin, just to rip my T-shirt.

"Did I miss anyone?" I ask to my team.

"You got them all, boss," Seth answers. Apparently, he's the only one brave enough to answer me after what I did to Joel and Amelia.

I walk over to the closest dead combatant and dig through his clothes until I find his wallet and phone.

"Get to work cleaning up this mess," I tell my team as I take the wallet and phone back to the house.

I pull my earpiece out and pocket my gun, now that the danger has been squashed.

I consider letting Phoenix know that it's safe to come out. *Do I really know it's safe until I find out who's behind the attack and deal with them?*

Plus, I really want to be alone right now.

I run up the stairs, taking them two at a time.

I head to my dresser and find the finger scanner below the top drawer, revealing another hidden gun and a laptop.

I pull out the laptop and bring it to my bed, ignoring the images of Liesel that flash in my head like perfect snapshots.

Stitching up her shoulder.

Holding her in bed.

Her tied up.

I shake my head like a magic eight ball, like I can just shake away my thoughts.

I start typing the name on the driver's license into the computer while I scroll through the phone, finding his most called numbers.

The first number is labeled 'Mom,' so I ignore it.

But the second number has no name associated with it.

This is going to be too easy. I really could use a challenge someday. Maybe that's half the reason I decided to go after Liesel's inheritance.

My head falls back in frustration against the headboard.

I only wish I were just looking for a challenge, and that's why I need Liesel's money. Then I could step away whenever I wanted.

I take a deep breath and then open my eyes. The top search of

Edgar Jacobs lists him as a car salesman. Clearly, he's not. It's a front. Just like the bars Enzo and Kai own are fronts for their business. Places that look like normal businesses, but are really the offices of a criminal organization if you look closely.

I'm ninety-nine percent sure that I've found the location of the man who ordered the attack.

I hit call on the nameless number in Edgar's phone.

"Is it done?" a man answers.

Jesus, this is too easy.

"Yep, I killed every single one of your pathetic men."

Silence.

I think he might have hung up, but apparently, this idiot really thought he had a chance to bring me down.

"Now that I have your attention..." I brush the dirt off my nails, barely even thinking about this conversation. My voice holds enough of a threat to let this man know that I'm serious. "...you will not attack me again.

"I now have men monitoring your every movement. If you do anything out of the ordinary, if I suspect in any way that you are going to attack and come after me again, then I will have you killed. Along with everyone who works for you, everyone you love, everyone you've ever met. Do you understand, Mr. Tirkel?" I say as I pull up the name associated with his number on my computer.

He's speechless, but his breathing is heavy and nasally, so I know he's still on the line.

"Mr. Tirkel? I need confirmation that you heard me."

"I—uh—I heard you."

"This is your only warning. And you should know that I don't give warnings often. The only reason you are getting one is because I don't want to bother with sending someone to kill you. That's how little you mean to me. But make one wrong step and I will."

"Yes, I understand."

"Good. And oh, Mr. Tirkel? Next time you try to take down a stronger man than yourself, don't send your men in to fight for you. Grow some balls, man up and fight yourself. If you're not capable of doing that, then you shouldn't order the attack in the first place."

I hang up the phone, putting no more thought to Mr. Tirkel.

He's an idiot with no skills and no money. He won't be attacking again. His attempt smelt of desperation. He needed money for his organization so badly that he was willing to try me.

I lean my head back again. The sun has begun to set.

I have a choice to make. Stay here with Phoenix and hope that Liesel obeys me by coming back tomorrow, or go out and search for Liesel myself before she slips through my fingers.

I'm pretty sure Liesel isn't coming back. She may want answers, but she's too stubborn to listen to anything I say. I should have told her to never come back, and then she might show up on my front door tomorrow.

But I'm not one hundred percent sure. She's tired of the lies too. She wants answers as much as I do. Although, we each have our own reasons for wanting answers.

I give her a ten percent chance of coming back on her own.

I won't go hunt her.

I'll wait and let her make her move. I'll let her decide her fate. If she comes back, I'll be more lenient on her. But if she runs...my brain fills with all the things it wants to do to her.

I won't be doing any of them. I'll do the smart thing. The thing that hits her where it hurts and gives me what I want.

I should get up and go talk to Phoenix. Just five more minutes of relaxing and then I'll go to her.

A lightbulb goes off in my head.

I know what Liesel's going to do.

I pull out my phone and stare at the names of all the contacts Liesel knows in our dangerous world.

Enzo.

Kai.

Zeke.

Siren.

Who would she call for help?

The answer is obvious. She knows me better than anyone, but I know her better than anyone too.

I dial Siren's number.

"I'm not going to help you keep Liesel hostage. If you want to talk, you can talk to Zeke. I'm not talking to you until you let her go," Siren huffs into the phone.

"Wait!" I say before she can hand the phone off to Zeke.

"You have three seconds."

"Liesel is going to call you for help."

There's a silent beat before she answers. "What do you want me to do?"

"Help her."

LIESEL

"That fucking bastard! I'll have a plane there in two hours," Siren says when I finish telling her everything.

I let out an audible breath.

I'm getting rescued.

"Thank you."

"Of course. And don't worry, Langston is going to get a mouthful from me next time I see him. He's an asshole for thinking he can just kidnap you like that, even if he'd never actually kill you. He's just trying to bully and intimidate you into doing what he wants."

I can't wipe the smile off my face.

"You have no idea how much I appreciate your help. I'll pay you back—"

"Don't you dare. You have nothing to pay me back for."

"Not even by going with you on a girls trip?"

I can feel her smile through the phone. "Kai would kill me if I didn't use this opportunity to persuade you to go on a girls trip with us, but I don't think persuasion will be necessary. You'll want to vent after all of this is over."

"You're probably right." I won't be venting to Waylon about my time here, that's for sure.

"Hang tight. I'll have you off his island in two hours." Siren hangs up the phone.

Two hours until I'm free.

I stare down the road that leads toward Langston's house as the sun begins to rise. Even if Langston comes for me before I'm rescued, I trust Siren. She'll find me and make Langston release me.

This is truly the end of this nightmare.

Wait...

I didn't give Siren my location. *How does she know where I am? And where am I exactly?*

I shake off the weird vibes. She probably just knows because she knows where Langston has been living lately and the location of his beach house. I'm sure he's told those he's close to before. I'm just not one of those people anymore.

I sit back down in my hut and wait.

♡

THE SUN HAS FULLY RISEN WHEN I HEAR THE ROAR OF AN ENGINE. I step out of the hut, hoping I'm not dreaming up the sound of the airplane and it's not just Langston's car or another attack.

I refuse to think about who those men are or why they were attacking Langston. It's been a while since I've heard any explosions or gunfire—not a good sign. That means Langston is no longer occupied by fighting. He could be searching for me.

I shield my eyes and look up.

A plane.

I hold my breath while the plane lands, begging it to be Siren's team.

Finally, the plane rolls to a stop, and the side door lowers. Siren sticks her head out the doorway.

I exhale. She's here. I wish she had sent a team to pick me up instead of doing it herself, but I'm happy that she's here. It means I'm getting off this island and away from Langston for good.

"Any sign of Lanston?" Siren asks as I jog toward the plane.

I shake my head.

"Good, let's get going before he figures out I'm here. I'll deal with his dumb ass later."

I smile.

Siren pulls me into a hug even though I'm covered in dried dirt, leaves, and sweat.

I wince when she hugs me too tightly, agitating the wound on the back of my shoulder.

"I'm sorry, are you okay?" Siren asks as she holds me at arm's length and looks me up and down.

"It's okay; I've been sleeping on the jungle floor. I'm just sore." I don't want her to know I'm wounded. I want her to know as little as possible.

She nods. "There is a bathroom in the back with a small shower. The water won't stay hot for long, but you can at least clean up. I'll put a change of clothes outside the bathroom door for you."

"Thanks, looking forward to getting off this island."

"I'll go talk to the pilot and get us out of here as soon as possible. Be careful showering during takeoff."

"Of course." Although, I'm not worried about getting knocked around during takeoff. I've been through hell; a possible bruise as I bump into the shower door is nothing.

I walk to the back of the plane and find a small bathroom. I don't know whose private jet this is—probably Enzo and Kai's. Siren and Zeke have money, but I don't think they own their own private jet to my knowledge. Or she chartered this.

The bathroom is just big enough for one person to fit in. It has a small sink, toilet, and corner shower. I take my clothes off, letting them fall to the floor. I don't dare look at myself in the mirror. If I did, I'm not sure whether I'd see a strong, determined woman or a frail, broken one.

Instead, I flip the water on and step under the spray. The water is cool; I don't bother letting it heat up. I don't need it to be warm. Siren also said it won't stay warm for long anyway.

I let the water wash away the mud, the dried leaves, the blood from the bug bites and scratches. It also cleanses me of my pain and anger.

I can't believe Langston kidnapped me. I can't believe he threatened my life—all for a secret treasure he doesn't even need. He has his own private island and mansion. He doesn't need money. He just wants to hurt me.

We've been through a lot as kids, but I still feel like there is something I'm missing, something Langston is hiding. His rage goes far beyond the truth as I know it.

I feel the plane rising off the ground.

My body lightens, as if a weight has been lifted from my body as we takeoff.

I don't have to worry about Langston anymore. I don't have to spend another second thinking about him.

Fuck Langston and his stupid games. Siren won't let him come near me again.

I hear a light tapping on the door. I'm sure it's just Siren telling me she put clothes outside the door for me.

I don't stop showering, though, until I've used every ounce of water. Even then, I let the water droplets drip down my hair, face, and body.

I stare at these little miracles—tiny water droplets that brought me back to life.

After several minutes, I can't hide in the bathroom anymore. I dry off and wrap a towel around me before cracking the door open to grab the clothes Siren left for me.

I look at them closely—jeans and a black T-shirt, fighting clothes. I quickly change, even though my hips don't fill out the jeans like Siren's would. My breasts fill the shirt, stretching the material to its limit.

I run my hand through my wet hair—good enough.

When I step out in the main cabin, I find Siren sitting in a chair holding Cayden.

How did I miss her baby when I entered?

I was too worried about just getting on the plane and in the shower to wash off everything that happened.

"Feel better?" Siren asks with a tense smile.

"Yes, thank you." I make my way over to the captain's chair directly across from her and sit down. Cayden is asleep in her arms, and Siren seems content to just let him sleep there.

"Is Zeke here?"

She shakes her head. "It's just me, Cayden, and the pilot."

"What if Langston had gotten to me first?"

"You don't think I'm capable of getting Langston to do whatever I say?" Her eyes twinkle, and her face lightens with the knowledge that she's able to control a man she's not even married to.

My ribs clench, and my stomach drops in jealousy. If only I could control Langston as easily. It makes me wish even more that Siren wasn't here.

I stare out the window as we fly over the ocean. I'm not even sure where we are. I'm about to ask, but Siren beats me to speaking.

"This plane can take you anywhere. So, where are we going?" Siren asks.

I furrow my brows as I glance back to her. *We* aren't going anywhere. I'll only be able to stand Siren until this plane ride is over, and then I'll need her to head back to Zeke.

"Home."

Siren blinks rapidly, trying to digest my single word in disbelief. She sits up and slowly lifts Cayden off her lap, placing him on the couch across from us. Once he's solidly asleep again, she folds her arms and stares down at me like she's about to give me an order.

"New York? You can't go back there."

"Why not? It's my home. It's where I want to be." I stand up, wanting to be on the same eye level as her. I won't let her, or anyone else, bully me into feeling weak.

"That will be the first place Langston looks!"

I glance at Cayden as Siren raises her voice, but he sleeps right through it. I guess when you grow up in our world, you can sleep through anything.

"I'm not going to run anymore. I'm not going to play his games."

"Just hide out, take a vacation somewhere until I can talk some sense into that boy."

"No. I have Waylon to worry about. I have a job. A life. I'm not going to let Langston take anything more from me."

Siren's eyes flick side to side as she looks into my eyes, hoping to find something in my eyes to persuade me. She won't find anything. My decision is already made.

She lets out a long breath, blowing some of her hair out of her eyes.

"I'll tell the pilot we are headed for New York, and then you and I are going to talk."

She heads toward the front of the plane, while I take a seat again, feeling victorious, even though I know she's not going to let this go that easily. I close my eyes. Maybe if I pretend to sleep, Siren will ignore me.

"Nuh-uh. That's not going to work. You're not asleep. Start talking," Siren says as she plops back into her chair.

My eyes flick open. "I can't."

"Why not?"

"It's a long story."

"We've got time."

I close my eyes again. "Sorry, Siren. I don't want to lie to you, and that's all I'll do if I start talking. You're better off not knowing."

♡

I TEXTED WAYLON TO MEET ME AT MY APARTMENT, BUT I NEVER got a response. I don't know if he'll be here or not. I don't know if he called the police and filed a missing person report. I don't know if he's given up on me coming back.

I get to my apartment door and realize I don't have my key. I knock, hoping Waylon is inside, so I don't have to break into my own apartment.

I hear footsteps inside, and I fidget with the hem of my black T-shirt. *Will Waylon notice that I'm not wearing my usual power dress? Will he know that something's instantly wrong? Will he ask me a dozen questions about where I've been or what I've been up to?*

What do I tell him? How do I keep him safe?

The door swings open—the moment of reckoning.

"Baby, I didn't think you were getting back from your trip for a while. I'm so happy you decided to change your plans and head home early." He grabs me by the back of my neck and kisses me in a friendly kiss. His tongue parts my lips, his hand massages my neck, and he moans softly against my lips. It's a good kiss—a grateful kiss, but not an 'I was worried you were kidnapped, murdered, or dropped off the face of the earth' kiss.

"Yep, I missed you. Thought I'd come back early."

Waylon pulls me tightly to him, until I'm pressed up against him. That's when I get a whiff of him—a musky, sweaty scent. I scan him up and down and realize he's in a T-shirt and gym shorts. He must have just worked out.

"We are going to have to celebrate later, though. How about Noda for dinner in three hours? I need to shower, and then I have a quick meeting. After that, I'm all yours." He wiggles his eyebrows suggestively.

My body melts at his proposal. I need to let off some steam, and fucking Waylon all night is just the way to do it.

Waylon notices my body's reaction. He leans in and kisses me softly on the lips. The kiss is full of promise for tonight.

I want to protest and tell him I want him now, but a knock at the door interrupts my plea.

We both groan in annoyance at whoever is at the door, who interrupted our kiss.

"I really need to shower and get to my meeting. Soon, love," Waylon says, and then he's jogging down the hallway to the bathroom.

I turn to the door, hoping it's just a delivery. If it's Siren, I'm going to kill her.

I open the door.

Langston is standing in the hallway with a heavy scowl, dark eyes, and an evil grin twisted on his face.

"I told you to come find me," he growls.

My stomach drops as he pushes his way into my apartment and

back into my world in record time. There is no getting rid of him, not unless I kill him.

"Waylon is in the shower. You can't stay."

"Good. It's time I find out the truth. If he's here, you won't be able to lie about the status of your marriage."

CHAPTER 4

LANGSTON

As I step closer to Liesel, she retreats—backing away, but not backing down. Her scowl and ridges between her eyes shoot through my body. She doesn't want me here.

Well, too bad. I don't want to be here either.

If she hadn't forced my hand, if she'd at the very least stayed on the island, then I wouldn't be invading her apartment with her supposed husband in the next room.

I kick the door closed behind me, purposefully slamming it.

"Shh," Liesel hisses.

I tilt my head. "Why? Worried dear old hubby will notice?"

"Don't make fun of Waylon."

"I'm not making fun of him. I just can't imagine you're married to that fossil."

"I am," she says without hesitation, with as much conviction as she can muster.

"Well, that's the problem—I don't believe a word you say."

She shrugs. "That's not my problem. Now get out of my house."

"We had a deal."

"No, you kidnapped me and forced me to agree to your terms. So unless you're planning on kidnapping me again, we're done here."

Oh, I plan on kidnapping her again if I need to. But I'll take my time. First, I want answers. Then I can worry about what I'm going to do with her.

"It doesn't matter if you're on the island or not. Our deal remains. You will tell me truths, and I'll give you more time to live. You tell me lies, and I'll give you less time. You're down to eleven months. I took off a month after you ran and made me come after you. Now's your chance to earn some time back."

Liesel glances down the hallway as she bites her bottom lip. The shower is still running, so we have some time before Waylon joins us.

"Did Siren rat me out?" Liesel asks.

No, she didn't. But I won't let Liesel think she has any friends on her side. Liesel needs to know that she's all alone battling me.

I'll have to deal with Siren later, though. I can't have her intervening in my plan. It's probably time I told Siren the truth. Then I wouldn't have to worry about whose side she's on. She would be firmly on mine.

"Of course. You really think you could turn one of my best friends so easily?"

Her eyes narrow, searching for the truth in my eyes. In my words. In my body language.

I don't let my anger rise beyond my gut. I don't let my voice carry my pain. I don't let my eyes widen in worry.

Liesel sighs. "Maybe not, but she freed me. She's clearly not as close to you as you think."

I chuckle and step closer to her, forcing her to step back. "You think you're free?"

"I'm in my own damn house, and as soon as Waylon gets out of the shower, he'll kick your ass if you don't leave."

"Will he?" I take another step, and her back hits the wall.

She glares as she pushes past me and heads into the kitchen. She winces when her injured shoulder brushes against mine.

I stare at her back, wanting to ask about her wound. To take a look at it and make sure it's healing properly. To remove the staples.

But that would show that I care. It would be a weak move. And I'm tired of being powerless for this woman.

I storm after her, not letting her even catch her breath or grab a knife, which I assume is the only reason she's heading into the kitchen.

I cock my head and smirk at her as she pulls a knife out of a cutting block. "Really? You think a knife is going to protect you? You're so predictable."

"No, a knife won't protect me against a monster like you. You don't play fair. And you're more skilled at killing people than anyone I've ever met. If you want me dead, you'll kill me."

"Then why even bother grabbing it? Why fight me? Why not just tell me the truth? You'll live a longer, much happier life if you just give in," I say, standing on one side of the kitchen island. She stands on the other side, using the island as a barrier between us.

"You don't deserve the truth, killer. You don't get any more parts of me."

"But I haven't even gotten to taste the best part yet." My voice is low and throaty as I speak.

I swear I hear Liesel gasp.

We may both be married, but that doesn't extinguish the fire between us. That doesn't stop the pull of attraction. No matter how much Liesel hurts me, no matter how much she betrays me, on some level, my body will always want her. I just have to remember she's poison to me. One taste and she'll eviscerate me.

"You stole a kiss against my will—you don't get more. I'll cut off your balls if you so much as touch me without permission."

There's my feisty huntress.

I laugh. "I don't have to take anything—before I'm done with you, you'll be willingly giving in to me. You'll be begging me to kiss you, to fuck you."

"I have a wonderful husband just down the hall who is more than capable of satisfying my every need. He kisses like a king and makes me come like a servant. Why would I need a schmuck like you? You wouldn't even be able to find my clit."

Her words are firm and defiant, but I notice her chest heaving up and down. She's all hot and bothered inside. I remember the explosive orgasms she had with Waylon. I remember the sounds she made, the faces. *How much of that was real and how much of that was fake?*

"Now you make me wonder if Waylon is the one who doesn't know where your clit is."

"Just like Phoenix doesn't know how to suck you off, huh?"

Her eyes glitter with jealousy. She doesn't like that I'm married to Phoenix any more than I like her marriage to Waylon. Not because I want to be married to her, but because she's mine. She doesn't get to belong to anyone else.

"I'd be happy to let you try if you think you can do better. But let me tell you, no one sucks me off like Phoenix."

Her grip on the thin knife tightens, along with the lines around her eyes and harsh frown of her lips.

"Just leave; neither of us is going to tell the truth. We aren't going to say that we lied and that we aren't married. That you don't have any freaking kids. Just go. We don't have to keep hurting each other."

I take a step toward her, expecting her step away from me, keeping the island between us.

She doesn't.

"You really think you're going to stab me if I get near?"

"You'll have to come closer to find out." She smirks and twists the knife around casually in her hand like it belongs there.

She forgets that I know the real her. She doesn't like wielding a weapon. The only time she holds a knife is when she's cutting into her food. She wouldn't even be able to flick her wrist in my direction before my reflexes would stop her without even thinking.

I take another step.

She still doesn't move.

My heart beats wildly in my chest, wanting to be near her, even though the only part of me that Liesel could actually damage is my heart. She has no idea the amount of torture she's caused me. She thinks I'm the devil. I am, but I have nothing on her.

One more step and I'm standing face to face in front of her.

Her breathing is erratic. I can't tell if she's scared or turned on.

"Are. You. Married?" I ask. If she is, then she could go after the treasure without me. I want to know for my own personal reasons. I want to know so I know how to destroy her.

"I already told you I am."

"You sure about that?" I study her for any signs that she's telling the truth or lying, but all I can focus on his her breathing in and out. Her chest is rising and falling beneath Siren's black T-shirt.

"Yes," she says sharply, expecting me to call her out.

I inch closer, just leaning into her personal space. I won't touch her without her permission or invitation, but I can do a lot without touching her. And I'm not planning on leaving until I get this single truth.

I take a deep breath, breathing in her scent—lavender and something floral. When I exhale down her neck, I watch her shiver.

I put my hands in the pockets of my jeans to keep from touching her.

Not yet.

Soon, though, I'll be able to touch her.

It won't take long to break her—to get her begging to be touched.

My eyes run down her body from head to toe. I linger over her hair —long and wavy and slightly frizzier than usual, untamed. My eyes heat over the curves of her breasts and hips and then down her slim legs to her oversized boots. She doesn't look like the Liesel I've known all my life. She's not wearing the right clothes, and her makeup isn't caked on. But somehow, standing there with that damn knife in her hand, she's never looked more incredible.

My eyes snap back up, meeting hers.

She shivers once again.

"Cold?"

"Hmm."

I shrug my jacket off and drape it over her shoulders. I let my fingers graze her arms as I pull the jacket tighter in front of her. My hands grip her hips before I even realize I'm touching her.

"Better?" I ask.

"Hmm."

I've made her speechless. Although, I'm not much better. I only got one word out.

I have to take back control. I can't let her affect me. I have to beat her at her own game.

I lick my lips.

Her mouth parts.

The air changes—she's in a daze.

"Kiss me," she says suddenly.

She's lost her mind, but she doesn't have to tell me twice.

I press my lips against hers, reveling in how incredible her soft lips feel against mine. But I'm greedy, and I want more than just the softness. I want the taste of her sweetness, the battle of her tongue with mine, the moans she makes when I make her feel alive.

This kiss is just as mind-blowing as our last kiss and so much more. This kiss isn't about chasing demons away. This kiss is about need, desire, want. It's about taking back what's mine.

I don't give a damn if Liesel is married or not. I can steal her back either way.

"Tell me to stop," I say against her lips.

"Sss..." She doesn't make it past the first letter before she's kissing me again.

I smirk against her lips, slowing her kisses. As much as I would love to lose myself in this kiss, I can't. I'm here on a mission, and I won't let earth-shattering kisses stand in my way.

"So, you're a cheater, then?" I ask as I pull her hips tightly against mine, pressing my hardness against her jeans.

"Huh?" she moans.

"You have an open marriage? Waylon doesn't mind you kissing strange men?"

"What? No."

She puts her empty hand against my chest.

"Tell me to stop," I repeat.

She breathes hard and fast, her lips devouring over mine. She rocks back and forward, letting our hips rub before falling back.

She wants this.

She wants *me*.

But something is holding her back. Is she really married? Is she just dating that asshole? Does she not care about him at all?

"Sto…" She takes a deep breath. "Stop."

"That took far too long for a married woman. Unless you don't mind being a cheater?"

"I'm not a cheater," she growls, getting her voice back.

"You're the one who asked me to kiss you." I don't back away. My hands are still on her hips, and hers are now both on my chest, still holding the knife. But she doesn't push me away. She lets me stay close.

"I. Am. Not. A. Cheater."

"Then you're not married?"

Liesel looks at me with a fierceness in her eyes. She's about to try and use the knife on me because she's pissed I won. That I got in her head and got me to kiss her.

Just like I knew she would, she throws her arms up, trying to strike me with the knife in the neck. But I catch her wrist and hold the knife suspended in the air between us.

Her face is locked on mine. She's trying to be a shell. She's trying to keep her emotions off her face, but I notice the lift of her lips in a hint of a smile before her lip quivers, and her eyes widen.

"Please," she trembles.

My eyes search hers for answers. *Why did she just flip a switch? How did she go from lust to anger to fear in three seconds?*

"Get your hands off my wife," Waylon says from behind me.

And then Liesel can't keep the smirk off her face. It flashes for only a second. Only long enough for me to notice, but not long enough for Waylon to see it.

She got the knife to frame me.

She asked me to kiss her to force me close, so that in Waylon's eyes, it looks like I'm attacking her.

I have a decision to make. *Do I let her win—go and walk out the door? Or do I fight back?*

Liesel knows that if I wanted to take down Waylon right now, I could. *Did she just sign Waylon's death sentence, all for a chance to beat me?*

"We aren't finished. I'll let you win this round, but I still want answers. And your time is running out. You have twenty-four hours to decide if you want to finish the game here or back on my island. But remember whom you are risking if you choose to finish our game here," I whisper so only she can hear.

I let go of her arm.

I half expect when I turn around for Waylon to have a gun pointed at my head. For him to be holding a bat, something.

Instead, he's standing there in a suit. His graying hair is slicked back, and there is a drop of blood on his jawline from where he cut himself shaving.

"I called the police. Get out if you don't want to spend the rest of your life in jail," Waylon says.

I shake my head. *Lawyers—they are all the same.* Cocky smart-alecks who think the police will step in and save them. They don't know that if the police showed up, they'd just look the other way as soon as I paid them off or whispered my name.

The only thing protecting Waylon right now is that I want to know who Waylon truly is to Liesel before I kill him. Whether he's truly her husband, the love of her life, or just a man she fucks because she's lonely. I'll figure it out.

I don't speak as I walk out the door like a stranger back into the night. The man isn't worth my words.

The door slams behind me. A heaviness weighs me down as I ride the elevator down.

Wife.

Waylon called Liesel his wife.

She had to have warned him before I got here to call her that, to pretend they are married. *Right?*

Liesel Dunn can't be married.

Can't. Be.

My steel heart hardens. It won't break. It won't even crack. Not for her.

Liesel may think Waylon calling her his wife is confirmation that she's married, but it's not. I want her to tell me the truth. Sure, I could look up her marriage license with the city, *but what fun is that?*

No, after her little stunt, I'm going to pull every truth I can from her, until the truth kills her.

CHAPTER 5

LIESEL

Langston walks out the door, and then it slams shut.

I stand frozen—pretending I'm in shock. I am, but not because Langston threatened my life. In fact, he offered to give me more time if I told him the truth. He gave me a chance to save my life if only I answered one question.

The only problem is that I don't know the answer because I don't know the question. I don't know what specific truth matters above all others. The one that matters beyond the secrets only I know from the ripped paper.

None of that is the reason I'm in shock.

That fucking kiss.

Waylon runs over to me and consumes me in his muscular arms, yanking me against his hard chest.

"Shh, I've got you. I've got you. I won't let that man or anyone hurt you," Waylon says.

I should feel safe with his arms around me. His thick chest is as protective as any armor. His soothing voice normally eases my tensions.

Instead, I feel rattled. My body trembles, and I feel empty.

My brain is trying to process Waylon's words. I'm trying to come up with a plan to explain Langston to Waylon. To figure out how to defeat Langston while keeping myself and Waylon safe.

But.

That.

Kiss.

I planned it, knowing that it would knock Langston off balance. It would bring him in close and help me set a trap where Waylon would find us close.

But I was the one knocked askew as soon as our lips touched. The spark at our touch took hold of every nerve ending and brain cell in my body. The entire time he was kissing me, I forgot about my plan. I forgot that Langston is the enemy.

"You're trembling. It's okay, baby. Try to take a deep breath. You're safe," Waylon says.

He doesn't realize that I'm not safe. I'm never safe.

I take a deep breath—trying to shake the sparks still shooting off my body. My adrenaline is up, which is probably why I'm shaking. I crave more kisses, more of his touch, just more.

I won. I won't let the memories of Langston take the victory from me. He doesn't get to win by taking my thoughts, my cravings, my body.

I grip onto Waylon's forearms while I lean back, looking into his eyes.

He smiles down at me sweetly. He really is a sweet, kindhearted man. He's what I need, not Langston.

"Kiss me," I whisper. I meant to speak stronger, more assertively, but I'm too shaken up. As much as I want to get rid of Langston's touch, I also want to wallow in it, no matter how much pain it will eventually bring me. I don't want to forget Langston's kiss, but I need to.

Waylon, who can never deny me, leans down and plants the softest kiss, barely brushing his lips against mine. That won't be enough to wipe Langston from my memory.

I reach up, grabbing onto his sculpted neck and parting his lips with my tongue, pushing deep inside his mouth, begging for him to kiss me with all of his passion.

Waylon takes the hint. He's so perceptive, always listening to the little clues I give him.

He pushes me back until my ass is against the counter. His hands grip my hips firmly but not in a controlling way. His thick, hard muscles push against me until I feel his cock pressing against my stomach. His tongue sweeps in my mouth, commanding my attention as it dances over mine.

I should feel that all-consuming, heart-stopping, breathless emotion. That emotion one step below love or, at the very least, deep lust.

This kiss is barely getting my heart thumping, though. My body didn't come alive. The spark didn't fan into flames. And worst of all, it didn't wipe any memory of Langston's kiss from my brain, my body, my heart.

Langston is just a good kisser. That's all it is.

There is no way a man like that kissed me while married. If he is married, he sure as hell isn't in love. You can't kiss another woman if you love your wife.

"Liesel?" Waylon asks, searching my eyes for my thoughts as he pulls away.

I shake off the memories, but that will only last for a moment at best before Langston will weasel his way back into my head. It's clear Waylon must have asked me a question, but I didn't hear it.

"Sorry, I'm still a little frazzled. What did you say?"

Waylon's hands are still on me, afraid I'll fall to pieces. He's probably right, but it's because of that damn kiss, not because I had a knife pressed against my neck.

"Can you tell me what happened before I actually call the police?" Waylon asks.

I take a deep breath as I prepare the lie. "There was a knock at the door after you went to the shower. I assumed it was a package being delivered. When I opened the door, he grabbed me and held a knife to my throat. He told me he wanted money and information about your campaign plans. And then you walked in."

"Oh, baby. I'm so sorry." Waylon pulls me to him again.

"It's okay. I'm okay now, but I think we should hire some security." Security won't stop Langston, but it might slow him down.

Waylon nods. "I agree. I'll double the amount of security we were planning. And I think we should start my campaign for governor as soon as possible. Actually being on the campaign trail will make a statement to those trying to attack us that we aren't afraid. That we have security who will protect us and throw any criminal who comes at us in jail."

"I don't think we should call the police."

"Why not?" Waylon wrinkles his forehead.

"We don't want anyone to know we were attacked. Our security team can find the man who did this without a public investigation."

His eyes roll up for a minute, and then he lets out an exacerbated breath. "You're right. It just means you can't go anywhere without security or me by your side. No more answering doors by yourself. Are you okay with that?"

I suck in a breath. *No, I'm not okay with that.* It means giving up control to someone else, relying on someone else for protection. It's what I did when I was part of Enzo's gang of minions. I vowed to never do it again.

But this isn't about keeping me safe, not really. It's about doing everything I can to protect Waylon.

"I understand."

Waylon's raised shoulders relax as he exhales.

"You have no idea how terrified I was watching that man hold a knife to your throat. I never want to be that scared again. I'd give up everything—my work, my campaign, my money, my life to never have you threatened again. I can't lose you, my love."

I put my arms around Waylon. "I can't lose you either."

He kisses the top of my head in a move that's meant to make me feel safe and loved—two things I've never been.

"I need to make some calls. You going to be okay?"

I nod. "I'm going to shower. Then you can talk to me about your plans for our security and your first campaign events."

"I'm so lucky I have you."

"Me too."

Then I walk down the hallway to the bathroom.

I close the bathroom door and take a deep breath as I slink to the floor. I close my eyes, trying to push Langston out, but he floods my head.

His hands on mine.

His body pressed against mine.

His lips...

STOP! I can't think about any of that.

Langston's body is replaced by his words in my mind. He said I have twenty-four hours to decide if I want to finish the game here or back on his island. But if I choose to finish our game here, he threatened Waylon.

I don't want to risk Waylon's life, but it's not about choosing between keeping him safe or not. Langston will hang Waylon's life over me no matter where I fight Langston.

This is about choosing between the two men. *Who do I trust? Whose side do I want to be on?*

The choice is easy—Waylon.

It has to be Waylon. I can't choose Langston.

All that's left to do is to convince my body it wants Waylon, not Langston.

I shower and get dressed.

I listen while Waylon talks to me about hiring security and starting his campaign.

Then I kiss him goodnight. I should fuck him, remind my body whom it craves.

I can't.

I'm exhausted, and my body is buzzing for another man. I need space and time. Only then will I be able to reconnect with Waylon.

"I'm here if you need me, but I need to finish some calls before I come to bed," Waylon says.

"I'm going to take a long, relaxing bath, and then I'll meet you in bed."

"You deserve to relax."

I walk to the bathroom and start filling the tub when my cell phone rings.

If it's Siren or Kai, I'm not answering. I'm pissed at Siren for ratting me out, and I don't want Kai's sympathy. If it's anyone calling about any of Waylon's plans, I'm too tired to listen.

I stare at the name. I intended to turn the phone off, to not answer.

But with one flash of his name, my heart skips, and my insides warm.

My thumb hovers over the button.

Just turn it off. Turn off the phone and enjoy your bath.

Somehow, my thumb brushes against the answer button. I bring the phone up to my ear, and I speak.

CHAPTER 6

LANGSTON

Liesel answers the phone.

I wasn't sure if she would or if I would have to sneak over in the middle of the night to drag her out of bed and force her to talk to me.

"Hello," her voice is breathy as she answers.

"Have you decided? Are we finishing this here or on the island?"

She shakes her head on my monitor screen. I'm watching her from my hotel room across the street from her building. "Really? We aren't even going to talk about the fact that I tricked you and won? How does your *wife* feel about you kissing me?"

"My wife is none of your concern," I snap back.

She turns off the tub faucet but keeps the phone near her ear.

"I have eighteen hours left to decide according to you. I won't give you an answer until then."

"But you've already decided."

She frowns but doesn't speak, which only confirms my guess.

"Are we done? I'm sure you'll find me when my twenty-four-hours are up so you can get my answer then."

"We aren't done."

"I would like to enjoy some peace and quiet, so can we hurry this along?"

"Why? Anxious to get into that bath so you can touch yourself to the memory of our kiss?" My voice is a low, deep timbre that practically vibrates through the phone and down her body.

She shivers at my words.

"You're watching me?"

"Yes," I hum.

More shivers. Her cheeks pink. Her eyes search the bathroom.

"Where did you put the camera?"

"Does it matter? Are you planning on putting on a show for me?"

"I'm planning on showing you what you will never have."

She grabs the hem of her black T-shirt, stretches it over her body, and then her breasts are staring back at me.

Fuck, I shouldn't have called her when she was headed into the bathroom. I'm not going to be able to concentrate on pulling the truth from her when her body looks like that—smooth, curvy, and welcoming.

I close my eyes when I see her start on her jeans, but they only stayed closed less than a second. Then they are glued to the screen, watching her jeans slide to the floor, followed by her panties.

She's standing naked in the bathroom with the phone still to her ear. "I hope your wife walks in and sees how hard I make you. I hope she slaps you and takes all of your money before she leaves your cheating ass."

"I don't cheat."

"So you aren't really married, then?"

A beat passes.

She smiles like she won again before she steps into the tub. Her body disappears under the water's surface while resting her head against the tub's edge.

I exhale—her spell on me breaks as she slips under the water, her body no longer as visible to me.

"We are going to continue our little game. You tell me the truth, and I give you more time to live. You tell me a lie, and I give you less time. I don't care if we are here or back on the island. The battle continues until I pull every last truth from you, or you run out of time."

She smirks, her seductive eyes glancing up, looking right at me. "What makes you think I'll answer you? I'm not your captive anymore."

"Because I'll start hurting and killing people you care about. And I'll automatically take a month off your time every time you don't answer me. Your time will run out very quickly if you don't start talking."

She closes her eyes and leans her head back on the back of the edge of the tub. "What do you want to know?"

I was expecting more of a fight. Apparently, I've knocked all the fight out of her, at least for tonight.

"Tell me the truth of how you and Waylon met."

She keeps her eyes closed, which makes it hard for me to read her expression or emotion. When she does finally speak, the tone of her voice is my only clue as to whether or not she's telling the truth. Doing this from a distance is going to be difficult.

"A blind date," she finally says.

I narrow my eyes, trying to read her.

Her eyes softly open. "We are both lawyers. We run in the same circles. We have mutual friends. Waylon was looking to settle down, for someone serious to help him build a long-lasting political career where he could make a difference. I was looking for a partner with power to keep me safe from men like you."

I laugh at her comment about Waylon being able to protect her. I don't even think Liesel believes that. Even if Waylon could keep her safe, she wouldn't want that. She wants to control her own safety.

"You really think Waylon can protect you?"

"He has power—that's as much protection as I can expect from a man."

At least that's the truth.

"What did you do on your first date?"

Liesel adjusts herself in the tub, and I get a glimmer of cleavage as she lifts slightly out of the water. My cock throbs at the sight.

"The usual drinks at a bar and then dinner at a nice Italian restaurant."

"Was it love at first sight?"

She laughs as she sinks back into the water. "He ordered my drink and meal for me. What do you think?"

"I think you castrated him right then and there." I smile just imagining what Liesel would do if a man tried to control her like that. *But then how did she end up married to the ass?*

"I ordered the most expensive champagne on the menu, and then I threw it at him."

"Not scotch?"

She scoffs. "Would I ever waste scotch?"

My smile grows to my eyes. I haven't smiled this big in a long time. It almost feels like we are kids teasing each other again—almost.

"No, I don't imagine you ever would."

Liesel smiles so openly I can see every one of her white teeth. It makes me almost not want to ask her my next question, but I need to know.

"What happened next? How did you end up on a second date if the first date ended in such a disaster?"

Her smile immediately drops from her face, almost as if it was never there in the first place. She takes her time before she speaks, the movie of those events flashing before her eyes.

She's trying to decide if she tells me the truth or if she tells me a lie.

"You lose two weeks from your life if you lie," I warn.

"I was at a bar. A man sat down next to me and started up a conversation with me," her voice is soft, and her bottom lip trembles as she speaks.

I hate this man, whoever he is instantly.

"The man seemed nice enough. He was a typical suit—nicely groomed, a banker with warm eyes. He was charming, and I was lonely and frustrated with my lack of a sex life, so we got a hotel room."

Jesus, so many awful things happen to this woman. It's like she's a magnet for evil men.

"In the elevator on the way up, I started to get some bad vibes from him. I made a phone call and said I had to go..."

Her voice trails off as she looks down at her hands like she's embarrassed.

"He was in the wrong, not you," I say, trying to make her feel better before I realize that's not my job.

The corner of her mouth lifts in gratitude for my words. "He forced me into the hotel room. Ripped my clothes. Tried to rape me."

"Tried?" My heart stops.

"The call was to Waylon. He was the only person I could think of who might be close. He was an asshole, but I didn't get the same vibes from Waylon as I did from Frank."

"He rescued you?"

"Sort of. I was able to knee him in the balls and break free."

I smile, knowing I was the one who taught her that move.

"Waylon was in the lobby by the time I made it down. He called the police. We went and got some greasy burger and fries from a dive next door. He made me laugh. He tried to protect me."

She gave Waylon a second chance. *Why could she never give me one?* I sigh.

"How did you and Phoenix meet?" Liesel asks.

"I picked her up at a club. She was the only woman, not on the dance floor, trying to get my attention."

She smiles again, happy that I'm talking.

"I fucked her in the dirty bathroom. It was the hottest sex of my life. Nine months later, she had our first child."

Liesel's smile snaps off her face, replaced by a scowl. "Liar."

I hear the hope in her voice. She doesn't truly believe I'm lying, she just hopes I am. Whether she will ever admit it or not, she wants me. It hurts her to hear that I'm with another woman, especially one related to her.

I don't care if she believes me or not. What I care about is figuring out if she's lying. I don't think she is, but I also don't think she's telling the full truth.

"Do you trust Waylon?"

"Not going to ask if I love him?"

"I don't care if you love him or not," I lie. "I care if you trust him."

"He's my husband."

"That's not an answer."

"I've already answered my question for tonight," she says, dodging the question.

Interesting.

"Last chance to tell me why, Liesel. I'm done asking. This is your last chance to save your life. Just give me one good reason for what you did and this can all be over. I'll leave you alone, if that's what you want. You'll never hear from me or see me again. Just tell me why," I say.

I'm so completely desperate. I need this answer more than I need anything else. I would trade all of her truths for this one single bit of information. I'll give her up; I just need to know why. I need to know why she did the cruelest thing that anyone in our group has ever done. We all work for a criminal organization; we've done some fucked up shit, but nothing like what Liesel did.

"Why?" I repeat.

She blinks; it's the only clue I have that she even heard me. She looks right at me, finding the camera. "I have no clue what you are talking about. Maybe if you'd ask me an actual question, I would answer you."

I run my hand through my hair in frustration. I need to know, but her refusing means I get to keep her. I get to kill her for her sins once I get all my answers. And I still plan on getting this answer from her, no matter how long it takes.

"Ten months," I say, letting her know how much time she has left, and then I end the call.

CHAPTER 7

LIESEL

I should be listening to Waylon's speech, but all I can think about are Langston's words last night.

I've done a lot of horrible things in my life, but I have no clue which specific monstrous thing I did that Langston wants me to explain.

"With my beautiful, intelligent Liesel by my side, we will win the race for governor!" Waylon finishes his speech.

I smile brightly as he lifts my hand up, doing my part. I didn't have a speech to give today, but I will at future events.

I'm glad we've started the campaign in earnest. Waylon thinks it will stop us from being attacked with the amount of visible security he hired, but it will only slow Langston's kidnapping attempts.

Hand in hand we walk off stage, waving to the crowd and smiling so wide that my cheeks begin to hurt.

As soon as we are off stage, Waylon is swarmed by his team of people.

"I need you to look over the prenup and sign it ASAP," Nolan, his campaign manager, says to me as he thrusts some papers into my hands.

I sigh but take the papers.

Nolan is closer to my age than Waylon's. I have never seen the man not in a suit. His blonde hair swooshes over his head in a perfect wave, and his blue eyes pop with brilliance.

I haven't decided yet if I trust him or not.

"I already told you, the prenup isn't the problem," I say as I make a show of signing the damn prenup.

"You should have a big, extravagant wedding. It will bring in lots of donors and make a big splash."

"We've always discussed having a small court wedding and not making a big fuss. That way, we can show that Waylon cares about the important things. Downplay how much money he has and show that he works for the people." Also, if we have a big, splashy wedding, there is no way for me to hide it from Langston.

"Just make sure you're free three weekends from now." Nolan walks away in a huff.

I flip his back off.

I'm tired of men running my life. Waylon and I will decide when and where and how we have a wedding.

Waylon is busy talking with Nolan. I glance at the clock on my phone as I yawn. I didn't get any sleep last night.

I need some caffeine to wake me up.

I search for cafes on my phone and see a coffee shop across the street.

"Maxwell, I'm headed over to get a cup of coffee while they finish up here. You coming?" I say to the brute man in an all-black outfit. This man has nothing on Zeke, who is basically a giant, so a man like Maxwell doesn't intimidate me.

"Yes, Mrs. Brown. Wherever you go, I go."

"It's Ms. Dunn."

Maxwell frowns as he walks next to me out of the event hall.

"I'm sorry, Ms. Dunn. Nolan told me to start calling you Mrs. Brown so I wouldn't slip up when you get married, since it's happening so quickly. He said I might as well start calling you Mrs. Brown."

"I won't be changing my name even after we're married, so please call me Ms. Dunn. Or better yet, Liesel."

Maxwell stops in his tracks. "Do Mr. Brown and Nolan know about your plans? I don't think you keeping your own name will help the campaign."

"Don't worry about the campaign, Maxwell. Just worry about keeping me safe. As long as you do that, Waylon and Nolan won't have anything to complain about."

I jog across the street rather than wait at the crosswalk, forcing Maxwell to choose between almost getting hit by traffic or waiting on the sidewalk. It's a test.

He passes.

He puts his hand on the hood of a car slamming on its breaks to avoid hitting us.

I open the door to the coffee shop, and Maxwell grabs it to hold it open for me.

"No more running into danger. If I'm going to protect you, I need you to tell me your plans. I don't need you to make my job any harder than it already is."

I smirk. "That was a test. I don't usually run into danger."

His shoulders relax.

"But danger does usually find me."

And then I walk to the counter.

"Can I get a large coffee, black?"

The woman smiles at me. "That will be $3."

I hand her my credit card from my sleek white purse that pops against my navy pencil skirt and jacket.

She swipes the card a few times. "I'm sorry, but your card keeps getting declined. Do you have another one?"

I frown as I pull out another card and hand it to her. I have a sinking feeling in my stomach.

"I'm sorry, this one isn't working either."

I take the card back. I have two more cards we could try, but I suspect the same thing will happen. A line has formed behind us, and I don't have any cash.

I look to Maxwell behind me, who pulls out a ten-dollar bill and hands it to the barista.

"Keep the change," he tells her.

I walk to the other counter to wait for my drink.

"Something wrong with your card? I can tell Nolan to have the credit card company to send you a new one."

"No, that's okay. I can call myself."

Maxwell nods.

"Mind taking me to the bank?" I ask, suspecting this might be more than just a credit card issue.

"Of course."

$0.00

That's what my bank account reads.

Zero.

I haven't had an empty bank account since high school. My credit cards all have a $0 credit limit too.

I had millions saved. Millions I earned by starting my own law firm, by winning lawsuit after lawsuit.

I struggled my way through poverty, became friends with the richest boy in all of Miami, studied my ass off in college, and fought through a male-dominated world until I made my way to the top. I did all of that while wrestling with a dark past that haunts my every waking moment. I did all of that with unbearable pain. I did all of that after starting over and moving my entire life to New York.

I earned every cent, and now it's all gone.

I don't have to do any investigating to know who stole my money —Langston.

Waylon has no need for my money. I just signed the prenup. He has no right to my money any more than I have a right to his. The only money of his I can access are campaign reimbursements. We don't even plan on sharing a residence once we are married. I'll keep my apartment, and he'll keep his.

Now, I have no idea how I'm going to pay for my apartment. I can't even afford a coffee, let alone the thousands of dollars in monthly rent for my apartment.

Maxwell drives me back to my apartment as I think through my options. I refuse to rely on a man. I refuse to put myself in more debt.

I won't ask Waylon for help financially. I don't even know how I'd explain to him what happened to my money in the first place.

"You okay?" Maxwell asks, raising an eyebrow in the rearview mirror as he drives.

"It was just a mixup at the bank. They recognized some fraudulent charges on my credit cards, so they canceled them. It's all sorted out now. I'm just tired."

Maxwell nods.

"Please don't mention any of this to Waylon. I don't want to worry him with something so little when he has so much going on."

I'm not sure who Maxwell is loyal to—me or Waylon. Technically, Waylon pays his salary, but I'm the one who gives Maxwell orders. Waylon made sure that Maxwell knew his job is to protect me and follow my orders no matter what. It will be an interesting test of his loyalty.

"Of course, Liesel."

He stops the car outside my building and then steps out, opening the door for me after handing the valet the keys.

I don't really need him to walk me to my door, but he won't leave me alone until I'm safely inside my apartment. I let him walk with me up into my building and up the elevator.

Once we reach my door, I expect him to come inside and search the apartment before I enter. That's what Langston would do.

"Do you need anything else, Liesel?" Maxwell stands to the side of the door as I insert the key.

I smile. "I'm good. Thanks, Max."

He grins at the nickname. "I'll be in the apartment down the hallway monitoring your door. If you need anything, just text. Otherwise, have a good night."

I walk inside and shut and lock the door behind me.

Maxwell is sweet enough. He's a decent bodyguard who I think I can trust, but he's no match for Langston or anyone who works for the Black empire.

It's an illusion of safety.

Maxwell said that he'd be monitoring the hallway, which should make it tough for me to leave without him noticing.

But he isn't the only one watching me.

I walk into the apartment, making it seem like I'm going to bed. I pull out my phone and do a quick search of surrounding hotels until I find the one Langston is staying at. It's the most expensive and closest. I know without a shadow of a doubt that he's there.

"I assume you draining my money was because you wanted to talk to me and calling me on the phone wouldn't work."

I stare up at the camera in my bedroom, talking directly to Langston.

"Meet me in the hotel bar in fifteen minutes."

I walk into the bathroom to change out of the professional-looking jacket and skirt and into something that will work to my advantage. I take my time changing into a tight black dress with lace at the hem and the neckline. I apply a dark line of eyeliner, sweep a darker shade of eyeshadow across my lids, and then pull a scarlet red lipstick out to paint my lips.

I strut out of the bathroom and fluff my hair as my eyes meet the corner of the bedroom again.

"Make me disappear," I whisper. Then I walk out of my apartment, knowing Langston will ensure that Maxwell thinks I'm still safely inside my apartment.

LANGSTON

If looks could kill, I'd be dead right now.

Liesel struts into the hotel bar exactly fifteen minutes after speaking at me via the security camera in her apartment.

Her dress screams sex. It's black with lace and fits her like a second layer of skin. Her eyes are a darker shade than she usually wears, making her irises pop. Her red lipstick taunts me. As much as I want her lips pressed against mine, or better yet wrapped around my cock, that won't be happening. Liesel is far too pissed to let me touch her.

Even though I'm bigger, stronger, more skilled—the look in her eyes lets me know that right now, she'd win in a fight. I have to tread carefully with her.

She walks straight to the bar and sits down in the barstool next to me, her eyes never leaving mine.

"You found me. I'm impressed. I wasn't sure you still had it in you, huntress."

She growls. "I've always been the better hunter. I know you know I found you that day in your hotel room. You were hiding in the damn ceiling. The only reason I didn't climb up there and yank you out was that I came up with a better plan."

"You're welcome," I say when she finishes ranting.

She turns to face me with red eyes and flushed cheeks. "You're welcome? Are you serious? You have ruined my life more times than I can count."

I grin. *Good, I need to ruin every aspect of her life. I need every tiny thing of hers I can get my hands on before I eventually kill her. I need that to live with what she did.*

"You're welcome that I ensured Maxwell didn't see you leave. You don't have to worry about what to tell him."

She flags down the bartender with her finger. "What can I get you?" the bartender with a trimmed gray beard and piercing blue eyes asks.

"Your most expensive scotch, and put it on his tab."

He nods at her with a smile and then goes to make her drink.

She ordered the exact same thing I already ordered myself.

One minute later, he slides two glasses of scotch neat in front of us.

"Thank you," Liesel smiles at him as she takes her drink, purposefully letting her hand slide against his.

He winks back, and I suspect he'll leave his number with her by the end of the night.

"So, you like the older types?" I ask.

Liesel rolls her eyes and takes a drink. "I didn't come here so we can talk about the kind of men I find attractive. I came here to tell you to stop stealing from me." Her voice drops in revenge and pent up frustration. Her fingers tighten around the glass as her rage with me consumes her.

"Did I steal something?" I lean back in my chair, keeping my eyes on hers instead of letting myself explore every inch of her body. I have to have discipline. I have to focus on my mission.

"Don't play dumb. You stole every penny I had."

I purse my lips. "Oh, right. I did do that. But I wouldn't call it stealing."

"What would you call it?"

"I'd call it taking what I'm owed."

"You're a self-serving demon. What gives you the right to take anything from me?"

You have no idea just how much of a right I have to that money, huntress.

"You seemed to lack motivation. Taking days, months, years of your life from you wasn't working, so I took the one thing that every human responds to—money."

"You think by taking my money, I'll be forced to tell you the truth? I think you've forgotten everything I've gone through. How poor I used to be. How much of a survivor I am. I built everything I have from nothing, and I can do it again."

"Or you can marry that rich fiancé of yours."

"Husband," she says firmly.

I pull out my phone and open my browser to the announcement before sliding the phone on the oak counter in front of her.

"Liar," I whisper, cutting through the noisy bar with the single word.

Liesel freezes as she realizes she's caught in a lie.

"That little liar," she says.

"That would be you."

She slides the phone back across the bar, her frustration apparent.

My reflexes kick in, and I catch my phone before it slides off the bar.

She's glaring at the phone, not at me. I'm completely lost.

"Who's the liar?" I ask.

"No one."

"The correct answer is you—you're the liar."

"Fine, I lied, but so did you."

"I'm not the one caught in a lie. And I'm not the one who has to tell the truth in order to live—that would be you."

"Just kill me and get it over with. I'm tired of your damn games. Nothing you do will make me tell you the truth. I will go to my grave hiding my half of the letter."

"Well, you have six months left to decide."

"Six months? You took off four months for one little lie?"

"One big lie."

She downs the rest of her drink, and that's when I know that I'm getting to her. It bothers her that I'm willing to kill her.

"Whatever," she says. She pulls her own phone out and starts scrolling through news articles about her engagement announcement in frustration. It's then that I realize she hadn't agreed to the announcement. Waylon did this without her consent.

I suspected all along that Waylon isn't a good person. There is something he's hiding. I don't know what it is, but I'll figure it out long before Liesel does. I may want her dead, but I want to be the one to inflict pain. I don't want Waylon to beat me to it.

"I wouldn't trust Waylon if I were you."

"I trust him more than I trust you."

"He didn't even have your agreement before announcing your engagement. Sounds pretty untrustworthy to me."

"At least he hasn't threatened to kill me. He doesn't try to control me, unlike you."

I lean in close, getting a whiff of her sweet perfume. It's intoxicating, but I won't let it affect me.

"But does he love you?"

Her eyes narrow, her pulse races, her body stills. "He loves me more than you will ever love anyone."

"Maybe so, but I wouldn't call that love. He's just as controlling as I am. He announced your wedding without you. He made you sign a prenup. And you can't even tell him about me. It doesn't sound like true love to me."

"The announcement wasn't him—it was Nolan, his campaign manager. I had just as much money to lose as him. I don't want a man to take care of me. I want to take care of my own damn self. And not telling Waylon about you is to protect him, not because I can't.

"Waylon and I may not be head over heels in love, but our union will outlive the best marriages because we know what we are getting into. Our marriage doesn't rely on falling in and out of love. Our marriage relies on mutual respect and understanding."

I chuckle. "You don't even know who Waylon is."

Now it's her turn to lean toward me.

I hold still and try not to breathe, so I don't inhale her scent again. I can't help myself anymore, though, so I take a deep, unsettling breath.

"I know exactly who Waylon is. Just like I know who you are. I'll take my chances with Waylon."

"You don't have a clue who I am anymore. You haven't cared about my life in years."

"I know you. You're a liar, just like me."

I grin and feel her eyes on my dimples that drive her mad. "You don't have any proof of my lies, do you? You have no idea if I'm married with kids or not."

She smirks and moves her hand to mine, until she's stroking the inside of my wrist. Her eyes tilt down to my crotch.

"I don't know if you are legally married or not. I don't know if you've sired a string of bastards that are genetically related to you. What I do know is that you want me. One touch and your cock is as hard as steel. One kiss and I'm all you can think about. It doesn't matter if you're lying or not—you want me."

I remove my hand from her grasp. "I want you dead."

Her eyes dart back and forth. "I'm pretty sure that's a lie too."

"Pretty sure? That's a weak statement to bet your life on."

She stands. "My entire life has been a series of bets on my life. Somehow I've survived them all. I can survive you."

"Maybe. But right now, you have a lot less money to fight me with unless you plan on asking Waylon for help."

"I won't be asking any man for help. I've built a small empire before. My only mistake was not ensuring it was better guarded. I won't let that happen again."

"Tomorrow, I want answers. Real answers, not lies, or I'll steal more from you until you have nothing left."

She whips her hair over her shoulder. "I guess I'll just have to steal right back from you. I hope you aren't lying. I hope you are really married with kids. Because I will destroy them all. If you have a heart to break, I'll shatter it. This is war, killer."

She pauses. "And unlike you, I won't wait six months to kill you. The first chance I get, you're a dead man."

I smile. "You can't kill me, and you don't have any money to hire someone skilled enough to lay a finger on me."

Her smile is bigger than mine, which scares me. "I'll have more money than you can imagine soon enough."

With those parting words, she leaves.

Not five seconds after she leaves, I see a man I didn't expect to see here—Maxwell.

I frown; maybe he's more skilled than I thought.

CHAPTER 9

LIESEL

I have a plan.

Langston declared war. He has no idea why I'm with Waylon. He has no clue about all of the struggles I've been through to get the money he so easily stole from my bank account. He has no idea what I will do to continue to survive.

Six months—that was the death sentence Langston gave me. I don't give a damn about the time. Not anymore. But I do care about finding the truth.

Langston just sparked a fire in me.

This is war.

That was his goal in taking all of my money. He wanted to make me desperate. He wanted to make me beg him or Waylon for help. Dependent—that's the one thing I vowed I'd never be again. I'll do anything to protect myself before letting a man take care of me again.

Now, I want the truth, too. I want every damn secret Langston is keeping from me, and I want to use every single word against him. I want to drown him in his lies. I want to tear apart his family, his life.

I want everything from him.

But most of all—I want to know why Langston hates me. Why he started this war. *Why?*

I'm missing a crucial piece of the puzzle, and I'm tired of being left in the dark.

I'm a powerful woman. All the shit I've been through has made me invincible to pain. I no longer have fear. I no longer cry. That makes me stronger than Langston's weak ass.

He still cries. He can still feel pain. I'm stronger than him.

I have a plan.

First, I need an unlimited source of money.

Then, I'll lay my trap.

I know exactly where I'm getting the money. Thank god I signed the prenup already.

"Good morning," Waylon says as he enters my kitchen in his suit, already dressed to head into the office.

"Good morning," I say as I hold my cup of coffee and stand at the counter.

Waylon comes over and kisses me softly on the cheek. Then he heads to the coffee pot and pours himself a cup in a travel mug.

"What do you have planned for today? Headed into the office?" he asks as he secures his coffee lid.

"No, the office is running smoothly, but I thought I'd get away for the weekend."

Waylon freezes. He knows what that's code for. We have an agreement, he and I. I have needs he can't satisfy and vice versa.

He can fuck whoever he wants. I can do whatever I want. We live separate lives when we need to. Our future marriage is about mutual gain. It's about helping each other with our careers, our image, our lives. And it's about having a steady fuck in each other's bed. It's not real love, but it works for us. It's a modern relationship that doesn't hide the fact that one single person can't possibly fulfill every single one of our needs.

It's been a while since I tested the arrangement, though. Before, it was just a verbal agreement. Now that we are getting married—it's a legal contract in our prenup.

"You'll take Maxwell with you. That isn't an option."

I nod. "I agreed to security. You should have the guys over this weekend to keep you company while I'm away." That's my way of saying he should invite a whore over to fuck since I won't be here.

Waylon walks over to me and tucks a strand of hair behind my ear. "Now that I'm running for governor, I shouldn't be seen doing such things."

His eyes bore into mine, letting me know that if I get caught, there will be consequences.

"Understood." I nod back.

"You have to tell Nolan, though." He steps back, leaning against the counter across from me.

"No way, you hired him. I'm not telling Nolan."

"He's my campaign manager. He needs to know your whereabouts in order to protect the campaign from any misunderstandings that may happen."

I glare at Waylon. "I signed an agreement with you. There is nothing in it that says I have to be the one to arrange things with your employee. You deal with him."

Waylon grins. "There is the woman I love. You know how much I enjoy your fiery spirit."

"I'll see you Monday. Take me out to dinner before the campaign event on Tuesday."

"I have the perfect place."

We exchange words back and forth with our eyes. Promises. Threats. Arrangements.

Our entire conversation is in code. Langston won't know what we are talking about. And he definitely won't know what we aren't saying with our eyes and bodies.

But we know.

I nod.

Then, Waylon comes over and kisses me on my forehead. "I look forward to our dinner."

I swallow hard, before forcing my body to breathe.

I'm doing this to keep control, to earn unlimited amounts of money. Waylon may not be perfect, but he's not the devil. That label belongs to Langston.

There is a knock at the door. Waylon heads to the door and answers it.

"Come in, Maxwell. Liesel is almost ready. It seems you will be headed on a nice weekend trip."

"Yes, sir."

"And let me remind you if anything happens to Liesel or if her identity gets out, it will be you whom I take my wrath out on."

"Understood, Mr. Brown."

Waylon looks back and winks at me before he heads out to work.

"Where are we going?" Maxwell asks me as he enters my kitchen.

"Straight to hell."

♡

I PULL MY SILVER MASK DOWN OVER MY FACE AS MAXWELL PARKS the car in front of Pier 40 at Hudson River Park.

"You sure about this, Liesel?" Maxwell asks with uncertainty in his voice.

I take a deep breath as I stare at the yacht tied to the pier. I hate the damn ocean. It reminds me too much of my past. Langston will always have the advantage on the water, but this weekend is about earning back power. And the only way to truly have power is with money. Once I have money, I'll be back on equal footing with Langston.

"Yes," I answer, stepping out of the car.

Maxwell steps out as well with his own mask on. He's in a tux, and a black mask covers his sculpted face, but it doesn't make him any less intimidating. He extends his arm to me, so we look like a couple as we walk up the ramp to the yacht.

I'm wearing a long dark wig to cover my blonde. That, combined with the mask and my bare ring finger, will mean no one will have a clue who I am here. That is unless Langston decides to make an appearance. I could wear a full prosthetic, don a wig, disguise my voice, and he'd still know it was me. Our connection is too intense for him to not recognize when I'm in the same city, let alone the same yacht as him.

"Nervous?" Maxwell asks as we walk up the ramp.

I nod. I'm nervous, but not for the reasons Maxwell thinks. I'm not nervous about what I plan on doing tonight or about getting caught. I'm nervous to see Langston tonight and what that could possibly mean.

"Don't be. My only job is to protect you and your identity. I'll keep you safe. You don't have to worry about that. I won't let any man hurt you or even lay a finger on you unless you want them to."

"Thank you," I say with a weak smile. I truly think Maxwell might be the only good person in all of this, but he's no match for Langston. If Langston wants to hurt me, Maxwell won't be able to stop him.

"I could protect you better if you told me your plan," Maxwell says.

My smile drops. "Sorry, Max, but I have to keep my intentions to myself."

"But Mr. Brown knows?"

My eyes cut to Maxwell as we reach the top of the ramp.

"Miss...?" A man on the yacht with a tablet asks as I approach.

"Ms. Juliane White," I say, giving a fake name.

"It's a pleasure to meet you, Ms. White. And you are?" The man turns to Maxwell.

"Mr. Maxwell," he gives me a confused glance out of the corner of his eye but goes with the flow. He doesn't know what tonight is about or what kind of yacht we just boarded. He doesn't know that he's going to have to earn his keep this weekend when some of the most powerful and dangerous men on the planet will all be gathered on this yacht.

The man nods at me. "I'll escort you to your rooms. Play starts at midnight."

I bat my eyelashes at him. "I can't wait."

The man leads me and Maxwell to two adjoining rooms, complete with a balcony and jacuzzi tub.

"You'll find everything you need inside. If not, dial one on the phone, and anything you need will be provided. The yacht leaves in two hours. As I said, play starts at midnight." Then the gentleman, who never gave us a name, leaves.

Maxwell stands frozen with his hands in his pocket, staring at me in disbelief.

"Liesel, what the heck have you gotten us into?"

I remove my mask, knowing that it will be one of the few times this weekend that I can. "Not us—me."

"I'm on the damn ship, same as you. You just gave a fake name while boarding a ship without any luggage for a weekend. What the hell is going on?"

"I pay you to follow orders, Max, not to question my decisions."

"Liesel, I'm speaking as a friend. What is going on?"

"Something was stolen from me. I'm just ensuring I get it back and that nothing else is ever stolen from me again."

CHAPTER 10

LANGSTON

I stand on the pier, looking up at the giant yacht. Never have I been so hesitant to set foot on a boat.

Liesel came here because she needs money. Apparently, she thinks boarding this boat will help, but I've never found less information about an organization before stepping foot on their yacht than this one.

I scoured the internet but found nothing on this group. I don't even know who owns this boat, or who runs whatever excursion we are about to embark on.

My guess is this is an exclusive poker tournament or betting ring. Liesel thinks this is the fastest way to earn a lot of money since she won't ask her fiancé for money.

Their conversation the other morning was quite intriguing. So much unspoken in between them. I don't understand why they are together—*love, lust, power? What draws them together?* It can't be love. At least from Liesel's side, the woman is incapable of the emotion.

"You sure about this, boss?" Enzo asks, standing next to me in a tux and black mask—the only requirements listed to board the yacht.

"I'm not the boss. That would be your wife," I say.

Enzo shakes his head with his hands in his pockets. "We've all taken turns being in charge. This is your mission—we are here to support you. That means you're the boss, and you have to take responsibility for your actions and any lives lost."

I swallow down the acid creeping up in my throat. Almost everyone I love is standing behind me, waiting to get on this yacht if I give the order.

Kai, Enzo, Zeke, Siren, and Beckett. The only one missing is Nora, but she's watching the kids. Phoenix also stayed home to watch our kids. If I send us into a trap, five little kids could lose their parents. Nora could lose the man she loves. Phoenix could lose me.

It's a big decision to make when I don't have all the facts, but we know yachts more than we know anything. Once on board, we'll hack into the security system and figure out just what the hell is going on. And we have a crew nearby on one of our own yachts prepared to follow this one. We'll be safe—safe as we can be, anyway.

"I'm sure," I say and step forward onto the boat's boarding ramp. I hear footsteps behind me, and I don't have to glance back to know that my entire team is following me. I'm not used to being the leader or worrying about anyone except myself, but I vow to keep every one of them safe. No one gets hurt on my watch.

"Name?" a man at the top of the ramp with an iPad asks.

I could give a fake name, but my name, and the name of everyone behind me, is feared. Our names help to protect us. We won't hide.

"Langston Pearce," I say.

The man nods and gestures to a woman beside him. "Kala will see you to your room."

I start to follow the woman as the man asks Enzo his name. She leads me downstairs and through multiple hallways.

"Here is your room for this evening," the woman finally says, opening the door to a room for me before handing me the keycard.

I step inside the plain room and examine its simple bed and connected bathroom.

"Play starts at midnight," the woman says, and then she shuts the door without explaining anything else.

Play? I guess this is some type of high roller poker tournament.

I scan the room, looking for any clues. After going through every cabinet and drawer, I find nothing.

I pick up the phone.

"Do you need anything delivered to your room, Mr. Pearce? Food? Drink?" a man starts speaking as I pick it up.

"No, I'm good."

I hang up.

Hmmm.

I pull out my phone to try and hack into their system. We weren't allowed any bags, so there was no real way to sneak a laptop onto the yacht.

After scanning the room, the hallway, and the deck outside, I realize there is no system to hack into. There are no security cameras.

Strange.

I suspect there are plenty of rich people here that will need to feel protected and safe. *Why are there no cameras?*

Three quick knocks at the door.

I walk over and open it. Enzo spills into my small bedroom, followed by everyone else—Kai, Zeke, Siren, and Beckett.

"There are no cameras, are there?" Enzo asks.

"No, only the control systems in the wheelhouse to drive the yacht. There is nothing else to hack," I answer.

"So, what's the plan?" Kai asks, stepping in front of the sliding glass door to look out at the night sky.

"We keep Liesel from getting money. She's desperate. I need her that way to end this."

Kai and Siren exchange glances.

Beckett nods in agreement—I've always liked him.

Zeke shows no emotion. He's always ready to do what I ask; no questions asked—even after everything that has happened between us.

Enzo studies Siren, like he's begging her to be the voice of reason.

"No kidnapping or hurting her to get what you want. There are five of us. We can stop her from getting money or harming us without hurting her. Liesel's on our side. We just have to remind her of that," Siren says, her look threatening death if I disobey her.

Siren's wrong—Liesel isn't on our side. I don't think she was ever on anyone's side except her own.

"Promise me, no hurting or kidnapping Liesel. We've all betrayed this family at one point or another to protect ourselves or someone we love. That's all Liesel is doing. Just remind her that we all love her and want her to join us again," Siren continues as she walks to me.

I frown as she puts her hands on either side of my face. "Promise me."

There is no getting around this. Siren won't stop until I promise. And she knows I won't break a promise—not with her. I won't risk my relationship with her. Our connection is too strong. I need Siren in my life.

"I promise I won't kidnap or hurt Liesel unless she's trying to hurt or kill one of us. I will protect everyone in this room above everything. But if Liesel tries to hurt one of you, I will stop her with whatever means necessary."

"Liesel won't try to hurt us," Siren says.

Everyone else in the room exchanges glances. Liesel has already hurt the rest of us. Siren just hasn't felt the same level of pain because she knows Liesel the least.

"She might," Kai says.

Siren's head whips to her. "You're not helping."

"I'm just being honest. Liesel is always welcome in this group, but only if she chooses to put our family first. She's not doing that right now. We don't know what she's gotten into. We don't know how dangerous she is," Kai answers.

I pull Siren to me, holding her tight against my chest to try and reassure her. "I promise I won't hurt her unless I have to."

She nods, and a soft sigh escapes her lips.

I'll do my best to keep my promise to her, at least while we are on this yacht. But someday, I'll be forced to break my promise. There is no way this ends without Liesel dead. She's done too much.

♡

AT MIDNIGHT, WE ALL LEAVE MY ROOM AND HEAD TO THE CENTER of the yacht. We are all wearing tuxes, fancy dresses, and masks to cover our faces. Although, we don't really need to hide who we are.

We are greeted by one of the employees as we walk down the hallway.

"If you could head to the top deck, you will be given more instructions from there," a man in a sharp suit says.

Wordlessly, we climb to the top deck, where several people are already gathered. There is a small bar set up with drinks. We all walk over to get one to hold in our hands, not because any of us will be partaking. We need to be completely clear-headed for whatever we have gotten ourselves into.

"Where is she?" Zeke asks, holding a whiskey drink in his hand as he scans the deck. Everyone is dressed like this is the most extravagant party they have ever attended. And everyone has a mask on. Even so, I can spot some politicians, athletes, and models in the crowd.

"I don't see her yet," I answer.

"She better be here. I don't know what we've gotten ourselves into, but I don't like it," Zeke says.

"She will be," I say.

I tracked her phone here. She's here.

I take a sip of my scotch. I guess I'm going to be needing a bit of alcohol to get through tonight after all.

"Jesus," Zeke mumbles under his breath.

I turn to follow his gaze as chills creep up on my arms.

At first, all I see is a glimmer as her dress sparkles under the moonlight. Then my entire body adapts to Liesel being in the same space as me. She dominates everything—my attention, my breath, my heartbeat, it's all hers.

I've never seen a more sexy woman. Liesel may not care for makeup and dresses and all the foo-fooey things some girls like, but damn does she know how to wear it well. The dress is the perfect mix of skin, silk, and lace. I can see the outline of her body through the thin material—her nipples are already hard.

I finally force my eyes off her body to her face. She's wearing a glittery mask, like everyone else here. The shine of the mask makes it difficult to get a good glimpse of her eyes. That, combined with the jet black wig she's wearing, would make her almost unrecognizable to anyone else who knows her.

But she could be wearing a head to toe Mickey Mouse costume and I'd still know it was her underneath. She can't hide from me.

"Wait, I thought Kai was wearing a green dress, and what is she doing with that guy?" Zeke asks.

I snort. "That's not Kai, that's Liesel."

"Wow, she looks deadly," Zeke says.

My lips thin. "You have no idea."

I turn my attention to the man at her side—Maxwell. He's dressed like us in a sharp suit that shows off how many muscles he has beneath his jacket, and a plain black mask covers half his face. His jaw is tight, his lips showing no emotion, and his eyes scanning everyone in the room. He seems as unsettled as I feel.

It hits me all at once that he doesn't know why we're here any more than I do. I know it's about Liesel getting money to fight me, but I don't know this game we will be playing.

"Ladies and gentlemen, thank you all for coming," a man in a suit says. He's the only one not wearing a mask as he makes his way to the center of the deck.

The stars are sparkling overhead, making it feel like this is meant to be a romantic night with some rich fuckers. But I have a feeling that's part of the lure, to get us to relax and let our guard down before this game starts.

"Does everyone have a drink?" he asks, scanning the crowd of people.

Most people are nodding their heads, yes. For the few that don't have drinks, bartenders are quickly bringing around glasses to fill their hands.

Once the man in the center is assured that everyone has a drink, he continues.

"My name is Mr. Reyes. I'm here to oversee this weekend's games. I recognize a couple of familiar faces, but for the majority of you, this is your first time. I want to assure you that you will be well taken care of for as long as your stay lasts."

Enzo gives me a tight glare as we both try to figure out what's happening.

"The game is simple. The last one remaining wins the twenty million-dollar prize."

Fuck—Liesel could do a lot with twenty million. No wonder we are here. She would instantly regain everything I took from her in one weekend if she won.

"As you know, there is no buy-in. No money is required to enter. The winnings are generously provided by the ship's owner. The owner enjoys watching people get pushed to their limits. The owner and a very select group of people are the only ones watching the games along with the game's remaining participants."

So someone is watching, which means there are cameras. I just need to find them.

"What is the game exactly? I'm sure you're all eager to know."

Yes, spill, old man.

"The game is simple. Each round, you will be drawing names to be paired with. Sometimes it will be a one on one competition. Other rounds might be a group of four competing. The goal is to push your competitor to their sexual limits until they withdraw from the competition."

Fuck.

My eyes find Liesel. She's standing casually in the same spot she was before. Her heart isn't thumping wildly, her lips are relaxed, and she takes a quick sip of champagne.

I frown. She knew exactly what she was walking into and did it anyway. These are sex games. Liesel can't give up control when it comes to sex, so I don't know how she expects to win.

"The game lasts two days. Most of you won't make it past tonight's rounds. You can withdraw at any time for any reason. But if you withdraw tonight, you will be leaving us. You will not get to stay to watch tomorrow's events. If you make it to tomorrow, even if you withdraw, you can remain and watch the final rounds if you so choose."

Everyone is eerily silent as Mr. Reyes speaks. There are a few people who seem unfazed—the ones who have been here before. Others are licking their lips in anticipation of what is about to happen.

And still, others are jittery, shifting their weight in the spot where they stand or tapping their fingers or heels to try and get the nervous energy out.

I don't have to glance at my family to know that they will all end up withdrawing by the end of the night unless they draw the names of their spouses. None of them are prudes, but I can't imagine Enzo sitting by watching Kai getting fucked by some stranger here. Nor Zeke watching Siren. Nora may not be here, but I suspect Beckett won't push things too far if he wants a chance with her. That means it'll be up to me to remain in the game.

"What about security?" Maxwell asks.

"I assure you this yacht is completely secure, and my team is here to ensure no one gets hurt who doesn't want to. You will be pushed to your limits if you remain in the game, but you will have a safe word to use at any time that will alert my team to get you out of here quickly and safely.

"Everyone here must participate in the game or go home. We don't allow bystanders to just watch or protect. If you feel that you need to remain to protect someone in the game, then you must participate and advance."

Maxwell frowns and almost kills the guy with one look.

I feel his pain. Maxwell won't last the night, but I will. Tomorrow he won't be here to protect Liesel.

"If there are no more questions, we will begin. Everyone's name and safe words are already in this bowl. I will randomly draw two names at a time to match partners for the first round. Let the games begin."

CHAPTER 11

LIESEL

I knew there was a chance that Langston would be here, but seeing him standing in a suit and black mask has my heart skipping beats so often that I'm afraid I'm going to flatline and die right here right now.

It was a risk I took coming here to earn my money back. My win was almost guaranteed if I was here alone, but having Langston in the game changes everything.

I can't stop looking at him in his tux. His chiseled jaw, sharp eyes, and smooth hair would make it seem like he spends every weekend in a tux. In reality, he wears jeans and boots and kills people every day of the week. He's not comfortable in a tux, in this wealthy, extravagant world. I need to remember that and try to use it to my advantage if I can.

Beat, my reckless heart. Beat hard and steady—I'm going to need every drop of blood and ounce of oxygen in my body to flow through me if I'm going to win.

What surprises me the most is seeing the rest of the gang all here, flanking Langston like he's the leader instead of Enzo and Kai.

They had no idea what they just walked into. Their tense bodies and guarded expressions make it clear they want to be anywhere but here.

I smirk, raising my champagne glass meant to make me look girly and feminine instead of the scotch I really want. Adding them to the game will make it easier to win if I'm matched with one of them. None of them will be able to withstand watching their partner get fucked.

No, the only threat to me is Langston—for so many fucking reasons.

Maxwell leans over to whisper in my ear. "I'll try to stay in as long as I can. I promise I'll at least make it to tomorrow."

I tilt my head up at him. "Don't worry about protecting me. I can protect myself here. Stay if you want to stay, but don't do anything that will wreck your soul for my sake."

I said the wrong thing. Maxwell's face morphs into a horrified expression. He's beyond worried.

I laugh. "Just fuck some women if you want to, Max, but don't do it on my account." I pat his chest, trying to calm him, but his heart is beating wildly out of control.

He clears his throat and exhales.

Poor, Max. I doubt he lasts the first round.

A woman brings a large glass bowl out, while a man brings a small table. The table is positioned, and the woman sets the bowl down upon it.

"Round one is a partner game. I'll draw two names who will be competing against each other and the clock. There will also be your individual safe word on the paper as I draw them. Memorize this safe word. If you mutter it, you are withdrawing from the game. Your challenge will immediately stop, and you'll be escorted out. Round one will take place here on the upper deck as there is the most amount of room."

Mr. Reyes tries a comforting smile on his face as he scans the crowd.

"Let's begin." He reaches into the glass bowl and pulls out a name.

"Ms. Laine," he says the name of Laila Salo, an actress using a fake name.

She walks over and takes the card with her name on it. Her breath hitches as she waits for her partner to be drawn.

"Mr. Fray," he says.

A gentleman almost twice her age walks over to her.

Her smile falters for only a second, but she recovers before almost anyone notices. This is a game of bluffing and chicken more than anything else. Most people think they would be willing to do anything for twenty million, especially sexual things with mostly wealthy and good-looking people. When it actually comes down to it, they are dead wrong.

Mr. Reyes pulls out another card. "Mr. Pearce."

I raise an eyebrow as my eyes go to Langston's. He gave his real name. *Ballsy.* That or he thinks using his real name will intimidate people more.

My heart, my breath, and all other bodily functions stop as I wait for Langston to walk over to collect his card and wait for Mr. Reyes to announce his partner.

Anyone but me.

"Ms. Fraser."

I gasp, sucking in oxygen, trying to restart my body.

"Are you okay?" Maxwell asks me.

I nod silently as a pretty redhead approaches Langston. He gives her a tense smile, and then they move to the side as more names are called.

"Mr. Kane."

"Mrs. Kane."

Zeke and Siren smile at each other, happy to be partnered with their spouse. It will ensure they last this round, but that's it. Once they are re-partnered, they will be gone.

"Mr. Maxwell," Mr. Reyes says.

"Good luck," I whisper to him as he walks forward.

Maxwell is paired with a woman in her mid-fifties, and he doesn't hide his disgust well.

I smile behind my glass. He won't last round one.

I'll be truly on my own after this round.

"Mrs. Black."

Kai walks forward like she owns the room, the most powerful woman here.

There are whispers and gasps as she steps forward, proudly using her name and being herself.

It's all a facade, though. She won't so much as kiss another man, or let any man but Enzo fuck her.

"Mr. Ito."

A tall, handsome gentleman steps forward. He's good looking, but he glances in fear at Enzo as he walks. I wouldn't be surprised if the man simply dropped out so that he didn't have to deal with Enzo's wrath for touching his wife.

"Mr. Beckett."

"Ms. Abara."

Beckett wordlessly and expressionlessly takes his spot by his partner, who looks like she is about his age.

"Ms. White."

That would be me. I step forward and feel everyone's eyes on me as I collect my card.

I don't bother to glance at the safe word as I tuck the card into my bra. Everyone notices, and there is a collective hush around the room.

I will look at the safe word later, but I won't be needing it this round. I know my limits, and really, I only have one. This round won't be the one where that limit is crossed.

I feel Langston's stare more intensely than anyone else's. He has questions. He wants to know why I chose a fake name. He wants to know what a rape victim who has trouble fucking anyone is doing in the middle of a dangerous sex game.

Just more secrets I'll be taking to my grave.

"Mr. Black."

My eyes cut to Enzo as a smug smile crosses my lips.

Jesus, could this first-round be any easier?

Enzo walks stoically toward me as he collects his card. He, unlike me, looks at the safe word. He's going to be needing it.

We stand to the side as the rest of the names are called.

"What did you get us into, Liesel?" Enzo asks me.

"I didn't get you into anything. This is Langston's fault when he stole everything from me."

"You could have come to any of us for money, and we would have given it to you."

"But then it wouldn't have been mine. I would have owed you a debt, and I'm tired of owing men debts."

His eyes narrow as he tries to find the meaning behind my words.

"Round one is limited to thirty minutes. Enjoy your time together. Push the limits. But remember, the word 'no' has no power here. You can say no, but that doesn't mean your partner has to stop. The only word with any power to stop the madness is your safe word. Use it, and your time here ends. Keep the word from your mouth, and you'll move on to the next round, where more pleasure awaits you, but so does more pain. Round one starts now."

Round one isn't where things get interesting. There are too many people in the game that have no sense being here. People are too timid in round one. I plan on making it to the end, so I won't hold back.

I've fucked Enzo Black and been raped by his father. There is no limit too far when it comes to him. I'd love to enjoy making him bleed, but I doubt I'll get the chance to take things that far.

"So, what happens now?" Enzo asks as people around us nervously start talking, some touching or tentatively kissing.

I down the rest of my champagne, letting the sweet liquid burn my throat, and then I calmly place my glass on one of the little cocktail tables.

Enzo is still gripping his scotch glass.

I take Enzo's free hand.

"Liesel, I'll give you the money, you don't have to do this."

I kiss the palm of his hand, knowing I won't get a reaction from him. But I want to draw some blood before he calls out his safe word like the pussy he is. The only way to do that is to take my time with him.

"What? You think I'm whoring myself out to make money?"

The tick in his jaw confirms that is exactly what he thinks of me. He doesn't realize the way to win this game is to push your partner before they push you. Keep the upper hand, the control, the power, and you win. Lose it for a second, and you might as well forfeit because there is no way to come back.

My gaze finds Kai's as my teeth sink into Enzo's wrist like a vampire drawing blood.

He winces as my teeth pierce his skin, but he doesn't surrender. He's a man who can handle pain. He's lived it just like me.

He grabs me by the neck and yanks me to him. "Don't play games with me, Liesel. You'll lose. You've lost every time."

"I lost because my protectors failed me. But I don't lose when I'm protecting myself."

My hand shoots down his pants, and I squeeze, hard.

He releases my neck, and I plant a wet, passionate kiss on his lips as my hand strokes his cock.

His hands are at my shoulders in a second, and he shoves me harshly back. I stumble back in my heels, but I'm not pissed. I just won.

"Pergola," Enzo says, saying his safe word.

Two men come over to immediately escort Enzo out.

I wave at him as the men put hands on his arms to lead him out. He shakes them off, gives me a glare vowing his revenge, and then walks out on his own accord.

Kai is staring me down.

"You're welcome," I mouth, knowing that she doesn't want to watch her husband kiss another girl.

She stands frozen, not sure whether to thank me or kill me for touching her man, even if it ensured that no other woman would touch him.

Kai turns back to her partner, and they chat. The man doesn't touch her. He's too afraid of what will happen. She'll remain in this round, but eventually, she'll be partnered with a man who isn't afraid of her husband.

I glance around at the other couples.

Zeke and Siren are holding each other and whispering, most likely a plan, to each other.

Beckett has his girl on her knees, pulling his cock out and stroking him.

Interesting, he might be better at this game than I thought.

Maxwell's partner moves to undo his pants, and he calls out his safe word. He turns to look at me to apologize.

I laugh and shake my head. *I knew he wouldn't last.*

And then I see Langston. He's making out with his model partner. His hands are all over her. He's completely in control. Every time she tries to touch him, he grabs her hands and stops her. Forcing her hands behind her back, he spins her around and kisses down her neck.

She seems to be enjoying herself. But then he whispers something into her ear, and her face turns white.

She gulps like she can't get enough air. That's when I realize he's gripping her neck, too. She can't breathe.

I frown. This is one of the many reasons I don't want Langston in the game. He's smart and controlling and sexy—all weapons in this game.

Men have an advantage in the initial rounds because of their strength. Like Langston is doing now, they can overpower a woman to win.

But women have an advantage in the later rounds when that strength is taken away. With restraints, it becomes about limits. If you can read your partner and identify their weakness, that's when you have the advantage. Knowing if they can handle pain themselves or if they'd rather be the one inflicting it.

Langston releases the woman's neck as he kisses her so tenderly. He smirks at me, knowing I'm watching him. Half of the room is watching him. Neither of them is undressed compared to the majority of the room. Some brave souls are already fucking their partners. But Langston demands attention. He sucks in all the air around us, drawing us all to see what he will do next.

He raises her dress until her ass is visible. He slaps it hard, hard enough that water stings her eyes. Her mascara starts to run down her cheeks.

Langston fists her hair as he whispers something else into her ear.

She sucks back the tears.

He's playing with her, like this is a random Tuesday. This is ordinary for him.

He slaps her ass again, and this time she calls out his name loudly. So loudly that the few people that were fucking and not paying attention stop and turn to watch them too.

This woman could be a submissive, someone who craves pain, and it wouldn't matter. She would still lose. At this point, all Langston has to do is tell her to say her safe word, and she will. She's completely under his control.

Langston notices the attention he's getting. It's a power move so that whoever he's partnered with next knows to desire and fear him in the same breath. And yet, I think the only reason he's putting on a show is because of me. He wants me to know that he won't play around. That married or not, he's in this game, same as me—to win.

I drag my eyes away, forcing myself to look out at the ocean instead of him. I hear another slap, and I can feel his hand on my own skin. My fingers trace over my collarbone, trying to distract myself, but it's a useless endeavor. Whenever we're in the same room, all I feel is him.

Now that he's purposefully trying to pull my attention, my entire body is screaming to touch him, to kiss him, to want him.

"One-minute warning," Mr. Reyes says.

That's when I hear the woman Langston is partnered with call out her safe word.

The room gasps as she says it, not because she's being tortured or pushed, but simply because Langston told her to.

"That's the end of round one. Congrats on making it through, but the night isn't finished yet. We will give you ten minutes to regroup before the next round begins."

I'm standing outside on a yacht in the middle of the ocean, and yet, I can't breathe. I can't get enough oxygen. Not with Langston so near and smelling like sex. I want to jump into the ocean and swim until I can't any more, but that wouldn't solve any of my problems.

Instead, I grab a glass of scotch and head to my room to get myself off. Ten minutes isn't a long time, but I need a release if I'm going to survive the next round. I just pray I'm never partnered with Langston, because that's the only way I might lose. And I can't lose.

CHAPTER 12

LANGSTON

"That's the end of round one," Mr. Reyes says.

Thank fuck.

I'm so wound up, every nerve in my body is firing, overloading my brain. Lust, want, fear, desire, anger, pain—they all mix together.

But the one single thing that sticks out is that by the end of this game, I know my soul will be lost to the fires of hell. Not because I'm going to fuck complete strangers, or take advantage of them until they are screaming to stop. We are all adults here. No one is forcing anyone. People attend parties like this because of the excitement, the danger.

They just didn't expect a sick fucker like me to show up. One who doesn't give a damn about anyone except the blonde in a dark wig who just ran out of the room, taking my soul with her. Somehow, she stole it, and I haven't been able to get it back.

At least it's not my heart.

I have ten minutes until the next twisted round.

Enzo is out.

Maxwell is out.

By pure luck of the draw, Kai, Siren, Beckett, and Zeke remain.

Zeke flashes me a look, gesturing to come strategize with him. He's going to warn me that there is no way any of them are going to last another round. They won't stand by watching their spouses fuck a sick bastard just to try to protect me, or stop Liesel from winning.

I don't want to spend my ten minutes talking to them. I already know they can't help.

Instead, I chase after the woman who is always running from me. The woman who has my soul locked in a cage somewhere deep in her body and set it on fire. Together we burn. Neither of us will survive like this, but I have to survive.

I have to free my soul and every other part of me she's tried to claim.

I run downstairs and look left then right when I get to the hallway of bedrooms.

Which way did she go?

Right.

I walk down the hallway, listening carefully like I'm going to be able to hear her heart beating through the thick doors.

I might if it's beating anywhere as loudly as mine.

That was intense. Not the woman I had my way with—she was nothing. But Liesel's eyes on me—being able to feel her from across the room, I've never felt anything like it.

And I'm not sure I can win if we don't break the connection now.

I try knocking on several doors, but I get no answer. Either she's not in these rooms, or she's not opening the door to me.

I get to the end of the hallway, and I know before I knock that this is her room.

Gently, I let my knuckles tap against the door and hopefully rattle her.

There is a hiss of breath coming from the other side, as if she just got burned. *I know the feeling, baby.*

A minute later, Liesel opens the door.

She tugs on her dress, trying to straighten it out. Her cheeks are pink beneath the glittery mask, her eyes wild.

I glance past her, almost expecting a man to be in the room. There is no one else.

I take a deep breath and then smirk.

"What are you doing here?" she asks.

"I turned you on so much that you couldn't even wait ten minutes for your next partner to get you off. You had to do it yourself?"

Her cheeks turn a bright shade of red, but her eyes tighten to slits trying to break through my skin with her gaze.

"No."

I grab her hand and lift it to my nose. "Liar, I can smell your cum on your fingers."

She yanks her hand away. "Just trying to satisfy myself since I know no man here will. It helps me keep a level head during play."

"You've been here before, haven't you?"

She doesn't answer my question. "I guess asking you if you're married is a moot point. If you are, it's only on paper. No man would touch a woman like that if he were in love or even getting regular sex at home."

"I guess Waylon is just a man you can use for power. Why stay with him when you can just whore yourself out for money?"

She slaps me.

I could have stopped her, but I like her all worked up and angry. It will make it harder for her to win if she can only concentrate on me and nothing else.

"Quit now, Langston. You and all of your friends need to use your safe word and get out of here. This isn't a good place to be. Tonight is nothing. Tomorrow..." she lets her voice drop as she brushes past me.

I let her because our time is up; we both need to get back to the top deck if we are going to be on time. Something about the way she spoke has me on edge. It's more than her just wanting to win the money to get back on equal footing. There is something I'm missing.

Liesel has definitely attended these games before. *Did she win? What the hell happened to her? Why does she look like she's seen a ghost? And why does it feel like she'd be here even if I hadn't stolen all her money?*

I jog after her and make it to the top deck just as Mr. Reyes starts up the next round.

"Ms. White, Mr. Kane, and Mr. Young. You three will form the first group."

Liesel, Zeke, and a man who looks twenty all stand together to the left of Mr. Reyes.

He continues to draw names. Apparently, we are forming groups of three this time. I must have missed the first set of instructions.

"Mrs. Kane, Mr. Pearce, and Mr. Lloyd will be the next group."

I groan as I walk over to Siren and a middle-aged man.

"Mr. Beckett, Mrs. Black, and Mr. Cole."

A couple more rounds of names are given.

"You have one hour together. Enjoy yourselves. Test your limits. Remember the reward at the end if you win. This will be the final round of the night. Whoever makes it through this round will make it to tomorrow, where everything will change. Begin."

I glance around at the two other groups I care about. Beckett, Kai, and a random man. Kai will lose, but Beckett will protect her for as long as he can.

Then, I find Liesel. She's paired with Zeke and another man who is almost as big and tall. The two men could gang up on her. They could tear her apart, rip her to shreds. Bruise her, gag her, hurt her. It's two against one. I don't like her odds. The only thing working in my favor is that Zeke won't want to do anything sexual to Liesel. But he'll have no problem holding her down while the other man fucks every one of her holes and suffocates her to within an inch of her life.

"Zeke won't hurt her," Siren whispers to me.

I grunt. "He's hated her since we were kids. He'll enjoy hurting her."

"That was before he knew you were in love with her."

I laugh. "I'm not in love with her."

"Then why else are you going through all this trouble? I know you say for the treasure, but that's just stupid. Why?"

"Maybe it's because I hate her, and this is the best way to make her pay."

"We only have an hour. Are we going to get started, or you two going to waste everyone's time? Because I have no problem using my shirt as a gag if it will shut you two up," Mr. Lloyd says.

I size the man up. He's tall and lanky. Built like a swimmer's body. He has muscles, and he's fit, but he doesn't have the bulk strength that

I do. I also doubt he has the intelligence. That's not me just being cocky; I'm smarter than almost everyone else I know.

"If you're so impatient, then you start. But if you go anywhere near my asshole, I'll punch you until your lights are out. Got it?" I say.

He chuckles. "You aren't going to make it long if you can't handle some anal play from another guy. First time?"

I don't answer. I don't have a problem fucking anyone—woman, man makes no difference. Sex is just that—sex.

But I don't like anyone else taking control. Liesel and I have that same problem.

I looked at Liesel less than a minute ago, and yet, I'm already finding her again. Just as I suspected, Zeke has Liesel's arms tied behind her back while Mr. scumbag is running his hands up and down her body.

I growl. *No one touches what is mine.*

I want to run over and stop the man from touching her. She doesn't want this. There is no possible way she'd ever let a strange man touch her. She does the touching, the kissing, the fucking. She didn't even let Waylon, her fiancé, take control during sex. He was her submissive puppy.

I'm about to break all the rules and go over and put a stop to this when Liesel glances my way. There is a twinkle of mischief in her eyes, and I realize she's completely in control. I don't know what her plan is, but it's there.

That twinkle immediately disappears as soon as Siren puts her hands around me from behind and begins unbuttoning my shirt.

"What are you doing?" I hiss.

"Making Liesel jealous. Her look says she suspects we're going to breeze through this round because she already thinks you and I have fucked."

I curse.

Siren kisses my neck like we are lovers, like she's already intimately acquainted with every area of my body.

"Zeke isn't going to like it," I whisper back as Mr. Lloyd starts walking over to join in on the fun.

"Let me worry about Zeke. Just keep me away from Lloyd."

I roll my eyes. "You're going to owe me."

Siren whips me around, grabbing onto my tie. "No, you're going to owe me."

I won't be able to hold off Mr. Lloyd forever, and I can't fuck Siren. I can't take things that far. Zeke would have my balls and my head. He probably will no matter what. But I sure as hell can make Liesel think that there is something between Siren and me. I can make her fucking insane; then, I might be able to get some answers tonight.

I slip my jacket off and toss it at Mr. Lloyd.

"I'm not your coat rack," he growls, tossing my jacket to the floor.

"Let me have my way with her first. Then you can have a turn before we take her together."

"I'd rather fuck your tight ass," he smirks back.

"Fine," I hiss. "Just give me ten minutes with her first."

Mr. Lloyd grins. "I'm going to enjoy the show."

Siren raises an eyebrow in surprise. I frown in return.

Really? You think I'd ever let him fuck me?

Siren laughs. "This is going to be fun."

"Not when Zeke hangs me by my balls later." I grab Siren's curvy hips and yank her to me hard, taking her breath away.

"I enjoy a jealous Zeke. He fucks me so much harder when he's angry."

I grab her hair and yank her head back, exposing the skin on her long neck. "Can you not talk about you and Zeke fucking? I don't really want to know that I'm turning you on." I let my tongue lap down her neck, like a dog thirsting for water. Tasting Siren like this does nothing. She's a beautiful woman, but I think of her as a sister. She's my best friend. My soulmate. My partner in crime. She's not my lover.

"Eww," Siren says but the way she says it makes anyone looking on think I just made her come with my tongue on her neck alone.

Her hands go to my shirt, and she continues to unbutton it as her lips kiss my chest. "Are they watching?"

I can feel Liesel's heated gaze. "Yes."

I let my eyes cut to them, and I about fucking lose it.

Liesel's dress has been ripped from her body. Zeke is using the remnants of her dress to tie her arms together, while the other guy slobbers on her neck.

"We need to up our game," I tell Siren.

Her eyes cut to them. "He won't hurt her."

"He will if he thinks I'm fucking you."

Siren yanks off my shirt and then goes to work on my belt. I face them as I shove Siren down on her knees in front of me. I won't strip her of her clothes, but I sure as hell am going to let her go further than I ever thought I would.

This isn't chicken between me and Siren. It's chicken between me and Zeke.

I look at Liesel, who is cringing with each kiss, biting her lip in disgust.

"You want Zeke to hurt Liesel?" Siren asks when she has my pants undone. I know what she's asking. *How far do I want her to go?* She's willing. She'd do almost anything for me after everything I've done for her.

I want Zeke out of the games. I want a more fair match between Liesel and the other man. She has no chance as long as he's holding her back and letting the other man do whatever he wants to her.

"Yes," I blow out.

In that second, she has my cock out, and her lips are wrapping around it.

"Jesus," I curse too loud.

I was expecting her to pull my cock out, and maybe fake touch me. I wasn't expecting a fucking blowjob.

Slap.

Zeke slaps Liesel so fucking hard across the cheek. All I see is red. Sure, my cock is hard, but there are a million naked hot people around me all moaning. Liesel is standing basically naked in front of me. Of course, I'm turned on.

You're a deadman, I mouth to Zeke. How dare he touch my woman.

Without thinking, I grab Siren's hair and fist it in a ponytail. Then I pump her head back and forth over my cock.

I'm numb. I don't feel her warm lips, wet tongue, moist saliva. All I see is Zeke's hand across Liesel's face.

Surrender, asshole. Or I'm going to take this too far.
Zeke screams pineapple.
What?
It's then that I realize it's his safe word.
I release Siren.
She removes my cock from her mouth and whispers her word.
Even as quietly as she whispered it, a man walks over to escort her out with Zeke.
"I'm sorry," I whisper to her as she stands on her feet.
"I'm not. Zeke's going to fuck me so hot tonight." She winks, and then she's led out behind Zeke.
I glance over to Liesel, who now has the man she's with tied up and on his knees.
Thanks for your help, she mouths in my direction.
"You're a sucker. I don't know who that woman is to you, but you just fell into her trap. She couldn't manipulate two men, so she had you get rid of one for her," Mr. Lloyd says behind me.
I know he's right.
"Now, about that asshole," he continues.
Like hell, I'm going to let anyone near my ass right now.
I turn and grab Lloyd by the neck.
"Ooh, you're into erotic asphyxiation? Me too," he says.
"Soon, you won't be."
I squeeze hard around his neck as I shove him toward the railing. He'll either die from lack of oxygen, or I'll throw him overboard. Either way is a win-win for me.
I lean in close to him, so no one can see that nothing sexual is happening between us. In the darkness, it looks like we are kissing. There are no rules, but I'm guessing that whatever you are doing has to at least be perceived as sexual. If not, this would just be a fistfight to the end.
Lloyd's eyes bulge and his hands grip mine, scratching them until I release enough for him to speak.
"Ready to say your safe word yet?"
"Not fair. You have to be doing something sexual. Otherwise, I can tell the owners, and they will remove you from the games when I

remove myself."

Dammit.

I force my lips over his as I squeeze around his neck again. This is actually better. I can assure he can't breathe if I've sealed his mouth and blow carbon dioxide in his face.

I don't take a breath. My mouth is locked over his. My tongue dances at the seam of his lips that feel swollen from lack of oxygen.

Finally, I release him.

He mutters a word—his safe word.

I release him and walk away.

I find Liesel. Her man has her leaning against the railing, and his head is buried between her legs, tasting every inch of her.

My mouth waters at the sight as her eyes roll back. But just as she predicted, he can't get her to completion.

Her nails dig into the poor man's back, drawing blood.

"My turn," I can hear her say.

The man's eyes light up like he's just entered heaven.

She kneels in front of him.

Don't fall for it, man. The devil lives in her eyes. I wouldn't let her near your man parts right now.

She takes his cock into her mouth in one deep swallow, and he's down her throat. It's not that impressive since the guy isn't that big to begin with.

Suddenly, she bites down.

I wince at the sight as a blood-curdling scream echoes through the ship.

A man walks over to him. "I need you to say your safe word if you want to end your games."

Liesel still has her mouth around his penis as his blood drips down her chin.

The man is still screaming hysterically, but he can't seem to remember his safe word.

"Say your safe word, and this ends," the man is basically pleading with him to use his safe word.

"I can't...remember." He stutters.

"It's pterodactyl."

"Pterodactyl!" he screams.

Liesel takes her time releasing the man. When she finally unsheathes him, two more men rush over to carry her victim away.

Liesel stands up with blood dripping down her chin and onto her bare breasts. She's completely naked, covered in the man's blood with his saliva dripping between her legs.

I grind my teeth together.

"This ends tonight's game. There are eight of you left. The games start tomorrow at midnight. Enjoy the rest of your night and day tomorrow, but make sure you get plenty of rest. Tomorrow's games last as long as it takes to crown a winner."

As soon as Mr. Reyes finishes speaking, Liesel takes off. Everyone moves aside, too scared of her to stand in her way.

I chase after her, through the hallways, down the stairs.

She's about to slam her bedroom door shut, but I catch it.

My eyes take in everything—the fucking sexiest woman I've ever seen. She looks like a vampire. I have no doubt she's more powerful right now than any vampire in any novel or movie I've ever seen. She's fucking glowing with strength.

"You should have said your safe word, killer. Tomorrow, you'll be the one I'm taking a bite out of."

I shake my head. "I would worry about tomorrow later if I were you. Tonight, we are playing my game. Tonight, I want to hear a lie. Tell me all the lies, because I can't wait another night to kill you."

CHAPTER 13

LIESEL

He wants me to lie.

I must have really gotten under his skin. And now he's here getting under mine, taking in every ounce of my nakedness.

I still have blood on my face from biting Mr. Young. I'm sweaty and sticky from being manhandled and his failed attempts at making me come.

My hair is wild, and my makeup must be dripping from my face. The only piece of clothing I still wear is my mask.

Langston is shirtless, and the top of his pants are still undone, but he has a lot more clothes on than I do. He's sweaty, but no blood covers him. He looks almost dignified.

"We should both get some rest. Tomorrow night is going to take every ounce of strength," I say.

He forces his way inside my room, and I push the door shut behind him.

"But by all means, please come in."

He snorts as he turns to look at me with his heady eyes, hooded and dripping in lust and desire.

He's just as turned on and unsatisfied as me. That's why he's looking at me like this. Not because he finds me attractive, I remind myself.

I want to get dressed, put a robe on at least. I feel weak without clothes on, but I can't let him know that. Tomorrow if I get to wear any articles of clothing other than my mask all night, I'll be lucky. I need to get used to it. I need to feel powerful naked.

Somehow though, being nude in front of everyone else makes me strong. But in front of this man, with his eyes dancing over my body, I feel powerless.

My memories flutter through everything that has happened tonight, but only playing the parts that included Langston. Him kissing and groping the first woman, completely in control. Siren down on her knees, pleasuring him. Him threatening his male partner.

"She really loves you, doesn't she?" I ask out of nowhere. It's the only thing I can concentrate on.

"Who? Phoenix?" Langston says sheepishly, like it's too much for him to think of Phoenix while he's living this life.

"No," I shake my head. "Siren."

There is a beat of truthful silence as Langston and I trade breaths.

"Yes. Siren loves me, and I love her."

I can feel how heavily his heart beats for her. How he'd do anything in the world for her and she him.

"What is it like? Loving someone and being loved?"

"It's the most incredible and terrifying thing in the world."

I nod.

"Don't get it twisted, though. Siren and I aren't lovers. Until tonight, we'd never touched each other and never kissed."

"I know. It's not a sexual thing between you. It's not what Siren has with Zeke. It's different, but it's still love."

Langston nods as he turns and looks out the sliding glass door behind him. I walk up beside him, and we both stare out at the stary night.

"Phoenix—" Langston starts.

"It doesn't matter if you are married to her or not. It's clear you don't love her. Not after I've seen what you loving a woman looks like. You don't have that with Phoenix as far as I've seen. And no man who truly loves his wife would be able to stomach what you did tonight. That's why Enzo and Zeke dropped out so easily." I smile, thinking about what Siren did. "Zeke is going to punish Siren for touching your cock, isn't he?"

Langston chuckles. "Probably. Siren thinks it will spice up their sex life. I, for one, don't want to think about it."

I stare at his dimple and the twinkle in his eyes. For a split moment, he's happy. He's content. He's not thinking about how to get the treasure. He's not thinking about my lies. He's not thinking about killing me. He's just living in the moment.

Langston reaches into his back pocket and pulls out his phone. After a couple of swipes, he hands it to me.

"My marriage to Phoenix is legal. It may not be a fairy tale. It may not be love, but it's real."

I stare at the photo of his marriage license. I have no reason to believe he faked this. It looks real enough, and it doesn't matter. He signed a legal document, the same way I'm going to in a couple of weeks. That doesn't mean he's in love with her.

Would it matter if he was?

I don't want Langston to ever fall in love with me. I could never fall in love with him. *Maybe if he loved another woman, it would make our relationship easier? Maybe he'd be able to focus on her instead of whatever this feud is between us?*

Slowly, Langston turns to face me. His hands touch the bottom of my glittery mask. The mask makes me feel beautiful and mysterious, even though it doesn't hide who I really am.

He pushes the mask off my face and tosses it on the bed.

Then he tugs gently on the black wig I'm wearing.

"I don't like this," he says.

"No?"

"No."

His hands pull the wig off next. I've never felt so bare and so seen.

My blonde hair is up in a bun.

With his eyes locked on mine, he tugs the elastic, and my hair falls in waves down my neck.

"Better," he says.

We both stare at each other, breathing deeply. He said he came here for me to tell a lie so he could take more time off my life. But right now, it seems he came here to see into my soul.

"About the lie...we should talk so I can shower and sleep," I say.

He frowns and takes my hand.

"First, I need to wash the blood, sweat, and saliva from your body."

"Then?"

He smirks. "I'm going to enjoy the 'then' step the most, probably for quite a while. After we do that, you will tell me a lie to soothe my rage at this mess you got us all in."

First, he wants to wash me.

Then, he won't say.

Lastly, he wants me to tell him a lie.

I don't think I'm going to survive this night.

"Why?" I ask.

His jaw ticks. His teeth grind. Langston doesn't like to be defied. He doesn't give orders often, but when he does, he wants them obeyed without question.

"I hold your life in the palm of my hand. If you want to survive the year, you'll do as I say."

I bite my lip. He has no idea how wrong he is.

Langston walks to the bathroom, and I follow.

Maybe I follow out of survival.

Maybe I follow out of curiosity.

Maybe I follow out of desire.

The bathroom door reveals a giant jacuzzi tub.

"They gave you a nice suite," he says.

"Yours doesn't come with a hot tub?"

He shakes his head as he flips on the water and pours some nearby bath salts into the water.

I'm already naked, and I assume the tub is just for me, so I move to climb into it, knowing the water and bit of bubbles will make me feel more covered up.

Langston holds out a hand, stopping me.

I frown.

My eyes bulge as he undoes the zipper on his slacks and pushes them down until he's naked in front of me. His cock strains in my direction.

My mouth waters, looking at the large veins on his member pointing in my direction. I've never been so jealous of Siren. She got to taste it, touch it, suck it.

My heart is beating wildly in my chest. *Does he expect me to fuck him?*

Silently, he steps into the tub. Then, he holds his hand out to me.

I take it. My brain is mush, unable to think through any decision. He could tell me to jump off the balcony into the ocean right now, and I'd probably do it.

We are standing face to face in the tub as the water fills to just below our knees. I've seen Langston shirtless before, but never naked like this. His muscles are a perfect sculpture of man. Leonardo da Vinci couldn't have sculpted a more perfect specimen. But it's offset by scars, cuts, bruises that show why he really has the muscles. It's not because he wants to look good; it's out of necessity.

I want to bask in the view of his cock again, but I'm too afraid. Not of what Langston would say but what I might accidentally do if I let myself go there. I'd be a goner.

Langston turns me around until I'm no longer facing him, and then we both sink down into the water, my back to his front.

I purse my lips, trying to breathe slowly out. I need to slow my breathing, my heart rate, everything if I'm going to have a chance of keeping my lust in check.

"Relax. I'm just washing you. I won't rape you."

I'm not sure if he touched me right now, it would be rape. I'm pretty sure my body would be begging for it, and my mind would go right along with it.

I still don't know why he's washing me, spending time with me tonight. *Trying to get under my skin? Learn secrets that will help him tomorrow?*

There is a sponge lying on the edge of the tub. Langston grabs it and wets it before he squeezes it over my head to wet my hair and face.

Once he does that, I can breathe again as the iron taste of blood begins to wash from my lips.

I can't believe I bit that guy's penis, but whatever it takes to survive. I will survive at all costs. I made that promise a long time ago. I'm just afraid I'll break that promise sooner than I ever imagined.

"I'm in awe of you right now. That's why I'm equal parts pissed and drawn to you," Langston tells a truth, surprising the hell out of us both.

"Why? We played the same game. We both did things that we had to in order to make it to the next round," I say.

He turns my head back to face him. His eyes carry a heaviness as he puts the sponge up to my bottom lip to wash the remnants of blood away.

"No, what I did doesn't compare to you."

I clear my throat, unsure of what to say to that. I never thought we'd be in a tub like this together, sharing an intimate moment. Even though I can feel the hardness of his cock against my ass, he hasn't tried to touch me inappropriately. He hasn't tried to kiss me, turn me on, or fuck me.

"I need to wash between your legs. I need you to be clean of any place that man touched before we get to the 'then' part."

I suck in air, knowing I'm going to need all of it. While he's touching me so intimately with the sponge, I won't be able to breathe.

I realize he's asking me for permission. This isn't something he's willing to take.

I nod.

His hand reaches around my waist with the sponge in his hand, and then he moves it in slow circles between my legs. The soft bristles cause enough friction that little zips of energy flutter in my stomach. Or maybe it's because of the man sitting behind me, caressing me so carefully.

"He also sucked my nipples," I say.

He growls low and even as his hand moves up to my breasts, and he rubs the sponge over each. This time harder than he did between my legs.

I bite back a moan. It shouldn't feel this good. Nothing this man does should feel good.

Without thinking, I grab his wrist when he tries to pull away.

I immediately release him, though, but not before he mutters 'fuck' under his breath.

I affect him just like he does me.

Even if we were good, kind, do-gooders, we shouldn't be together. He's dynamite, and I'm fire. You can't combine the two without destroying everything and everyone—ourselves included.

Langston puts the sponge down on the edge of the tub.

First, he wants to wash me.

Then, he wants to...

"Then?" I ask, not sure I can handle his answer.

"Then, we both come."

CHAPTER 14

LANGSTON

I knew sitting in the tub would lower her guard, make her more willing to do the next part we both crave. But I didn't think it would also lower my own defenses.

I can't think around Liesel.

All I can do is suck in air by the gallon and hope it's enough to survive.

Neither of us has spoken since I said the word come.

We can't.

Our brains are consumed with scolding fire and hurricane winds fighting through our bodies. That's how badly we both need to come.

I haven't decided whether we will be making the other come or doing it ourselves.

I don't fucking care.

I just need to explode in this tub, and I need to see her come undone more than I need my heart to keep thumping. I wouldn't live long if my heart stopped, but seeing her face as she falls apart in a glorious orgasm would be worth it.

She scoots away from me in the tub, and I let her. She wants a few moments to process what I just said. As much as I hate the cold feeling as she leaves my skin, I let her go to the other side of the tub.

"What did you say?" she asks.

"You heard me."

"Tomorrow night is going to be non-stop sex. I don't think we need to worry about a release tonight."

I raise my eyebrows. "Do you really think any man or woman left has the ability to make you come? I'm not even sure all that moaning with Waylon was real. You're a difficult woman to please, Liesel Dunn."

She glares at me. "And you think you are capable?"

"I am, but that's not what I'm saying. I can make you come, or you can do it yourself. But I want to know what you really sound like when you come. So tomorrow, when you are moaning and faking it, I'll know the truth."

She licks her bottom lip, and I know she won't say no. Even though she made herself come earlier, she reacted so sensitively to my touch. She's still too wound up to sleep, same as me.

"We shouldn't," Liesel whispers.

She doesn't say why we shouldn't—we both know. *It would ruin everything.*

Things we know.

Things we don't know.

Things we assume but haven't spoken aloud.

But there is also a twinkle in her eye, a mischief, a wanting desire that the girl I used to know would give me. The woman in front of me now shows it in a much dirtier way.

She wants to come as much or more than I do.

I watch as her hand dips into the water between her legs. Her hooded eyes look up at me, and her breath slows and shallows. She doesn't wait for me to start, for me to tell her touch herself. She took control of the situation.

Clearly, the only way she can come is if she's in control.

I'll let her have that control tonight, because I want to watch her come in pieces. I need to hear the ecstasy she feels as she moans and calls out—in person, not over a monitor. Not through a closet.

Tomorrow though, I'll use this little tidbit against her. All I have to do to beat her is take the control.

Liesel is already broken, so taking control won't break her; it will just burst the stitches holding together the illusion that she's whole.

"Are you going to touch yourself, too, or am I doing this by myself?"

I chuckle.

"Need to see my cock in order to come?"

She bats her eyelashes. "I don't need a man for anything. But looking at your filthy cock won't hurt, even if it's not as impressive as the guys I'm used to."

My hands grip the side of the tub as I raise myself above the water and sit on the edge, so she can see just how unimpressive my cock is, according to her. I smirk, and my eyes threaten of what I want to do to her, of what I should do to her.

She gasps when our eyes meet.

"Killer, don't...not tonight..."

Tomorrow.

We both know we will make it to the finals. Tomorrow we will finally fuck each other, hurt each other. Fight each other to win the battle she entered us in.

I nod solemnly, agreeing to her terms.

She exhales harshly, her shoulders slumping.

I grab my cock, holding it loosely in my hand.

Her eyes are locked on my hand as she rubs between her submerged legs.

"Show me," I say. I won't be able to keep my hands off her if I can't see her come.

She licks her bottom lip, considering my command. Then she hops up on the tub edge opposite me. She spreads her legs wide as he lifts one leg up onto the side of the tub, giving me an even better view.

Her lips are swollen pink. Her pussy is bare. Her perfectly manicured fingers slip between her legs and into her tight slit. When she removes her two fingers, I can see the sticky evidence of how turned on she is on her fingers. Her moisture is dripping from her pussy down to her ass.

"Fuck," I breathe.

She smiles at my reaction. "Like what you see?"

I glance down at my cock that has somehow grown harder. *Painfully harder.*

I pump my cock, showing her how much I appreciate the show.

Her soft moan hits me in the chest, making me ache to touch her. *God, why did I agree to not touch her again?*

"Do you like it soft and slow or hard and fast?" I ask.

"I like it in control, without pain, but then you already know that. You?"

"I like being in control, too."

She rubs over her clit, her head falling back until she's no longer looking at me. "Which is one of the many reasons why we shouldn't ever fuck. We can't both be in control. All we'd end up doing is hurting each other."

I snort. "We hurt each other plenty without fucking."

Her eyes roll back to me. She's breathless, her cheeks are a light pink, and the way she's biting on her bottom lip and no longer speaking shows how close she is to coming. She stops moving her fingers quickly over her clit. She slows to the point there is no way she'll come.

"You first," she pants.

"I thought it was ladies first?"

"I'm not showing you how incredible I look when I come until you show me how much of the devil escapes your soul when you do."

I pump faster, letting my gaze roam her body and pretend her hand is the one stroking my cock. I have no problem being the one who comes first.

Faster, faster I stroke until warm white liquid shoots from my cock, splashing in the water between us.

As soon as I come, she loses it. One more circular motion of her fingers over her clit, and she's crying out in soft explosive moans.

I try to soak in everything. Her face opening wide as if she's letting all of the pain out. Her breasts heaving up and down. Her opening is contracting around her fingers, soaking them in her come.

It's too much and too little. I want more. I want to feel her as she comes. Taste her. Smell her.

For now, seeing will have to be enough.

Slowly, she comes back to earth. While she came, she was her most vulnerable. I could have asked her any question, done anything to her, and she would have let me.

I tuck that secret away for another time. I'm not sure I'm strong enough to take advantage of her like that, but I will if I have to.

I lean forward.

"You got it wrong. The devil doesn't escape me when I come. More of the devil enters my soul until I'm more evil than anything else."

I grab her hand where her fingers are still buried in her pussy. Slowly, I remove them, watching her body reluctantly release her fingers and spill out cum. Then I lift her hand to my mouth, and I suck her fingers clean.

I got to see her come. I got a taste and smell of her cum. Now all I need is to feel.

That will be the last thing I take from her.

She swallows hard, like her throat is on fire.

"I think I liked the then part the most," she says.

I agree.

"Finally, I want to hear all your lies. This changes nothing. I still want to kill you."

CHAPTER 15

LIESEL

Every sexual encounter with Langston is hotter than the previous.

He didn't even touch me until after I had already come, but rubbing myself while he was watching me, while he was stroking himself, while he was so close—*fuck me.*

Those words almost slipped from my lips so many times.

My body was screaming for Langston to fuck me.

Fuck me.

Fuck me.

Fuck me.

For the first time, I wasn't sure if it mattered if I was in control or not. It didn't matter if Langston tied me up and stripped me of all my power. It didn't matter if he pushed his cock between my lips, in my ass, or in my cunt. All I wanted was his cock inside me. His lips kissing me. His hands touching me.

Every time I'm around Langston, I want more.

And every time I realize just how bad things would get if we were to cross that line into more.

Langston steps out of the tub and grabs a fluffy towel from the nearby shelf. He doesn't grab one for me or help me in any way.

I stand and grab another towel. I dry quickly before grabbing the single white robe hanging on the back of the bathroom door and wrapping it around me. I walk into the bedroom after Langston.

I don't see him.

Did he leave?

My heart flutters at that. I both want him to have left and want him to still be here.

I turn to the right and see Langston out of the corner of my eye, sitting in one of the two chairs on my balcony.

I exhale.

He didn't leave.

I hesitate before I walk over to him, trying to prepare myself for the conversation.

Langston wants me to lie. He wants me to give him another reason to hate me, to eventually kill me.

I'll lie alright. But it will be closer to the truth than he'll ever know.

I slide the door open and step outside. Wordlessly, I take the seat next to him.

When I glance over, I see he's shirtless with only the towel wrapped around his waist.

Jesus.

How does he think I'm going to be able to focus on anything?

"So tell me, how does a girl who grew up with a whore for a mother decide the only way to make money is to whore herself out now?"

I slap him again.

He's made comments like this before, but I'm not tolerating it.

"I am not a whore."

He smirks. "Why did you enter this game, then? You've been here before. You've played before, won before. Why?"

I drag my eyes from him to the ocean. "Is this the part where I'm supposed to lie so I can fuel your sick rage to eventually kill me?"

He shrugs. "Ultimately, it's up to you whether you tell the truth or lie."

"Lie it is then," I say.

His jaw ticks, but otherwise, he remains stone-faced.

"I've been living in hell since I was eighteen years old." The year that Langston left me. That was the year my world changed. Since then, nothing has been the same.

"Liar. You thrived after I left you," Langston says.

He has no idea what happened after I left, the deal I made. And he never will.

"Be quiet and let me tell the story. Otherwise, I'll stop talking right now."

He rolls his eyes but doesn't speak again.

"As I was saying, I'd already been living in hell for years. My entire life has been dealing with the flames of the devil. Some years were harder than others, but then I met Duncan."

"Who is he?"

"So impatient."

"Duncan is the man who brought me here."

Langston frowns. "Against your will?"

I laugh. "I don't do anything against my will, not anymore. I wanted money—knowing it was the only way I could ensure that I never had to do anything against my will again."

"So you whored yourself out?" he asks.

"Do you want me to slap you again?"

He chuckles and puts his hands up in surrender.

"I didn't know I was whoring myself out. He brought me here. Told me there was a game he thought I'd enjoy, and I could feel in control. He said it would bring me enough wealth that I would never have to worry again."

"Did he tell you what you were signing up for?"

"Yes and no. He asked how far I'd be willing to go to earn unlimited freedom. I said as far as it takes."

I pause.

Langston's body is hard as stone, and his eyes have rage spelled out in his pupils.

"I understood what he wasn't saying. I could read between the lines. It was my choice to come here, to play the game."

"And he demanded a cut?"

My eyes gloss over. *Yes. No.* I can't think about that—about all of the fucking pain. I'd break more than I already have. I may not be able to get through tomorrow or tonight as it is.

"No, I took everything I won." A sly smile spreads. "And I won everything."

Langston's lips turn up into not quite a smile, but I know he's impressed by me.

"Where's the lie?" he asks after a beat.

"That's for you to figure out."

Everything. Almost everything is a lie, yet not enough is.

We sit in uncomfortable silence for a while, both staring out at the ocean.

"So how much time are you taking off? Another month? Six months? You plan on killing me tomorrow?" I finally ask, not hiding the disdain in my voice.

He sighs, and there is an emotion on his face that I haven't seen since we were kids—fear.

"What happens tomorrow, huntress? How do you survive if I don't save you like I did tonight?" Langston asks, referring to him kicking Zeke out of the games.

I shake my head. "You don't understand how different tomorrow's games will be."

"Tell me."

"It's not something I can tell. It's only something you can experience."

He frowns. "Huntress..."

"You can't save me. No one can. And I don't need you to. Only I can save myself."

Langston gets up and walks to the sliding door.

"What happens when we both make it to the final round?" he asks as he pauses at the door.

I lose.

"I hope you make it to the final round with me. I'd love to see you go through hell," I reply.

CHAPTER 16

LANGSTON

Why did I go see her last night?

It was a mistake. Now I can't do anything but think of her. Of her body, the sounds she made when she came. She has crept into every part of my body all day.

It's more than that, though. I've played her little story in my head over and over, and I can't figure out the lie. I also can't figure out who Duncan is.

It's probably because he doesn't exist. That's the lie—his name. That way, I can't look up to see who she's working with.

I throw my phone in frustration after once again coming up empty on my search for information on the owners of this yacht and fucked up game.

There is a knock at my door.

I huff as I stand and walk over to it.

"Yes?" I answer while throwing the door open.

Beckett is standing in my doorway with a stack of two to-go coffee cups and a raised eyebrow. I'm always impressed with how he's adapted to a life with only one arm.

"You look like hell," he says as he pushes the top cup into my hands and walks inside my room.

"Thanks," I say. The hot liquid runs down my throat while I hope it turns everything around for me. It's only a couple hours until midnight, but I'm going to need the coffee to stay awake all night, especially since I haven't slept.

"Couldn't sleep?" he asks.

"Yea, Liesel got into my head." I run my hand through my hair, messing it up even more.

"Women." Beckett shakes his head like he doesn't understand why I'd ever let a woman bother me. "You and Liesel aren't together though, right? So why do you let her affect you so much?"

"Our relationship is complicated. I want to kill her most of the time."

"But you also want to fuck her?" Beckett says with a grin.

"Something like that," I grump.

"But you don't love her?"

"No." *I could never love her.*

"Hmmm, then fuck her and get over her."

If only it were that easy.

"What about you and Nora? Isn't she going to be pissed that you let some woman suck your dick?"

"I actually fucked the second woman."

I frown. *Nora will kill him.* "You need to withdraw. I don't want to ruin any more relationships than I have to. I'll be alright. I don't need anyone to stay in the game just for me."

"Nora and I broke up. I'm a free man. And I plan on staying and helping for as long as I can. So far, I've quite enjoyed myself."

I chuckle. "Well, I'm sorry about you and Nora."

He shrugs. "I'm not. It was fun while it lasted, but we were never meant to be together."

"You don't have to be loyal to me just because I work with your brother."

"I'm not. You're as much a part of this family as I am. And we protect our family."

I nod, thankful that I have someone here. I have no idea what tonight holds. Beckett and I have never been as close as any other pair in the group, but I'm thankful nonetheless.

"Don't push yourself too far tonight to defeat Liesel. If she wins, we can steal the money again like before," Beckett says nonchalantly.

We can't.

And I'm beginning to think I need to win for more reasons than just keeping the money from Liesel. Something feels off about everything Liesel said last night. It feels like she's begging for help, for a way to escape. I want her dead, but at my hands. No one else gets to bury Liesel except for me.

A few minutes later, Beckett leaves. I take my time getting dressed once again in my suit that has somehow been dry cleaned and delivered to my room. Then I don the mask, tying it around the upper half of my face.

The mask is supposed to make me feel invincible, discreet and hidden. I hate hiding, though. I'd rather fight head-on. I didn't give a fake name when we boarded, because I'd rather everyone know exactly who I am. Hopefully, I can take my mask off in the final round.

I glance at the clock in my room—a quarter till midnight.

Showtime.

I walk into the hallway and up the stairs, the caffeine buzzing through my body, making me feel alive and ready.

I'm ready for whatever I face tonight.

When I reach the top deck, the air feels different than last night. Last night everyone was chatting; there was a nervous, excited energy about the crowd. Tonight, it's all anxious nerves. There is no small talk between the eight remaining participants. Only about half the people up here even have a drink in their hand. Everyone has a solemn, ready to go to war look in their eyes.

Everyone left came to win.

"It feels eery up here. I feel like everyone here knows what's about to happen except for us," Beckett whispers.

I nod. I feel the same.

There are five men, including Beckett and myself.

Two women.

And...

Liesel.

I tried to ignore the pull I felt when I stepped foot up here, but it's here, plain as day.

She's wearing a different dress than last night. This one is all black, and she has a black mask. The only thing that isn't black on her body is her dark red lipstick.

How did she get a new dress?

Everyone else here is wearing a dry cleaned version of what they wore the night before.

What game is this, Liesel? Why did I let my anger out last night? I should have demanded a truth instead of a lie. Then I might have a damn clue what this stupid game is.

I look at Liesel, trying to gain any insight from her expression. I find nothing. She's solid stone. Expressionless and unbending.

I stare her down. *I'm going to destroy you, and then I'm going to take you back to my island, and we are going to finish what we started.*

"Congratulations, everyone, on making it to the second night," Mr. Reyes says, holding a glass of champagne in his hand.

An employee carries a tray of champagne glasses around the deck, offering a glass to everyone.

I turn it down. I don't want to drink sweet champagne right now.

"Tonight will be much different than last night. Last night was about dipping your toes into this world. Tonight, you'll dive headfirst into the deep end." He smirks like he knows a secret that will ruin all of us.

I grind my teeth and my hands fist. *Out with it!*

"Last night you had complete control over the situation. Tonight, you'll lose all control. The only power you'll be able to wield is the ability to say your safe word and leave the game."

I glance at Liesel again. She can't lose control. I can't lose control.

How are we going to survive?

Liesel looks into my soul. *We won't.*

Fuck.

"Tonight, I'll draw names to decide your partner each round, but that partner won't be the one pushing you. The owner of the game will be selecting a challenge for each of you. You won't be fighting against each other. You'll be fighting against yourself. Your worst demons. The darkest part of your soul."

I've fucked plenty of women in my life. Phoenix and I may be legally married, but we aren't tied to only fuck each other. We aren't lovers in that sense. *Have we fucked? Yes.* But it's never crossed to love or loyalty to each other.

I'm a free man. I can fuck whoever and whenever and however I want. I can't imagine a sexual act that I wouldn't be willing to do, not if it meant destroying Liesel a little more.

Bring it on.

"The rules are also different tonight. There are two ways you get knocked out of the game—either by using your safe word or by not completing the challenge. Once you are knocked out, you will get to watch the rest of the games from a safe room. Any questions?"

The room is silent. I have so many, but I'm not going to ask any of them. I'm not going to appear weak in any way.

I haven't been weak since I was a boy.

Never again.

Mr. Reyes starts pairing off people, until there are only four of us left: Liesel, me, Beckett, and another man.

I exhale.

I don't even know who I want to be paired with anymore.

"Ms. White and Mr. Beckett."

Liesel and Beckett are paired together.

Beckett gives me a cocky wink as he walks toward her. I don't think I can handle the two of them together.

A low growl escapes. It's a territorial growl, but Beckett takes the hint.

He nods once.

That leaves me and the remaining man to be paired.

I have nothing against men fucking each other; I'm just not gay. But I have a feeling this isn't about who you're partnered with. This is going to be different. I just don't understand how.

"The first and the last couples drawn will go first. Each of you will be led to the two rooms where you will be completing your challenges, while the rest of you will be led to the viewing area. Once the challenges are finished, you'll swap places."

That means Liesel will be able to watch me, and I'll be able to watch her.

"Gentleman, if you'll follow me," a woman in a simple black dress says. She's not wearing a mask, the clue that she's an employee and not a player.

We follow her down from the top to the bottom deck. It feels like we are walking down into a dungeon, possibly to our deaths as we descend deeper into the ship.

She opens a door and holds it open for us as we step inside. The room is about twice the size of the bedrooms on the ship. It has a king-sized bed in the center, but otherwise, there are no whips, chains, bludgeons—nothing that makes it seem anything other than an ordinary bedroom. The only light comes from two light shades on either side of the bed. There are no windows or other light sources I can see.

The woman steps in after us and closes the door behind her.

"Mr. Pearce, this challenge is for you. You'll have five minutes to mentally prepare, and then the challenge will start. You are required to do and accept everything on the card to complete your challenge. Understand?"

"Yes."

She smiles tightly. "Here you go. You have five minutes." She hands me a standard-sized index card.

I read through it quickly as my skin turns pale.

How?

I'm going to kill Liesel. She had to have told someone who I am and about my past. That's the only way they could have picked out this specific challenge for me. Although, I stupidly gave my real name and made it simple for them to find me.

The card is basically all of my fears thrown into one twisted game.

They know I was beaten as a kid.

And that's exactly what I have to do—beat another and then get beaten while climaxing.

Who thinks up these sick challenges?

I glance up in the corner of the room, looking for a camera, but I find none. My eyes cut around the room; the wall seems completely flat. I don't see any indication of a camera, but there must be one somewhere.

The man who is partnered with me sits on the edge of the bed. He wasn't given any instructions. He doesn't know what my challenge is.

I have less than five minutes to decide if I'm going to do this task or not.

Liesel, what did you do? What horror will your task be?

She'll do it, whatever it is. She's done it before. This round can't be any worse than what she's already done.

Why?

What the hell am I missing? There has to be easier ways to get money.

I close my eyes in thought. I'm already going to hell; *what difference does it make if I do this?* This man is a man, not a boy. He can say his safe word and stop. This is for millions of dollars. This is to stop Liesel. This is for so much more...

When I open my eyes, it's like the room has transformed.

Smoke has started to billow in, making it hard for me to see anything except a small table that has been placed in front of me with a man's belt lying on it.

They couldn't even give me a whip; they had to give me a belt—my father's tool of choice.

You can do this. This is just like any other time you've beaten a criminal for information. This will be no different. The man who is playing isn't a good person. If he was, he wouldn't be here.

I walk over to the table with the belt. There is a single white card attached to it. I yank it off.

20 LASHINGS WITH THE BELT.

20 with your fist.

Repeat until he breaks, until he uses his safe word.

FUCK.

This is about me or him.

Either I win or he does.

Don't show weakness. You're giving a grown man a lashing—something you experienced nightly as a child.

Liesel was right; I'll be living through hell. As much as I don't want to do the first part, the second part is what is going to fuck with my mind. The second part is going to try and twist my worst nightmare with sex. I may never be able to fuck normally again.

The smoke parts, and I see my partner. Except I'm not sure he's my partner. He looks younger. He's no longer in a suit; he's in shorts and a T-shirt. He seems smaller, weaker. He wears a new mask, one that isn't as dark. This one is white, pure.

He's a grown man. He's not a child. But damn did they do a good job of tricking my mind.

"Begin," a man's deep voice comes through a speaker in the room.

At the sound of his unfamiliar voice, I decide I'm going to see this through. I realize the voice must somehow be that of someone I know. If he's the one in charge of these games, then the only way to meet and destroy him is to win.

I'm now more determined than ever to win.

I smirk.

I probably look like a sadistic asshole. But when I do this challenge, all I'll be thinking about is the voice. How he screwed up by letting me play these games. I will win and will end his life.

I pick up the belt.

It feels strange in my hands. My head wants to start making the connection to my father, but I don't let it.

All I think about is him—the guy behind the voice.

He used his voice to threaten me. To make me feel small, but it fueled everything inside me.

I crack the belt across the man's back—striking with everything I can. The best way to win is to start strong. To make him think this is only my first gear, that I can go higher, hit harder. Put the fear into him. Fear that he won't be able to survive. That he won't know when this stops. He didn't get a card. He has no clue how long he has to endure, which I realize must be his challenge.

He doesn't know that if he survives, the roles will be reversed except so much worse for me. I have to find a way to make my body come while enduring the pain.

Stop thinking.

I hit again—two.

Three.

Four.

Five.

I act cool and collected with each strike. I don't grunt or show any sound of strain as I use the belt to hit him. I'm silent. I'm composed. In my head, I'm thinking of all the ways I'll kill the voice.

Twenty.

Now for twenty hits with my fist.

This is actually easier for me. I'm used to fighting with my fists. It actually makes it less personal. And maybe the guy will fight back—that would make me fight on instinct instead of hitting him because a damn card told me to.

I carefully place the belt back on the table, hoping I won't have to pick it up again. And then I walk toward the man, every footstep loud and heavy, telling him of his impending doom.

Say the damn safe word, my steps say.

I won't.

You will.

Say it, and I won't beat you to within a second of your life.

Say it, and you get to live.

I should hit him while he's down. That's how you beat a man, but I'm not my father.

I yank him up by the back of his shirt until he's standing in front of me. I see the blood on his back, soaking his white T-shirt. That's why they made him dress in white, so I could see the pain I inflicted on him.

When I look at him, face to face, I realize that he too got instructions somehow. He wouldn't be staying here if he didn't. He doesn't want to lose his challenge, but tears are streaming down his cheeks.

"Welcome to my world," I mutter sadly. This man would have broken a long time ago if he had to face my life. I've had a lifetime of this. He's endured five minutes.

"Fight me, it will make it easier to take," I say. That was a lesson I learned too late. I used to grow quiet, meek when my father raged on me. I used to just submit and obey. It took me too long to realize that it didn't lessen my suffering. It didn't make him hit me any lighter, and by submitting, I just felt helpless.

My eyes glisten with the truth.

I know he sees it.

He lifts his fists in front of his face, and I know he wants to fight me. But then he immediately drops them.

If I wanted confirmation that this is part of his challenge, I just got it. He's not allowed to fight. I don't know what his demons are, but this is part of it.

Jesus Christ.

This is sick.

But it's him or me. And a twisted part of me knows this is for the greater good. If he were to win the whole game, he wouldn't be able to take the bastard down. I would. I don't have a choice but to win.

I ball my hand into a fist, giving him my only warning.

Say your damn safe word, and let's end this.

He closes his eyes.

I sigh; that will just make his fear worse. His body won't be prepared for the hit.

I swing with everything I have, aiming for the hinge of his jaw. I hear it crack. He falls back, blood spills from his mouth, and he lands hard on his ass.

I know how painful it is. I've broken my jaw before. It was a pain to reset and heal. The best way to do that is to stitch it shut for weeks at a time, not something I was willing to do. I assume that's why my smile is more crooked than it ever was before.

I wait for him to move, for him to get back up so I can knock him down again. That will mess with his head and soul. That will defeat him quicker than any pain will.

But he doesn't get back up.

I walk over to him and lean down, putting a finger to his neck.

There's a pulse, but it's weak. His breathing is shallow.

His eyes don't open.

He's unconscious.

I stand up and look around the room.

The card said to continue until he breaks. Until he uses his safe word.

The sucker is definitely broken, but he won't be saying his safe word any time soon.

I'm the devil, but I'm not so monstrous that I'll hit a man when he's unconscious, especially a man whose sins I don't know.

I take a deep breath. I'm barely breaking a sweat even though I'm still wearing a suit and living my nightmare.

"Mr. Pearce, you have a five-minute break. You can clear the room while we tend to Mr. Newman. Then we will continue," the vile motherfucker's voice says again.

The smoke fills my lungs and burns my eyes as I walk to the door at the back. Even though I can't see, I walk straight to the door.

It unlocks as I push on it, and then I'm in the hallway, able to truly breathe for the first time.

I only have five minutes. I don't know where to go or what to do with that time. But I decide to climb, to get fresh air, to look out at the sea—the place that saves everyone in my group when we need it the most—Kai, Enzo, Zeke, Siren. It's saved all of them at different times. Now it's time it saves me.

I cling to the railing as I stare out at the ocean. For a split second, I consider jumping. But I don't. I just hold on, preparing myself for what comes next.

"I'm sorry," her soft sweet voice comes next to me.

I don't know if she's real or a hallucination.

"I shouldn't have come back here. I forgot how bad it can get. This is only the beginning. It can get so much worse," she says.

"How do we survive?" I ask the same question I asked before.

"We don't. Only one of us does, and that person will be haunted forever. Let that person be me. You don't deserve this pain."

♡

LIESEL'S WORDS MEAN I HAVE TO WIN EVEN MORE.

She'll never tell me the truth of what this place is or what happens when you win, but I have to know. I need to know.

I enter the room once more, still not completely sure if Liesel showing up was real or a hallucination I formed to help me deal with this traumatic cruise.

Once I'm back in the room, though, any thoughts of Liesel disappear.

In here, the only way to win is to stay focused.

The room is still filled with smoke when I re-enter. I blink, trying to keep the smoke from my eyes. My nose immediately fills with the haze, making it hard to breathe.

Messing with our senses is meant to strike fear, but my fear is gone.

I walk further into the center of the room, where I once again find the table with the index card. I pick it up. It has more detailed instructions for the second half of the challenge.

Take a beating. Endure any pain given to you. This round ends when you come or say your safe word.

I glance around the room, but I don't find anyone. Mr. Newman is gone. I'm guessing he's still unconscious, and hopefully, a doctor is attending to him.

Who will be giving me my lashing?

I don't see the belt I used before, but I'm guessing it's somewhere. I also don't see the bed.

"I hope you are ready for this round, Mr. Pearce. This will be your biggest challenge yet. The games begin, now," the voice comes over the speakers again.

I want to flip him off, run through the ship to find him and kill him. But I'd never get to him before he killed me. He's too secure where he is. The only way I find the voice at the other end of the speaker is to win.

Let's get this over with.

People run into the room in a flurry. Between the smoke, rush of people, and now lights flashing in my face, it takes me a moment to count how many people are in the room.

Four.

Two men.

Two women.

Jesus, this isn't just a man whipping me like I did to Newman.

Before I can fully process what's happening, the two women are removing my coat jacket, then one is unbuttoning my shirt, while the other works on my pants.

It's not the women I'm worried about. I can overpower them easily. It's the men.

I was told to endure and come, but no one said anything about not fighting back.

Within seconds, I'm stripped of my clothes, and then the women are gone. I think they are still in the room, but they are no longer touching me now that my clothes are off.

I focus in on the guys. They are boxing me in on each side. I could take the two of them.

No.

Let them come.

Let them hurt me.

That's what has to happen for this to be over, in order for me to win.

I let them attack.

They run at me like they are afraid I'll put up a fight. It takes everything in me to not knock them both out, to not resist.

I close my eyes, but that only intensifies their movements in my head. I try meditating as they come for me. I think they are going to tie me up, but they stop just short. That's when I feel the cracking of belts on my back.

The familiar feeling of my dad's belt on me creeps back into my muscle memory. I feel everything just like I did as a child.

They aren't hitting me that hard. The pain is doable. The problem is the haunting memories playing in my head like a movie.

My dad's voice.

His hand grabbing me.

His belt hitting me.

I open my eyes, hoping the memories will fade.

I jolt forward as a belt hits my back. This one was harder than the previous ones, but still not enough to make my eyes water, my pulse to race, or my body to send signals to my brain to fight back.

The two women start approaching me, and I remember the other part of my challenge.

I have to come.

I glance down, but I don't have to to know that I am zero percent turned on. Coming right now seems almost impossible. Even if both women start sucking and licking and giving me the best strip show of my life, it won't be enough.

I should give up now, rather than be tortured like this.

But his voice.

Knowing who he is...

I have to win. I don't have a choice.

I welcome the women in as I collapse to my knees with my cock in my hand. I try to stroke my cock like I did only hours ago in Liesel's bathroom.

My body doesn't respond. My cock is limp in my hands.

"We can help you out there," one of the women says as they reach me. They are wearing lingerie. One has a black, lace bra and thong complete with a garter. The other woman is wearing a white flowy number.

I suppose they are supposed to fulfill whatever my fantasies are. Whether I like a bad girl or an angel—I have both.

Their hands start roaming over my chest as the men continue to hit my back over and over with the belts. Not exactly inflicting pain, but delivering a constant thread of nightmares.

I try to focus on the women.

Their touch.

Their smell.

Their bodies.

I can't feel any of it.

I'm back in the house I grew up in. My father is beating me because he ran out of beer.

The back door opens just as my father is about to hit me again.

Liesel is standing there, except she's no longer a child; she's the woman I know.

"What are you doing here?" I ask.

"Saving you." She smiles.

And then, she's running to me.

She scoops me up from the floor and carries me across the street to her couch.

Finally, I can breathe. My father can't hurt me here. Liesel's protecting me.

I half hiccup, half sob.

"Shh, it's okay. There is nothing to fear, not anymore. I'm here."

I nod.

I'm safe because of her.

Liesel climbs on top of me.

"What are you doing?"

"Loving you. We both need love. This is the only way."

The only way to what?

But then she's kissing me. Her long blonde hair is spilling onto my cheeks and brushing against my neck as she kisses me. It's everything I wanted it to be and more.

So much more. It pushes out all the pain until all I feel is her.

And then I feel her hand grip my cock.

My eyes roll back. I've never been touched like this before.

It's heaven. It's everything.

It's...

CHAPTER 17

LIESEL

I stifle my gasp by biting my lip and swallowing it down until it burns my throat.

I'm sitting in a room with six other participants watching Langston fall to the floor.

He passed out.

I look over at Beckett out of the corner of my eye, trying to gauge his reaction. But he's just as good at hiding his emotions as I am.

Beckett doesn't so much as speak.

I glance back at the large screen in front of us. The men whip him one more time after he collapses, and I want to barrel through the wall and rip their throats out.

Finally, they stop after they realize he's passed out.

The women step back.

I don't know what happened.

Watching him broke me more than whatever I will face next ever could.

I would've called out my safe word if it had a chance at stopping his madness. I don't know how they know our greatest fears and weaknesses, but they always find them here and exploit them. They did the last time I was here too.

Get up.

Get the fuck up, killer!

I watch, but Langston doesn't get up. *Does that mean he's disqualified?*

"Mr. Pearce will be advanced to the next round," the voice says. A voice that always sends chills down my spine.

How will Langston advance?

I stare at Langston more closely, and that's when I see the drop of cum on the floor.

Technically, he came.

A part of me wishes he had lost now. The rest of me wants him to win so he can kick everyone involved in this organization's ass.

But I need the money. I need to win.

Langston is the only person standing between me and victory. Right now, all I can do is beg him to wake up. To show me he's still alive—that this didn't ruin him forever like it did me.

Finally, a couple of men walk over to him. Langston's back is covered in red welts, and there are a few drops of blood, but it doesn't look like they did any permanent damage to his back.

They hook their arms under his and lift him up.

I lean forward in my chair as I stare at a man I thought could never be broken.

Please, don't be broken. Please, please, please.

Langston is slumped in their arms, only being held up because of the men's strength, not his own. He's completely naked. He looks like he just walked through hell, and his limp body is all that is left of him.

I want them to cover him up, to show him some dignity. I know they won't, though.

Slowly, Langston starts to awaken. His head rolls side to side. At first, he doesn't have the strength to even lift his head. But he won't let anyone see him as weak.

It takes everything in him, but he lifts his head up, and then it's like he's looking right at me into a nearby camera. He's telling me he's fine. That he isn't broken. That he survived. And I was the one who helped him survive.

Me.

I'm whom he thought about to get through it.

Not Phoenix.

Not Siren.

Not some other whore.

Not his kids.

Me.

I don't know what to do with that information. It's a lot to take.

Finally, Langston is led out of the room, and we can no longer see him. I know from experience he will be given a room where he can shower, take a hot bath, eat some food, and drink some coffee. There is also a screen to watch the rest of the round if he so chooses.

He's safe now.

Just for now, not for later. Later is the opposite of safe.

What did I do? Why did I bring him here?

I didn't, he followed. This isn't my fault.

At least, that's what I keep telling myself.

"Ms. White and Mr. Beckett, your turn," Mr. Reyes says, entering the room.

We both nod, but don't show any emotion. Soon one or both of us is going to be as beat up and broken as Langston. I hope Beckett realizes what he's gotten himself into now.

He can still stop this before it goes too far. I don't know what his trauma is, but everyone has trauma. Everyone has a past they are running from—Beckett is no different.

I only know pieces of his story. He's the half brother of Enzo Black. Their family is darker than any I know. Beckett's full name is Eli Beckett, but he's always gone by his last name. I know that he's close to Enzo's kids. I don't know how he lost his arm, just that he helped to save Enzo and Kai. Once he did that, he became more a part of the group than I ever could be.

I don't want to belong to their criminal gang. I've tried most of my life to get out, to stop belonging. Now I finally succeeded. They all entered the game just to show me how much they hate me and are on Langston's side.

Beckett remained till the end. I thought he had a woman he cared about. *Nora, was it?* Apparently, they aren't that close.

"If you're ready, you can follow me, Ms. White and Mr. Beckett," Mr. Reyes says.

We both stand at the same time. Beckett holds his hand out to indicate I should go first.

I follow Mr. Reyes while Beckett walks behind me.

I have a few ideas of what awaits me in the room now that it's my turn. I've been here before. They know my weaknesses, my strengths, and my fears.

We enter the room, and Mr. Reyes locks the door behind us.

Beckett and I exchange glances, knowing the lines we will cross if we both try to win this game. I don't give a damn who tortures me, who fucks me. As long as it's not Langston, it doesn't matter.

There are two white, labeled cards on the small table in the center of the room. We walk over and pick up our respective card, neither of us letting the other see what's on our own card.

I read mine:

WHITE,

You already knew what this round would be—a rematch of your last round here. You survived once, but can you survive again?

X

I GRIP THE PAPER TIGHTLY IN MY HAND, CRUMPLING IT INTO A little ball.

I never got over what happened here the last time. To relive it would be my greatest hell. It's one thing to go through it once and survive. It's another to know exactly what's coming, to have visions of the last time haunting my head while it's happening again, and to not mutter my safe word.

I still haven't looked at my safe word. I won't until the final round. I've already made the choice. I'll finish this round. I'll either die or win. There is no pulling myself out.

I glance over at Beckett, who has a stern expression under his black mask.

He doesn't like what's on his card either.

I don't care if he stays or leaves. My card will be carried out whether he continues the game or not, just like what happened to Langston.

I try to think of Langston, try to let my thoughts drift to him, soaking his wounds in a warm tub right now.

It makes me smile.

Langston may be my enemy, and he may be the devil, but he's slipped through my defenses to wiggle a tiny piece of himself into my heart. I can't help but care a little about the bastard.

Plus, holding onto any positive thoughts of Langston for as long as I can will help me. Or it will twist him deeper into my soul and make me hate him more...

"You have five minutes to prepare," the familiar voice announces.

I don't need five minutes, but it gives me time to be in control.

I reach behind my head, and I remove my mask, lying it carefully on the table. I kick off my heels, too. Unfortunately, I'm going to need Beckett's help for the next part.

"Can you help me unzip my dress?" I ask him.

He stands frozen, looking at me like he thinks he just imagined me speaking. He's probably in shock from what is on his card.

I sigh, *poor man.*

I walk over to him and take his card.

"What are you doing?"

"Saving you for the next five minutes."

I crinkle his card into a ball and toss it on the floor. It makes a satisfying bounce as it slides away from us. Then I take Beckett's hand.

"Help me, and I'll help you."

He frowns.

I smile.

"The only thing I need help with is unzipping my dress."

"Did your card say...?"

I shake my head. "My card didn't say that I couldn't undress before it starts. If it isn't clearly on the card, then it's fair game. Now, are you going to help me?"

He nods.

I release his hand and turn around, lifting my black hair up. I hate the stupid wig, but it's necessary.

I feel his cold hand graze my back as he unzips my dress.

I turn back around and face him. "Thank you."

Then I shimmy out of the dress.

Beckett trains his eyes on my face as I stand naked in front of him, which makes me grin even wider at his adorableness.

"If you can't handle looking at my naked body, you should just say your safe word and get out now," I say.

He shakes his head as he removes his jacket and then starts unbuttoning his shirt. It's impressive how he can tackle things I take for granted with one hand. Everything is harder for him, doing everything one-handed.

Finally, he's naked in front of me too.

I, unlike him, let my eyes explore his body. I see the painful-looking scar where his arm was cut. I see the wounds on his torso that mix with the ripples of his abs and V. His long toned legs. I even look at his cock. In a matter of minutes, it could be inside me; it's only fair that I get to look at it. It's a good cock—thick, long, and veiny. But I don't get a thrill in my stomach looking at it. There is only one cock that has ever done that.

I'm sick.

"Say your safe word before this starts, Beckett. I don't need you to protect me. Neither does Langston. If you do this, trust me, there is no going back to the life you had before. This will be your life. Everything will bring you back to this."

He frowns, and then he leans in, so there is no possible way the cameras could pick up his next words. "I'll say my safe word, but only after I ensure you're safe first."

"Why are you protecting me?" I breathe.

"Langston will hate me if I don't."

It's because Langston asked him to, not because Beckett considers me part of the family. That is reserved for Langston.

"I'm warning you, Beckett. You saw what the game did to Langston. It will do the same to you."

He gives me a smug smile and then holds out the stub that is all that is left of his arm. "I survived this. I can survive anything."

I hope he's right.

"The challenge begins now," the haunting voice says. A voice I've tried to rid my brain of so many times, but it's permanently etched into my ears.

I look at Beckett, and he looks at me.

No one enters the room, so I know what is on Beckett's card, what his first task is.

I won't hate him for it, but I won't be able to go near him after he does this. He'll set off my worst nightmares like no one else can.

I should make this easy on Beckett, but my body literally can't. I know the rules, and I can do anything—fight, try to escape, anything. I just have to survive.

I don't know how long I have in here. As long as it takes to break me once again, that's how long.

"Please," I whisper as Beckett takes a step toward me.

He stops at my word, like he wasn't expecting me to make this hard for him. He thought I'd submit. I'd let him tie me up, take all my senses away.

He doesn't know me at all if he thinks I'll just take that. I can't.

I have to fight.

I made a promise to myself I'd never stop fighting. I'd always be in control. I chose this game. I chose to be here. This isn't rape. And yet, I'll fight while they tie me up. I'll fight while they do unthinkable things to my body. It's the only way I can make sense of everything in my mind.

"Beckett, please."

My eyes water—they won't spill tears, but they'll get close.

His hand balls into a fist, his legs remain planted, his eyes dart side to side, trying to make sense of what I'm not saying.

But then he takes a step.

One single step toward me.

I run.

I know the door is locked, that it's a waste to try and break the door down. I learned that the last time. The only way I survive this is to run and outsmart Beckett.

I start running, knowing the smoke will start soon, which might assist me in hiding from him.

The smoke creeps in, but all it does is make me break out in nervous hives—memories flood my head.

Out!

I stay focused on my goal—run until I can't run anymore. I hope to find a bed, some piece of furniture I can use either as a weapon or to hide under while I make my next move.

I find nothing.

It will be exactly the same as before.

You are strong.

You are powerful.

You are in control.

You can block out all evil with your mind.

I feel Beckett's hand grab onto my hair.

I was so close to getting caught. Luckily, I'm still wearing the black wig, so all Beckett grabs is the wig, and I keep running.

That was too close.

My time is running out.

Beckett is better than the last man who chased me. He's faster, smarter.

I should give up.

I can't give up.

I run.

Run.

RUN.

My hair falls from the bun—loose and free. Something I'll never be.

It will be my downfall—I know it before it happens.

I feel the tug on the back of my head, my feet stop in their tracks, and my body slings back as Beckett pulls me tight to his body, still holding on by my hair.

"I'm sorry," he whispers.

"Me too," I say back. I'm already broken. Technically, I've been broken since Enzo's dad raped me. But it didn't have to be this way for Beckett.

He starts dragging me by the hair. I grab onto his hand with mine and sink my nails into him.

He hisses but doesn't release me.

"You know you can save us both. Just say your safe word, and I'll say mine as well," Beckett moans in my ear as I feel little droplets of his blood dripping from his hand.

"I can't."

"Yes, you can."

"I don't know my safe word. I won't read it until the final round."

He gasps. "Fuck."

I feel him loosen his grasp, and I try to scramble away. My hair starts to slip through his fingers, almost to the end before he tightens his grip again.

Beckett's decision has been made. He'll do this for as long as he can, until he's pushed to a limit that Langston would kill him for crossing.

We both look at each other through the smoke. It's the last moment that we aren't truly enemies. From this moment on, we will hate each other. We will never be able to look at each other the same.

I'm done begging. And he's done talking.

He yanks me hard until I fall to my knees, and then he resumes dragging me. Once again, I try to dig my nails into his hand, but I end up just grabbing onto his wrist to keep him from ripping my hair out as he drags me.

Suddenly, he stops.

I know why.

Fear builds inside me like a windstorm. If only I had magical powers that would allow me to release the storm inside me on this room. I could destroy everything so much easier that way.

I know Beckett has to release my hair to grab my arms, my legs. So I wait patiently for my moment.

He releases.

I try to run. I scramble onto my feet and start to dive.

But he's smarter than me. He anticipates my move and kicks my feet out from under me. As I'm falling, he grabs one arm and twists it behind my back so forcefully that he's about to pop my shoulder out of its socket.

I can feel the tears welling, the pain radiating through my arm and down my spine.

"Give me your other hand," he growls.

No. I won't give in.

"Break my arm if you have to, but I won't ever submit to you."

My other hand reaches out, trying to find the chains I know he plans to tie me to. *Maybe if I grab one, I can use it as a weapon against him?*

I find a chain.

I sling it as hard as I can at Beckett's head.

I feel the weight hit him.

But he's like me. He must be used to the pain. He doesn't even react.

Instead, he once again kicks my feet out from underneath me. I reach out with the hand he isn't holding to try and catch myself from hitting the ground.

No.

I feel the cold metal clamping around my other hand.

He won.

I can keep fighting, but there is nothing I can do now. I can't break the chains holding me.

With one arm encapsulated, he grabs my arm on the floor and yanks me up. I try to kick, to fight, I even spit to try and get him to stop. He's relentless.

My free hand goes into the next handcuff over my head, and finally, my arms are locked in a wide V over my head.

I get in several vicious kicks as he slides down my body and moves to grab my ankles. But I'm weak compared to him. He attaches a chain with a metal cuff to each ankle until my legs are spread apart, and I can't move.

And then he's standing in front of me looking solemn. I know what comes next, and it's the worst. He still won't look beyond my eyes to my naked body. I stripped myself of clothes rather than have someone else strip me, but that was the only control over the situation I have.

"Please," I say, one last time.

I can hear him swallow, hear the pain in his throat, see the heartbreak on his face. But he won't stop.

We both know it.

Then I feel the gag against my mouth. I open—I'm the one making this decision, not him. He ties it tightly around the back of my head.

One more sense gone.

I can't move.

I can't talk.

I try to turn off my hearing before he places the earplugs into my ears, cutting off all sound.

I can't move.

I can't talk.

I can't hear.

There is one step left, and it's the worst of them all.

I close my eyes—trying to gain my composure before the blindfold goes around my eyes. Once it's on, I open my eyes. I can't see anything.

I can't move.

I can't talk.

I can't hear.

I can't see.

The only sense left is smell, and I'm pretty sure they'd cut that sense off too if there were another way for me to breathe.

He's taken everything from me. I no longer have any control over my body. The only thing I could do is try to cry out a safe word. That would get my gag removed long enough to see if I was using my safe word or not.

But that would only be a temporary solution. Once they removed my gag, and I didn't call out my safe word, they'd resume.

I take a deep breath through my nose, trying to gain any knowledge of who is in the room or what's going to happen next. I don't smell anything except smoke. I never got a good whiff of Beckett, so I don't know what he smells like. I'll have no idea if he's the one touching me or someone else.

Right now, no one is touching me.

The not knowing, the waiting—that's the worst part of this all.

I try to meditate in my head, but I've never been very good at meditating. I can feel my pulse rushing, my body warming, sweat bubbling on my forehead and neck.

And then it starts.

Hands...

So many hands touching my body that I can't keep track.

Being sensory deprived like this makes it impossible to tune out the touching, the feeling. It all becomes more intensified. A light brush of a hand feels like a million nerve endings bursting. A rough grasp feels like a bone breaking. A slap feels like a gale-force wind hitting my face.

I can't anticipate a touch or a slap.

I can't decipher if the feelings are enjoyable or perverted.

I can't fight back.

I'm helpless.

The one place I never thought I'd be.

Hands start invading my body. Gripping my breasts. Spreading my legs. Dipping into my pussy, my asshole.

Make it stop.

Make it all go away.

Langston. Think about Langston. Think about what you are doing to him, for him. Think about all that you've lost. Think about who you are doing this for.

CHAPTER 18

LANGSTON

'm dragged out of the room by my arms. I don't know where I'm being taken, and I don't care. My mind is on a loop of all things Liesel.

My brain has decided for the moment that Liesel's snarky comments are my favorite thing about her, replaying her highlights.

"One touch and your cock is as hard as steel."

"One kiss and I'm all you can think about."

"This is war, killer."

I smile at the last one.

A door opens in front of me, and the men turn us sideways so we can all fit through. Then, I'm being shoved into a tub. Warm water and bath salts sting my back, but I don't even have the energy to hiss or protest.

"Stay in the water for at least a half-hour. It will help. To your left, there is a tray of food for you to eat and a remote to turn off the TV if you prefer not to watch. The next challenge starts in five minutes," one of the men says.

And then they leave.

I tilt my head up. I'm in a bathroom, soaking in a large tub filled with bath salts that have started to soothe the ache on my back.

Why do I feel so weak? I don't remember them doing anything that should make me feel this terrible.

I inhale and get a whiff of a burger.

I turn to my left, and I find a gourmet looking burger, a milkshake, fries, a pizza, a salad, and some cake looking thing. I want it all.

I grab the milkshake first, knowing I'll be able to get those calories in with the least amount of effort. Then I can move to what my stomach is really craving: that damn burger.

I suck down the milkshake. Within seconds, my headache is gone, and my head clears.

I feel like I've been drugged, and the drugs are just starting to leave my system.

Maybe I was?

The screen in front of me starts flashing, and then I see the room I was just in. I cringe looking at it. I can't watch whoever goes next.

I see Liesel walk in, followed by Beckett, and I know I won't be able to tear my eyes away.

I watch them read the cards.

Please, just get out. I want to scream at them that it's not worth it.

Beckett's hand is on the back of her dress, and he's unzipping it.

Motherfucker.

I told him not to touch her, not to fuck her.

The next thing I know, they are both naked, and I'm terrified. *Why did they willingly get undressed?*

Why?

WHY?

Then, the monster's voice starts the challenge.

Liesel runs.

Why is she running?

Beckett chases her.

There is so much smoke initially; it makes it hard to see. My own eyes begin to water just thinking about how it feels to be in that room.

Then the smoke lessens as Beckett catches her.

She keeps fighting.

My Liesel.

I'm so sorry.

You are mine to play with. Mine to torture. Mine to kill.

You owe me penance, not him.

And yet, she'll pay the price all the same unless she mutters her safe word.

Save yourself.

Save me.

This is torture watching her suffer. It might be worse than going through it myself.

I should turn the screen off. I can't help her, and this will just hurt me. But I can't leave her alone.

We may be enemies, but she's *my* enemy—*mine*. No one else gets to touch her.

And then my heart stops. I wouldn't be shocked if I died from a stroke or heart attack watching Beckett restrain her.

My chest rages with pain; my heart thumps hard then slow, fast and quiet. It doesn't know what to do; it's just yelling at me to get my ass out of the water and go save her.

But I can't save her. Only she can save herself.

Beckett has her tied, her arms and legs spread in the center of the room.

She can handle this. She's strong.

And then I see what comes next.

A gag around her mouth.

Earplugs.

A blindfold.

She must be going crazy inside being so sensory deprived.

I'm going to lose it.

My chest pounds for her. I don't know what I feel for Liesel other than possessiveness, and anger at her fucking sins.

But this...

This is unthinkable for her to endure.

Except, she's endured it before. And she came back. *Why did she come back?*

I look at Beckett—it's obvious what he's required to do next, but he's just standing there still as a statue, unsure. *Does he touch her and endure my wrath, or does he say his safe word and leave her vulnerable?*

He looks to the door.

A moment later, three men have entered.

They look similar to the men who beat me.

Don't fucking touch her!

But of course, that's what they are there for—to ravish her. To make her feel out of control and so overwhelmed that she can't think straight.

To many other people, this might be their wildest fantasy—tied up, blindfolded, and fucked senseless by four hot men.

To Liesel, this is her greatest nightmare. I've seen her fuck. She has to be in complete control. I don't blame her. I'm much the same way, which is one of the many reasons why we'd never work together.

The men start touching her, groping her, and Beckett follows suit. He runs his hand down the curve of her waist and then grips her hip while a man penetrates her with his finger.

I can't watch.

I can't *not* watch.

I run out of the tub and go to the door. Water drips all over the tile floor, and I almost slip on my ass. I yank the door handle, already expecting the door to be locked.

I have to get to Liesel.

I have to stop this.

I pull harder, determined to get the door to budge. All I end up doing is pulling my side of the handle clean off. I throw my body against the door. I kick as hard as I can, but this isn't an ordinary door. This one is thick, most likely bulletproof.

I slink to the floor as my tears fall. I can't save her.

I hear a slapping sound, and that motivates me to get my ass off the floor and run to the screen.

Liesel's cheek is pink from where she was slapped.

Beckett steps up to her and slaps her.

I'm going to kill him.

And then I watch as a man slides his cock into my woman and I'm lost, so fucking lost.

Watching Waylon fuck her drove me mad—but this, this will change me in a way I haven't even figured out yet.

Does watching her get punished like this wipe her clean of the greatest sin she could commit?

No.

But it does weaken me, make me feel like she's suffered more than anyone. When I kill her, I'll be merciful. I'll make it painless and quick. Not torturous, like this.

This is pain.

There is only one time I've felt this much pain: when Liesel betrayed everything I thought I knew about her.

I never thought helplessly watching her put herself into a situation like this would make me feel anything for her. I thought my heart had closed to her permanently, but I was wrong.

This.

This...

It changes everything.

I have to win. I can't let her endure more than this. I don't know how many rounds are left, but if she doesn't mutter her safe word now, I have to get her to early in the next round. I have to convince her. Hopefully, this experience will remind her to not push any further.

Maybe if I promise to give her the money when I win, she'll stop?

I don't know if she'll believe me, but I have to try.

I can't fucking go through this again.

I can't.

I crumple to the floor, glued to the TV as my heart breaks more and more for the girl who used to live across the street from me. To the girl who, at one point in my life, meant everything. *Maybe she means more to me now than I'll ever admit to myself?*

Tears continue to stream down my face. I realize that Beckett's task is to repeat one of the men's actions on Liesel. When there is nothing left for Beckett to repeat but fuck her, he says his safe word.

When he turns and looks at the camera, there are tears in his swollen eyes. He hardly even knows Liesel, and he's a fucking mess.

I'm not going to survive this.

I scream my own safe word, wishing that I could make it stop, but no one is listening to me. No one will come.

I pray to God that this is fake, that this is all a show Liesel is putting on to show me how much I fucking care about her.

I know it's not, but my brain is trying anything to make sense of this.

I'm broken.

I was already broken, but this—this is as bad as it gets.

I don't know how long it goes on. I don't know when it stops, but at some point, I look at the screen, and she's no longer on it.

That's when I collapse again. I fall into the darkness of sleep, and that's where I plan on spending the rest of my life: swimming in the dark.

CHAPTER 19

LIESEL

I'm barely conscious as I'm dragged out of the room, but I survived.

Now, I get a break. A hot bath and warm food. I won't be watching any of the other rounds. I don't care. I just need to refocus before my next round.

A door is opened in front of me, and I'm pushed inside.

There is a body on the floor.

"Sorry, we went to the wrong room." The men start to turn and lead me away.

"Stop. I want to stay here."

The men look at each other and shrug. Then they leave me barely able to stand on my own two feet. Langston better not have eaten all the food because I'm going to need something to eat.

As soon as the door is locked behind me, I stumble forward to Langston's body on the ground, and I collapse next to him.

I can hear him breathing. *He's alive, just passed out.*

He looks so beautifully broken lying on the floor. I reach out and stroke his hair back off his forehead. I want to press my lips to him. I want to feel him moan against my mouth after everything we've just been through—I need something warm and comforting.

He opens his eyes.

"Are you real?" he asks.

I smile. "I'm real. I survived, just like you."

"What are you doing here?"

"A room mixup, but it worked out in my favor."

He finally smiles. "Mine too."

"Think you can sit up?"

"Do you think you can?"

I sigh. "As long as you promise to feed me lots of pizza."

"That I can do."

We both inch up slowly until we are in a sitting position leaning against the base of the tub. Langston reaches back and grabs a towel and hands it to me. It's only then I remember I'm still naked.

"Thanks," I mumble as I wrap the towel around my body. He ties a towel around his waist.

Then he pulls the tray of food in front of us. I grab a slice of pizza, and he grabs the burger. We both eat, trying to regain some strength.

"You care about me," I say.

He stops mid-bite.

"No, I don't," he says.

I smile brighter. "Liar. You care about me."

He frowns and shakes his head. "I don't."

"You can't lie anymore. I know the truth."

"How?"

I grin around a bite of pizza as he stares deeply into my eyes. I can feel my cheeks blushing like a schoolgirl who just found out her crush likes her.

"You called out your safe word."

He frowns. "And that means I care about you?"

I nod. "You would have only said your safe word to get them to stop hurting me."

"Explain."

I laugh. "My challenge was to last until someone said their safe word to try and get it to stop. You were that person. You stopped my suffering Langston, which means you must have been suffering a lot watching me."

It was the same rules last time, but last time I was here, there was no one here that personally knew me. It took much longer for someone to say their safe word to try and stop my pain.

"Does that mean I'm out of the game?" Langston asks.

"No, you didn't say it as part of your challenge. You're still in. But if you want out, just say it at the beginning of the next round."

He nods.

I go back to happily scarfing down my pizza.

"I care."

His words make my heart skip a beat.

"I care about you. But I still hate you," he says.

I bite my bottom lip to hide my pleasure at hearing those words.

"Same," I say.

His eyes light up at my voice.

We both finish eating all the food on the tray.

"Get in the tub. You must be aching," Langston says.

I nod.

He turns the hot water on to warm up the tub and then holds out his hand to me. I take it, and he pulls me up into a standing position.

I let my towel fall to the floor, but this time, Langston doesn't take in my body.

"It's okay, you can look at me," I say.

He shakes his head. "If I do, I won't be able to stop. I'll run my eyes over every inch of your body, looking for all the ways you were hurt. And you don't need to be violated again, even by me."

What happened in there broke him more than it broke me. Maybe because I'm already in a million pieces.

I step into the water and sink down, expecting Langston to join me, to wash me, something.

He doesn't.

He can barely even look at me.

"What happens next?" Langston asks with a heavy voice.

"The final round."

"And that round is worse than this one?"

I shrug. "It can be."

"When it starts, I want you to say your safe word immediately. Say it and end this. I'll give you all the money I stole back. I'll give you more than that if you want. I'll make our fight fair again, just end this."

I close my eyes. *I wish it were that simple.*

"I can't."

"Yes, you can." Langston grabs my hands, and I open my eyes to look at him. "You entered this for the money. I'll deposit the money back in your account, plus a couple of extra million. Just say your safe word."

I touch Langston's face. For a moment, he looks like the boy I used to know. Bright, warm, and a little bit mischievous, with a haunting brokenness behind his eyes.

There is a knock at the door, saving me from more conversation. A man enters holding our clothes.

"Be ready in fifteen minutes for the final round," he says, placing our clothes on the back of a chair.

We both nod at him.

"We need to get dressed," I say, getting out of the tub and drying off. I don't care if Langston is watching me or not. We both get dressed, and I find the note with my safe word attached to the inside of my dress.

I pull it out and read it.

Unicorn.

Langston studies me. "You didn't even read your safe word until this moment, did you?"

I shake my head.

"I should have called you my wild thing instead of huntress," he says, impressed.

I smile. I like hearing him call me his anything.

"Promise me you'll use your safe word if things go too far," Langston says.

"I promise," but it's just another lie. There is only one thing that will stop me, and he's standing in front of me in a tux.

LANGSTON

I want to kill Liesel for what she did. But I'd also die to protect her.

It's confusing, but it's how I feel.

Liesel is once again in her swanky black dress. I'm in my tux. We only have minutes left until the final round begins. I don't know how many competitors we face, or if we are the only two left. We'll find out soon enough.

"How do you feel?" she asks, while she traces her hands up my forearms to my biceps, sending chills up my body.

"Better when you do that."

She smiles. "I'm serious. Did you get enough to eat? Did you soak long enough? Did—"

I lean down and kiss her. She tastes like marinara sauce mixed with lavender, which makes me grin into the kiss. Her lips are soft and warm; they respond immediately to my touch. I'm the only man who gets to kiss her. That may be how it should be, but it's not reality. I hate that this can't be our reality.

My tongue pushes into her mouth, and she jerks back. But as my tongue massages her bottom lip, she lets me into her mouth. The attack of her tongue against mine proves that this is what our mouths were always meant to be doing—kissing each other.

I can feel the minutes and seconds ticking by; we don't have forever. Our time together is precious. Soon, there will be a knock on the door, and this kiss will be nothing but a memory.

But I hope it's a memory I'll be able to take with me long after. In the middle of the challenges we are about to face, I hope this brings us peace.

"Thank you," she says as my lips leave hers.

"Don't ever thank me for kissing you. Kissing you is a gift to me as much as it is for you."

I tuck a strand of her hair behind her ear. "No wig tonight?"

She shakes her head. "Beckett pulled it off in the last round; everyone knows I have blonde hair. So tonight, I'm going in as me."

"Whatever you say, Ms. White."

She blushes, and her eyes sparkle.

"Turn around."

She does, and I help her fasten her mask to her face. My fingers brush against her bare arms when I'm done, and I watch her goosebumps rise. A small part of me is excited about what this round could entail. It could finally give me a reason to fuck Liesel.

I don't want this twisted game to be the reason that I sink my cock into her. But my cock is excited all the same.

"Turn around," Liesel says, repeating my words.

I do, and she stands on her tiptoes to reach my head where she can fasten my mask.

There is a knock at the door just as she finishes.

Instinctively, I step in front of her, and my hand reaches back to hold hers, to protect her.

"If you'll follow me this way, we are about to start the final round," the man says and then starts walking.

I don't let go of Liesel's hand as we start following the man out of the room. The man leads us down the hallway to the same room we both faced our previous challenge.

I stop and turn to Liesel before we enter.

"I will do everything I can to protect you. I can't fail—not again."

She releases my hand. "I can't let you protect me," she whispers.

Then she walks past me and into the room like she's the CEO entering a boardroom—full of sass and determination.

I walk in behind her with her words ringing in my ear. *She won't let me protect her.*

Well, too fucking bad. After the life we've both lived, she deserves my protection. I'm the only one who gets to kill her.

To my shock, we are the only two in the room. I glance to Liesel, who looks just as stunned. *Are we the only two who made it to the final round?*

The voice appears. "Welcome to the final round. Only two contestants remain. Each of you have cards lying on the table. The final round begins in five minutes."

Liesel and I both walk over to the table with the cards.

We pick up our respective cards in unison.

I'm dying to know what's on her card, but I doubt that's allowed.

So instead, I focus on reading mine:

A WOMAN YOU KNOW WILL BE TIED TO A BED. FUCK HER SO THAT YOUR competitor thinks you're hurting her. You will have thirty minutes to strike fear into your competitor. You will then receive new instructions. If your competitor shows no fear, you've failed.

I JUST HAVE TO MAKE LIESEL THINK I'M HURTING THIS WOMAN, NOT actually inflict pain. I don't know who the woman is, but it doesn't seem so terrible. Although, Liesel will hate me more than she already does.

Liesel finishes reading her card. She doesn't show any emotion. I don't know what her card says, but I'm guessing something similar to mine.

Just please don't let it involve her being tied up again. I won't be able to sit by and watch that happen.

Smoke starts billowing into the room, the indication that the game is about to start.

"Your thirty minutes start now," the wicked voice says.

Liesel and I exchange glances through the evaporating smoke. Apparently, the smoke won't be hanging around this time.

Two beds appear side by side in front of us.

"Phoenix?" I ask, looking to the woman tied to the bed right in front of me. *It can't be. Did they kidnap her?* She would never agree to be here.

"Waylon," Liesel whispers.

My eyes cut from Phoenix tied to the first bed to Waylon tied to the other.

What the hell is going on?

I look to Liesel, like she might have an explanation for this. If this happened last time, she could have at least warned me.

Liesel isn't looking at me; she's walking toward Waylon's bed. His arms and legs are tied in an X to the bedposts, same as Phoenix.

I run to Phoenix's side.

"It's okay," she whispers. "I agreed."

My heart clenches. I don't know if she understands what she agreed to or not, but her words at least comfort me. Now isn't the time to ask questions, though.

I look deep into Phoenix's eyes, letting her know what is about to happen as best as I can with just one look.

Phoenix and I aren't as good at understanding each other with looks as Liesel and I are, but it's pretty clear what I'm asking in this situation.

"Yes," she whispers, her voice aching.

My eyes cut over to Liesel, who is already undressing Waylon. Her lips are pressed to his, just as they were to mine a few moments ago.

My stomach twists, wishing it were me tied to her bed.

Liesel doesn't look over at me. She just keeps kissing and moaning. *Jesus, I can't focus on that.*

But how am I going to strike fear in her if she won't even look at me? If she looks at me, she'll know I'm just doing whatever is on my card. She won't be any more afraid of me than she already is.

Phoenix is tied to the bed loosely with rope—rope I can easily pull off. I can fuck her in any position in any place in this room.

My mind races, thinking about what I can do to scare Liesel.

I remove my jacket and then roll my sleeves up.

"Lang—" Phoenix starts, but I throw my hand over her mouth, silencing her.

She takes the hint and doesn't speak when I remove my hand.

Liesel and Waylon, on the other hand, are a non-stop moan-fest. All I hear is moaning and groaning coming from their direction.

I try to shut them out, but that's impossible. My fists clench, and my body fills with adrenaline and rage. I actually think it's going to be easier than I thought to get Liesel to fear me.

I growl. It's loud, demanding the attention of everyone in the room as I grab the ropes at Phoenix's ankles and rip them hard. The ropes break free from the posts at the end of the bed.

Phoenix gasps, but she's used to my loud, controlling behavior. I can be as rough as I want, and it won't bother her. She'll welcome it.

Phoenix is wearing black leggings and a long-sleeved black shirt. She has a black mask over her eyes. Strangely, the mask only adds to Phoenix's outfit—like she should always be wearing a mask.

Even though I've fucked Phoenix plenty of times, it feels strange, almost immoral to do it now.

She chose you. She came to you. She wants you.

I glance over at Liesel on top of Waylon. She hasn't removed any of her clothes, but I know his cock is about to slide between her legs.

Focus on Phoenix, on fucking her.

But what if she isn't the one I crave anymore?

I grab Phoenix's legs with all my rage and flip her over until the rope at her arms twists, tightening the bindings.

She gasps at the sudden movement, at her body twisting in an uncomfortable way. But that's what this is about—fucking her so forcefully and so painfully that Liesel is terrified of me.

I climb onto the bed and rip her leggings back until her ass is showing. I slap her ass red.

She grunts, but when I reach between her legs, I feel how wet she is.

She likes it.

She would be the perfect match for me, unlike Liesel, who would be horrified if I touched her like this—untamed and wild.

I unzip my pants, pull myself out, and roughly enter her from behind. My hand reaches out to grab her face and shove my fingers into her mouth, pulling on her cheek. Her saliva drips down her chin as I pound into her.

Don't look at Liesel.

Focus on fucking Phoenix. Focus on making it blissful for Phoenix; that's the best way to frighten Liesel. If she sees Phoenix loving how rough I am, Liesel will be mortified.

I have no doubt what the next challenge is—fucking Liesel. I'm not sure I can handle it. Not after she just fucked Waylon. Not after I just fucked Phoenix. *Not like this.*

I want to win.

I want to protect Liesel.

How do I do that?

The bed creaks and breaks beneath us; that's how hard I've been fucking Phoenix. In such a trance that I didn't notice her sobs, her tears, her pain.

Phoenix likes the pain, though. I didn't break her.

One glance over at the single tear floating in Liesel's eye tells me I broke her.

CHAPTER 21

LIESEL

his is all a game.
    A twisted.
    Fucked up.
Evil game.

Langston may not realize how dangerous this game is yet, but he will soon.

I ride Waylon's cock like I have an unhealthy level of love for him. My body pumps over his harder and faster; my eyes are wild with love and lust. I even let my eyes water a little. I haven't cried in years, but this—seeing Langston next to me, pretending to hurt his wife while I pretend that fucking Waylon is my favorite thing in the world, makes me insane.

It pushes me to the edge of spilling my heart. To telling every rotten truth. To stop the lies between Langston and me. But if I did, we'd both be destroyed.

So I keep pretending. I like Waylon—truly, I do, but I don't love him. I'm incapable of love.

Yet, by the way that Langston keeps shooting me dirty glances, it's clear he believes I love the man whose cock is inside me.

Mission accomplished.

That was what I was supposed to do according to my card. Make Langston think I'm in love with Waylon. And I'm sure Langston's told him to make me afraid of him.

I don't really fear Langston any more than I did before we started, but still, I wince at every slap.

Maybe I'm lying to myself? Maybe I do fear Langston?

No, I'm just afraid of what will come next. I can't be with Langston in that way…

Waylon moans, and I turn my attention back to him. I feel him close to coming. I rock my hips against him, pushing him closer to orgasm.

"Come with me, baby," he says.

I smile at him and stroke his hair like his words are melting my heart.

I nod. "Together."

Then I feel his warm cum inside me at the same time I yell out his name—faking an orgasm, something I've perfected over the years.

Once he's done shooting cum into my body, I lean forward and kiss him tenderly on the lips.

"Thank you," I whisper.

"My pleasure. I love fucking you here where everyone is watching, knowing that you can have another man's cock in you, but that you belong to me, no one else."

"Yours," I whisper against his lips.

I feel Langston's hot stare on me. I hear his growl and the rough slapping of skin as he fucks Phoenix with everything he has. Every noise bites into me.

He's taking out his frustration with me on Phoenix. And instead of feeling pity for the woman, I feel jealousy. I wish I were the one Langston was fucking that hard.

But my body and mind couldn't handle it. Langston is too much for me. Maybe that's why I chose Waylon—he's safe.

I continue to kiss Waylon sweetly until our time is up. I've already completed my mission, and I'm just trying to focus on anything else except Langston going to town on Phoenix.

The slapping.

The kissing.

The grunting.

The moaning.

The smell of hot sex.

It's impossible to shut out.

I sigh into Waylon's lips.

"I love you, baby," he says.

I kiss him. I never say the words back because our time is up.

"You both passed the first round. You have five minutes to collect yourself before we proceed," the voice says.

I take off. I need out of the room. I need to breathe without smelling Langston. Need to think without Langston popping into my mind. Touch without Langston's lips branding into my memory as he kisses me.

I want to run to the top deck to get some air, but Langston will find me there, and I need some space away from him to make sure I know what I'm doing.

I dart into one of the bathrooms and lock the door behind me.

I take deep, hard breaths, filling my lungs with warm oxygen as I grab onto the sink and look at myself in the mirror.

I'm doing the right thing.

I'm going to win.

I have to win.

CHAPTER 22

LANGSTON

I really do hate Liesel.

And yet, I've never wanted her more.

As frustrating as that was, it was also the most erotic moment of my life.

I've spent my entire life needing to fuck Liesel and yet not having her. That was the closest we've ever gotten, and it was nowhere near enough.

Hearing her, smelling her, seeing her, but not being able to touch her, that was my own special kind of hell. One I hope to rectify soon.

Five minutes.

That's how long we have to the next round. I watch Liesel dart out of the room. Immediately, I sprint after her, leaving Phoenix still tied to the bed.

Of all the ways I've imagined Liesel and me fucking for the first time, this isn't what I'd choose. Minutes after we were both forced to fuck other people in the same room while being watched by strangers isn't exactly ideal.

Five minutes isn't long enough either, but at least it would be our choice.

I chase Liesel down the hallway.

She slams a door shut.

I run after her.

My pants are still undone as I chase her.

I grab the doorknob and turn, but it doesn't open.

She locked it.

"Huntress?" I ask through the door.

I wait for her to answer.

She doesn't.

I press my hand against the door as I feel the seconds ticking by. Our time to choose is ending.

If we both want to continue the game, we'll end up fucking each other. It's what I want, what I need, but I didn't want it this way.

But nothing between Liesel and me is ever what I want.

Five minutes tick by before Liesel opens the door.

She's not surprised I'm standing here. She knew.

She knew I was here. She knew and chose to keep the door shut.

Her eyes are full of apology.

I nod.

"Ready?" I ask.

"Are you?"

I have no fucking idea. The woman I've wanted all my life is about to agree to fuck me in a wicked game. I have no idea how to feel about that.

A soft smile spreads on her lips as she reads my thoughts.

"Me too," she says, and then she walks past me. Her hips sway extra hard, like she's trying to seduce me.

Although, she's had me under her spell since I was thirteen. She doesn't need to try to get me to fuck her. All she has to do is say yes.

I walk down the hallway, redoing my pants even though I know they are probably going to be ripped from my body soon.

What will it feel like to fuck Liesel? Like a fucking atomic bomb going off.

Liesel walks back into the room two seconds before I do. The setup is the same, but now Phoenix and Waylon are gone. I should be worried about Phoenix, but I'm not. She told me she came here voluntarily, and she can take care of herself. Plus, I don't want to think of anything else while I'm with Liesel.

"Read your cards, and the game starts in five minutes," the voice says.

We see the cards with our names on it once again on the table, and exchange glances at each other. After this moment, everything is going to change.

I pick up my card reluctantly and flip it over.

FUCK HER LIKE YOU'VE ALWAYS WANTED TO. TAKE NO MERCY. MAKE HER hate you. Make her fear you. Make her say her safe word.

I SUCK IN A LONG BREATH. SOMEHOW, I KNEW WHAT WAS ON THE card. I knew the card would make her hate me if I were to succeed. The one positive is that Liesel already hates me, so that part wouldn't change if I complete my challenge.

I don't know if I'm going to be able to fuck in her a way that makes her say her safe word, though. She's been through a lot, me taking her control away and fucking her hard wouldn't force her to quit.

Fuck her like you've always wanted to.

That was the first order. So first, I can fuck her how I've always wanted to—a loophole.

First, fuck her like I want to.

Then, fuck her to make her fear me, to get her to say her safe word.

I'll worry about the second part later, but I've been dreaming about the first task since I hit puberty.

Liesel doesn't look at me. She's still staring at her card; her lips are moving along with the words. I've never wished more that I could read lips.

Look at me, huntress.

She doesn't.

She drops her card and stares at it on the ground as our time ticks down.

"You may begin. You have as long as it takes until one of you says your safe word," the voice says.

I take a step toward Liesel, and she takes a step back.

I frown.

She's already afraid of me.

That or her card...?

I take another step. She takes another step back.

"I'm not going to hurt you."

"Yes, you will, killer."

Her words sting, but they are also the truth. I'm always hurting her. *Why would she think this would be any different?*

I take another step, and she trembles.

I may have done too well in the previous round if she's this afraid of me.

"Huntress, I won't hurt you." *I won't do anything you don't want me to do. Someday, I'll have to kill you, but that day isn't today.*

Another step, and I have her boxed into a corner. There is nowhere for her to go.

"Trust me," I whisper.

I reach out my hand slowly to touch her, and she cringes away.

It crushes me.

So instead, I grab her wrist and place it against my heart.

"I'm scared too."

She swallows her pain, trying to lock it inside. Really, I want her to unleash it on me. I deserve to feel her pain as much as I need to feel her pleasure. I've fucked up as much as she has. I deserve to die just like she does.

She closes her eyes, keeping her hand on my heart.

I let her hold her hand there for as long as it takes. This challenge can last as long as we need. I'm not going to rush our first time. I'm going to let every moment linger. I'm going to memorize every little thing because I don't know if I'll ever get this chance again.

I close my eyes too—just feeling her warm hand through my shirt.

My heart aches for more, but also for this moment to last forever.

Once I feel that Liesel is ready for more, I reach my hands out and grab her face, lifting it gently toward mine. I open my eyes, watching her reaction as my lips hover over hers.

I want this kiss more than I want to breathe. And my body craves what comes next more than anything else. I'd trade life itself for a chance with her.

Her eyes open, and for a moment, it feels like old times. We share a direct connection between our hearts, souls, and minds.

I win, her eyes say.

I frown, not understanding.

What did her card say?

It doesn't matter. She can win the game for all I care; I just want her. That's me winning.

I lean closer, closing the gap until my lips all but brush against hers.

"Unicorn," she whispers.

I raise an eyebrow in confusion.

"That concludes the game. Mr. Pearce is the winner," the voice says.

I stare at Liesel, but she's no longer looking at me.

I grab her chin, trying to force her to look at me. I don't understand how she could go through what she did and yet couldn't endure a simple kiss from me.

Her face has morphed, and she is no longer open to me. I can't see what she's thinking or feeling.

Two men enter, grab onto Liesel's arms, and lead her out of the room.

Suddenly, I'm alone.

I won.

I don't give a shit about the money.

"I'll escort you to meet the owners, Mr. Pearce. There you will be able to collect the twenty million dollar prize," Mr. Reyes says.

I nod. "Lead the way."

CHAPTER 23

LIESEL

It's over.

I take a deep breath, unsure of my actions.

It had to be done. I didn't have a choice.

But I know how this ends.

That makes me smile, even though he's going to hate me even worse than he already does.

The men continue to hold onto my arms as they lead me out of the room and up to the top deck. There is a small dingy boat waiting to take me to shore. They lead me to it and release my arms once I'm inside the small raft-like boat.

"Thank you for playing, Ms. White. You'll be taken back to shore now," one of the men says.

I nod.

They continue to stand there until the raft is lowered into the water, and there is no way for me to escape and climb back on board.

"I'm Kyo. We should be back to shore in the next twenty minutes," he says.

"Thank you, Kyo."

He starts the engine once we've hit the water, and we pull away.

I did the right thing.

I did the right thing.
I did the right thing.
Those words continue to play over and over in my head the entire twenty minutes the dingy takes us to shore.
I did the right thing.
I did the right thing.
I did the right thing.
I can't look back at the yacht. I can't look back, hoping to find Langston. What's done is done.
I did the right thing.
I had no other choice.
I already know how this ends. He'll be fine.
The dingy stops back at the dock, and Kyo helps me off.
"Your ride will be here shortly. Can I get you anything else?" Kyo says when we are both standing on the dock.
I shake my head and then walk down the dock to where Maxwell is standing outside of a limo.
"Did you win?" he asks.
"Yea. Yea, I did."
He smiles. "Good. Now don't give me a heart attack like that again."
I smile back.
He helps me into the back of the limo, before heading to the front to drive me.
I lean my head against the headrest and close my eyes, trying to forget everything.
I should be happy. If I'm lucky, I'll have a few days of freedom.
A child's squeal jolts my eyes open.
I stare out the window and see two kids playing together with a ball in a nearby park. Phoenix is standing nearby, watching them with a smile on her face.
Kids.
Two beautiful, healthy kids.
Langston wasn't lying. He's a father. These are his kids.
I fucked up.
I did the wrong thing.

CHAPTER 24

LANGSTON

"This way," Mr. Reyes says.

I follow Mr. Reyes out of the game room and down a hallway. He leads me through the ship to a thick, sealed door that has all of the highest tech—facial recognition, thumb scanner, and multiple external-facing cameras.

The door unlocks, and Mr. Reyes holds it open for me. I step inside cautiously, knowing a trap when I see one.

The door locks behind me. I don't even jump. I knew it was going to happen, and I accept it. I want to meet the owner of this operation. I want to look him in the face and demand answers for what he did to Liesel. I know she didn't do this willingly the first time. I'm not even sure she did this willingly the second time.

I wish I had a gun, a weapon. I always feel less anxious with a gun on me. But I'm thankful that at least Liesel is off the ship. I don't feel her presence anymore.

The coward I'm about to meet had to ensure that I met him in this room, the only room on the yacht strong enough to hold me. He knew the only way to get me here was if I won, if I saw all the darkness that he forced Liesel to endure—that alone would motivate me to meet the man behind the voice, behind the darkness.

He's not the devil. The devil is cunning; he has a plan. This man is just a vile pansy who will spend his life rotting in hell.

"Congratulations on your win, Mr. Pearce," the man says. He's sitting in a chair in the shadows, so I can't see his face.

But I can finally hear his voice unmodified, and I recognize it.

"Show your face, you coward."

"Why? I'm sure by now you've figured out who I am."

"I have. I want to look you in the eyes when I kill you."

He laughs.

I scan the room. It seems like it's just the two of us, but this man must have set the trap ages ago. He will have everything planned. I have to be careful and find the perfect timing.

"What do you want with me? Why set up this elaborate game?"

"You claim Liesel belongs to you, but she's always belonged to me. Always."

"And how did this game prove that?"

"We've been playing these games for years. She's always required to win, always required to do as I say. This is the first time I told her to lose."

"Why?" This isn't just about Liesel. This is about so much more. It's about that damn letter Liesel and I accidentally split in half when we were eighteen. This man seeks the treasure—he might have known about it from the moment he met Liesel. He might have been playing her all along.

But does he control her?

Or is she playing him like she so often plays me?

That's a question for Liesel. This bastard needs to die.

"I guess I'll just have to kill you without seeing the whites of your eyes. It makes no difference to me." I goad him, giving him one last chance to step forward.

He doesn't take the bait.

"I won't be the one dying tonight," he says.

I make my move.

I dart forward into the shadows, not sure what I'm going to find. He could be holding a gun aimed at my head for all I know, but I've faced worse. Liesel lost on purpose, so I would end up here. I've failed Liesel too many times; I won't disappoint her again.

I go for his head, grabbing him by the neck. I squeeze and hold on with everything I have, tackling him to the ground and out of the shadows.

Waylon Brown.

The fucking bastard.

There is so much I don't understand, but what I do know is that he's a sick fucker who hurt Liesel and is using her to get the treasure.

I punch him in the eye before I feel a bullet hit my back.

A second bullet.

A third.

It doesn't stop me from trying to strangle Waylon.

Now, it's just a matter of time.

Will I lose consciousness and bleed to death, or will Waylon stop breathing first?

His face is red.

My body is strong.

I can kill him before I'm taken down.

I can.

I must...

CHAPTER 25

LIESEL

"Stop the car!" I yell.

The limo continues moving forward. I don't think Maxwell can hear me, and I'm not going to wait to figure out how to find the button that connects me to the front of the limo.

I open my door and roll out, hitting the pavement hard in my dress and heels. I scramble to my feet quickly and start to run in Phoenix's direction. I need to get to her before she realizes who's coming for her. If she recognizes me, she'll run away before I get a chance to talk to her.

Luckily, she's facing the kids playing in the park. I can't see the kids easily, but it's not them I need to convince. Although, I'd love to get a closer look at the two young kids—bask in the traits that are Langston.

I don't have time for that.

When I'm almost to Phoenix, I speak.

"It was a trap," I say, not sure how many words I'll be able to get out and choosing the most important ones first.

She turns and looks at me with wide eyes and a puzzled expression.

I huff and grab her arms, hoping I'm stronger than her or the skills Langston taught me as a kid will be good enough to force her to listen

457

to me. The only problem is Langston has probably taught her the same tricks.

"Get off of me," she tries to shake me off her arm, but I don't let go.

"Listen to me. I'm trying to help you."

"Help? You don't know the meaning of the word. Langston will be here soon, and he'll kidnap you and drag you back to the island. Or better yet, kill you."

"No, he won't. I set him up. It was a trap. He might escape, but it won't be anytime soon, and while he's gone..." I nod in the direction of the kids.

"The kids are in danger," Phoenix finishes my sentence with a gasp.

"Go, get them out of here. Somewhere safe," I say.

She turns, and I think she's heard me and is going to go protect her kids when she suddenly turns back. Her hand flies up, slapping me hard across the cheek.

I feel the sting all the way through my body. I deserve it. I deserve so much more. I didn't believe the kids were real. I thought it was all a lie. But now I know, and I would never put children in danger for my own benefit.

I don't know if it would have changed what I did. I had to do it, but I would have ensured the kids were safe, that Phoenix was safe.

Phoenix gives me a smug smirk, and then she runs toward her kids, yelling at them to get in their car.

Satisfied that Phoenix will keep the kids safe, I run back to the limo. Maxwell is now out of the limo and walking toward me.

"What the hell? You could have been seriously hurt," he says.

"Drive me to Teterboro airport," I say, marching to the car.

"What happened?"

"It doesn't matter. Just drive me to the airport."

He shakes his head. "Not until you tell me what's going on. My job is to protect you; I can't do that if I don't know what's happening."

I don't trust him. There is no way I'm telling him anything. "This isn't negotiable, Max. Give me your cell phone, then get in the car and drive."

I hold out my hand, and Maxwell eventually tosses his phone to me before I stomp to the back door, open it, and climb in.

I watch from the window as Max curses and then eventually returns to the driver's seat and starts to drive.

I call Enzo.

No answer.

I leave a message saying Langston is in trouble.

I call Kai.

No answer.

I leave a message saying Langston is in trouble.

I call Zeke.

No answer.

I leave a message saying Langston is in trouble.

I call Beckett.

No answer.

I leave a message saying Langston is in trouble.

That leaves...Siren.

I hate her. She betrayed me. But right now, I need her to be there for Langston above everything else.

I call Siren.

No answer.

I leave a message saying Langston is in trouble.

"Shit," I curse as we drive toward the airport.

I don't know who else to call for help.

A second later, Maxwell's phone starts ringing in my hand.

"Hello?" I say.

"Liesel, what's going on?" Siren's voice replies.

"Langston is in trouble. I fucked up. He won the game, but it was a trap." I don't include the fact that I set the trap in the first place.

"Fuck," Siren says.

There's a pause. "I'll make sure Kai and Enzo know. They'll put together an extraction team to get Langston out of there."

I sigh, relaxing. "Thank you."

"Where are you now?"

"I was headed to the airport to come persuade you guys to get your asses here to save Langston."

I can feel her smile through the phone. "Head to your apartment. Zeke and I will head to you. You need to be protected."

"I have..." I'm about to say Maxwell, but he's not really protection. Not like Zeke and Siren would be. "Thank you," is all I end up saying.

I find the button that connects me to the front of the limo. "Maxwell, take me to my apartment."

He sighs. "Will do."

And then I'm alone in uncomfortable silence. The ride to my apartment takes over an hour. I assume Zeke and Siren are back in Miami, and will take a while to get to me, but I'm not sure.

Maxwell goes up in the elevator with me, and when I get to my apartment door, he asks if I want him to come in with me.

"No, I'm exhausted. I just need to get some rest."

"Of course."

"Goodnight."

"Goodnight."

And then I open the door and walk inside. I flip the lights on. Nothing seems out of place.

My feet wobble as I walk. I need rest. This weekend was too much.

I head toward my bedroom, planning on just collapsing into bed with Max's phone, hoping that Siren calls soon to let me know they got Langston.

I flip on the lights.

And scream.

Waylon is lifeless on my bed, covered in blood.

CHAPTER 26

LANGSTON

I yank on the chains that have held me for the past twenty-four hours. The yacht has long ago stopped moving; I don't know where though.

I allowed myself to be tied up. I took that as the only option when I was bleeding out and too weak to fight.

But the bandages have stopped the blood from flowing, and my body has regenerated plenty of new red blood cells. These chains won't hold me much longer.

I test their strength once more. The chains are solid—only a person of abnormal strength might be able to break them. Unfortunately, I don't have that strength.

I stare at the locks around my wrists. I smile. I do, however, have the ability to pick any lock.

I glance around for something I can use to pick the lock. I don't have much to work with—the clothes on my back, a fork, a plate, and a coke can on the floor that they left me to eat.

I pick up the can and fork. *This will work.*

Five minutes later, I've carved the aluminum of the can into a lockpick.

A moment later, the locks release on my wrists, then my ankles. I'm free.

I'm being kept in a small dark room at the base of the ship. The door looks bulletproof, but when I try the handle, it's already unlocked.

Strange.

I look for something I can use as a weapon as I move up the floors of the yacht. When I make it to the kitchen, I find a drawer of knives. I put several into my pockets and then grip the largest and hold it out in front of me as I continue to creep around the ship.

After making it to the top deck, I haven't run into a single person. *Why are there no people? What the hell happened?*

"Looking for a ride?" Enzo says suddenly from above me.

I smile brightly as I shield my eyes from the sun and look up at him. A helicopter has landed on the upper deck—my escape.

"I assume you are the reason no one is on board?"

He shrugs. "We might have had something to do with it."

"But you couldn't free me?"

He sighs. "We were working on it, but we thought your prideful ass would want to save yourself."

I chuckle as I climb up the stairs to where he stands. "That's code for you couldn't get through the door."

He growls. "We were working on it."

I pat him on the shoulder. "It's good to see you. Let's get the hell out of here."

ONCE IN THE AIR, ENZO TENDS TO MY WOUNDS.

"There are no bullet fragments inside. It looks like they were shooting you with rubber bullets. They left some serious marks, but nothing as bad as it could have been."

I put on the clean black shirt Enzo hands me. "Rubber bullets? Why would they do that?"

He shrugs.

"Where is everyone?" I ask.

"Phoenix and the kids are in a safe house. Kai is giving orders back home. And Zeke and Siren are protecting Liesel."

Liesel.

"Where do you want to go?"

I should say to Phoenix, to check that she and the kids are alright.

"Liesel."

He nods.

I stare out the window of the helicopter. I have so many fucking questions for Liesel, but all I want to know is the answer to one.

Did she refuse to fuck me because she didn't want to? Because she was afraid of me?

Or did she refuse because Waylon required her to lose the game?

We fly out further into the ocean instead of closer to land. I turn to Enzo.

"Where are we going?"

"They are on a smaller yacht a few miles from here. Zeke and Siren said something about it being safer than at Liesel's place. I don't know, it wasn't my decision. We won't be able to land the helicopter on it, though."

"That's okay. You can just lower me down."

He nods.

I see the small yacht floating in the distance. It's not one of the boats I recognize from Enzo and Kai's fleet. My guess is it doesn't have all the safety features that one of our regular yachts have.

So why would they bring Liesel here to keep her safe?

I find a rope in one of the storage compartments and tie it around a bolted hook then hand the rest to Enzo.

With a slight nod of our heads, he's lowering me down while I hold onto the rope. It takes a few jerky moments for Enzo to figure out the speed to lower me, but soon I'm close enough to let go and land on the upper deck of the boat.

"Siren? Liesel? Zeke?" I shout as I look around. I should have armed myself with more than a pocket of knives before I got here, but I don't think any enemies are on-board.

I head below deck and round a corner and then freeze. My eyes blink rapidly, not sure I believe the sight in front of me.

Zeke is tied up sitting in a corner, so tightly bound he can't move a muscle.

But that isn't what has me worried.

Siren is also tied up. And with tears streaming down her face, Liesel is pointing a gun at Siren's head.

I put my hands up slowly as I approach, not entirely sure what I'm walking into.

"Huntress, talk to me. What's going on?" I ask, my voice soft, soothing, and trusting.

She sobs, louder.

"If Waylon is forcing you to do this, you should know he's dead. He can't hurt you anymore."

"I know." She sobs more.

I gaze dumbly from her to Siren. I try to reassure Siren with my eyes, but Siren will barely even look at me, she's so disappointed in me.

"I think it's your turn to tell a truth about the letter, killer. Tell me something."

"Okay, I'll tell you whatever you want. Just don't hurt Siren."

"Tell me," her voice shakes. This is about more than that stupid letter we ripped in half all those years ago, but I'll appease her if it will calm her down.

I think through all the secrets I could tell, but the one I choose is obvious. She'll figure it out soon enough if she hasn't already.

"When your father dies, the secret will be told. Others will start looking for the treasure. You will have a choice—do nothing and let them take it, or go after it and protect it."

"My father died a month ago."

I nod, already knowing that. But I wasn't sure if she did.

"So all these attacks have been people coming after the treasure?" she asks.

I nod again.

"You thought Waylon was coming after the treasure? That's why you killed him?" She's sobbing again.

"I killed him because he was hurting you."

She shakes her head. "You don't understand. Waylon would never hurt me."

"You didn't love him, Liesel. You can do so much better than that guy. He was using you."

"You don't understand. How could you? Waylon was *everything* to me."

Her words stun me. *How could she care about Waylon?*

"You killed the one person I needed in my life, so I'm going to do the same to you."

"Liesel," my voice is a warning. I start surveying my options. I don't have a gun, but I have a knife in my back pocket. That's my only option to stop her.

"I thought about killing Phoenix, but then I remembered you don't love Phoenix. You love Siren."

"If you do anything to stop her, I'll kill you," Maxwell says from beside me a second before I grab my knife. My eyes cut to him in surprise, and I see the gun he has pointed at me.

Liesel had help, that's how she was able to pull this off.

I have to reason with her. That's all I can do.

"I'll tell you everything. Everything on my half of the letter. I'll trade your life for Siren's, just don't kill her. I'll do anything," I say.

More tears stream down her face as she looks at me.

"Huntress, please."

"You've always said I was the huntress who could never kill. You're the killer; I'm the huntress. Today, the huntress becomes the killer."

Then I watch in horror as she pulls the trigger.

FATED LIES

PROLOGUE
LIESEL

I've always wondered what my fate would be.

Would I someday fall in love or would my life be filled with hating enemies?

Would I spend my life alone or with a group of close friends to call family?

Would I marry or enjoy the single life?

Would I have kids or be focused on my career?

Would I find someone to love or spend my life regretting having loved and lost?

Would I live long or die quick?

After living as long as I have, my fate isn't rosy. I'm destined to suffer every agony life has to offer—to die young.

For a long time, I thought I could change my fate. That I could take on the world and win.

I know better now. My fate is not to love. It's not even to survive. My fate is to protect him...

CHAPTER 1

LANGSTON

I've seen death so many times that it's as routine as breathing for me. Usually, death occurs at my hand.

Not this time.

This time it's happening at the hand of a woman I thought would never see murder. I thought if I did the killing, it would keep her pure, innocent, and intact.

I was wrong.

Liesel Dunn is just as savage as I am. She can kill in cold blood as easily as I can, and that's terrifying. There is no stopping her now. Now she'll come for every single one of us.

Liesel pulls the trigger, and my world stops.

I didn't think she had it in her. I really didn't think she did. But the tears, combined with her pulling the trigger on one of my best friends, one of the only people I love, has me convinced.

Fuck...

Everything happens in slow motion and at double speed.

My lungs and heart slow down so much that my body is basically a standing corpse, not getting enough oxygen or blood. While Siren falling to the ground happens so fast that I don't even notice where the bullet hits her.

471

Siren can't be dead.

No.

There is no way I'll believe it. I've seen death. I've seen close friends 'die,' but they turned out to be fine. So even though I'm watching Siren drop with my own eyes, it doesn't mean she's dead.

I drag my eyes to Siren's chest. Her chest is rising. She's still alive—for now.

I want to run to Siren. To stop her suffering, to help her stay alive, but Maxwell still has a gun pointed at me. Liesel still has a gun on Siren. If she hasn't already killed her, another shot could. I have to make my next move carefully.

It's impossible to think, though. All I can feel is Liesel's pain. Unbearable, devastating, just lost the love of her life kind of pain.

She really did love Waylon.

That suffocates me. My own airway begins to strangle me with her tears, her agony pulsing off her in waves. It's the purest thing I've ever felt.

How could she have loved him? It doesn't make sense to me. Nothing I noticed between her and Waylon told me she loved him.

Except she fucked him like she loved him. She was going to marry him. She wouldn't take his money. She wanted to be his equal. *Maybe I was very wrong about her and Waylon's relationship? Maybe he didn't hurt her? Maybe he was trying to protect her from me?*

I can't process it. I'm overwhelmed by her pain and mine. We are two broken hearts who just lost the love of our lives.

No—I didn't lose Siren, not yet. I can still save her.

Zeke has the exact same idea and is hopping in his chair with his legs still tied together, but his arms free toward Siren and Liesel.

I take the moment to disarm Maxwell as Zeke tackles Liesel and wrestles the gun away from her. She doesn't put up much of a fight. She's too broken—completely heartbroken.

The threat is over. Zeke and I both have the guns.

I return my gaze to Liesel as Zeke aims the gun at her.

"This is for Siren," Zeke says.

My heart stops.

Zeke should get to kill Liesel for what she just did to Siren.

Whether or not Siren dies, Liesel deserves it—not to mention her other crime...

I turn away.

I can't watch.

But suddenly my body is flying. I'm not thinking straight. I'm not thinking at all. I run as fast as I can, knowing that I'm fast enough. There is nothing that could ever stop me from getting to Zeke, from stopping him from hurting Liesel.

"Get the fuck off me. She deserves to die," Zeke yells, a man who hasn't yet accepted what has happened to the love of his life.

"Put the damn gun down, Zeke," I say as I point my gun at him.

I won't let him hurt Liesel, my huntress. He can't hurt her. He can't kill her.

"No—no more games. She dies today, not however many months you want to wait to get answers. She'll never give them to you. She dies today."

Liesel is ignoring our fight. She doesn't give a damn if she dies or not. She's drowning in her own tears. She would probably prefer us to kill her and make the pain stop.

"Liesel isn't dying today," I say, still holding onto Zeke's back. Zeke is twice the size of me. Physically, he's stronger. The only way to beat him is to outsmart him, which in his grief just might be possible. But he's not the only one grieving. My brain isn't functioning at the moment.

Boom.

The gun goes off.

No.

No, no, no...

I look over at Liesel. She's still alive. I don't see any blood. I follow her gaze to my leg, and that's when I see my own blood spilling out.

I exhale, thankful the bullet hit me. No one else I love will die.

I can't feel the physical pain. All I can feel is the heartbreak.

Zeke sees the blood, and finally, I'm able to wrestle the gun from him.

"Why did you stop me?" Zeke whispers.

My heart clenches. Because I care about Liesel more than I will ever admit out loud. More than I care about Siren. More than one can care about another person. And yet, I still want to kill her for what she's done.

My plan failed, in so many fucking ways. I need to rethink everything when it comes to Liesel. There are so many pieces that I'm missing. At least now I have some of the truth. I need to lay it all out like an unsolved crime to figure out the rest of her lies.

"Go to Siren. She needs you right now," I tell Zeke before he tries to grab the gun from me again.

Zeke slinks on the ground to where Siren lies. I think he was too afraid to go to her. Too afraid that he might find her dead.

I watch as he lifts her bloodied head into his large lap with his rough hands. He strokes her face and whispers something into her ear.

Her chest is still rising and falling.

Siren is still alive.

She has to be my first priority. I have to make sure she's alive. That's all that matters right now. I need to keep my family intact and alive. The rest I'll figure out later.

I look to Maxwell, who isn't much of a bodyguard unarmed.

I hold up one of the guns I now possess and aim it at him. He doesn't even flinch. He's prepared to die.

Interesting.

"Get Liesel off the boat—now. There is a small speedboat at the back. Take it."

Maxwell nods, and then he calmly walks toward Liesel. I keep the gun aimed at him, unsure if he's going to try something stupid.

He bends down in front of Liesel, who is in an entirely different world. She has no tears left; there are just dry streaks on her cheeks where her tears once were. But her crying won't be enough to get her torment out. It will live with her for a long time.

I've felt the death of someone I loved before. It never leaves you. I feel for Liesel, I do. But right now, I have to make sure that I don't have to endure the same level of pain with Siren.

Maxwell says something to her that I can't hear. She doesn't react.

He carefully slips his arms underneath her, afraid that she's going to lash out or do something to get them both killed.

He lifts her up, cradling her honeymoon-style.

I continue to aim the gun at him, as my heart explodes, watching Liesel so vulnerable in another man's arms and not going to her. *How did things get so fucked up? How did the girl I used to do anything to protect become this?*

Because I failed to protect her from the danger.

Maxwell carries Liesel past me, and I don't turn to look at her. I pocket the gun, and then I turn back to Zeke and Siren. She's still breathing, but there is so much fucking blood. It's all over Zeke's lap.

This isn't something that Zeke and I can fix. Only the best surgeon in the world, with the help of a miracle, would be able to save Siren.

I run up to the top deck and wave Enzo down in the helicopter, knowing that's the fastest way to get Siren to shore.

Finally, I'm able to feel the rage for the possibility that Siren might die.

That can't happen.

I turn, just as I see Maxwell and Liesel disappear out of sight.

In a split second, I've changed my mind. Liesel has to die for what she did to Siren and for what she did before. I can't wait much longer to kill her.

"One month."

CHAPTER 2

LIESEL

My stomach heaves up and then slams down.

Over and over.

That's what rough waves will do to you—make you lose your stomach until you eventually vomit.

Losing someone you love will also do it.

I'm sure I'm in shock. That's what's happening. It's why I can't feel anything. I'm numb to touch, to motion, to the sea salt splashing in my face.

"Twenty more minutes," I hear Maxwell say, but his voice sounds far off in the distance. I can hear him, but his words don't matter.

I just lost everything.

I lost everything I've ever cared about. Everything I've ever fought for. Everything I've ever considered loving—I lost it all.

I've lost a lot in my life.

My parents.

My innocence.

My child.

Langston.

But this time—it's different. This time I had a chance to love what I lost. This time I fought to try and save it. And I lost.

I need to shut out the pain. I need to push it away so that I can focus on what I need to do next, but I can't. It's in every muscle, bone, and nerve in my body. There is no hiding from it. It's all I'll ever feel again.

I see the shore in the distance.

I'm going to have to function like a human soon, but all I can focus on is how the waves launch our tiny speed boat into the air and then slam us back down. That's my life. I get one brief moment of happiness, of joy, of positivity—only to have life slam me with the worst thing imaginable.

I don't want anything positive, not anymore. Every good thing has been taken from me. I don't want hope. I don't want love. I reject it all. I will not allow myself to feel anything close to love ever again.

The boat stops.

I look around and see Maxwell tying the boat to the dock.

I should get out, but I can't move. My brain can't even function well enough to tell me to stand. My mouth is incapable of speech. My eyes don't really see beyond the haze.

Maxwell must know that because he doesn't ask me to get out. He doesn't ask what's wrong with me.

After he finishes tying the boat, he climbs back in.

"I'm going to lift you out of this boat and get you in a car. Just tell me if that isn't okay, but otherwise, I don't need you to speak at all if you don't want to." His words are soft and soothing.

How does he know exactly what I need?

I give him the tiniest of nods, and then he once again lifts me gently like I'm a broken doll, and one wrong move would end me. It probably would. That's how fragile I am right now.

He carries me to a car. I don't know how he got a car here, but he did.

He lays me sideways in the backseat before he closes the door. Then he carefully walks to the front seat and starts driving.

He doesn't ask me for a destination, and I honestly don't know where I would tell him. He just drives.

I close my eyes, trying to get a moment to breathe. But all I can see is the blood on my bed, Waylon's lifeless body, and what that means.

The car stops suddenly, my eyes fly open.

Waylon drove me back to my apartment.

"I've got you," he says, lifting me out.

He carries me into the lobby before he realizes he made a mistake.

Flashes blind us as reporters swarm us with their microphones and cameras.

"Jesus," he curses. Maxwell is sweet enough, but he's not the brightest. Of course, the media found out that Waylon is dead. A man running for governor showing up dead in my apartment makes for an excellent story.

"Miss Dunn, were you upset that your fiancé was cheating on you? Is that why you killed him?" one brave journalist asks me.

Maxwell growls. The reporters take the hint and back up half a step, but that's as much room as they give us.

"Maxwell!" Nolan shouts from across the lobby.

Maxwell turns his head as Nolan pushes through the crowd to us. "Take her to my house. We have a whole team setup there. You can't go to her apartment anyway; it's a crime scene."

Nolan looks at me with disappointment, like this is somehow my fault.

Quickly, Maxwell has me out of the lobby and back in the car. This time, Nolan sits in the passenger seat, and they both discuss me like I'm not even here.

"Has she been like this the whole time?" Nolan asks, like he can't believe how weak I am.

"Pretty much. She's completely distraught. But can you blame her? She thought she was going to marry Waylon and spend the rest of her life with him. Cut her a break. No one reacts well in this situation."

"Well, I need her to do a press conference soon," Nolan says.

"Why? Waylon is dead. You don't have a candidate to support anymore. Your job is done."

"My job is far from done," Nolan says.

He's heartless. I don't know what Nolan has planned, but if I didn't know that Langston killed Waylon, Nolan would be my number one suspect. He's up to something—I just don't have the energy to figure out what.

My eyes glaze over as Maxwell drives us away. Building after building passes by. Car after car. Tree after tree. None of it registers. I don't even know where Nolan lives.

I see the city disappearing behind us, and yet, we keep driving.

The car slows as we turn down a car-lined suburban street. I don't know how this is going to help keep me away from the press, but maybe that's not the point. Maybe the point is to force me to talk to the media.

"Pull into the garage," Nolan says.

I exhale a deep breath I've been holding since we turned down the cul-de-sac. I won't have to talk to the press.

I don't pay attention as Maxwell pulls the car into the garage. As soon as he parks, he'll open my door and offer to carry me again, but I'm tired of being carried. I'm tired of relying on someone else. I know better than to trust another man.

As soon as Maxwell stops the car, I open my door and climb out. Nolan opens his door at the same time and walks toward the house door. I follow him inside.

"You okay?" Maxwell catches my arm just before I step inside.

I nod.

Reluctantly, Maxwell lets go of my arm, and I enter the house.

"I'm so sorry about your loss, Mrs. Brown," a woman in a suit comes up to me and says.

I give her a tight nod as I push past her in the hallway and into the kitchen.

Big mistake.

A dozen eyes stare at me, and each pair begins to approach me.

"I just can't believe he's gone. You must be so devastated," a woman in a black dress says, gripping my hands.

I stare down at where she's touching my hand and pull my hands abruptly away before pushing past her.

"I'm Toby Cox, I was working on Mr. Brown's campaign. I'm so sad he's gone. Please, accept my condolences," a man in suit pants and a buttoned-down white shirt with the sleeves rolled up says to me.

I frown at him with my eyes.

Then I let my daggers cut through everyone in the room, warning them to stay the fuck away from me. I'm hurting. I'm in pain. I'm in shock. I'm still reeling from the loss. And these people have the audacity to approach me, to speak to me.

I don't even know these people. They worked with Waylon on his campaign or in his law office. We aren't friends. We aren't family.

I run out of the room. I don't know where I'm supposed to be staying tonight, and since Nolan hasn't escorted me to a room, I'll take whatever room I want.

I reach the stairs and run up, all the time feeling odd stares from the room.

"Leave her alone. She needs space to mourn. She just lost her fiancé," I hear Maxwell trying to defend me.

I don't care what anyone thinks of me.

And I don't need a man to protect me.

I run down the hallway to the farthest room from the stairs and peer inside. It looks to be an unoccupied guest room.

Thank god.

I open the door and slam it shut behind me. I find a lock on the door.

Perfect.

I lock the door and then walk to the bathroom where a large free-standing white tub sits. I flip the water on, intending to wash the pain away. But as the water runs, I collapse onto the floor and cry.

I've already forgotten how it feels to cry—to let warm, wet tears flow down my cheeks.

So many people came up to me apologizing for my loss, but none of them understand the depth of what I just lost.

Langston won.

I lost.

It's over.

I hope Langston is in as much pain as I am. I hope he's lying on a bathroom floor somewhere crying his eyes out with all hope lost.

But I don't care. Even if he is, he won. He just doesn't know it yet.

CHAPTER 3

LANGSTON

I shed one last tear.

In that tear, I feel everything. Its warmth and wetness fills the corner of my eye, fogging my sight of the ocean from Enzo's balcony. It burns until I finally release it. It starts its quick journey rolling down my cheek until it hits the scruff on my chin. The tear slows and pinballs between each fiber of hair on my face until it reaches the edge of my chin. There it drops onto the deck where my feet stand.

That is the last tear. I've already decided that I can't keep spending my days crying. I need to take action. My tears won't save Siren. They won't protect my children, my wife. They won't make Liesel tell me the truth. They won't put an end to my suffering.

So I stop crying.

I hear footsteps approach. Even though the man is capable of walking without sound, he lets me know he's coming to talk.

I'm not sure I'm ready to talk, not after everything I've been through in the last few weeks, but Enzo Black won't give me a choice. He's one of my best friends. I've known him since we were kids. We've protected each other. He made me filthy rich. He's my brother in every way that matters.

But right now, I don't want to hear his opinion because I already know what it will be. Punish Liesel and then let her go.

Enzo leans on the railing next to me. He's a patient man, more patient than I am. He could wait me out, and I'd start talking.

"Why?" Enzo asks, still staring straight ahead. If he doesn't look at me, maybe I'll answer more honestly. I haven't had many reasons to lie to Enzo or any of my friends, but lately, I find myself lying more than telling the truth.

When I don't answer, Enzo sighs and then turns and looks at me.

I stare back. His eyes are swollen, his dark hair disheveled, and he's wearing sweatpants and a grey hoodie. He looks like he hasn't gotten any more sleep than I have. He doesn't look like a boss; he looks like a broken man.

"Why go after the treasure? Why not just let Liesel and whoever else finds it have it? We have more money than you could ever need. And if you need a raise, just ask."

It's not about the money. It was never about the money. I wish I could tell him the truth, but it would endanger him and his family. If I told him the truth, he'd murder me for risking his family—something I'd never willingly do.

"I can't tell you."

He narrows his eyes, trying to figure out what I'm not telling him. He won't figure it out. I'm a fantastic liar.

"Are you going to make Liesel pay for what she did?" he asks. He doesn't give away if he wants me to punish her or not. There was once a time when Liesel was his friend too. He knows her more intimately than I do, but Enzo is also a man of honor. He won't let someone hurt his family without consequence, and Siren is his family.

"Yes," I say.

"Good," his voice is strained as he says it like it hurts him, but he knows it has to be done. "Liesel used to be part of this family. She used to get our protection. Not anymore. She chose to leave. She chose to hurt this family. That is the one thing I will never forgive."

I nod, and then I look at him with all the pain of our past. "This is our fault."

"How do you figure?"

"We failed her. We didn't protect her when we should have. Time and time again, we failed to save her from the darkest among us. From your father. From others…"

Enzo turns back to the ocean. It's too painful to know the part we played in making Liesel this way.

"We did fail, but we were kids then. Since then, we have done everything we could to protect her. She made her choices," he finally replies.

"We were never kids, never given the choice to be innocent. We should have protected her. There isn't any excuse that's good enough. Someday, we will pay for that sin." I run my hand through my hair, feeling the salt from the ocean turn my hair into blonde waves. "And I'm not sure we didn't fail again as adults."

"We've had an eye on her this entire time."

"I know, but how did she end up in that twisted game on that boat the first time? How did we miss that?"

"Because she wanted us to. Listen, Liesel isn't innocent anymore. She's a woman who can make her own decisions. You have to let her go. Punish her, get Siren justice, but then let her go."

I can't.

I frown.

"What do you need from us?" Enzo asks.

"One month. I need you to give me one month to get some answers from Liesel, and then I'll end this."

Enzo nods and then pats me on the back. "I'll hold you to that. You have one month, and then I don't want to ever speak of Liesel Dunn again."

He walks back into the house, and I know I won't be able to keep my promise to him. Even if I accomplish everything I need to in one month, I won't be able to give Liesel up. She's in all of my thoughts. She's in my soul, and dare I say it—my heart.

♡

I don't waste any time. Enzo gave me a month before he intervenes. That's how long he's willing to put his family, and me, at risk before he makes me give Liesel up.

I stand on the floor of the convention center with a crowd of people who have come to mourn Waylon Brown.

Nolan, his campaign manager, is on stage speaking about how great Waylon was and all the amazing things he would have done as governor.

I resist the urge to roll my eyes. The man was a monster who lent out his soon to be wife to play in a sick game for his own twisted pleasures. The man would have run this state into the ground.

"Let's all have a moment of silence to honor Mr. Brown," Nolan says.

The room goes quiet, and that's when she spots me.

Liesel is wearing a black lace dress sitting in a chair on stage to the right of Nolan. She plays the part of heartbroken fiancée well.

That's because she is heartbroken, even though I'll never understand why she fell for that old, fucked up man. He had to have brainwashed her.

Our eyes meet through the silence.

This is war, I say with mine.

Good, I'm ready for this to end, hers say.

I smirk as Nolan begins talking again.

I don't focus on him. I focus all of my attention on her, trying to form a plan of how I'm going to kidnap her. I see Maxwell standing to the side of the stage with a large security team. He's not the best, but he has more talent than I originally gave him credit for.

Still, I can easily slip past him to grab her.

How do I want to do this?

Tie her up?

Drug her?

Drag her kicking and screaming?

Threaten her?

So many choices. But this time, when I take her, she won't be leaving my sight, not again.

"Now, I'd like to give Miss Liesel Dunn the stage to say a few brave words. She's the strongest woman I know. And to prove that point, she's decided to continue Mr. Brown's legacy and run for governor on his platform. Miss Dunn, everyone!"

The room breaks out in giant applause.

My gaze stays locked on Liesel's. Her eyes widen until the whites of her eyes are more visible than the hazel. Then her teeth grind in anger as she looks to Nolan, who is applauding her with a smug grin. The bastard forced her hand again.

I smirk. Nolan messed with the wrong woman. She is going to squash him like the bug that he is. He might have political aspirations, but Liesel won't be manhandled.

She stands from her seat and takes her time walking to the mic.

"Thank you, everyone, for your warm welcome. As you know, this moment is the time to mourn Waylon Brown, a man I loved very much. A man who would have done this state proud. A man who was brutally murdered and taken from us too soon. That is the focus of today."

The crowd is silent as she speaks, completely entranced with her. Liesel has always been a good speaker. She knows how to pull anyone to her side.

"While I would love to announce today that I'm running for governor in my late fiancé's place, today isn't the time or place to make such an announcement. Today is about Waylon. I can pledge this to you, though. I will do everything I can to honor Waylon. If that means running, I'll run. If that means dedicating my life to catching his killer and protecting this state, I will. That is the promise I can make to you today."

The crowd applauds her and then starts chanting, "Dunn, Dunn, Dunn."

They are obviously encouraging her to run. Of course, they want a beautiful, intelligent woman who has lost the love of her life to run. She'd easily win.

I doubt she will, though.

Liesel is a strong woman, more than capable of doing the job, but she's cynical. She doesn't believe the world can be changed from a political office. That's one of the many reasons I was surprised to learn she was with Waylon to begin with.

Liesel believes the world is a dark and dangerous place—and the most she can do is survive it. It's the most any of us can do. Anyone who thinks they can change it is just naive, chasing a dream that will never happen.

Liesel introduces a minister to say a prayer, and she once again takes a seat back in her chair.

Everyone bows their head as the minister begins his prayer.

Everyone except Liesel and me. She looks at me like I'm her savior.

I cock my head, not understanding. I must be interpreting her look incorrectly if she thinks I'd be willing to save her after what she did. The only thing stopping me from killing Liesel today is because I need the secrets she has locked away.

She smirks.

Dammit, what is she doing? What don't I know?

I look around the room like maybe she has the place rigged to blow. Liesel wouldn't kill a room full of innocent people, though. *No, if she plans on killing me, it will be personal.*

The event ends, and Liesel and the group on stage wave before heading backstage.

The crowd begins to move toward the exits, but I slowly walk toward where she disappeared, trying to decide how I'm going to kidnap her, once again.

"Sir, if you aren't with the campaign, then you need to exit through the back, please," a man says. He's wearing all black and has white lettering that says security on the front of his shirt. I could easily take him out, but I don't want to cause a scene.

I'll just have to wait outside. I open my mouth to apologize but am interrupted.

"It's okay, Oliver, he's with me," Liesel suddenly says from behind him.

I frown. This is definitely a trap. I don't like this at all.

Oliver nods at me, and I walk past him toward Liesel, who is now walking quickly down the hallway. *What is she doing?*

A few people give their sympathies to Liesel as we pass. She nods politely and thanks them but doesn't introduce me, even though they all stare at me, expecting an introduction.

I don't know what she's going to do if we run into Nolan, Maxwell, or someone who actually has the balls to ask who I am.

Finally, we get to the end of the hallway, and she pushes me into a room before slamming the door shut behind her. She doesn't turn on the lights, but I realize from the cleaning smell that we are in a janitor's closet.

"Kinky. You want to fuck me in a closet at the memorial service for your fiancé. I didn't think you had it in you, but I'll be more than happy to oblige."

"You're disgusting. And if that's what you really think, you're no better. I just killed your best friend, and you're still willing to fuck me? Always thinking with your cock instead of your brain."

I grab her by the neck and shove her hard against the wall, until the beautiful sound of her struggling to breathe hits my ears.

"I didn't come here to fuck you. I came to kidnap you. It's time we end this."

She tries to say something, but she can't.

I release enough for her to speak.

"Good. Take me to your island. Let's finish this," she says.

Of all the ways I imagined kidnapping Liesel, her willingly agreeing to go with me wasn't one of them.

I smirk. "Who said anything about going to my island? My island is too good for you. No, where we are going is much darker, much more dangerous, and only one of us will come back alive."

CHAPTER 4

LIESEL

This should be my nightmare—trapped in a dark closet alone with Langston, the man who killed my fiancé. The man who kills as easily as he breathes. With his hand on my throat, I know he can feel my pulse. It should be racing out of fear, but after everything that has happened, I know he's not here to kill me, not yet.

No, my body is screaming for a fucking kiss. For him to steal a kiss from me because if I gave one willingly, it would be a betrayal to Waylon. Now that he's dead, it's almost more important that I don't betray him.

All I can do is lean into Langston and hope he closes the space.

He won't, but that doesn't stop our bodies from edging closer to that ominous cliff. Once we fall over, we won't ever be the same. We won't be able to go back. Perhaps that's why we've never crossed the line. Never done anything other than kiss and play with each other. Never fucked. Never made love. Never been that intimate.

Flashes of him being that intimate with Phoenix are permanently branded across my eyes.

Langston is married to her, but he doesn't love her. That should be enough to ease my pain, but it doesn't.

I will never admit it out loud, but I want Langston all to myself. I want his every breath, every heartbeat, every kiss, every touch, every orgasm. I want it all, as much as I want to kill him for what he's done.

"Where are you taking me, if not the island?" I ask. It's a stupid question I know he won't answer.

"Why? Changed your mind? Not willing to go with me? Because it doesn't matter. If you don't come willingly, I'll enjoy dragging you out of here by your hair."

I don't want to stay here with these horrible people. I don't want to run for governor. I don't want my devastation to be paraded around for political gain. I don't want to deal with Nolan. I don't even want Maxwell following me around anymore. I'm done with this life.

"I'm ready to finish this—whatever this is between us."

"Good." He removes his hands from my neck. And then I can't feel or hear or see him at all. His breath goes silent, and due to how dark the room is, I can't even make out his outline.

He could kill me right here, and I wouldn't even see it coming. *That's how I'd prefer it.* Take me in the night death, without me seeing you hiding in the shadows.

But as the door creaks open, I know that death won't be coming for me today. I won't be gone in the darkness without pain. No, I have to keep suffering over and over. I have to carry my agony with me every day. But that's why I want to end this with Langston. I'm tired of the pain.

We are at the end of the building. It should be easy enough to sneak out. The main problem is the press. If they are waiting for me to exit the building, they'll see us. I don't want to be photographed with Langston; it will draw too many questions from Nolan and Maxwell.

I should tell Langston all of this, but then this is what he does for a living. He knows how to sneak out of any building. He knows how to be invisible.

So I don't say anything as he opens the door and the light shines onto my face once again. It also hits his face, and for a moment, neither of us is sad or mourning our losses. For a moment, the light reflects off the golden specks in his eyes, and he's the happy boy who once protected me.

My heart clenches, missing that boy so damn much. That's the worst part of having Langston in my life—knowing how incredible he can be. Knowing how amazing he must be to Phoenix, how he protects her. Knowing that he's an incredible father to his kids. Langston can be the most protective, caring man, but only to those he chooses worthy. I lost that title a long time ago.

Langston takes my hand roughly in his, but it doesn't stop the sparks from flying. *Why can't my body hate him as much as I do?* That would make this so much easier.

He yanks me hard into the hallway. In the light, his eyes take in my body roughly, and he frowns.

I glare back. I know I look good, so I don't know why he's frowning at my appearance.

"Don't deny that I look fucking hot."

"I won't, but your black dress screams widow. You're too recognizable."

He's right.

"What do you suggest?"

He smirks, and then he shoves me hard into the wall. His hands run up and down the curves of my waist and hips.

"If you were going to touch me, you should have done it in the closet, not here where everyone can see us."

"I'm in charge, not you. And in the closet, I couldn't see you."

In the hallway, we're both illuminated. His eyes covering my body is torture as he now has his hands planted on my hips, no longer exploring my body.

He's wearing a black leather jacket that he shrugs off and then holds out to me. "Put your arms through."

I turn around as he helps me put the jacket on, my body tingling as I feel his warmth and smell his husky scent in the jacket. He spins me back to face him as he zips the jacket up, hiding most of my dress. Then he grabs the hem of my dress, and I hear a rip.

"What are you doing?" I breathe.

"Making you uncomfortable."

I roll my eyes as I realize he's separating the lace layer from the black material underneath. He rolls the lace of my dress up and ties it around my waist until it's hidden beneath the jacket.

I smile at him.

He frowns, staring at me.

"What's wrong now?"

"Your hair."

I grab at my blonde tendrils. He's not cutting them off; I won't let him.

"Relax," he winks. "Stay here."

He leaves me leaning against the hallway wall for support as he walks back into the closet. A second later, he reappears with a hat.

"How did you know there was a hat in there?" I ask.

"I can see in the dark."

Then he plops the hat on my head, tucking any loose strands of my blonde hair until the hat hides it all.

"Let's go." He yanks me hard into the side of his chest as we walk back down the hallway and out of the convention center, looking like a couple attending. No one pays us any attention. No one knows it's me.

We walk to his parked car down the street. I willingly climb in, knowing that this could be the last time I step foot in New York City if Langston has his way.

I smile at that. New York wore me down more than I ever want to admit. Langston makes me feel alive, even though he's the one man who could finally end me. But until that time comes, I'm going to enjoy the fleeting feeling.

CHAPTER 5

LANGSTON

"**W**here are we going?" Liesel asks as I start driving away.

"You really think I'm going to answer that?"

She smirks. "No, and honestly, I don't care. As long as it isn't this city."

I frown. *Why does she stay here and build her life here if she hates the city?*

A tear builds in the corner of her eye again. I've never seen Liesel cry before I killed Waylon. Now it seems she doesn't know how to stop.

I still don't understand why she cries for him. *How she could have loved him?*

That and a million other questions are what I plan on finding out.

I drive toward the docks, and Liesel moans.

"Really? Back on the water? Can't you take me anywhere else? A filthy dungeon somewhere swarming with cockroaches and rats?"

I stifle a smile. Liesel always hated the water most of all. I never learned why.

"Why do you hate the water?" I ask.

She looks out the window, and I doubt I'm going to get an answer.

I stop the car and pull into a parking spot next to the dock. We step out of the car, and to my surprise, Liesel speaks.

"The ocean took you away from me," she answers.

My breath catches. She's right; the ocean took me away from her. The ocean led me to Enzo. To earning enormous wealth. To killing.

But I can't be the reason she hates anything. Me getting taken away from her was a blessing for her, not a curse.

My phone buzzes in my pocket.

Phoenix.

I frown. She knows not to call me unless it's an emergency.

I answer. "Siren?" I ask, hoping there's good news. I can't think of the worst.

"No, sorry, it's Rose."

"What happened?"

"I'm taking her to the children's hospital. She's lethargic and in pain. She's asking for you. I told her you have to go on a very important trip, but—"

"I'll meet you there in twenty minutes," I say.

I can hear her relief through the phone. Phoenix is great with the kids, but they've always been closer to me. We share a bond that no matter how much I've disappointed them by having to spend time apart, they still love me. It's why I can't fail them, not in the ways I failed Liesel.

I end the call and look at Liesel, who is staring at me curiously.

"Leaving?" she asks.

I take a heavy breath. I don't want to leave Liesel here. I don't trust she'll be here when I get back, but I have to go. I won't abandon my kids.

"Yes, but you aren't."

She gives me a sad smile. "Where are you tying me up?"

"I'm not."

Her head turns sharply in my direction like she doesn't believe me. There are too many dangerous people after us. She still may not understand that yet, but the treasure that only she and I have all the clues to are infinitely valuable. And she doesn't yet understand that I won't let anyone hurt her, not until I have every secret she holds. She will only die at my hand.

"You're taking me with you?" She raises an eyebrow.

I can't do that either. I can't let her anywhere near my kids.

"No."

"Then what are you going to do with me?"

I pull a gun from my waistband and hold it out to her.

She recoils. She hates guns almost as much as she hates me.

"Take it."

Reluctantly, she takes the gun in her hand. I try to push the last time she held a gun out of my head. *Don't think about Siren.* She's strong. She'll survive.

But I can't help the rage that forms seeing Liesel holding a gun again. I can't believe I'm doing this. I can't believe I'm letting her live.

Not for much longer.

"Don't worry, I won't kill anyone else," Liesel says, trying to get me to explode and end this sooner than I planned.

"Don't push me, Liesel."

"Why? You won't tie me up. You won't kill me. You won't hurt me. You've already taken everything from me. There is nothing left you can do to hurt me."

I run my hand through my hair. "There is nothing left you can do to hurt me either."

"Not Phoenix? Not your kids?"

"I care about Phoenix, but she knows what she signed up for. She knows her role and that it's a dangerous one. Losing Phoenix wouldn't hurt, but then you already deduced that."

"But hurting your kids would hurt you."

I growl, losing my control. I run at her and tackle her to the ground beneath me. "My kids are untouchable, even to you. They can't be hurt. They are more protected than anyone on this planet. You may be a monster, but you won't hurt them."

"How do you know I won't?" She wheezes as I crush her beneath the weight of my body.

"I see through you. You're not the devil you claim to be."

Then I stand up and walk back to the car.

"What am I supposed to do?" Liesel shouts at me as she sits up on her elbows and watches me get in the driver's seat.

"Stay alive until I get back."

"What if I want to run?"

"You don't. But run if you must, I'll enjoy the chase."

Then I slam the door and drive away, knowing that Liesel won't run. She'll be here when I get back. She's tired of running, just like I'm tired of begging for a different, less painful life.

♡

"Daddy!" Rose says as I enter her hospital room.

Everything else in my life fades away with one word. My little girl is sitting in a hospital bed that makes her look tiny and small, smiling up at me like she's meeting her favorite Disney character, instead of just her father coming to tuck her in.

I walk into the room where Phoenix is sitting next to her. She looks over at me with a worried expression on her face. She stands up and touches my shoulder, telling me everything with that touch. Then she walks out of the room, giving us some privacy.

I sit down on the edge of Rose's bed, and then I tuck her blonde curls that match my own behind her ear. I eye the cast covering her arm.

"Fell out of a tree?" I ask with a wicked smile. I should be angry that I had to risk my entire plan to come here and be in the hospital with Rose, all because she has a far too adventurous spirit for a normal seven-year-old.

She blushes. "Mom told me not to, but there was a robin that fell out of the nest. I had to help it back."

I smile, completely in love with my little girl. She's fearless, compassionate, and kind—everything I'm not.

"You know you should listen to your mom when I'm not around."

"I know, but you would want me to save the robin. I knew you would be proud of me, so I had to climb the tree. I had to be brave, just like you always tell me."

I laugh as I pull her into my chest. She's going to continue to be a handful as she grows up. Boys are going to line up for a chance with her, but she's too strong-willed to let any boy into her life.

And I have no doubt she's going to take on the world. I have no idea what she will be when she grows up—a doctor, a veterinarian, a lawyer, an activist, the president. Whatever it is, she's going to make a positive impact on the world and most likely spin it on its head.

I just hope I'm around long enough to see it.

"Dad!" Atlas yells, as he runs inside Rose's hospital room.

I wink at Rose, knowing that Atlas is about to lecture Rose on how careless she was. That's my son, the complete opposite of Rose. While Rose is outgoing, bright, and adventurous, Atlas is introverted, quiet, and serious. He lives life carefully, ensuring that each decision he makes is the right one. He doesn't run head-on into danger like Rose does.

I scoot Rose over as Atlas climbs up onto the bed. I pull him into my other side until I'm hugging both of my kids. If only I could live the rest of my life here like this, holding my two kids—the only people in my world I truly love anymore.

"Rose climbed a tree even though Mom told her not to," Atlas says.

"So I've been told. And what did you do?"

"I tried to catch her when she fell, but I wasn't strong enough."

I notice now that Atlas has some scratches on his arms and his clothes have dirt spots on them.

I smile. My kids are perfect for each other. Rose gets into trouble, while Atlas tries to rescue her. I love them both for exactly who they are. As they grow older, they will continue to look out for one another, getting each other into and out of trouble.

"You did well, Atlas. What do I always tell you?"

"To help Rose. Are you sure I shouldn't have ratted her out and told Mom what Rose was planning?" He gives Rose the evil eye, like she's the reason for all his problems. It's not true. He loves Rose and would do anything for her.

"No, your job is to rescue her when she needs your help."

"I do not need rescuing, ever," Rose pouts.

I bite my lip to hide my smile as I touch the tip of her nose. "I know you don't, but sometimes it's nice to have the help of someone who loves you. You can do great things on your own, Rose, but just imagine how much more you can do with the help of someone who loves you."

She thinks about it, and my words sink in.

I pull them both tightly to my body, hugging them as hard as I can.

"Look out for one another. Love one another. Don't rat each other out. Don't turn on each other. Protect one another. Can you both promise me that?"

"Yes, Dad," they both say at the same time with bright smiles.

"Good."

"Do you have to leave again?" Atlas asks.

"Not until you two fall asleep. But yes, I have to go. This is for the last time, though. Someday soon, I won't have to go anymore."

"I'm never going to sleep then. That way, you won't ever leave," Rose says.

I kiss her forehead as she yawns. I'm sure the doctors have her on strong pain medication and she'll be asleep very soon.

"I'm going to sleep just like you say. The sooner I go to sleep and you leave, the sooner you'll return," Atlas says.

I kiss his forehead as well.

"Tell us a story, Dad," Rose says, yawning again.

So I do. I tell them the same story I always do about a prince and princess who save the world. It's a true story. Maybe the prince and princess don't actually save the whole world, and maybe technically they aren't royalty in real life, but in my world, they are. And they saved me. Now it's my turn to save them back.

I watch as Langston drives away, leaving me with nothing but a gun and the clothes on my back.

The only thing I can think of that would make him leave me right now is something happening to Siren. He spoke her name. *Does that mean she's dying? Already dead? Did I finally succeed in killing someone?*

It doesn't matter. He's gone, which means I have nothing to do but wait until he returns. He left me here because he knows I won't run. I'll stay and fight.

I put the gun into the pocket of the leather jacket, and then I walk down the dock to Langston's yacht. This is the safest place to be, at least until Langston returns. Then anywhere Langston is is the least safe place to be.

I climb onto the yacht and then down to the bedrooms. There is a security system that requires facial, handprint, and a code to enter the bedrooms. The bedrooms are designed to be the most secure place on the yacht.

I frown, knowing I'm not going to be able to break in. I'm going to have to sleep on one of the lounge chairs on the upper deck instead of in one of the secure bedrooms.

The laser begins scanning my face, and I put my hand on the scanner. To my surprise, the light turns green. The only thing left is to enter a code.

I enter my old code that used to work, and the door unlocks. Langston never had my codes revoked. He never ended my access. He never stopped hoping that I would return to redeem myself.

He was wrong to wait for my return. He should have known that I would always betray him, just as he's betrayed me.

I walk into the room and climb into the bed, my eyes instantly closing to prevent more tears from escaping.

And then I wait.

I DON'T HEAR ANYTHING, AND YET MY EYES FLY OPEN. THEY ARE flooded with tears, as is my pillowcase. I wipe the wetness from my face quickly. So much for sleeping to keep the tears at bay.

I sit up in bed and dig the gun out of the pocket of the leather jacket I'm wearing as I listen carefully for the intruder that I feel in my bones is here.

Stay alive—that's what he said.

I almost want to die just to disobey him.

I hear nothing.

No footsteps, no creak of the floorboard or door, no talking.

It was nothing. I'm just being paranoid.

Goosebumps form on my arms even though I'm plenty warm enough with Langston's jacket wrapped around my arms.

I smile at the reaction, knowing exactly who is on the ship.

The door opens, and I don't even bother to lift the gun to aim.

"That was quick," I say.

"I didn't trust that you could keep yourself alive without me. You have a hankering for getting into trouble whenever possible."

My smile lifts higher. He's right—danger is constantly following me.

Langston steps further into the room. He doesn't turn the light on, but I can make out enough of his outline and the whites of his teeth. He's smiling. He seems happy. Wherever he went made him happy.

"Did you go see Siren? Is she doing better?" I ask, risking changing his mood in an instant for bringing up my latest sin against him.

He growls and walks around the bed before plopping down next to me. He hasn't changed out of his clothes. He stares down at my outfit, recognizing that I haven't changed out of my dress or even taken off my heels.

"They haven't told you how Siren's doing, have they?"

He looks at my face, and I know it's true. They are keeping Siren's status hidden from him so he won't spiral.

"Why didn't you aim the gun at me just now?" he changes the subject.

"Because I knew it was you."

His brows furrow. "How?"

"I always feel when you're near. And only you, Enzo, and Zeke are able to sneak around without making a sound. I knew it was you."

"All the more reason you should have pointed the gun at me."

I shrug. He's right.

"Where were you?" I ask, not expecting him to answer.

He leans his head back against the headboard with a soft smile. "With my kids. My daughter broke her arm climbing a tree, and I needed to make sure she was okay before we left for a while."

He turns to me. "I promised her it would be the last time I left her. I hate leaving her."

"She sounds like a spirited little girl."

"She is. She's the troublemaker, the adventurer. She has to right the wrongs of the world. My son is more cautious, he's the protector."

My ovaries ache listening to him talk about his children. That's when I realize he isn't being kind by sharing facts about his children with me. He's rubbing it in that he gets to be with his children, while I will never see my child again. It's torture.

I pull the jacket tighter around me like a hug. Even though the jacket belongs to Langston, it still makes me feel comforted.

I feel Langston's eyes on me—he's watching me, trying to read my emotions in the dark. He doesn't have to look at me to feel my torment—it's in the air between us.

He's going to say something else cruel and heartless. Right now, I can't handle it.

"Don't. I know I've hurt you, and you've hurt me, but just don't. I can't right now," I say.

He doesn't speak. I close my eyes to try and block out the pain.

I feel a brush against my hand, and then his fingers wrap around mine until he's holding my hand, comforting me.

"Why are you being nice?" I whisper, my eyes still closed. I'm too afraid if I open them that the tears will spill, and he'll see how weak I am.

"Seeing my kids reminded me of the kids we once were before everything got so damn complicated. Sometimes I wish we could go back to that time and change everything."

I open my eyes. "Me too."

He nods.

"Do you regret setting me up in the game on the yacht, knowing that I killed Waylon?" he asks.

I frown; my answer could reveal too much. It could lead to more questions I'm not ready to answer.

"Do you regret killing Waylon?" I ask, stalling.

His eyes dance left then right across my face, trying to read what I'm not telling him.

"No, I don't regret killing Waylon," he answers.

"I don't regret setting you up, even though I knew the outcome."

He blinks rapidly, like I surprised him.

I guess I did.

"What now?" I ask. We are still holding hands like old friends instead of the enemies we have become.

"We have one month to figure that out."

One month—Langston doesn't have to spell it out for me. We have one month to learn each other's secrets, and then he'll kill me. He'll kill me for whatever sin he thinks I committed against him in the past. And even if he learns that wasn't true, he can't let me live for what I did to Siren.

And I can't let him live for what he did to Waylon.

I yawn. I don't know what time it is, but based on how I feel, I'm guessing the middle of the night.

"Sleep, huntress. Tomorrow we fight. Tonight we sleep."

I sink down onto the pillow, knowing that Langston will sleep next to me. I shouldn't feel safe next to him, and yet it's the safest place I could be. He won't kill me until our month together is up. Until then, he'll protect me from every danger.

I drift to sleep, knowing it's the most peaceful sleep I'll be able to get.

Until a loud bang wakes me up.

CHAPTER 7
LANGSTON

I watch Liesel close her eyes and fall asleep. She looks so peaceful, so content, but I know that isn't true. Just like all my worries slipping away when I stare at her—it's not reality.

In reality, we are both enemies locked in a battle that will only end in one of our deaths.

I've had a lot of practice watching others sleep over the years. Ever since my kids were born, I've been watching them sleep and ensuring they're still breathing as they snuggle their favorite stuffed animals—Rose, a dragon and Atlas, a traditional teddy bear.

I get the same feelings watching Liesel sleep as I do my children. Liesel feels like my whole world. I have blinders on when it comes to Liesel. I don't see, hear or feel anything but her.

I should sleep. I'm going to need my energy to match her tomorrow. I can't afford for her to outwit me and once again escape or lead me into a trap.

But it's impossible to close my eyes when watching her sleep soothes my soul in a way that I didn't even realize I need. I reach out and touch her face.

She doesn't stir.

That's when I sink down into the bed and wrap my arms around her body. If I can't keep my eyes on her all night, at least I can hold her.

I don't feel the rage I expect by holding her in my arms. I don't want to destroy her for hurting Siren, or for what she did before. Holding her makes me want to protect her, care for her, even love her.

"Why don't I hate you?" I whisper in her hair. I don't understand—she's done some of the worst things possible against me, and yet, I don't hate her. I'm angry—*yes*. But hate...*I could never hate her.*

But still, I have to ensure that Liesel never commits another sin. I have my kids to worry about. I can't let her anywhere near them. I still can't believe I talked to her about them. I have to protect them from her.

But dammit, do I wish she could meet them. She'd love them. Maybe meeting someone so pure, innocent, and kind would persuade Liesel to my side.

A loud banging noise startles me, and I jump up.

Liesel jumps up as well.

"What was that?" she whispers, wrapping my leather jacket tighter around her. She hasn't taken it off. I want it to be because the jacket comforts her and makes her feel like I'm wrapped around her, protecting her. But she also hasn't changed out of her dress or heels, so I can't read much into her still wearing my jacket.

"Someone's on the boat," I say back.

I find the gun I gave Liesel and hand it to her once again. She takes it weakly, like holding the gun disgusts her.

"Have a problem holding a gun? You didn't seem to have a problem using one to shoot my best friend," I growl at her, still pissed off.

"I hate this world," she mutters almost to herself as she readjusts how she holds the gun like a pro. She may resist this world. She may act like she doesn't belong. But the way she holds a gun and carries herself, combined with her devious and conniving methods means she belongs as much or more than any of us.

"Stay here. I'll go take care of the danger. The bedrooms are the safest place. I'll put it in emergency lockdown mode. I won't even be able to get back in without you unlocking the door."

I stand up and pull out my own gun. I'm sure it's just another failed attempt to get information about the treasure from Liesel or me. I'll be able to squash whomever this is quickly, but I should move the yacht out to sea to make it harder for us to be attacked.

I consider calling Enzo or Kai to let them know we are being attacked in case I'm wrong and I need their help, but I think better of it. I don't need their help, and I don't want them to worry, not when they should be taking care of Siren and making sure she lives.

I walk to the door before I hear Liesel's strong voice, "Stay."

I turn and look at her.

She's breathing hard, her eyes wild, and she climbs out of bed and runs over to me.

"If this is the safest place to be, then stay. We can wait whomever out."

I smirk. "Worried about my safety?"

She frowns. "No, but I know what it's like to grow up without a father, and I don't want to have to find your kids a new one because you are too proud to call for help when you need it."

Liesel's worried about me. It warms and pisses me off at the same time. She has no right to care about me.

"Liar," I say. She can pretend she's looking out for my kids all she wants, but I know the truth. She only ever looks out for herself.

She blinks like I just slapped her. "Is it so wrong of me to care?"

I touch her cheek. "It's only wrong of you to say you care because of my kids. You're selfish, Liesel. You care about me because you are the one who wants to destroy me."

She shakes her head angrily and steps back. "You're right. I lied. You are my only chance at killing the danger outside this door. I just want you to be smart so that I don't end up stuck in this room without food or water. This gun isn't enough to protect me, and I don't trust you to protect me."

"Don't worry, sweetheart. No matter how many attackers are out there, I'll be able to protect you. I never lose."

And then I kiss her to piss her off.

The kiss starts that way as she tries to push me back with her hand on my chest. Her lips push me away as she bares her teeth, but when her back hits the wall, she moans. She slips up and parts her lips just enough for my tongue to push between her full lips. And her hand grips, instead of pushes, at my shirt.

And then we are kissing, not fighting. It seems the only time we aren't fighting is when our bodies are pressed together. I want more and more and more.

Her moans prove she doesn't want the kiss to stop either.

A loud booming sound jerks us away from each other as we both pant hard.

"Why do I enjoy kissing you so much when all I want to do the rest of the time is end your life?" I say, talking to myself.

"Because I'm an excellent kisser and you're a man. You only think with your cock."

I shake my head. "You're a huntress whose main strategy is to attract her prey with honey and lure them into her trap. I'm no prey. You can't trap me, and we already know you are incapable of killing me."

"I killed Siren."

I grit my teeth and fist my hands. She's trying to goad me. To knock me off-balance so when I leave this room, I won't be on my game. I'll be thinking of killing Liesel instead of focusing on my task.

"Siren isn't dead."

"You don't know that." She smirks.

"I know that if she is, you're a dead woman."

"I'm a dead woman either way."

The way she says it with such a softness and certainty hits me to my bones. She's right, but I didn't expect her to surrender to that truth so soon. I expected more of a fight from her, but maybe killing Waylon did that to her.

"Stay here and use that gun on anyone who tries to get through the door."

Then I open the door and quickly shut it behind me, before keying in a code that puts the whole ship into emergency lockdown. It will keep Liesel safe. I just don't know if she'll ever let me back into that room when the danger has cleared.

I listen carefully, trying to get hints of who and how many attackers are onboard. I don't hear any footsteps, but I do hear a loud banging sound from upstairs, like someone is banging on a door trying to get in.

I crack my neck. After my conversation and kiss with Liesel, I need an excuse to kill someone. It will help get out some of my rage.

I pull out my phone to check the security feed, but no one shows up on any of the cameras.

I frown; whoever is attacking knows how to hack into my security system to make themselves invisible. That's not an easy feat. Not impossible, but not easy.

The assailants are more skilled than I first thought. *But why are they so brazen to make loud noises?* It's almost like they are drawing me out on purpose.

I consider turning back and checking on Liesel, but I don't want her to win. I don't want her to know I have a single feeling for her other than hatred.

Plus, Liesel is completely safe locked in the bedroom.

I head upstairs slowly, even though I want to rush in and start shooting. I want to get my adrenaline pumping. I have to be smart if I'm outnumbered, though.

I inch forward room through room, floor through floor, but I find no one. I reach the top deck, thinking I may have imagined the threat.

I look around the top deck and find no one.

I sigh.

Maybe I'm just being paranoid?

I turn to head back down with my gun at my side when I feel something sharp hit my neck.

I reach back, and I feel a dart in my neck. I yank it out, but whatever drug that was just pushed into my system works quickly. My legs weaken, my heart races, and my eyes spin.

I turn my head, trying to get a look at my attacker, but all I see is the darkness, the moon, the stars. I don't see anyone.

And then I collapse.

CHAPTER 8

LIESEL

My head pounds as I open my eyes, and I know things are very, very wrong.

A chill hits my spine despite me still wearing Langston's leather jacket. There must be a hole in the back, letting cool air in.

I blink several times, and then I lift my hand to my head to try and soothe the pounding headache. That's when I feel the weight of chains on my wrists. I look around the room to assess the danger, although I see nothing but darkness.

I'm no longer in the safety of Langston's yacht.

I've been taken.

Did Langston do this? Is this the place he was taking me to get answers out of me?

It must be.

I take a deep inhale, but all I smell is sweat and blood. I try to examine myself, but I don't see any signs of injury, so I don't know where the blood smell is coming from.

There is a quiet drip of water hitting the stone floor. It's the only sound. I don't hear anything or anyone else.

I'm in a prison by myself. I should be thankful I'm no longer on

513

the yacht, that Langston did what I asked and moved me to a dank dungeon.

I lean my head back against the stone wall to try to keep my head from spinning. I can't remember anything from last night—nothing after Langston left the bedroom to go check on the intruders.

Whatever drugs Langston used are strong.

I move my legs and realize they aren't chained, just my wrists to each other. After my head stops spinning, I force myself to stand and explore my new room. I'm sure there is no weakness. No hole that I can make bigger. No breakable door. No escape. Not this time. But I still have to check.

My hands trail over the wall as I walk around the room. The room is a circle of stone, and my mind creates a medieval tower. I reach up, but I don't touch the ceiling. And after I've walked for a while, I suspect I've walked in a complete circle several times but never found a door.

I frown as I look up. The door must be above me.

"Dammit, Langston! Really? You think you need to lock me up like this to get answers? You coward! Show your face."

A moan.

My eyes dart back to the ground. There is someone in this room with me.

How did I miss him?

I've walked all the way around the room, touching the wall as I go, but I didn't explore the center of the room.

Carefully, I take a step, then another toward the center. I can't see anything, but eventually, my foot hits a soft lump, and I stop, dropping to my hands and feet.

"Hello?" I say as I reach out to touch the person.

He moans once again.

"I'm not going to hurt you. Are you injured?"

The man doesn't answer me, but he slowly sits up. I'm guessing he's recovering from the same drugs used to knock me out.

I sit patiently by him while he comes to. It's going to take him a moment to process everything.

Finally, I think we're face to face. "Liar. You've already hurt me. I'm sure you'll do it again."

I gasp.

"Langston?"

"Yes, huntress. It's me."

I bite my lip as I stare into his golden eyes. It's dark, but my eyes are slowly adjusting enough to make out the tiny specks of his hair falling over his eyes. It's Langston, and I have no idea what we are both doing locked in this dungeon together. Maybe he locked us both in here so I would have nowhere to run, no safe place to hide for even a moment between him torturing me for truths.

"Please tell me this is your dungeon," I say, realizing I'd prefer that to be the truth than the alternative. I can handle Langston as my enemy. I know him. I know what I'm up against. But an unknown enemy—I don't know how to face that. And if we are really stuck in here together, I don't want to have to fight with Langston by my side.

He winces as he sits fully upright. "This is my dungeon."

"Liar," I breathe.

He curses once again as he tries to move.

"Where are you hurt?" I ask, moving the heavy chains as I reach out to Langston to find the wound.

"Why do you care? If I'm hurt and die, then you win."

I roll my eyes. "Because I'm stuck in a dungeon with no door. My hands are bound together with a heavy metal chain. Unfortunately, you are my only hope of getting out of here alive. So tell me where you are injured so I can make sure you stay alive long enough to kick our attacker's ass."

"I'm not injured. It's just the drugs. Everything hurts when I move."

"Wimp," I say with a smile.

"Yes, I'm a wimp. Sorry, I don't like pain."

Now, I'm smiling.

"Are your arms chained?" I ask.

He lifts them, and I hear them rattle together. "Yes."

"Legs?"

He shifts, and I hear nothing but his feet moving against the stone. "Nope."

"Good." I take a deep breath, trying to think. "What do you remember? Who attacked us? Who is holding us captive?"

There's a beat of silence. "I don't remember anything after I left you alone in the bedroom."

I frown. "Nothing?" *Is he lying to hide facts from me? So he can escape without me?*

"Nothing. Whatever drug we were hit with is strong. We might remember as time goes on. That is, if we live long enough."

Chills hit me again, and I shudder.

"I'll live long enough."

He chuckles. "Not without me, you won't."

"Good thing you want to be the one who kills me then instead of me dying from starvation or hypothermia."

"Good thing."

"I've felt around the whole room. There is no door. I think it must be above us. The entire room and floor is made of stone, so I don't know if you will be able to dig us out or not. There is water dripping on the far side against the wall. That might mean there is a weakness in the structure on that side. What's your plan?"

"To rest."

I frown. "Seriously, what's your plan? We have to work together if we are going to have a chance to escape."

"To. Rest."

"We can't rest. We are trapped in a dungeon. We have to escape. We—"

"Need to rest. You just said there are no doors. There is no way to dig under the walls. We are both weak from being drugged. We need to rest to regain strength. We need to wait and be patient. Whoever is holding us captive will make themselves known soon enough. People are easier to break than walls. Once we have all the facts, then we will be able to escape."

He starts to crawl away from the center of the room until he hits one of the walls, and then he leans against it. His breathing is heavy, and I suspect he is really hurt, he's just not telling me. That's why he suggests we rest.

I move until I'm sitting next to him, leaning against the wall. I try to think of who could be holding us captive.

"Whoever it is, it's about the treasure, isn't it?"

"Most likely."

I close my eyes. "I should have told you the truth. Maybe then you could have gotten it, and everyone would be going after you instead of both of us."

He doesn't answer.

"They are going to torture us for information, aren't they?" I ask.

He doesn't answer again, but I know that's what is going to happen. And I know I'm going to be seen as the weakest. They will torture me, rape me. They'll try to use my pain to break Langston, but it won't work. Even if I told all of my truths, it wouldn't be enough to save me. Langston has the other half of the secret. My secrets alone wouldn't be enough.

Stop thinking like that. For now, I need to do what Langston said. I need to rest. I need to save my strength so that when the bastard shows his face, I'll be strong enough to face him.

And then I hear Langston speak before I drift back to sleep. "I won't let them torture you. I won't let them hurt you. I'll only let them torture me."

His words should comfort me. But he's told me that before, and he failed me. He didn't protect me. I doubt he can now.

CHAPTER 9

LANGSTON

I lean against the wall of our dungeon—a tower made of stone with no door, no escape. The room is pitch-black, but I've lived my life in the dark. That I can adjust to. I can see almost as easily now in the dark as I can in the light.

I wish I could say I have a plan to escape, that I know exactly who took us and how to defeat them. But I can't even remember how we were taken. I don't remember anything after kissing Liesel.

I don't know how much danger we are in, but I suspect whoever took us is serious about getting the treasure that only we know the truth about. They took us without a fight, wiped our memory with a drug, and then dropped us in this impossible to escape tower.

Nothing is impossible. I haven't tried to escape. We will be free again. I just need to regain my strength first.

I don't want Liesel to worry, though, so I don't tell her the truth. I don't tell her of the pain in my back that agonizes me with every breath. I don't tell her that I don't have a plan. That I'm not sure I'm strong enough to protect us both.

I just have to protect her. That would be enough.

Flashes of Rose and Atlas pop in my head. *I have to protect us both, for my kids.*

I told Liesel that we should rest, that that was the only thing to do. Really, it was just an excuse to not talk and reveal the extent of my injury to her.

Liesel closes her eyes and, judging by her steady breathing, drifts to sleep.

There is no way I'll be able to sleep with the amount of pain I'm in.

"Are you asleep? I can't sleep," Liesel suddenly says.

I chuckle.

"Can you not tell that I'm not asleep?" I ask.

She bites her lip. "Not all of us have adapted to see in the dark like you."

Good, I like that I can see her, but she can't see me very well. It gives me an advantage. When it comes to her, I'll take every advantage I can get. It was wrong to assume I could just bully her into telling me everything. She's a worthy opponent, playing her own game. Her odds of winning are as strong as mine.

"Let's play our game then since you can't sleep."

"I can't tell you about our secret. Whoever is holding us could be listening. You can't punish me for not telling you the truth when it could endanger our lives."

"No, but you can still tell me a different secret."

She sighs. "Fine, I'll answer a question, but only if you answer one of mine as well."

"That's not how this works."

She folds her arms. "Then kill me. We are trapped in a dungeon for who knows how long. There is nothing worse you could punish me with. You aren't going to kill me until we escape and you get all your answers out of me, so your threats won't work here."

She's right. "You answer one of my questions; then I'll answer one of yours."

"With the truth?" she asks.

"That's up to you to figure out."

She smiles knowingly. "Fine. What's your question?"

I have a million, but one pulls at me more than any other. One I still don't understand.

"Did you love Waylon?"

She stills, not expecting that question. Her eyes glaze over as memories flood her head. She's no longer in this room with me; she's lost to her thoughts.

I give her time to think about Waylon, about how she's going to answer me.

I study her every feature looking for clues as to how she feels about the man. She was so distraught that I killed him that she tried to take one of the most important people in my world from me. Her actions speak louder than any words, and yet, I still feel like I'm missing something. I didn't think Liesel was capable of loving another man, loving anyone.

"Love is weakness. I have no use for love," Liesel finally speaks, not looking at me, just staring out into the darkness.

"That doesn't answer my question."

"I'll answer you honestly because I have a question I want you to answer with the truth." Her eyes flick to me. I know she can't see anything but an outline of my body when she looks at me, but that doesn't stop me from feeling like she can see everything I'm thinking.

"I tried my entire life to not fall for a man. I tried to keep love out of the equation. I tried...and failed."

Tears water her eyes, but it's nothing compared to how my heart aches. She drives me mad, and yet there is nothing in this world I want more than to hear she has feelings for me. To hear her admit she has feelings for another man is going to break me.

"I changed my mind. I don't want to hear your answer," I say, admitting my own weakness to her.

"I loved Waylon." She plunges the knife into my heart.

She loved him, and I took him from her.

"You loved him even though he sold your body for money? Even though he made you suck other men's cocks to set a trap for me? Even though he wasn't strong enough to protect you, you loved him?"

"Yes, I loved him. I'll always love him."

"I didn't think you were capable of love, huntress."

"I didn't think you were either, killer."

"And yet, we both fell in love."

"Do you love Phoenix?"

"Is that your question?"

"No," she quickly replies.

I don't answer her, but she already knows I don't love Phoenix. I've never felt romantic love. I love my kids. I love Siren as my soulmate. I love Enzo, Kai, Zeke, and even Liesel as friends, but I've never been in love, never fallen for another human.

"How did you fall for him? What was it about him that made you surrender to your feelings?"

"It wasn't a choice. It just happened. I tried to fight it, but I couldn't. It was everything—his charm, his kindness, his loyalty. The more I spent time with him, the more I fell. I didn't even realize I was falling until it was too late. I never said the words to him. I never told him I loved him. I don't think I realized how much I loved him until he was gone."

I shake my head. "Ironic then that me killing him revealed your true feelings for him."

She scrunches her nose, narrowing her eyes, as she tries to understand what I'm not saying.

"You would have let him live if it meant that I never revealed how much I loved him?"

"No, I would have still killed him." I had to. He would've ruined her.

She sighs defeatedly and then leans her head against the stone.

"Your turn," I say.

"What?"

"Your turn to ask a question."

"Oh."

She hesitates for a moment, and I suspect she's going to ask about my feelings. Is there anyone I love outside of Siren and the kids? I wouldn't know how to answer that because I don't understand my feelings toward Liesel.

I implore her to ask any question other than that one. I don't want to lie to her anymore. If I lie, she'll lie in return. And then I'll never get what I want.

My teeth grind together as the pain consumes me again. Any time I'm not completely focused on Liesel, the pain returns.

I turn my head and look at Liesel, letting all my stray thoughts I almost never let myself think into my head.

I let Liesel's beauty strike me; I let myself admire every feature that I usually try to ignore. Her bright eyes and red lips are my favorite, but I miss her smile, her laugh. And I have no idea how to make her do either of those things anymore.

I'm the man who makes her cry for the first time in years. I'm the monster who stole the love of her life away from her. I'm the man she will never forgive even though I know I did the right thing for her. Waylon Brown was a bigger monster than me. He would have destroyed her.

You're going to destroy her, too.

"Stop looking at me like that," Liesel says.

I frown, not believing she can see me well enough to know the thoughts in my head.

Still, I drag my eyes away from her face.

"Where are you hurt?" she asks.

"What?"

"My question that you have to answer honestly. Where are you hurt?"

My eyes drag back to her, and I realize her lie. She can see in the dark as well as I can. Or at least, better than she let on.

I shake my head, annoyed with her. "You little liar."

She smiles, smugly. "I know you too well, killer. You can't hide your winces, your tense pained smile, or..." She touches the stone near my back and then lifts her hand up to my face. "...the blood that you are leaking."

She raises her eyebrows at me.

I take her hand covered in my blood and bring it to my lips. I wait for her to fight me, to try and wiggle her hand out of my grasp.

She doesn't move.

I put her fingers in my mouth, and I suck—tasting the iron of my own blood, but more importantly, getting to touch her.

She closes her eyes, and I can see how much I'm turning her on and how hard she's trying not to let her body be excited.

I pull her fingers out of my mouth as I suck them clean. "I should have known that I can't hide anything from my huntress."

She pulls her hand back into her lap. "Turn around," she orders with hooded eyes.

I do as she asks until my back is facing her and I'm sitting cross-legged.

"Let me know if anything hurts," she says, and then she places her hands on my shoulders.

I suck in a breath, not from pain but from agony. My body aches with needing more of her. Needing her touch, her kisses, her everything.

My eyes squeeze shut, and my body trembles as she lifts the hem of my shirt up so she can touch my skin directly.

"Sorry, did I hurt you?"

I shake my head, unable to form coherent words.

She hesitates, like she doesn't believe me. But then her hands are on my bare skin. Gently, feeling over my back, looking for the wound.

I hiss when she hits a spot about halfway up the left side of my body.

"I think I found it."

I nod, knowing she did.

She leans close to my back until I can feel her hot breath on my back, sending fiery goosebumps up my spine. My body is as conflicted as my heart and mind are. I'm not sure if I welcome Liesel's touch or if I want to run away from her as fast as I can.

"It doesn't look like a bullet hole, but I should feel inside and make sure there isn't a bullet fragment inside."

I nod again. This woman has made me mute.

"Tell me about your kids."

"Why?"

"Just do it." I know she's rolling her eyes at me in annoyance even though I can't see her.

"Rose is a free-spirit, always getting into trouble. I remember one time she jumped out of one of my boats into the ocean because she saw a bird dive into the water, and she thought it needed rescuing. She didn't realize that that is how some birds fish."

Liesel laughs. "What happened next?"

"Rose knows how to swim, but she was only six years old, and the waves were strong. I stopped the boat and was about to jump in after her, but before I could Atlas jumped into the ocean too, trying to save her." Now I'm laughing. "Him jumping in only made it more difficult for me to save them both. He was wrapped around Rose, trying to save her, but it was more like the weight of his body wrapped around her neck was drowning her. Neither of them was in any real danger; I got them out seconds after they jumped in. But we had to have a long talk about wearing life jackets and not jumping into the ocean without an adult's permission, no matter the reason."

"You know you and I used to swim in the ocean alone when we were their age."

"You and I did a lot of stupid, dangerous things when we were kids. It doesn't mean my kids get to do the same thing."

"You're a good father."

I don't know why her words make me smile. Apparently, I need her approval more than I realized.

"I didn't find a bullet."

"What?"

She pulls my shirt down. "I didn't find a bullet, but we should tie your shirt around it to prevent any more blood from escaping and try to protect the wound a little."

I realize now that she got me talking about my kids to distract me.

"Thank you." I pull my shirt off and hand it to her.

She takes it and begins wrapping it around my body before tying it off.

"Here," she says, shrugging my leather jacket off. "This will keep you warm."

I turn and stop her from removing the jacket. "Keep it."

"But you need it more."

"No, I'll let you know if I need it. Keep it for now." I like seeing my jacket on her. I like that at least part of me can protect her and keep her warm.

I don't know who is holding us captive. I don't know what their intentions are. But I do know that with me injured, and us both held in this stone tower, an escape is going to be difficult. We are going to have to hope that Enzo and Kai noticed our kidnapping and are on their way. I'm not sure I can get us out of this situation in one piece.

I've vowed to protect Liesel so many times. And each time, I've failed. I doubt this time will be any different. All I can do for now is to try to reassure Liesel that I can protect us, even when I can't.

The only people in this world I can absolutely protect are my children. These monsters can hurt me and Liesel, unfortunately, but they will not hurt Rose or Atlas.

CHAPTER 10

LIESEL

Langston is trying to be strong for me. He's trying to protect me, but he can't—no one can.

And he doesn't realize that I don't want to be protected, not anymore. There is only one thing in this world I care about, and that person is gone.

"We should sleep," I say.

Langston nods. "Come here." He holds out his arm, wanting me to snuggle against his chest.

"I can't. I don't want to hurt you." *I don't want to hurt me.* I don't want to get attached to him again like I did when we were kids.

I start to lie down on the ground next to him, when he reaches his hand out and yanks me to him.

"You can't hurt me, huntress. Not any more than you already have." His words strike me like he intended. But I'm not sorry for hurting Siren, just as he's not sorry for hurting Waylon.

"And you can't hurt me anymore. But if we both hate each other, why hold me all night?"

He holds me tighter until my head is forced onto his bare chest. I bite my lip, holding my breath and hoping he doesn't push me off of him because this is nice. It's comforting even though I know he can't, and won't, protect me.

"The same reason that you helped with my back."

"And what reason is that?"

"Sleep, Liesel."

He never answers, and I don't ask any more questions. For now, we are on the same side against a common enemy. We are going to have to work together to get out of here alive.

LIGHT SHINES IN MY FACE, AND I OPEN MY EYES. I'M STILL LYING ON Langston's bare chest; my hand is resting on his steel abs.

I let my eyes raise, but I can't see Langston's face. I can't tell if he's awake or still asleep. His breathing is slow and steady, so I assume he's still asleep.

That means I can explore his body without him knowing. My fingertips glide over his abs, feeling every ripple, every hard protrusion. My hand skips over his shirt tied around his torso. It's not completely soaked with blood, so the wound at his back must be healing. Then my hands stroke the thick muscle on his upper chest.

I try not to focus on how good he feels beneath my hand. He's just a man who has a lot of muscle that encases a steel heart—a heart that only softens for his wife and kids. It will never soften for me.

My hand moves up his neck to his face before I realize that his eyes are open and he's staring at my hand.

"What are you doing?" he asks.

I freeze, but that only means that my hand is lying awkwardly like I'm stroking his cheek.

"Checking to make sure you don't have any other wounds you're hiding."

He smirks and shakes his head slowly. "In the light of day, you can easily see that I don't have any wounds on my chest and face. But if you'd like to see if my cock has any wounds I missed..." he winks at me.

I roll my eyes and remove my hand from his face as I sit up.

"Phoenix is a lucky woman," I say sarcastically.

"She is—don't pretend to be offended that I would touch another woman while I'm married to Phoenix. You had a similar relationship with Waylon. Not every marriage is about passionate love."

"Why are you married to Phoenix?"

"It's not time for questions yet. You can ask me tonight in exchange for answering one of my own questions. Right now, we should eat."

"Eat? Unless we are planning on eating each other's limbs, we don't have anything to eat."

"You're such the observant one." Langston nods in a direction across the room.

I turn and see a tray of food is sitting on the ground opposite us.

"How and when did that get in here?" I ask.

He shrugs. "We were both asleep." He moves to get up, but I put a hand on his chest. He needs to save any strength he has to help us get out here.

I walk over and pick up the tray and then place it in front of us.

We both stare at the food—two sandwiches, two bananas, and two cookies, along with two bottles of water.

"Do you think it's poisoned?" I ask, hesitantly. My mouth is watering at the sight, and my stomach growls softly. It's been over twenty-four hours since I last ate. I'm hungry, but not so hungry that I would risk my life yet for food. But Langston could really use the food for strength.

"There's only one way to find out." Langston grabs one of the sandwiches and takes a big bite.

I stare wide-eyed before I grab my own sandwich and bite into it. It's peanut butter and jelly, I realize as I chew.

Langston shakes his head at me. "You were supposed to wait and see if I dropped dead."

"I don't want to be left in this dungeon alone."

Langston's face softens at my words. "Eat. We are going to need our strength."

We both eat in silence. We finish every bite, and every moment that passes reassures us further that the food wasn't poisoned.

"What are you thinking about?" Langston asks.

"How we could escape."

"Do you have a plan?"

I stare up, seeing a high window on the wall. "Maybe, but I'm not sure your wound is healed enough to try it. And I'm not sure I'm strong enough either."

Langston stares up at the window. "Let's try it."

We both stand up, and I remove the leather jacket so that I'm a little more mobile. I feel Langston's heated stare on me in my black dress. The jacket covered most of my curves, but now they are on full display and Langston is appreciating every inch of my body beneath the black fabric.

I clear my throat, and Langston's eyes meet mine. "Do you want to give me a boost, or do you want me to give you one?"

"Let's try you first; you were always a better climber than me," he replies.

I smile, but then I realize it will be hard to climb in this dress. I kick off my heels and hike up my dress until my black panties are exposed. I tie the dress just above my hips to give my legs more mobility.

"If you keep staring at me like that, I'm going to poke your eyes out. I'm not yours to stare at."

Langston walks over to me; brushing the hair off my neck until he thumbs my pulse. "Aren't you? You've always been mine, huntress. That's one of the reasons I'm so angry at you. You've always been mine, and yet you run off with other men."

I narrow my eyes as I glare at him. "Just like you ran off with other women. You got married. You had two kids. You don't get to be mad at me for falling for a man who isn't you. Not when you abandoned me. Not when you couldn't protect me. I've never been yours, killer."

He breathes on my neck, before he turns me around to face him with his hands on my hips. "That's where you're wrong, huntress. You've always been mine, since we were kids. But being mine doesn't mean that I'm going to gives you roses and pamper you. It doesn't mean I'm going to marry you and choose you over all others. Being mine means you are mine to do what I want with. To kiss, to fuck, to kill. Your life is in my hands—even here. Remember that."

"There was once a time when I might have been yours. But then you betrayed me; you failed me. From that moment on, I learned that I belong to no one, and no one belongs to me. I'm not property—I belong to no one. Not even you." I step back until Langston is no longer touching me. He has a scowl on his face, but he doesn't say anything else.

He walks to the wall, assessing the best strategy. "Climb on my back and then up onto my shoulders. I'll boost you as high as I can, and then you can try to climb from there."

I nod, agreeing with his strategy.

Langston leans down so I can climb on his back. I spot his wound that has bled through the T-shirt tied around his back.

I sigh and climb onto his back, careful to avoid hitting his wound. Although, he deserves for me to drive a knife into his wound, deep into the muscle until he can no longer walk.

Langston stands as I wrap my arms around his neck.

"Now, try to climb up to my shoulders."

I try to ignore how it feels to have his torso between my legs as I scramble up onto his shoulders until my legs are wrapped around his neck.

"Good, now can you stand up?"

I roll my eyes. "Of course, I can stand up. Are you strong enough to hold me up is the question."

He growls as I grab onto his head and press one foot into his shoulder. With a thrust of other my other foot, I'm flung up onto his shoulders.

I don't have to look down to know he has a smug expression on his face. I should know better than to doubt his strength. His body may be lean and injured, but he has an unlimited amount of strength when he wants it.

Standing on Langston's shoulders, looking up toward the window didn't give me much of a boost. I'm still a good twenty or thirty feet from the window. Even if I make it to the window, I'm not sure how I'll be able to get Langston out. A rope maybe, but if I can't find a rope, my only choice will be to run and try to get help. While Langston will be left here...

"On the count of three, I'm going to push you up until you can reach the rock jutting out. Think you can grab onto it?"

"Yes," I breathe, not wanting to think about how painful it would be if I fell and didn't grab onto the ledge.

"One, two, three."

Langston catapults me up, and I feel like I'm flying through the air as I reach up to the small piece of outreaching stone. When my hand touches the stone, I grip on hard and dig my feet into tiny grooves below.

My entire body is pressed against the cool stone, which helps to keep me from sweating and losing my grip.

"Nice job," Langston says with relief in his voice.

I tilt my head to look at him.

"Don't look down," he says.

I smile. "Why? You're the one who's afraid of heights, not me."

"Just focus. I'll help tell you where your next handhold and foothold is." His voice is stern and commanding, which only makes me smile brighter.

I look up, but all I see is an endless amount of stone bricks. There are no other large pieces of stone sticking out like this one. My handholds are going to get smaller and smaller going up.

I grit my teeth together, determined to reach the window. I'll find a way to get Langston out. I won't leave the stubborn asshole. I won't let anyone else hurt him; that's my job.

I start to reach up with my right hand to find the next handhold.

"A little to your left," Langston says.

I move my hand to the left.

"There."

I feel the hole. It's not much to hold onto. I lift my other hand.

"A little higher," I hear Langston's calm voice.

I move an inch higher until I find a crevice. I take a deep breath, and then I let go of the ledge and push myself up to my new handholds.

"Good job. Take a deep breath and then move again. You got this, Liesel."

I laugh. "Did you turn into a cheerleader?"

"The kids play all sorts of sports and dance recitals. It's just my dad cheerleader in me coming out," he chuckles.

God, what I wouldn't do to see Langston on the sidelines of his kids' soccer game, cheering them on like a regular dad. My heart melts.

As I cling to the side of the tower fifteen feet up in the air, I realize that I won't kill Langston. I have to protect him even though he's failed to protect me. I won't let any more kids grow up fatherless. His kids need him. And I need to get us out of here so he can go protect them.

I take a deep breath, more determined to reach the window.

I reach up faster this time than the last.

"Take your time; there's no rush."

I purse my lips and breathe out as I reach another handhold and then foothold. I hoist myself up.

I can hear Langston let out an audible breath when I pull myself up now at least twenty feet up in the air, but a good five to ten feet away from the top.

I can do this. I can reach the top.

I start to reach up, trying to find a handhold big enough that I can cling to. After testing a couple of spots, I can't find one big enough to get a grip.

"Try an inch higher if you can."

I reach higher, but the one Langston suggested is just as small as the rest.

"Climb back down and we can think of a new plan. Those holds are too small."

I hear Langston's voice, but I refuse to believe it. There isn't another way out. This is the only way. And we have to get out, for Langston's kids' sakes.

I refuse to give up so quickly. I reach up, take a deep breath, and pull myself up.

Somehow, I'm still holding onto the wall, but as I reach up again, I can cling onto the wall no longer. I'm going to fall.

No, I'm falling.

My nails try to dig into the wall as my body drops down, but it's no use. For a second before I hit the ground, it's freeing. *Maybe this is how I'll die, trying to save a man whom I care about more than I'll ever admit out loud?* I'll die fast and swift. That's too much to hope for. More than likely, I'll break a leg, an arm, a rib.

I close my eyes, relenting myself to my fate.

Suddenly I hit a soft lump instead of the stone floor.

"Oof," Langston says as I land on top of him.

I blink rapidly, not believing I'm still alive, let alone uninjured after that fall.

Then I look down at Langston beneath me. "Langston!" I shout as I roll off of him.

His eyes are closed as he lies on his back. I hold my hand over his chest. It rises and falls—he's still breathing.

"Langston Pearce, wake up right now!" I yell at him; my voice erratic and terrified.

I try to check him over without moving him, but I suspect he has a head injury, and I need to stop any bleeding on the back of his head.

I yank my dress off and slither it under his head to stop any bleeding and provide some support.

"Langston, wake up!"

An eye opens, and he moans.

"Shh, don't move." I sit back on my heels, a little more relaxed now that I know he's conscious.

He grins at me so large that I can see a dimple. "I'm fine, huntress."

He moves to sit up, but his eyes roll, obviously dizzy.

I grab onto his arm, slowing his movement. "Easy. You hit your head."

I reach back and grab my dress, pressing it to the back of his head where I see the blood coming from. I shake my head at him. "You buffoon, you should have let me hit the ground instead of trying to catch me. You could have been seriously hurt."

"If I'd let you hit the ground, you would have been seriously hurt."

"I don't understand you. You say I deserve to die for what I've done, and yet, you refuse to let me die when I should."

"You can't die until I get all of your secrets." That's what his mouth says, but his body says, *I can't let you die until I have you. Until you're screaming my name. Until I've claimed you as mine in every way.*

"Well, you can't die until we find a way out of here."

He smiles.

"How are you feeling?"

"I have a headache, but otherwise, I'm fine."

I scowl as I crawl to his back to take a look at his head wound. I remove the dress. "There's blood, but it doesn't look too deep."

I tie the dress around his head to apply pressure, but I think he's going to be fine.

"Here," Langston says, holding out the jacket to me. It's only then I realize I'm only wearing a bra and panties.

"Thanks," I say, taking the jacket back and putting it back on before zipping it up. I'm a little reluctant to put it on as I'm enjoying Langston's gaze, but he needs to focus on healing, not eye-fucking my body.

I sigh. "Now what? I don't see any other way out other than that window."

We both lean our heads against the wall. "Now, we wait for whoever is holding us to show themselves and their intentions. Then we try to find their weakness and exploit it."

I nod. I know it's our only option, but it doesn't sound like a good option. "Who do you think is holding us?"

Langston shrugs. "Someone after the treasure."

The window at the top opens, and a gun is aimed down at us.

"Liesel, get behind me," Langston says as we both scramble to our feet.

"No, we fight this together." If anything, I plan on jumping in front of him to take a bullet. He needs to stay alive more than I do.

"Liesel," Langston warns. His voice says he's going to kill me if I don't do exactly as he says, but that warning has never stopped me before.

A bullet rains down on us—we both move. We should be diving

out of the way, trying to duck for cover, but that's not how we move. We both lunge toward each other, trying to take the bullet to save the other.

That's the problem with Langston and me—we can pretend we hate each other, that we are enemies all we want, but in reality, we care about each other more than we'll ever say. Our actions speak louder than any words.

We both fall to the ground.

I look down at my torso. I haven't been hit.

"Langston," I whisper. He's taken all the injuries, while I've endured none. If he got shot, I'm not sure he'll have enough blood or strength to make it out of this cell.

I roll him over onto his back so I can examine him. His eyes are closed, but he's breathing. My hands race over his body, looking for the injury. I spot it in his neck. It's not a bullet—it's a dart.

I glance back up at the window just as another dart is shot—this time at me. I squeeze Langston's hand as the dart hits my arm. My eyes grow heavy quickly, and my breathing slows.

We're about to meet our captors, but I can't think straight. All I can focus on is holding Langston's hand as I collapse on top of him.

CHAPTER 11

LANGSTON

My head feels like I've been hit with a thousand bricks when I come to. I sit up slowly, expecting to no longer be in the tower, but as I look around, I'm still in the same dungeon. The sun is just starting to set and cast a shadow on the ground.

"Liesel," I breathe, but I already sense the loss. She isn't here. She's been taken out of this room while I was unconscious.

I scramble to my feet, and my body realizes instantly it's a mistake. I shake, my stomach writhes, and I almost vomit. But I push past all of that, just like I push past the pain in the back of my head and back. My body is slowly falling apart, but it's nothing compared to how my heart feels.

I failed Liesel, again.

I failed.

I've wanted nothing more than to protect her. She owes me an explanation, but she doesn't get to die at another person's hand.

"Liesel!" I shout, like she's somehow going to reappear out of thin air. Rage floods my veins as I spin around the room, trying to come up with something, anything, to save her from the hell I'm sure she's in.

I don't know who has taken us, but it doesn't take much to guess that she's currently being tortured by our captors while I sit down here useless.

There are only three options for trying to escape from this tower.

Climb out.

Dig out.

Or break out.

Climbing seems like the most likely option, but after watching Liesel attempt it yesterday, I don't think I'll make it very far.

Still, I move to the wall. I put my hands into the stone bricks and begin to hoist myself up. The climb starts easy enough, but quickly my fingers struggle to fit into the holds. No matter how determined I am to reach Liesel, I can't climb higher.

As hard as it is, I let go and land on my feet back on the ground.

I don't waste time. I move around the room where the wall meets the floor and look for any weaknesses that I could use to start digging my way out.

The best I can find is a small crack in the corner of one of the stones. Liesel's high-heeled shoes are lying on the floor. I grab them and use the heel to start digging. But after twenty minutes, I've barely made a dent.

I don't know what's happening out there, but I won't make it in time to save her from the worst of it, whatever she faces.

I stand up, considering my last option of breaking through a wall. I slam my body as hard as I can against one of the walls. I know it won't help, but it feels good to hit something, to feel something.

I yell at the top of my lungs as I slam my body again. And then tears burn my eyes as I collapse in a pile of worthlessness.

It's no wonder Liesel and I drifted apart over the years. I've failed so many times to protect her, to help her, to save her. This time is no different.

"Take me instead! I know more about the treasure than Liesel. Take me!" I shout up, hoping someone is listening.

I can't think beyond making sure Liesel is safe. I don't care what happens to me, but I can't stay down here, losing my mind while Liesel is being hurt upstairs.

My mind is going wild with all the ways Liesel could be tortured as

I collapse back onto the floor, grabbing Liesel's shoe and resuming my futile digging. It may be useless, but it's the only thing that allows me any progress in getting to her.

Images of her beaten, whipped, tied-up, tortured—they all flicker through my brain. Of her being raped, again.

Jesus, why did I think Liesel deserved death? She's already died a thousand times, and somehow she's survived. I can't blame her for her sins after everything she's been through.

If she survives, I should tell her the truth. I should tell her how I feel. I should...

I hear a creak of the window, and I look up.

"Let her go! Take me instead," I shout as I stand.

The dark shadow peering down from the window doesn't speak.

"Please," I beg.

The shadow turns, and then he's lowering something into the tower.

"Liesel," I breathe when I see her limp body being lowered to me.

I can't tell if she's injured or hurt; I can't even tell if she's alive. All I know is she's returning to me.

As soon as her body is low enough for me to reach her, I grab the rope and cradle her in my arms.

"Huntress, it's me. Wake up, baby."

She doesn't stir, but I can feel her warmth, her breathing, her heartbeat. She's alive, and from a quick glance, I don't see any major, life-threatening injuries. That doesn't mean she's not hurt, though.

I lower her to the ground and remove the rope from her body as I hover over her.

I should be focused on getting answers from the dark shadow above me. I should focus on figuring out who he is, but all I can do is focus on Liesel.

I grab her hand and hold it tightly. "I'm here, now. You're safe. I'm here."

I try to bring her comfort, but I don't even know if she can feel or hear me.

She's still wearing my leather jacket and her black panties, which brings me some relief. But there are plenty of things that could have happened invisible to the naked eye. Some of the most effective torture twists your mind more than your body.

I stroke her face as I hold her hand. I want her to wake up, to talk to me and tell me she's going to be okay. But I suspect after what she went through, sleeping is kinder than waking her up. If she's asleep, she doesn't have to face the pain yet.

Plus, I need to make sure there are no visible injuries on her body that I should take care of first. I start with her head and her legs. I don't see any marks, cuts, or bruises. I exhale to find no bruising between her legs. I unzip her jacket and gasp.

Black and blue bruises cover her entire torso.

My hands fist, the vein on my forehead pops, and my nostrils flare. I'm going to kill whoever did this to her.

I study the rest of her body carefully as to not injure her further. I don't find any cuts or lacerations—no external blood. But from the placement of her bruising—she's broken several ribs. It's going to be hard to move, to even breathe for a while. And there could be internal damage she'll never recover from.

What I wouldn't give for some ice or frozen peas right now. For some painkillers, anything that could help her. Instead, all I can do is watch over her. All I can do is watch and wait for her to wake up and hope the pain she feels is less than what I fear.

I pull her head into my lap, hold her hand, and watch her sleep. I pray that when she wakes up, she's not irreversibly broken.

Liesel's eyes flicker open, and my heart stops. I hold my breath, not sure what she's going to say, how much pain she's going to be in, or how my heart is going to break for once again failing her.

"I'm here, huntress. I'm here. I've got you."

Her head is still lying in my arms, and I'm still holding her hand. I doubt I, a monster in her eyes, am providing her any comfort. But I don't let go of her hand—I won't unless she does.

"Killer? What happened?"

I look at her with concern. I'm sure the drugs they shot her with made her memories fuzzy, but it won't last long. My memories came back quickly after I awoke; hers will too.

"How are you feeling?"

She blinks, trying to push through the fog. "My head is spinning, but otherwise, I don't feel too bad."

"Do you want to try sitting up?"

Her eyes look up at me. "Only if you'll hold me. I'm not sure I'm strong enough to sit up on my own."

I smile at her. There is no way in the world I'm letting go of her unless she begs me to. And even then, it would take all of my willpower.

"I won't let you go, not until you tell me to."

She nods.

Then I lift her gently until she's sitting up, leaning her back against my chest.

She hisses as she moves.

"Your ribs?" I ask.

She nods.

"It feels like I'm being stabbed with a hundred knives while being sat on by a thousand-pound elephant."

"I'm pretty sure you have several broken ribs."

She looks down at the jacket that I zipped back over her body. She finds the zipper and slowly opens it. Then she gasps.

I look over her body and notice the bruising looks worse than when I first examined her. This is because of me. Every terrible thing that has happened to her is because of me.

"I'm sorry," I whisper.

"You have nothing to be sorry for. You weren't the one who did this."

"Do you know who did this?"

"No."

"Then how do you know I didn't do this to you?"

She smiles. "Because you would never hurt me."

"I've hurt you dozens of times. I've threatened to kill you. I would definitely hurt you."

"Not like this."

"Tell me what you remember," I say. I need to know what happened. I need to know every detail so we can put the pieces together and hopefully find a way out of this.

She takes a deep breath, and I can sense how much it hurts her to just breathe. Although, she tries her best to hide her pain. She tries to hide her moan, her wince, her agony.

"Don't hide how you feel from me. Please, I need to know so I can help you."

"Help me move so I can look at you."

I help her adjust in my lap so that I'm still holding her, but I can see her face. She doesn't hide her moan this time. She lets it out.

It breaks me.

She notices my reaction, but we don't speak about it. I'm not supposed to feel anything for her. I'm not supposed to care. And I can't admit that I do, ever.

"What do you remember, huntress?"

I stroke her face, and she shivers, which makes her cough in pain.

I withdraw my hand from her face, resisting the urge to comfort her in case it might bring her more pain. But I keep holding her hand. I still haven't let it go from the moment she was lowered back into our dungeon.

"I remember the gun being aimed down at us. I remember us both diving toward each other. I remember you being hit in the neck." She reaches up and touches my neck, examining me for any injury.

"I'm fine. I was knocked unconscious while you were taken, but I awoke here and alone, with no injuries."

Her hand runs down my neck to my arm, where I have some bruising, and she looks at me with an accusatory stare.

"I, um, I did everything I could to get to you. I tried climbing, digging, and even ramming myself into the wall to see if it would break."

Her eyebrows drop, and her eyes narrow suspiciously. "You shouldn't hurt yourself trying to save me."

I shake my head. She still doesn't understand that I would do anything to save her, even from myself.

"Tell me what else you remember."

"I remember holding you as you fell unconscious, and then I remember the dart hitting me in my arm."

I nod. "And then?"

She sits for a moment, staring off into space. "And then, nothing but black, coldness."

"What about after you were lifted up?"

She shakes her head. "All I remember is darkness."

"You don't remember how you got these bruises?"

She thinks for a moment, like she should be able to remember, but from her blank expression, she doesn't seem to have her memories yet.

"You don't remember being questioned?"

She shakes her head.

"You don't remember your attacker's face?"

She shakes her head, and then her hand brushes over the bruises on her body. It's one thing to be attacked and tortured. To be able to fight back. To try and defend yourself. To remember and plot your revenge. It's another thing entirely to have your memory of that event taken from you.

I pull her tighter to me, trying my best not to hurt her as I hold her. Liesel was tortured and doesn't remember. That kills me. It kills me that she went through something and didn't even gain the benefit of learning who her attacker was.

And yet, I can't help but think she could be lying to me. She might remember what happened to her, but it was so horrible she can't bear to tell me. By lying, she's trying to protect me.

Oh, my huntress, stop trying to protect me. We can't protect each other. All we can do now is survive together.

CHAPTER 12

LIESEL

I don't remember what happened after I was darted. According to Langston, I was taken out of the cell while Langston remained. When I awoke in the dungeon, I had bruising all over my torso like I was beaten for information, of which I have no recollection. I should examine how the rest of my body feels, but I'm too afraid to find that I've been violated in other ways without remembering.

Instead, I focus on how good it feels to be held in Langston's arms. He's been holding my hand since I awoke and hasn't let it go. For now, I hope he never does.

We are two broken souls intertwining our bodies where our hands cling to one another. In a way, it feels like our intertwined hands are the only thing keeping us together.

But I feel a shift after I tell Langston everything I remember. He doesn't believe me. *Why should he?* We almost always lie to each other. At the very least, we withhold the truth, keep our secrets, or tell half-truths when we share information with each other.

In this instance, though, I'm telling him the truth. Usually, it wouldn't matter if he believed me or not, but our survival depends on help from each other. The only way we are getting out of here is together.

Langston needs to believe me. He needs to trust that what I'm telling him about our current situation is the truth. And I need to trust him.

"Ask me a question."

Langston looks down at me, confused.

"I've already asked you about what you remember."

"No, I mean, ask me our nightly question. You ask me a question, and I'll ask you."

"We don't need to play our game tonight. You need to rest and—"

"No, we need to play our game." I sit up abruptly, looking him in the eyes so he knows how serious I am. "We need to play."

He looks stunned. His mouth has dropped, and he's speechless.

"I'll ask my question first, if that's easier."

He searches my eyes, trying to understand why I'm asking. Finally, he realizes why I'm insisting on playing. This is a game of trust. We need to regain some of the trust we once had as kids. It's the only way we'll survive.

He nods, telling me to go ahead.

"Why are you married to Phoenix?" I ask a tough question, one I need to know the answer to. If he answers, it will mean he wants to earn my trust the same way I do his.

"I can't, huntress. I can't tell you the whole truth."

"Then, tell me part of the truth. Tell me what you can. Don't lie to me. We need to relearn some trust if we are going to survive, if we are going to get out of here, together. We are on the same side for now."

"Are we?"

I nod as I look down at our joined hands. Langston stares too.

"I'm married to Phoenix because I needed her."

I frown as I stare up at him, not understanding. "You needed her as in you needed someone who cared about you? Someone you could be romantic with? Someone to love?"

"I've never experienced romantic love. Not like you and Waylon. I needed Phoenix's help with an outside matter. She was the only person who could help me."

"You mean you needed to marry a Dunn to go after the treasure?"

"That was an added bonus, but it wasn't the reason I married her."

I search his eyes for the rest of the truth, but I know this is as much as I'm going to get from him. He didn't marry Phoenix because he loves her. He didn't marry her so that he could go after the treasure. *Why did he marry her?* My brain is flooding with possibilities, but none of them make sense to me.

"Thank you for what you told me." I smile weakly as I stare back at our hands, wishing that his words would have brought us closer together instead of the opposite.

"I've never loved anyone, Liesel. The only woman I could have ever loved hates me, and so I will never love."

My heart aches at his words. He's talking about me. I'm the woman he could have loved if things were different. I know because he is a man I could have loved if things were different.

I swallow down the pain. "What do you want to know?"

He thinks for a minute, and I think he's going to ask me more about Waylon. "I know you wanted to hurt me. You know Siren is one of the most important people in my life outside of my children. But why? Why did you have to kill her?" His voice shakes as he speaks.

I know for a fact that he doesn't know if Siren is alive or dead. He's just guessing based on her condition and our luck.

His fingers start to pull away from my grasp. It's like he chose this topic because he felt himself getting too close to me and needed a reason to hate me again.

I don't let him pull away.

"Siren isn't dead," I say.

"What? How do you know that?"

I bite my lip, considering my answer.

"Do you have your phone on you? Are you in contact with anyone?" He tries harder to pull away. He's much stronger than me and could rip his hand from mine if he really wanted, but his fingers still cling to mine even as he backs away.

"No, I don't have my phone on me."

"Explain."

I hiss out a breath as my increased heart rate has me breathing too hard and makes my entire body ache. Despite the pain, I face Langston.

"Siren isn't dead because I didn't shoot her."

"What do you mean you didn't shoot her? I watched you. I saw her drop. I—"

"It was all a lie. I was angry. I wanted to hurt you for what you did to Waylon, but as you said, I'm a huntress, not a killer. I couldn't kill her."

"You faked her death?"

I nod slowly. "Siren agreed to help me fake her death. She was pissed at you for kidnapping me and threatening to kill me. Then when I saw Waylon dead in my apartment and Siren saw how devastated I was, she said she would do anything to help me. I needed revenge. I needed you to feel pain like I did, even if it was temporary. So she agreed."

"And Zeke, did he know?"

I nod. "He was pissed for you making Siren suck your cock. So he agreed to play along."

"I wondered why he never retaliated after I did that."

He glares at me, his eyes cutting through me like a blade to butter. And then his eyes soften. "I knew you were never a killer, huntress. I shouldn't have believed my eyes. I should have known to always follow my heart. And I should always count on you lying to me."

I gnaw on my bottom lip, not sure if he's more pissed that I lied and tricked him or relieved that Siren is alive.

His thumb brushes against my bottom lip until I stop chewing on it.

"Thank you for telling me the truth and putting me out of my agony."

"You're welcome."

His other thumb then brushes against the back of my hand as our fingers tighten their grips on each other.

"Now it's my turn to put you out of your agony."

"You're going to tell me the truth about Phoenix?"

"Is that truly the greatest thing causing you agony?"

Yes.

No.

I don't know.

I also want to know why he wants me dead. What sin I did that was too far.

I want to know about his kids.

I want to know why he wants the treasure.

He reads my face and knows that I have too many unanswered questions. Too many to choose from to figure out which one brings me the most pain.

He raises an eyebrow as I once again wince. "I don't think I can reduce your pain with even my most guarded truth."

Langston thinks I shared one of my most important truths with him. I didn't. My honesty about Siren didn't even scratch the surface of the important things I've been lying about. But it was a big enough truth to regain some of Langston's trust. Enough for him to believe me when I say I don't know what happened when I was darted like an animal and raised out of this cell.

His hand is under my chin, lifting it until I'm looking at him.

"Let me help you ease the pain."

"What? How?"

He leans down and brushes his lips against mine, so hesitantly like he thinks I'm going to reject him.

I should—just like I should have rejected every one of his kisses. But I don't want to. His kisses alone are enough to take away most of my pain. His kisses bring my body back to life.

I fall into his lips, demanding more from him. It doesn't take much convincing. His lips consume mine, his tongue pushes into my mouth, and his hand cradles my neck.

As long as his lips are against mine, I forget the burning pain in my lungs, I forget that we are locked away in a tower, and I forget that this is where we will most likely die.

Langston leans back with a sad glimmer in his eyes. It seems he hasn't forgotten about our perilous situation, and he doesn't know how to save us both.

I squeeze his hand, letting him know it's okay. I'm okay. A soft whimper escapes my lips, as his hand glides down the side of my body.

"You're not okay. No matter how much you try to pretend you're not in pain, you are. Let me help you."

I take a slow, deep breath, trying to keep the agony from taking over my every breath, but it's impossible. All I end up doing is grimacing and moaning through every breath.

"You can't help me."

He smirks. "I can."

"How?"

"My kisses make you forget for a split second. Imagine what the rest of my body can do."

I blush, but that can't happen. I can't fuck Langston. I can't even if my body sings to life at the very thought. Even if just imaging him fucking me eases my discomfort, I shouldn't.

"I'm not fucking you, killer."

He grins. "I'm not asking you to fuck me."

"Then, what are you asking?"

He tucks a loose strand of my hair behind my ear. "I'm telling you to let me make you feel good. To let me loose on your body. To let me make you come with my hands, my tongue. Let me help you."

My tongue sweeps across my teeth. My body heats, begging me to say yes. I ache between my legs at the thought of his touch. *How many times have I imagined his touch? Wanted it, but thought it could never happen?*

It's a horrible idea. We are already crossing too many lines. Kissing Langston is one thing. Knowing how it feels for him to make me come is another. My body will crave him in an entirely new way—a way I'll struggle to resist.

"Just this one time?" I ask.

He nods slowly, as his tongue runs over his bottom lip. It's clear how much he wants me to say yes, even though I don't know what he's going to get out of this. He doesn't get to fuck me. He doesn't get to feel any pleasure outside of giving me pleasure.

I smile seductively. "You can help me—that is if you are capable of making me come."

He grins back. "Challenge accepted."

CHAPTER 13

LANGSTON

Liesel agreed to let me touch her. To make her feel good. To make her come.

It's something I've dreamed about a million times but knew it would never happen. I'm in a state of shock that she said yes.

I'm in a state of shock about a lot of things. Siren is alive. Liesel didn't shoot her. It was all a game. I'm beginning to think I'm losing this game that Liesel and I are playing. I thought I held the most important cards, but I was wrong. Liesel holds more power and secrets than I could have ever imagined.

My thoughts on changing the game will have to wait. Right now, all I can think about is Liesel.

I wish we had a bed, something I could worship her body and pamper her in. Instead, all I have is a cold, rough floor.

Liesel smiles weakly up at me, and I realize it doesn't matter where we are. It doesn't matter the circumstances—all that matters is I have her.

I lean down and kiss her again. Her lips part automatically, and a soft moan purrs into my mouth as I kiss her. I can't believe how she lets me kiss her without asking, like this is the most natural thing in the world.

But just as the kiss deepens, Liesel pulls away. "What about Phoenix? I won't help you cheat on your wife. I won't be the other woman, even for one night. It's one thing to participate in a wild sex game while you're married. This is different."

I knew she'd have doubts about this if I let her think too much. Apparently, my kisses aren't as powerful as I thought.

I frown. "I don't love Phoenix. We are married but only out of necessity, not because we have that kind of relationship. Whatever we do tonight or any other night isn't cheating, and Phoenix knows that." I wish I could tell her that Phoenix and I aren't really married, but that would be another lie. And I'm tired of lying to Liesel if I don't have to.

She hesitates. "I wish I knew why you married her."

"I wish I could tell you."

"But you don't trust me?"

"I trust you more than you realize."

We stare at each other, our eyes getting glimpses into each other's souls. I do trust Liesel—and that's the problem. I trust her when I shouldn't. I want her when I shouldn't. I care about her when I shouldn't.

She grabs the back of my neck and pulls me back into a kiss. This time I know there won't be any more doubts. There won't be any more hesitation on either of our parts.

We've been so close to this before. So close to crossing beyond kissing. I've wanted to touch her, to taste her for so fucking long.

So many times, things have stopped us before. Our history. Our hate. Phoenix. Waylon. That stupid game. Our pride.

There will be no interruptions this time—no one to stop us. I don't care who is holding us captive. I won't let them stop us. Nothing can stop me from claiming another part of Liesel that has always been mine.

I devour her lips with everything that I have, ensuring I remember every second, every touch, every warmth of her lips as I kiss her. No one will interrupt us this time, but that doesn't change our future, our destiny. It doesn't mean we will end up together. It doesn't mean our fate has changed. I learned that a long time ago.

I tangle my hand in her hair as I tilt her head back to give me access to her neck. I kiss every inch of her skin and am rewarded with the softest whimpers of pleasure.

Liesel still has her shell up. I'm going to have to do more to break through than just a few kisses. And I'm going to enjoy every moment of persuading her to lower her guard for me, even if it's just for a moment.

As I kiss down her neck, I instinctively grab the zipper of her jacket. I pull it down to give me access to more of her skin and start kissing down her collarbone before I get a glimpse of her bruises again.

I stop mid-kiss.

"Don't stop," Liesel breathes. "Not if the world is on fire. Please, don't stop."

That's all I need.

I know I have to be careful, gentle with her, so I don't hurt her. I know she's still going to want control as much as I will need her to give up all of the power to me. But most importantly, I will make her scream my name so loudly that the men who hold us captive will want to check on us to see what happened.

Carefully, I tilt her back sideways in my arms as I resume kissing her collarbone and then down over the curve of her breast, encased with the black fabric of her bra.

She takes slow, shallow breaths, and I can only hear the hint of labored breathing that still consumes her pain.

I run my hands over her arms until I remove the leather jacket from her body. I roll it up and then place it behind her head as I lay her back on the floor.

She shivers as the cool floor hits her back.

I grin as I kiss her and feel her warming beneath my body hovering over hers.

"More," she breathes when I try to pull away.

"So bossy." I kiss her again and again and again. I could kiss her forever. But the rest of her body is calling me.

As gently as I can, I run my hand down the front of her body until I hit her bra. I push it up until I find the mound of her right nipple, then I circle my thumb over the nub, making it harden beneath my touch.

"Suck it," she says.

I grin against her lips. That was my plan, but I need her to give me some amount of control if I'm going to be able to take her mind away from the pain she's feeling.

I place my finger against her lips as I lower my head to her nipple. "Suck," I command as I push my finger between her lips.

I hover over her nipple, almost giving in to her order but not doing it until she gives in to mine. Her lips wrap around my fingers, and the gasp that leaves my mouth rattles through my body. I try to hide my reaction by taking her nipple into her mouth.

I try to focus on how supple her nipple is, how incredible it is to be the one making her whimper. But all I can think about is how much of a mistake it was to have her suck my fingers, because now my cock is rock hard and jealous.

She grins around my fingers, knowing the exact reaction she's provoking in me. I pull my fingers from her mouth, and then I swirl them around her other nipple. She cries out in pleasure from my touch.

My eyes rake down her body, watching her every reaction. Goosebumps are all over her arms and stomach. She's still cold.

I want to press my body over hers to keep her warm, but I don't want to hurt her.

Liesel sees the hesitation in my eyes.

"Don't hold back."

I groan. I want to do as she says, but she wouldn't survive if I did. Instead, all I can do is give her the impression that I'm not holding back.

I kiss down her body, even over her bruises, trying to warm her up as I move closer to her black panties. I grab them with my teeth and rip them down her legs to her ankles. Then I gasp at the sight of her pussy so close, so tempting, so mine.

"Lick my clit," Liesel says, still clinging to her control.

She doesn't understand that her body is mine. Even though I've never touched her, I've watched Waylon touch her, other men have her. I've studied her body and know what she wants, what she needs.

She thinks she needs to be in control to come, just like I do. The trauma we have both experienced makes it difficult to trust someone else with our bodies. The only way we allow another to be intimate is if we keep that control.

We aren't even fucking and we are already battling.

I want to take complete control. I want to cover her mouth so she can no longer give me orders. I want to tie her up so she physically can't persuade me to her will.

But I decide on a different route.

I kiss up her legs, moving closer to her clit. I will lick her as she commanded, but I'll take my time.

"Langston," she whines, needing me.

I glance between her legs; she's not ready for me to touch her there yet, as much as she thinks. My first kiss of her clit is going to be explosive. It needs to be in order for her to forget the pain in her chest.

I kiss her upper thigh, the closest I've gotten to following her order.

Her hands grab my hair, and she pushes my head to where she wants me.

I smirk, and her eyes twinkle.

"Lick me, or I'll stop this."

I act like I'm going to move away and stop this.

She growls.

I chuckle.

And then I take her by surprise and do what she asks—I lick her clit.

She moans like I just gave her an orgasm with the single lick. Touching her here is everything I've ever imagined. She's not touching me, stroking me, and I won't be fucking her with my cock, but damn do I feel everything she's feeling.

I lick her again, stroking my tongue over her sensitive bud.

She grips my hair tighter.

I've always enjoyed pleasuring a woman, having my head buried between her legs, but it's always been a prelude to what comes next. But this—this is the most incredible thing I've ever been a part of.

Her legs buckle as I move my tongue in circles around her clit.

She starts to speak, I'm sure to give me another order. But I'm in control of her body now.

I slide a finger to her entrance before she has a chance to speak.

Her breath catches as she waits for me to enter her.

One second. Two seconds. Three...

And then I push a finger inside. She arches her back, taking all of me in as I continue to lick, rippling through her nerve endings.

I push a second, then a third finger inside her, knowing she wants to be stretched—that she would take my entire body inside her if she could. She wants me. She's desperate for me.

I have no doubt that if I asked to fuck her right now, she'd accept. But that will have to wait for another time. Until I have no doubt it's what she wants. Until I can take her again and again and again. Until she's fully mine.

Something I doubt will ever happen.

So I'll savor this, and it will have to be enough. This is the most I will ever get of her.

I slide my fingers in and out of her as I lick, tasting every sweet drop as I bring her closer to the edge.

"Not yet, huntress."

She moans, and I know she wants to protest. To order me to finish, to make her come but she can't speak. All she can do is moan and whimper.

I continue to work her body, learning even more about her. How much pressure she likes. How deep she likes my fingers. How fast, how slow. I memorize everything about her body.

I feel her getting close. Her muscles are tightening around my fingers. Her breath is speeding. I bring her right to the edge, and then I stop everything.

Her eyes glare at me, and she takes a couple of breaths, trying to regain her speech. "Lang—"

I start again, sending a million shots of electricity through her body as I lick, suck, and slide into her.

Her eyes roll back as she grips onto my head, my shoulders, any part of me she can squeeze.

"Say my name, huntress. I want to hear you scream my name when you come," I order in between licks.

She purses her lips. She's so close, so fucking close.

I look into her eyes, and I know she's not feeling the pain. She's not struggling or fighting for control. She's here with me. Nowhere else. She's not having nightmares of previous terrors. She's basking in how good her body feels for once when she lets someone else take the reins.

But I won't let her come, not until she's given me everything she can give. Not until she gives me what's mine.

"Say it," I whisper as I suck and kiss her clit.

She bites her lip, most likely trying to hold back from screaming my name. From giving into my command. From giving me any control.

Liesel is so close to coming, but I don't think I've won our little battle. She kept her control as much as I battled to take it.

And then, I hear her whimper—the softest, sweetest sound.

"Killer," she moans.

I grin as I push her over the edge with my tongue. Her orgasm explodes around my fingers and ricochets off the walls of the tower.

"Langston," she cries as she comes back down, her body slowing from her high.

We stare at each other at the realization of what just happened. We both surrendered some control. We both claimed something from the other.

One of the many reasons we never thought we could be together was because of our joint need for control. We both thought we needed it above everything else, so we chose partners who were willing to give up control in the bedroom.

This changed things.

Liesel's eyes grow heavy, as I pull her into my lap and stroke her face.

I unroll my jacket that was lying underneath her and drape it over her body to try and warm her. Then I lean my head back against the wall, and I try to sleep, hoping that I took away her pain at least for a few hours.

From her soft snores, it seems that I have.

I hardly remember a time I was happier. But I also know in an instant that I made a mistake. I still hate Liesel for what she did. There is no amount of forgiveness that will change my feelings about her sin.

For a moment, I thought Liesel was truly mine. I thought things could change, and I could have her, but it was a mistake. I shouldn't have touched her, and yet, I don't regret a thing.

Suddenly, I feel a sharp pain in my arm. I look up and see a shadow standing in the window as I once again lose consciousness.

CHAPTER 14

LIESEL

I wake up with a huge smile on my face. I've never slept so soundly and content in my life, even though I'm sleeping on a gross stone floor.

I stretch my arms over my head instinctively before cringing at the pain in my side. In my bliss, I've forgotten that I'm still injured.

I move Langston's leather jacket aside to look at my injured ribs. I'm still purple and green and sore, but the pain isn't as sharp as yesterday. Today will be much better.

Still, I wish I could remember. It could give us some clue of how to escape. And I hate not remembering any part of my life. It feels like I've been violated in some way, even though I've only been hit in the ribs.

Speaking of violated—my mind goes to what Langston did, and I blush. I've wanted to know what it would feel like to have his lips on me for so long. It's hard to believe that it was real and not a dream—a wonderful reality.

I wasn't sure we could exist together. We're both too stubborn, too dominant, too controlling. I was right and wrong. Both of us needing control made it more exciting, made us more equals, and yet for the first time—I felt comfortable with a man when he took control. That's never happened before.

I roll over, searching for Langston, but find the spot next to me bare.

I sit up abruptly, gripping the jacket to my chest.

The room is dark, but I can see enough to know I'm alone.

"Langston?" I say into the darkness.

As expected, he doesn't speak because he's not here.

I stare up at the dark wall, finding the window high up. I don't see anyone, but I know he's been taken.

I slip the jacket on and zip it up before I start shouting, like that is somehow going to help.

"Langston! Don't you dare hurt him!"

I pound my fists into the wall. "Take me instead!"

There is no answer.

I look around the room for a door, or any other option to escape that may have appeared in the last five seconds. But of course, there isn't another means of escaping.

My options are to break through a wall, dig out underneath the wall, or climb out.

I'm not strong enough to break or dig out. My only option to try and reach Langston is to climb out.

I grip my side. It was hard enough when Langston gave me a boost, I was uninjured, and Langston was below to catch me. This is going to be impossible.

I stare up at the wall, more determined than ever.

I don't know what Langston is going through—torture, agony, rape. *Is he hanging onto the edge of death? Or is he spilling secrets to stay alive and return home to his kids?*

I have to get to Langston. I have to find a way to rescue him.

I grab onto the wall without another thought and begin to climb. I don't think about failing. I don't think about waiting until the light shines and makes it easier; there isn't a moment to wait. I don't think about falling and hurting myself. I just climb.

I'm completely focused on my task of inching myself higher and higher. My side aches and burns with each movement, but I don't care. Langston won't die, not this way. I can't let him.

So I keep climbing.

I've made it two-thirds of the way up the wall when I hear the window open. I try to look up, but it's hard to look without loosening my grip on the wall.

I consider speaking, but it's still dark, and I'm not sure whoever is at the window can see me climbing the wall. So I freeze.

I watch as a blob is lowered down next to me—Langston.

I stop breathing as I watch his lifeless body lower. The rope holding him breaks halfway down, and he drops to the floor.

I shriek.

I look up, but whoever is at the window is gone. Now's my chance to climb up and escape, but then I look back down at Langston.

There is no way I can leave him.

I start to climb back down quickly until I'm about four feet from the floor, then I drop.

"Langston!" I run to him.

He doesn't move or make a sound as I approach.

"Langston!" I shout again as I try to look him over for any injuries. I find none on a quick inspection, which gives me enough courage to flip him over onto his back without worrying too much about injuring his head.

I hear his barely audible breaths and sigh in relief.

"Langston, wake up."

He moans as I tap his cheek, but I know he won't awaken until whatever drugs are in his system have worn off.

I look him over carefully, but I find no bruises, no blood, no new injuries. He even has a new T-shirt on, and his pants are intact.

All I can do is cradle him in my arms and wait.

♡

THE SUN FLICKERS IN BEFORE LANGSTON WAKES UP. I'VE BEEN holding him in my arms for the last couple of hours, studying everything about his body. I have my suspicions about where he's injured, but I won't know for sure until he's awake.

"Langston?" My heart clenches as his eyes open. I've been worried all night about what happened to him, but I also know that he's going to be in pain now that he's awake. He might even remember the torture he went through. And watching him go through that pain is going to hurt.

"There you are, beautiful."

I run my hand through his locks as I smile down at him. "You must still be drugged up to call me beautiful."

He shakes his head. "You're always the most beautiful woman in any room, my huntress."

I blush. I'm not used to compliments coming from him.

"How are you feeling?" My smile drops, and a look of concern crosses my face. I'm hoping that I'm wrong—that he's not injured. That they just questioned him and then threw him back in this tower with me.

"Better, now that I'm in your arms."

A flicker of a smile returns to my face as I stroke his face. He grabs my hand, and I can tell his intention is to kiss the back of my hand, but the rough growl he lets out instead rips through my chest.

I grab his arm and hold it against his chest to keep him from moving it.

"Hold still."

Langston tries to sit up, but I push his chest, trying to get him to stay down.

He groans. "I need to sit up and figure out where I'm hurt."

"No, you need to lie down and relax while I work on fixing your shoulder and finding all your injuries."

"I need—"

"Lie down," I growl with a seriousness to my tone that finally makes him lie back down.

"You're bossy when you're concerned." He smiles so wide his dimple shows.

"And you make a terrible patient."

I hold his arm against his chest, suspecting that it's popped out of the socket.

"Try moving your left arm, slowly."

He does and immediately hisses.

Shit—both arms are injured.

He starts trying to sit up again and fuss with his arms.

"Stop moving." My eyes bulge at him, my voice stern. I try to hold his arms against his chest in one place as I look at his legs.

"Now, trying moving each of your legs slowly."

He lifts the right leg without any pain and then repeats the same process with the left leg.

"Legs seem fine," Langston says.

I nod.

"I think your shoulders are out of their sockets."

He shakes his head. "Just the right shoulder. The left hurts more in the elbow."

I examine both arms. I don't know what a dislocated shoulder or elbow looks like, so I have no idea how to verify it. And if either of his arms is dislocated, I have no idea how to pop it back into place.

He smiles up at me with a knowing look.

"What?"

"You're adorable when you're concerned about me."

"I'm not—" But I stop myself, because of course, I'm concerned about him. "Do you remember what happened up there?"

His smile drops. "No. I remember holding you in my arms. I remember the sounds you made when you came."

I blush.

"But, I don't remember anything after the drugs entered my system."

We both stare at each other, locking eyes now that we've been through a similar situation. Langston knows that I truly don't remember anything from being tortured, just like he doesn't remember.

"I'm sorry I doubted you," he says.

"Don't be, you had every reason. Just like I have every reason not to trust you—you're still planning on killing me at the end of all of this, after all."

Langston frowns but doesn't correct me.

"What do I need to do about your shoulder and elbow?"

"Nothing."

"Nothing? But your shoulder is dislocated, and your elbow is in pain. Shouldn't I pop it back in place or something?"

He grins at me. "Are you going to let me sit up yet, or do I have to wrestle you until you are pinned underneath me? I'd enjoy either."

I roll my eyes and then put my hands at his back, helping him up.

"Kiss me," he says.

I blink rapidly, my mouth agape. I want to kiss him. I want to do more than kiss him, but I don't understand where we stand. Every time I kiss him, touch him, get closer to him, I lose a little more of myself to him. I vowed a long time ago I'd never let a man have a claim to any part of me, especially not Langston.

He sighs and is about to give up on me, when I grab his head, turn him to me, and kiss him without any more doubts entering my head.

As soon as his lips hit mine, I'm lost to a fairytale land that only exists when I'm kissing this man. I don't understand how my world can be so perfect only if his lips are pressed against mine. They are soft, warm and oddly comforting, while also being exciting and passionate. They send my heart into a flurry of heartbeats.

With my eyes closed, my tongue pushing into his mouth, and our lips locked, I forget where I am or how few moments we might have left in this world. None of that matters because I'm happier than I can ever remember.

I hear a pop, and I try to pull away, afraid that Langston got hit with another dart and will soon drop. But Langston grabs my bottom lip with his teeth and sucks, keeping my lips locked to his. I melt and cradle his head, hoping I'm not about to lose him to the pull of drugs once again.

Finally, he lets me pull away.

"Thank you," he says.

I raise an eyebrow, not understanding.

"Don't thank me for a kiss."

His eyes cut down to his right arm. "Thanks for the distraction while I popped my shoulder back into place. Your kisses are better than any pain medication."

My eyes widen. "You popped your arm back into place?! You should have told me that was what you were doing."

"Why? Because you would have offered to suck my cock?" he teases.

"You wish." Although, my body heats at the idea of sucking his cock. My mouth waters and my hands itch to feel his long, thick cock in my hand.

"What are you thinking about?" Langston asks, but from his smug expression, it seems he's learned how to read my mind again.

"I'm thinking about how much of an arrogant ass you are."

"Sure, you are." His eyes twinkle at me. "Now, help me get my shirt off so I can use it as a sling."

I suck in a breath and hold it while I grab the hem of his shirt. Maybe if I hold my breath, I'll be immune to being turned on by his rock hard abs. I lift his shirt up his torso and then help him move his left then right arm through the sleeves. He doesn't wince once; he just stares at me as if he's seeing me clearly for the first time.

"What are you looking at?"

He shakes his head, clearing away his thoughts. "Help me tie it up as a sling for my right arm."

"What about your left?"

"It's just my elbow—probably a bruise or strain, I don't think it's dislocated. My right is the one that needs rest the most."

I nod, trusting his own judgment of his body. He's lived his life fighting and getting hurt with fists, bullets, and knives. I'm sure this is normal for him, but it's not for me. This isn't the life I wanted, but it was the life I was always destined to have.

I reach around his back to loop the shirt around and then tie it up on his left shoulder, careful not to brush my hand against his firm chest. Once I've tied the shirt, I help him place his right hand into the makeshift sling.

"You're good at that," I say.

"Good at what?"

"Not showing pain." But then he's been practicing not showing pain since he was five, long before he joined Enzo and his team.

"You make it infinitely easier, but then physical pain is easy to hide. It's the emotional pain that I struggle to keep hidden."

"Where did you and I go so wrong? How did we end up here—hating each other so thoroughly?"

"You're lying if you think we hate each other. We are supposed to hate each other, but that doesn't mean that we do," he says.

Langston's right. Despite him taking everything from me, I could never hate him. And despite whatever horrors he thinks I've done to him, he could never hate me.

"What are we going to do about our predicament?" I ask.

"We should figure out who our enemy is; then we will have the best idea of how to fight him."

"I wish we had something we could use as a shield to keep from being hit by the darts."

"I won't let anyone else drug you. I'll shield you," he promises.

He takes my hand with his left and once again grips it. I wish his words were true. Just like I wish there weren't any lies between us. I wish I could trust him with all of the truths I possess. I wish he could trust me with his.

"So, enemies? Should we go through our list of anyone we can possibly think of?" I ask, bringing the subject back to reality. As much as I want Langston to be my knight in shining armor, he can't be.

"Sure."

Langston scoots back until he's leaning against the wall, and I sit cross-legged in front of him. I'm not at as good as him at hiding my pain, but I try my best to stifle a groan.

"Liesel, are you—"

"I'm fine," I say sternly, not letting him redirect the conversation again.

He narrows his eyes at me.

"So people in my life who might do something like this are Enzo and Kai as retaliation against what I did to Siren if she hasn't come forward and told them the truth."

"Why would they kidnap me?" He raises an eyebrow.

"Okay fine, they wouldn't. Waylon doesn't have a lot of family that would retaliate for his death, but he does have several loyal employees. Nolan Price, his campaign manager, also used to work at his law office. I've always been suspicious of him. There are other men at the law office who were close to Waylon, who didn't think highly of me: Laurence and Christopher. I don't know about the enemies my father made, but I'm sure there are plenty. And then, of course, there are the countless strangers who think they have a right to the money my father hid."

Still such a strange thing to me—my father hid away a mountain of treasure, told me not to find it, and then made public the fact that said money exists. There has to be something I'm missing, something I don't understand. That or my father is just a cruel, conniving man who wanted to ruin my life.

"What about Maxwell?"

I frown. "Maxwell? My bodyguard? He works for me. He doesn't know about the money. He didn't really care about Waylon. Why would he go after us?"

"Just a suspicion. He was more skilled than he let on. He didn't always use his skills. Instead, he chose to pretend he was just an ordinary bodyguard and didn't have training. But that man could rival most of the men we hire."

"Hmm, how did I miss that?"

"Maxwell is an attractive man who is good at manipulating people. It was easy to miss when you spend your time drooling over him."

"Are you jealous of Max?" I bite my lip as I smile brightly, loving that Langston is jealous of Maxwell.

"Max? My point exactly, you didn't even call him by his full name. Clearly, you had a soft spot for him, which would make it easy for him to attack us."

I roll my eyes. "You're jealous of Max. I love it!"

"I'm not jealous of anyone." The vein in his forehead bulges.

He's totally jealous.

"Well, by that logic, Phoenix must have kidnapped us then. She's good looking, more skilled than you give her credit for, and she even married you so she could get close to you and kidnap you."

"Leave Phoenix out of it," Langston growls.

I smirk, happy to have hit a nerve.

"Then who do you think is holding us?" I ask.

He stares off past me as he thinks. For a moment, I think he's figured it out, but then he sighs. "I can't think of a specific person off the top of my head, but maybe that isn't what we need to be focused on. We should be thinking about the traits of the person holding us and how to fight back."

"Hmm, well, what do we know? We know they have a castle with a tower."

"We're deep in a forest."

"How do you know that?"

"The smell of pine."

I take a deep breath, and sure enough, I smell the pine. *How did I miss that before?*

I nod. "Okay, so we are in the forest or mountains somewhere, but not somewhere too cold."

"We know the man likes to hide his identity from us, so either we know the person or they're afraid we will eventually escape and don't want us to know who they are."

"That makes sense. We also know that they are trying to get information from us, which is why they keep drugging and torturing us. But they don't want us to remember the torture or their identity, hence the drugging."

"We can assume they are after the money or treasure or whatever your father left for you. Am I right?" Langston looks at me like he thinks I might be hiding something from him. I am, just like he is, but not about this.

"I can't think of any other reason."

We both exhale in frustration. We don't seem to have gotten very far.

I yawn. "Should we ask our questions now?"

"No, we should sleep. Tomorrow we need to come up with a plan."

I'm sitting across from him, not sure where I should sleep. *Should I move next to him and curl up on his chest, or should I just curl up in a ball where I'm currently sitting?* I still don't know where we stand.

"No. We need to keep talking until we've shared all our secrets, or until one of us is dead." I refuse to just go to sleep. Answering our questions is just as important as forming a plan. The only way we are going to be able to escape is to rely on one another, and we can't do that if we don't trust each other.

"Fine, ask your question so I can go to sleep."

CHAPTER 15

LANGSTON

I wish I hadn't started our little game. At first, I had all the power —asking questions and demanding answers. I could punish her and take time away from her life. Now that we are trapped and I have no control over her life, the only way I get answers is if I give her an answer myself. And I'm running out of truths I can share with her.

Not to mention I get no benefit from her answers. She either tells me a lie, which only tears us further apart, or she tells me the truth and destroys me with how much we've been hiding from each other. There is no winning. Neither of us will reveal all of our secrets. Neither of us will reveal enough to change our relationship. *So what's the point?*

The only reward from talking to Liesel I can think of is the distraction from my pain. Even though I'm good at hiding how much pain I'm in from other people, it still hurts. My shoulder feels like it's been ripped from my body and thrown haphazardly back together, while my elbow shoots a sharp pain up and down my arm. But when I look at Liesel and listen to her speak, the pain eases.

Liesel purses her lips, considering her question carefully. "How did you find out you were going to be a father? What went through your head?"

Technically, she asked two questions, but this is an easy one to answer. It's one I like talking about, too, even if I can't reveal the entire truth.

"Phoenix told me I was going to be a father. She was nervous, not sure how I would react. I didn't plan on becoming a father. I didn't plan on Phoenix being my children's mother. But when she told me, sitting nervously next to me on the couch, I didn't care that I wasn't in love with her or that she wasn't my perfect woman. All I cared about was that I was going to be a father."

Liesel smiles at me.

"I was terrified at first. I don't know what it looks like to be a good father. My upbringing wasn't something I would wish on my worst enemies. But the fear slipped away within seconds, and all I felt was overwhelming joy and happiness. My entire life flashed before my life, and I knew this is what I was always meant to do—be a father.

"I vowed in that moment to be the best father I could. I would protect them from the dangers of the world. Show them what it felt like to be loved. Give them a family. Always put them first. Being a father is the greatest accomplishment of my life."

"From what I can tell, you've been a great father," she says.

I nod. "Thank you."

She leans back on her elbows and looks up as the moon reflects off her blonde hair and hazel eyes.

"What about you? How did you feel when you found out you were going to be a mother?"

I already know the answer. She's already told me before, but it gives her a chance to talk about her feelings for the child she gave up.

"I never wanted to be a mother, and the world agreed. There wasn't anything to feel beyond some sadness at the situation. Unlike you, I knew I wasn't cut out to be a mother. The choice to give up my child was easy."

Liesel hides her emotions well. She's feeling more that she isn't telling me, but I won't force her to reveal more tonight.

"Ready to sleep?"

She nods.

I start inching down the wall, assuming she'll curl up next to me, but as I lie down on the floor, I find Liesel already curled up on her side with her eyes closed.

I sigh. I guess she won't be sleeping next to me, after all. And it seems our stupid questions game has once again pushed us apart instead of bringing us closer together. I should be happy; we've been growing too close these last few days, far too close.

Especially when the end of our relationship has always been fated —with one of us dead.

My sleep is restless between the cool floor, my aching shoulder, and Liesel sleeping so far away. I shouldn't be so needy. I shouldn't need Liesel snuggled up against me in order to sleep. I shouldn't need her at all.

And yet, in the short time we've been together, I've found myself needing her more and more. I'm going to have to detox from her if we ever get out of here.

I roll over and groan, forgetting that my left arm is just as injured as my right. I flip back onto my back and sigh. There is no way I'm going to get any sleep. I should start coming up with a plan to get out of here, but honestly, I can't think with the pain surging through my body. There is nothing to distract me now.

"Hmmm," I hear Liesel hum, and I glance over through the dark to where she's asleep on the floor.

I smile. I may not get to hold her in my arms, but at least I can listen to her while she sleeps.

The humming changes into a soft snore. I'm thankful that she can sleep. It will be easier to face tomorrow if she's rested.

"Are you awake?" she asks suddenly.

"Yes, but I'm fine. You should go back to sleep, Liesel."

Silence. I assume she's closed her eyes and is drifting back to sleep. She probably won't even remember waking up in the morning.

"Does this hurt?" she asks, as she touches my left arm.

I nod.

Even in the dark of night, I can see her brow furrow, and her lips turn downward.

"Don't look so sad on my account. I'm fine, huntress."

"If you were fine, you'd be asleep. How bad is the pain?"

"Not bad enough that you need to worry." I look at her chest. "How is your pain?"

"You can't change the subject that easily. We are talking about you, not me."

"I'd be better if you slept on my chest; that way, I can listen to your soft snore easier while I fall asleep."

"I don't snore," Liesel pouts.

I grin. "You do, too. Now come here." I hold out my left arm for her to snuggle against my chest. It will hurt my arm, but I don't give a damn about that. All I want is to feel her warm body against mine.

She moves to lay on my chest and then hesitates. "I don't want to hurt you."

"You won't." Although, that's a lie. She's already hurt me in every way that she can. It will hurt to have her lying on my arm all night, but not as much as not having her lie on my arm.

Slowly, she lowers herself down until her head is resting on my chest. My left arm hugs around her, and I force myself not to grimace when some of her weight pushes back on my arm.

"I think I'm beginning to figure out your tells," she says.

"What do you mean?"

"I can tell when you are hiding your pain. You don't show the usual reactions. You try to overcompensate so no one knows you're hurting. You smile instead of grimace. You talk instead of suffering in silence. You ask me to snuggle with you instead of asking me to hold you. You soften instead of stiffening as a way to cushion the pain. You don't have to hide your pain from me. I understand it more than anyone. I know how strong you are."

"You think I hide my pain because I'll look weak if I don't?"

She thinks for a moment, then nods.

"I hide my pain because I don't want to worry you. I don't want to be taken care of. It's the same reason you don't want me to know about your pain. If I'm nice to you, it erases some of our history, some of the evil things we've done to each other." I pause. "Taking care of each other now while we are under duress and have no one else to rely on doesn't change anything between us. After we get out of here, we'll go back to being enemies. Deal?"

She smiles softly. "Deal. Now, let me help distract you from the pain."

I pull her close to me, assuming she means by snuggling or, if I'm really lucky, by kissing me.

Instead, she lifts herself off my chest.

"Where are you going?" I reach out to tug her back down.

"You have to promise to do exactly what I say. You can't give me any orders. You can't boss me around. You have to promise to relax and just let me have all the control. Can you do that?"

My eyes narrow as I study her. I don't know what she's talking about.

"I don't like giving up control."

"You need to try if you want me to help to distract you."

"Liesel, I know you are trying to be coy, but I really don't know what you are talking about. So please just say it."

Her hand dances down my chest and then stops just above the waistband of my pants.

"I want to repay the pleasure you gave me last night. But only if you submit to me." Her eyes are heated, but I know there's some fear. Each time we cross the line, we inch closer and closer to the point of no return. But the fear isn't just about us growing too close; it's also about hurting each other.

Because of her past, she needs complete control when she's with a man. Me having any control when I touched her was just because of how I knew her body, not because she trusted me. Now, she needs that control back.

I grab her wrist, stopping her. "I don't need you to repay me. What I gave you I did because I enjoyed it."

"I know. Let me enjoy your body. Give me the control." Her voice is soft but certain.

I can't believe I'm trying to turn this woman down. I want her badly. My cock is already hard, and she hasn't even touched me. I've dreamed of her touching me so many times, but I don't know how many more times we can touch and kiss each other without actually fucking. It's going to drive me mad, even if I'm in no shape to fuck her tonight.

She moves her free hand over my crotch, feeling how hard I am.

"Huntress," my voice sounds in a warning. If she starts this, there is no going back. Another layer of protection will be stripped from us. This will continue to change and morph our relationship. More feelings will be involved than before.

Liesel Dunn is the one woman I've always wanted to fuck, and yet, I can't. Any time we get close to fucking, I remember why we shouldn't. Why I can't, we can't. But my resolve is slipping. I don't have much self-control left. And if I ever claim her as mine, I don't know if I'll be strong enough to do what has to be done.

"Let me touch you. Let me make you feel good. Let me help you forget."

She squeezes through my pants to my cock. I close my eyes, not believing how good it feels to have her touch me even through the fabric of my pants.

I should say no. I shouldn't give her any more control. I shouldn't push us closer to our inevitable end.

But there is no way I can refuse her, no way I can turn her down.

"You aren't fighting fair," I say, still gripping her wrist while her other hand teases me. I'm sure I could overpower her and capture both of her hands with my one hand to make her stop, but I don't want to.

"Give me control. Don't fight me. Don't order me. I'd tie you up to ensure you can't control me, but with one arm in a sling and the other injured, I don't think I need to. Give me your word." She stops rubbing and waits for my answer.

She tells me to give up control, but in this moment, the decision is entirely mine.

I release her hand as I exhale a shaky breath.

She notices and smiles, but I can see that her breathing is just as erratic as mine. She leans forward and kisses me. At first, the kiss is hesitant, like I'm not sure she wants this or is going to be able to take complete control. But then she grips my hair and forces my head back, kissing me roughly. Our tongues tangle, along with our moans.

"Stand up," Liesel says when she pulls back.

I frown. I don't want to stand. I'm exhausted.

She gives me a warning look to obey her, or this ends.

I start to place my hand down to ease myself up, when she hooks her arm under mine and helps me. Then we are both standing.

She smiles at me. "Good boy."

I growl. "I'm not a dog."

She laughs and rewards me with a passionate kiss that almost knocks me off balance. She grabs onto my hair to steady me, and I realize she has even more control with me standing weakly in front of her.

She breaks the kiss and starts kissing my neck, my chest, and then she kneels in front of me.

"Liesel, you don't—"

"I'm in control. I don't want to hear you speak unless you're moaning my name."

She grips my pants and yanks them down before licking her lips and staring at my naked body. My cock is hard and straining toward her. I want nothing more than to grab her hair and slide my cock down her throat, but she's in control, and I won't dare hurt her. Not in this way. She's been hurt by too many men. If there is one thing I want to show her is that some men can be trusted with her body. She just has to learn how to choose the right ones.

She leans forward with her eyes on me as her lips press a kiss to the tip of my cock. The single touch proves this is going to take all of my restraint to not take control. She's not the only person who has gone through trauma. Ours might be different, but it still controls us both the same—with flashes of nightmares, need for power, and inability to love.

"I want you, killer. Don't ever think I don't. Tell me that you want me," she whispers as she wraps her hand around my cock.

"I want you too, huntress." I don't speak because she commands me to, but because it's the truth.

I want to grab her. I want to wrap her legs around my waist and fuck her against the wall. Against the floor. With her riding on top of me. But I know that can't happen. I won't let our first time be under duress in this cramp tower. She deserves better than that. Better than me. Better than any man.

"Grab my hair," she says with her lips pressed against my cock.

"If I grab your hair, I'm not sure I'm going to be able to hold back," I croak out. I'm afraid I'll slam her head and pump her mouth over me too hard as I thrust into her mouth.

She grins. "Try to keep up with me."

Then she thrusts her mouth over my cock, taking all of me into her mouth until I'm halfway down her throat. I grip her hair, more to keep from falling over than to pump her head over my shaft.

And then she's sliding her mouth over me. Her pace is wicked as she hungrily slides her mouth and hand over my length. Her tongue swirls around the tip before plunging me back into her throat.

She takes complete control over my body, something I'm not used to. When I'm with other women, they like a man in power, and I like tying them up and being the violent monster they all think I am.

But watching Liesel on her knees in front of me, stroking me and me completely at her mercy—if I ever thought I could fall in love with a woman, I would right now.

Her eyes flirt up at me, knowing that even if I wanted to take control, I couldn't. She holds all the power. I'm weak for her, and I've never enjoyed feeling weak more than I do right now.

"Huntress," I warn through a rasp in my throat.

I don't know if she'll swallow my seed, let me come on her body, or spit it out. And for once, I'm happy to let her choose.

I grip her head harder as her she lets a hint of her teeth scrape against my sensitive skin. I feel like a feral animal as she pumps over me. She's awakened a wildness in me I didn't know existed—at least, not when I'm with a woman.

"Liesel!" I scream as I pump my cum between her lips, spilling the salty liquid onto her tongue. She takes every drop I give her as I shudder. Then she swallows my cum down her throat, but she doesn't remove her mouth from my cock. She takes her time sucking every last drop and then licking me clean.

I still grip her hair as she continues to kneel in front of me. I'm too dizzy and out of my mind to stand on my own.

She smirks, reveling in the effect she has on me. She grabs my hand as she stands and kisses me softly on the lips. She's afraid if she kisses me too hard, I'll faint, and I probably would.

"Now, we can sleep."

She leads me by the hand back to the spot where we've slept every night, and then she helps me to sit before retrieving my pants and tossing them to me. I wiggle them back on one-handed while she sits down next to me.

"Thank you," I say as the hormones flow through my body, easing any pain in either of my arms.

"Don't thank me for letting me take what I wanted."

I lean my head against her forehead, wishing we could truly take what we both want. Wishing our lies aren't so monumental. Wishing our secrets aren't destined to destroy what's left of our relationship. Wishing our fate is different, like what I once thought it could be when we were kids.

"Someday, one of us will take too much," I say.

"I know, but until that day, we should stop fighting what we want. Stop paying for our pasts or worrying about our futures. For now, let's just enjoy what we want from each other."

I hope she's right. I hope we can enjoy what is left of our time together.

She lies down, and I lie down next to her.

"Come here," she says.

I scoot next to her and put my arm out for her to curl up on my chest.

She shakes her head. "You're injured. I'm not sleeping on your arm and hurting you worse."

"You could never hurt me."

"You're wrong. I could hurt you more than you realize. But I don't want to. Sleep on my chest instead."

I frown. "I'll crush you."

She shakes her head. "You said you would give me control."

"Yes, but only when you were making me come."

"You said you'd give me control. That doesn't end yet, and you'll accept that if you ever want my mouth wrapped around your cock again."

My heart stops, but I surrender. Gently, I lay my head down against her soft chest. "Again?"

She blushes, and her eyes twinkle with thoughts of being my dirty girl again.

"I won't deny that I like your body, just like you like mine. It doesn't mean I like you."

"Of course, it doesn't."

"Go to sleep," she commands.

I close my eyes. Liesel has taken away my pain and replaced it with memories of her sucking my cock. Of her on her knees. Of her saying she wants a repeat.

Again.

I want more. I want to fuck her. Sink into her. Feel the deepest pleasures I can with her. But it's for the best that I don't. My heart and soul wouldn't survive it. She wouldn't survive it. But then again, we have always been destined to destroy each other.

He's mine.

That's the tale my mind tells me as I dream. Langston Pearce is mine. He's my match, my partner, my soulmate. He was always destined to be mine: my best friend, my lover, my husband.

But when I open my eyes, reality hits me hard in the chest. The same chest that Langston is currently lying and drooling on.

Langston isn't mine. He'll never be mine, despite how much I want him. There are countless reasons why Langston will never be mine, why I'll never have him beyond what we've already done.

For one, he's a bastard who has threatened my life.

Two, he's failed over and over when he vowed to protect me.

Three, he's married. Although, I'm still not sure of the exact status or reason for that marriage. He's still married. Unless he divorces, he can never truly be mine.

Four, the only reason he even gives me any time of day is because of the treasure. He still hasn't told me why he wants the money. I suspect to get back at me for whatever horrible thing he thinks I've done.

And five, he killed Waylon.

There is too much to forgive, to forget, and to overcome for us to ever be together. Fucking Langston now would only lead to heartbreak later. But I need to keep all the reasons I can't be with Langston fresh in my mind to fight my overwhelming feelings of lust for him. I've had a taste; that will have to be enough. I'm not sure my heart could take more.

"What are you thinking about so seriously?" Langston says without opening his eyes as he nestles into my chest.

"About how heavy your head is."

He chuckles. "I don't think I'm ever going to get up again. Your chest is too soft."

He rubs his head against my breast.

I roll my eyes, but don't brush him off me. I quite enjoy having him resting on me. I run my hand through his hair.

"How are you feeling?" I ask.

"Horrible. My arms are throbbing, and I have shooting pains up and down my arm all the way through my back."

He moans when I stroke his cheek.

"I'm so sorry. Do you want me to rub your back? Is there something I can do to help?"

He scrunches his face in agony. "I think a repeat of last night is the only way to relieve my pain."

I break out into laughter, and he does the same as I swat him on the head. We both sit up.

"You horny bastard." I playfully hit his chest.

He wiggles his eyebrows. "It was worth a try."

"There's a tray of food and water," I say, pointing to the corner.

Langston tries to get up, but I put a hand on his chest. "I got it." I walk over and pick up the tray before setting it down on the floor next to us.

Langston looks up, like he can't believe food was lowered without us waking and noticing. I can't believe it either.

Both of our stomachs growl, though, so any discussion of how we slept through the food being lowered will have to wait until we've finished eating.

There's a couple of pieces of dry toast, peanut butter, and bananas. We eat everything on the plate and drink all of the water.

"We need a plan," I say before I finish the last drop of water. We won't survive much longer like this. We are getting fed, yes, but not enough to sustain us. We've both already lost a couple of pounds. Our injuries aren't life-threatening so far, but that doesn't mean it will remain that way for long.

"Do you have any ideas?"

"Yes, actually."

He grins. "My huntress is always the best at coming up with the plans."

"I suspect that we will once again be darted. That seems to be our captor's MO. He doesn't want us to know who he is. I don't know if we can avoid being hit entirely by the darts, but we can pull them out as soon as it hits us, so that hopefully we don't get a full dose, and we can remember more about our torture. Our goal after we are darted and raised should be to gather as much information as we can."

"Your goal should be to run if you can. If you get an opportunity to get out, you take it. Don't worry about me."

I won't agree to that, not unless I think I can get help to rescue Langston.

"I doubt we will have that opportunity unless we can avoid getting hit entirely by the darts. If we are even partially drugged, it will make it hard to run."

"I don't intend for you to be hit with another dart," he says.

I shake my head. "You aren't going to be able to prevent a flying dart from hitting me."

"You vastly underestimate my abilities, huntress."

I smile, sadly. "That's because I've overestimated your abilities before and you failed me."

His face looks crushed. He couldn't prevent me from getting raped. He couldn't keep me safe. From that point on, my life was different.

Langston reaches out and grabs the back of my neck as his thumb strokes my cheek. "There is no reason you should trust me in this. All I can do is apologize for failing you. I was young and stupid and cocky.

I'm grown up now and have experienced the world. I won't fail you. If I make a promise to you, I'm going to keep it. Even if it kills me."

Everything inside me wishes I could believe him, but everything is screaming not to trust him.

LANGSTON

Liesel doesn't believe that I'll do anything to protect her, and she shouldn't. But it's a vow I'll keep all the same.

"Maybe we should tell each other everything on our half of the letter? Stop hiding secrets from each other, so we have all the information we need to steer our interrogators astray? Or at least if only one of us survives, we can have the information we need to go after the treasure ourselves," she says, suddenly, completely out of character for her.

"You're willing to give me the information that I've been begging for and threatening your life over, just like that?"

She stills and then blinks. "Yes."

"And how would I trust that anything you said was the truth?"

"You'd know, just like I'd know if you were telling a lie."

I don't know her true motives for wanting to discuss what we know. But even if she wants to tell the truth, it can't happen here.

"First of all, no one is going to die. I won't let that happen."

She sighs. "You aren't God; you can't control everything."

"I can."

She shakes her head with a smile. "Pompous asshole."

"That's me, but we can't talk about the truth of what we know about the treasure. Whoever is holding us might be listening, and no one but the two of us can ever know the truth."

She narrows her eyes, trying to understand what I'm not saying. She still doesn't know the truth of why I want the treasure, why I'm pressing the issue so much, and she'll probably never know.

"You're right. I don't know what I was thinking. I just can't sit down here day after day and wait to be drugged, tortured, and most likely eventually killed."

I know what she means. Even now that we have a sort of plan, I don't want to just sit and wait, filled with an unlimited amount of anxiety. I'm paranoid that every sound is them coming for us—coming to hurt Liesel.

"Then let's not just sit around waiting."

"What do you suggest?" Her cheeks blush, telling me the dirty thoughts she's thinking.

"You want to be honest with one another so we feel like we are fighting on the same side. Then let's be honest. Rattle off random truths. Simple truths that don't really matter but tell us something about each other."

"And if either of us lie?"

"Then, the other gets to steal a kiss." It gives me more incentive to lie than tell the truth, but we are both far more comfortable lying than telling the truth anyway. And Liesel needs more excuses to kiss me. Or maybe she needs an excuse to pull away from me. Either way, I'm going to learn more about her feelings for me this way than if I ask her questions directly.

"I love being a lawyer," she says.

"That, I believe. You always enjoyed arguing with people."

"I do, but as hard as it might be to believe, I also enjoy helping people, whether society says they deserved to be helped or not."

"Hmmm, I never would have taken you to have feelings for other people."

"Are you calling me a liar?" she asks. She's been walking in circles around the room, running her hand along various lines on the bricks, while I sit in the center watching her.

"No, just surprised to find out the ice princess has a heart."

Her eyelashes bat in my direction, like she's trying to hide more of the mystery of who she is.

"I hate my beach house. It's so big, and I prefer the cold of the mountains to the beach. I think I'm going to have to build a new dream house in the mountains."

Her mouth falls open at my words, and I think I heard a little of her heart breaking.

I grin, flashing her my dimple.

Her eyes change in realization. I told a lie so she could decide whether to call me out on it and earn a kiss. Of course, I love my dream house. I love the ocean. I wouldn't trade it for any palace in the world. She knows that. *But does she want to kiss me again in the daylight?*

"I hate the beach house, too. You locked me in a freaking closet. You locked me off from your real home with Phoenix and your kids. The views were horrible. You tainted my dream house by making it my jail cell. I hate it, too."

She holds back a smile as she says it. She's teasing and taunting me just like I did to get a response. But I won't be the first to crack. I won't be the one asking for a kiss. We both already know that I want to kiss her. It's her feelings that I'm trying to figure out.

"I have a favorite child. Atlas is so much more sensible than Rose. I hate how much trouble Rose gets into."

Liesel frowns and shakes her head, knowing once again that I'm lying, but she doesn't say it.

"I think Phoenix and I will become great friends. The best of friends."

Her lie is just as brazen as mine, but once again, I don't call her out on it.

"Good, because I think once you get to know Phoenix, the three of us will enjoy having a threesome."

"Liar."

I grin seductively. "Oh, yea? You think I'm a liar?"

"Yes," she breathes, barely able to get the single word out.

"Do you want to punish me by making me kiss you? Or would you prefer a different punishment?"

She stops circling me. "Stand up."

I do as she says.

"You're a cheating bastard, Langston. You lied on purpose to get a reaction out of me."

"Did I? But then, that's the game. Kiss me or don't. Either way, I'm a tortured man. Kissing you tortures me, dangling so close to what will never be mine. But at least I get to kiss you. Not kissing you breaks my spirit."

"We can't have that."

She walks over to me until we are standing face to face.

"What stops you from wanting me? From wanting to fuck me? From giving in to your lust?"

She purses her gorgeous red lips, that still look like they've been painted red with her favorite lipstick. Her lips have always been the thing I've found most attractive about her. Her mouth is capable of so many wonderful things—sassy comebacks, delicious kisses, and wrapping themselves around my cock.

"You're a married man."

"You've fucked plenty of married men."

"That's true, but..."

"I've told you countless times I'd never get married, and yet here I am—married."

She nods. "That's part of it."

"And if I got divorced, would that change your mind?"

She stops breathing, as do I. "No, we have too much history. I would never want to give you the pleasure of thinking I was yours, even for a night."

Our eyes lock back in our endless battle.

"What would it take?"

"There is nothing that you could give that would make me yours."

I pause at her painful words. Then, I say the only thing that might save me. "Liar."

Her eyes cut back to me, and I grab her hand, yanking her to me until she's pressed against me. "What would it take?"

"More than you are willing to give." And then she presses her lips against mine, most likely to shut me up and end the conversation. But

I'll take any kisses she's willing to give, even if she's trying to trick me again.

The kiss is intoxicating, as are all her kisses. I'm so consumed that I almost don't hear the window opening until it's too late, but I hear just in time.

I keep kissing her, ensuring that she can't play my savior. Then, at the very last second, I turn her and take the dart meant for her.

Her eyes widen, and she yanks the dart out of my back as soon as she realizes what I did. She tries to stare up to get a look at the shooter, but I block her. I only have seconds left until I fall unconscious.

"Stay beneath me. Don't let them shoot you, promise me."

I start to fall toward her, and she does her best to catch me. My body is still shielding her.

"I promise," she whispers as we collapse to the floor, with my body covering her.

"What if I told you I love you? That I've always loved you? Would that be enough to make you mine?" I say, as my eyelids grow heavy.

I never hear her response before the world goes black.

CHAPTER 18

LIESEL

What if I told you I love you?

Langston's words are all I can think about as he collapses on top of me. I should be focused on avoiding any more darts coming my way, but I'm entranced with Langston's words. I wish he could wake up and continue our conversation. There are more pressing issues, though.

Still...

What if Langston did love me? Would that make any difference?

No, it would make things worse.

I glance up just as another dart is sent down toward my chest. I move Langston's arm at the last second, so it enters him instead of me. Rolling his arm so that I can pull the dart out and lay it against my chest, I hope they'll think the dart hit me instead of Langston.

I look up at Langston one last time before I pretend to pass out, and I can't help but brush my lips against his. He doesn't kiss me back, but it doesn't matter. I like the soft touch and smell of him. I like being able to appreciate his body without worrying about how he interprets it.

Langston's silly attempt at getting me to admit feelings toward him didn't go unnoticed. I knew exactly what he was doing when he started the game. The problem is, everything is so damn complicated.

I close my eyes and let my head fall back, pretending to be hit by the dart. A few seconds later, I hear men's voices mumbling above us, but I can't make out what they are saying. A creak of the window and the thump of a rope follows. I so wish I could open my eyes, but I need to wait until we are above ground. That will give me the best chance of learning something that will help us escape.

I wish Langston hadn't been knocked unconscious, that we had removed the dart in time. When I kissed him, I felt nothing back, though. He wouldn't have been able to resist kissing me back if he was still conscious.

Langston's body is lifted up off of me a few minutes later. Despite how hard it was to breathe with Langston on me, I immediately miss the feeling of his body against mine.

Another man lifts me into his brawny arms before I'm set down again. I smell Langston's body immediately, and I know I'm lying on his body.

Before I can worry about damaging Langston's injured arm further, I feel a contraption swinging us in the air. I hold my breath to keep from shrieking as the rig swings hard to the left, nearly knocking us off. Somehow, I resist the urge to grab onto Langston and reveal myself.

The swinging stops as we are plopped on the ground. We are upstairs, above ground, no longer in the tower.

I feel hairy arms beneath my head and legs as I'm once again lifted from the ground, away from Langston. My heart aches at the distance between us. I hope that Langston is being carried right behind me and that we are headed to the same room. I'm not sure I can stand to be apart from him when he's so vulnerable while unconscious, not to mention his hurt arms.

The man carrying me walks for a while. Apparently, wherever he's taking me to be tortured isn't nearby.

A door is kicked open, and I'm desperate to open my eyes to see where I am. But I keep my eyes tightly closed and do everything I can to keep my breathing and heartbeat slow and steady.

I'm plopped down roughly on a couch as if to test if I'm awake. I don't react, even when one of my hands and legs fall off the couch. I let them hang uncomfortably, my body barely staying on the couch.

Footsteps retreat, and then I hear the door close.

Even then, I don't move.

I'm lying on a couch, but I know without opening my eyes that Langston isn't here with me. I'd feel him. It terrifies me where they could be taking him or what they could be torturing him with.

My fear makes me brave enough to open my eyes the tiniest of slits. I'm in a fancy room, in what seems like a castle. The walls are stone, just like the tower we've been kept in, and the furniture looks like it comes from the previous millennia. The couch I'm lying on has gold claw feet, matching the color of the chandelier over my head.

But the room is empty. I open my eyes further and lift my head. It's then I see one of the two doors is open. Through its opening, I see another door with an inset window revealing the outside.

I could run.

Langston told me if I got the opportunity, I should run.

My heart thumps so slowly and loudly in my chest; I'm sure everyone in the house can hear it.

I stare at the door.

Run, I tell myself.

But I don't. I don't even get off the couch. I sit and turn my head to the other door—the closed door, the door I must have been carried through. That's the way to Langston.

I hear Langston's voice in my head. *Run, huntress. Don't worry about me. Save yourself.*

My heart flickers to the closed door.

I should run. I know I should. This might be my only chance. And by running, I could go and get help. I could call Enzo or Kai so they could send a team to rescue Langston.

I don't know how much longer I have until someone comes to check on me. I don't know how many guards are outside the house. I don't know if I'll get this chance again.

I stand, trying to make my decision.

Left to freedom.

Or right to Langston.

The decision ultimately ends up being easy—I run toward the closed door, toward Langston.

I can't save myself without saving him. If I left, they could kill him before I brought anyone to save him, and I couldn't face that.

I get to the closed door and listen carefully for any sign of someone standing guard. I don't hear anyone, but that doesn't mean they aren't there.

Slowly, I open the door wide enough to look down the hallway. I don't find anyone, so I open the door all the way and step through. The hallway is quiet and empty.

I start walking down the hallway, hoping to find Langston or some hint of who is holding us. With any luck, Langston will have woken up by now, and we will be able to sneak out together.

I get to a fork in the hallway. I can continue on straight or turn to the right. There are no people straight ahead, so I push my head forward to look down to the right. It's empty as well.

My gut tells me to go right. There are a lot more doors to the right than straight ahead.

I continue down the hallway as silently as I can, looking for clues of whose house this is or where Langston is. All of the decorations look to be a century or more old and have no personal touches. I wouldn't be surprised if this is a rental property. That, combined with the seemingly lack of security cameras or guards, makes it feel like whoever is holding us doesn't have as much money or skill as we first thought.

I come to the first door and place my ear against it to listen. I don't hear anything, so I continue on.

I do the same to two more doors before I get to one where I hear a gentle moaning sound. I open the door, too quickly, and it makes a creaking sound. But I'm in such a hurry to get to Langston if he's hurt.

Langston is lying on the cold floor, but no one is watching him. They must think since they drugged us that they don't need to stand guard—what fools.

I race over to his side and gently pat his cheek.

"Langston, you have to wake up. We have to get out of here."

I tug on his arm and try to roll him over.

He moans but doesn't open his eyes.

"Sorry about this, but you need to get up."

I take his arm out of the sling and pull hard.

He growls and grips it, his eyes flying open.

I exhale sharply. "We have to get out of here," I repeat.

He looks around, completely confused, but we don't have time to explain or wait until his brain is fully functional again.

"Can you stand?"

"I think so."

He starts to push himself up with one arm but falls.

"I've got you," I say, looping his arm over my shoulders and lifting him up.

He's heavy, and his feet seem barely functional. I won't be able to help him far. Hopefully, his legs will start working soon. If not, we won't make it far without being caught.

"Well, well, how clever you are to have avoided a dart," a man says from the doorway. He's wearing a sharp-looking suit, apparently the king of this castle. It's almost like he's from another time.

He snaps his fingers, and two men run inside and pull Langston from my shoulder.

"Don't hurt him!" I plead as they throw him back down on the ground. He's too drugged up to fight. He can barely even lift his head.

"Well, that depends on you, Miss Dunn," the man in the suit says.

I continue to look at Langston on the floor. I'm completely helpless. I've failed. Now I know how Langston must have felt when he failed to protect me. It's a horrid feeling that creeps up your chest and throat, taking hold of all your senses.

"What do you want?" I ask.

"Come with me, Miss Dunn, and we can discuss what will be done about Mr. Pearce."

I bite my lip and hold back tears as I look at Langston, broken and weak on the floor. I want to run to him, hold him, protect him.

"Promise me if I go with you, you won't hurt him," I say.

The man smiles. "This isn't a negotiation. You are in no position to negotiate."

"You want information from me, yes?"

He shrugs. "From either of you. Whoever tells me what I need gets to live."

I shake my head. "The only way you get the information you need is if you let him live. Each of us only has half the information. You need both of us."

The man frowns. "I promise I won't hurt him until after we've talked. You have my word."

It's the best I'm going to get, so I take a step to follow him.

"No, Liesel," Langston says, trying to scramble to his feet to come after me.

I refuse to turn and look at him. I'm doing this to save him. I won't let him persuade me to let him suffer in my place with his puppy dog eyes or commanding voice.

The man in the suit looks past me to his two employees. "Make sure he stays here, unharmed until I say otherwise."

I exhale sharply in relief. The man starts walking out of the room, so I follow him like a loyal servant.

He doesn't speak to me as we walk down the hall, and I try to tune out Langston's moans and pleas.

Please, let me be doing the right thing.

The man stops in the original room I was laid down in. He puts his hand out, indicating for me to sit on the couch, so I do. I told him I'd do anything to keep Langston safe, and I will. I'll do anything, and that terrifies me.

I want Langston's kids to grow up with a father—that's the only reason I'm doing this. I don't care about Langston, not really. I just want his secrets, and I don't want to be responsible for making two beautiful children fatherless.

The man shuts the first door, then walks over to the second door that has a view of the outside door. He slowly shuts it, closing off my escape.

"You're very interesting, Miss Dunn."

"I sure am, Mr....?"

He smiles at me. His dark hair is perfectly combed over, his teeth are pearly white, and his sharp jaw is clean-shaven. He looks like he's about to go into a boardroom, not about to interrogate someone for information about stolen treasure.

"I don't think you've earned my name yet, Miss Dunn."

"If you are going to torture me, you might as well call me Liesel."

"Who says I'm going to torture you?" He sits on the arm of the couch and stares at me, completely in control of his pleasant facade.

"Just a guess based on the fact that I was taken against my will, locked in a tower, and the last time you brought me above ground, I ended up with some broken ribs."

"You exaggerate. I doubt your ribs were actually broken."

I narrow my eyes. "You dislocated my friend's arm and injured his elbow."

"Did I?"

"You did."

"Well, Miss Dunn, I prefer to talk over torture, and it seems you will be amenable."

"What do you want with me and Langston?"

"You disappoint me, Miss Dunn. You shouldn't ask questions you already know the answer to."

I frown. "What do I have to do for you to allow Langston to go free?"

"Now, that is a much better question."

"One that you intend to answer, or will you continue to talk in riddles?"

"I'm curious. He took all of the drugs for you, so that you would stay conscious. My men stupidly left you unattended in this room, with a clear escape route. Why didn't you escape and save yourself?"

I tilt my head. "You shouldn't ask questions you already know the answer to."

He cracks up like I'm the funniest thing in the world.

"You're quite amusing, Miss Dunn. I might just keep you for entertainment."

"I don't care what you do with me, as long as Langston goes free."

He purses his lips and puts his hand to his chin as he studies me. "I've done my research on you, and I thought you were a soulless creature who only looked out for yourself, but I'm afraid I was mistaken—you do have a heart."

Now it's my turn to laugh. "I don't have a heart."

"Then, accept my deal. You give me some basic information, and then I'll let you go."

"You'll keep Langston?"

He nods.

"What will you do to him?"

"Whatever it takes to get the information we seek."

I frown.

"And then, we'll kill him."

I gasp.

He smiles, getting more information on me than I might have otherwise admitted. He stands from the arm of the chair and walks over to me, lifting my chin to look at him.

"One of you has to die."

"Why? Why not get the information from us and then let us go?"

"Because as you said, you have half the information and he has the other half. Neither of you can go after the treasure with only half the information. Whoever has all the info gets the treasure, and I have to be assured that no one else has all of the map. If I let you both go, you'll tell each other your half of the secret to head me off."

I swallow hard and pull my head from his touch as anger pulses through me. I try to come up with a new plan to escape, but nothing comes to me immediately. All I can think is that the drugs they've pumped Langston with will wear off soon, and then he'll find a way to escape. Maybe Enzo or Kai are on their way here to save us—or at least, save Langston. Hopefully, because I have no idea how to get both of us out of here alive.

"Who will live and who will die? You or Langston? I'll give you some time to decide, Miss Dunn. "

He walks out the first door and locks me in. I run to the door and attempt to throw it open, but the door won't budge. I run to the second, but the handle barely rattles.

I slump to the floor with tears in my eyes. Only one of us is going to survive this—and I already know what my decision will be.

CHAPTER 19

LANGSTON

Why is Liesel trying to protect me? That's my job.

I've threatened her life.

Killed her fiancé.

Gotten married despite telling her I never would.

I've been awful to her. And yet, she still protects me. I won't let her. It's my job to defend her.

"No, Liesel," I plead for her not to do this, not to offer up herself to protect me in any way. I want to call her huntress, but I dare not use my nickname for her in the presence of these horrible men.

She doesn't even hesitate as she walks out of the room. It's almost as if she doesn't even hear me.

The door is shut after she leaves. A roar of pain rips through my body, but because of my drugged up state, it doesn't leave my stomach. My head spins with a fog, and my body doesn't function. I try to tell my legs to move, to stand up, but the signal gets lost between my brain and my legs. My muscles feel like jello.

I fall forward, trying to go after her.

"Easy there, don't injure yourself on our watch. We'll have our asses ripped if there is a single new mark on you," one of the guards left in my room says.

"Just wait until the drugs have worn off; you two will be the first to die," I threaten.

The man chuckles. "Who says we are ever going to let the drugs wear off? We know what you are capable of, which is why we have to keep drugging you. We aren't stupid enough to let that happen."

They plan on keeping me drugged.

Shit.

I'm not going to be able to rescue Liesel. I'm going to have to find a way to fight through the drugs. I can do this; I just need time.

Move, leg.

It moves. Not enough to get me very far or to fight, but enough to give me hope that with enough practice, I'll be able to fight through the drugs I'm given. If I can pretend I'm still under the influence for longer and longer periods of times when I'm not, maybe I'll regain enough strength to get Liesel out of here.

"Don't wiggle off," one of the men says as he hooks his arm underneath one of my shoulders. The other man does the same to my other arm, and I'm dragged to a chair. It's more comfortable than the floor but doesn't make it any easier for me to escape.

What is Liesel going through?

Is she being tortured?

Beaten?

Raped?

Is she going to survive this, both physically and mentally?

Liesel Dunn is the strongest woman I know, but strength has its limits. At some point, she'll break and won't be able to heal.

The time ticks by slowly, so slowly I'm not sure if time even exists. My body doesn't regain much strength as the minutes pass. I'm still as out of it as I was when I was first brought to this room.

My two guards spend their time smoking a cigar and drinking whiskey. They don't talk or provide me any entertainment, which only makes the time tick by slower.

I hear footsteps, and my heart begs for it to be Liesel. Not because her returning to this room would make her safer, but because I'm desperate to see her.

The door opens, and the suited man steps in. It's easy to tell he's in charge by what he wears and how he carries himself, with complete confidence and fearlessness. My two guards act like if they put one foot out of place, they will be castrated.

The man grins at me as he walks into the room. "I'm happy to see you're still in one piece."

I frown. "And I'm unhappy to see that you still are."

"Miss Dunn did put up quite a fight, but in the end, she relented."

I growl and try to jump from my chair, but my body doesn't function very well yet. The two men grab my shoulders and yank me back in my seat easily.

The man in the suit laughs, amused by my distress. He walks over to the small bar and pours himself a drink before taking the seat opposite me.

"Who are you?" I ask.

"Does it matter?" The slick man raises his eyebrows.

"No, I'll kill you all the same."

"I have no doubt that you'll try, and if I falter in any way, you'll succeed."

"Then why don't you seem more afraid?"

"Because as long as I have Miss Dunn in my possession, I have complete control over you."

I growl again. He's right, but I hate that he already knows my weakness.

"What did you do to Liesel? If you hurt one hair on her head, I'll torture you for years and only let you die once I've broken every bone in your body."

He smirks. "Liesel is still in one piece, don't worry. She's currently contemplating my proposition."

I hold my breath, terrified she'll offer her body in exchange for keeping me safe—something I couldn't live with. But from his smug expression, I'm afraid he's already touched her.

I scan his suit, looking for any signs he's hurt her. Claw marks, a ripped hole or pulling of fabric, anything from her struggle, but I don't see anything out of place on him. That reassures me slightly, but maybe it's my imagination and hope convincing me. He could have changed suits after he beat her, or he could have had another man attack her.

"What proposition?"

"As I'm sure you've guessed, I seek the treasure that only you and Liesel protect."

I nod. Of course, he's after the treasure. I can't think of any other reason why he would capture both Liesel and me.

"For yourself or for your boss?" I ask. He may not tell me, but maybe he'll give me a clue as to a man higher up than him coming after us.

"Your questions don't stop, do they?" He takes a slow sip of his drink. "You won't get any answers, Mr. Pearce."

"Don't worry, I don't need to ask any more questions. Only a man who has vowed his life to another doesn't answer questions when asked. You are just like the men to either side of me. You're a low-life in a fancy suit, and you'll never have any real power."

He frowns, and I know I've hit a nerve.

"As I was saying, I gave Miss Dunn a proposition, and I've decided to offer you the same deal. I can only make the deal with one of you, but again, it doesn't matter to me who it is."

I hold my breath. I don't care what the deal is; all I want is Liesel to be safe. I want to get on my knees and beg to keep him from hurting her. I would offer all the money I have to keep her safe. I'll give him the treasure, anything if he lets Liesel go.

"What's the deal?"

"You both tell me everything you know about the treasure. How to get it and what exactly it is."

"And in exchange?"

A Cheshire Cat smile spreads across his face while my heart thumps wildly in my chest. What will I have to give in order for Liesel to go free?

"And in exchange, I'll let one of you go free."

"Liesel will go free."

"You haven't heard the second half of my deal, so you might want to reconsider your chivalry."

I frown and hold my breath, waiting for him to drop the part he thinks will make me change my mind. He doesn't realize that nothing will make me change my mind. Liesel has to go free. I can't be responsible for her pain again, not when I have the chance to save her.

He takes another long drink, enjoying making me crazy as he draws this out.

"I'll let one of you go free—"

"Unharmed," I say.

He shrugs. "The person who goes free will be in one piece."

"They will be unharmed."

"You aren't in a position to negotiate. As I said, I gave Miss Dunn the same deal, and if she agrees to my terms before you do, then you will have no choice but to go along with it."

I frown.

"As I was saying before you rudely interrupted me, I will let one of you go free after I get the information I need. I'll kill the other one."

The blood drains from my face. "Why? Why not torture the other to within an inch of their life and then let them go?"

"I can't have the two of you exchanging information and fighting me for the treasure. I must be the only person who knows all of the clues."

I don't think I've blinked, taken a breath, or let my heart beat since he said he'd only let one of us live. I've been in predicaments like this before, life and death situations. Every time I've defeated the enemy. I've not only won but succeeded in killing the monster who dared to stand against me. I could do the same again.

But I've never been drugged like this and never had to keep Liesel safe at the same time.

If I choose Liesel to be the one to live, I won't be able to fight back until I know she's safe. By then, I could be dead. And I'm not sure I'm strong enough to fight the drugs. I don't know where Enzo and his team are, but my only hope is that they are close.

I'm made several vows in my life—to Phoenix, to my kids, to Liesel. I'm afraid I won't be able to keep all of them. I'll have to choose which vows to keep and which to break.

The man in the suit grins as he watches my agony. He's a sick, sadistic man who probably enjoys this as much as he will getting the information he needs to go after the treasure. The man finishes his drink casually, then stands and sets the glass back on the bar.

"Watch him, but don't injure him. Give him a half dose in a half-hour. I want him lucid when I return," he says to the two guards.

"Yes, sir," they both answer.

He looks at me. "I'll return in an hour to get your decision." He starts to walk to the door, and my heart speeds. *What if Liesel gives him an answer before me? Can I really let her decide both our fates?*

"Wait!" I shout as he opens the door.

He turns and looks at me with raised brows.

"You don't need to wait an hour. I have an answer for you now."

He smiles, satisfied.

"I'm sure you do, but I have a lunch meeting I need to attend, and I'll enjoy watching you squirm. You can give me your answer in an hour."

"What about Liesel?"

"I'll collect her answer in two hours if you don't give me an answer in one."

Then he leaves without giving me a chance to say more. He leaves me with my choice—an impossible one, but one I won't regret making. Not this time.

CHAPTER 20

LIESEL

Time creeps by until the man in the suit returns. I spend the entire time trying to break open the doors, but they're too thick. All I ended up doing was bruise my shoulder and hip.

I startle, stepping back when the suit opens the door.

"I know you may find my capabilities lacking, but I assure you, there is no escape from this castle unless I give permission for you to leave."

I shrug. "Do you blame a girl, destined to die, for trying?"

"No, I just thought you were smarter than that. I thought you knew not to waste your strength on a doomed task."

He shuts the door behind him, and I hear the faint lock as he does. We are locked in this room together.

"Would you like a drink?" he asks as he walks over to the bar in the corner of the room.

I've already raided it looking for water, food, anything alcohol-free to give me strength, but there is nothing but whiskey, vodka, and gin.

"No, thanks."

"Suit yourself." He pours himself a vodka and then sits on the couch.

I take a seat next to him, not because I want to, but because I need to preserve what little strength I have left. I feel practically naked sitting next to him, still only wearing Langston's leather jacket and black panties.

Did he have cameras watching what Langston and I did in the tower?

When he brought me up here before and bruised my ribs, did he touch me?

"What are you thinking about, beautiful?"

"Why did you call me beautiful?"

Goosebumps pour over my arms, uneasiness rocking my body.

He grins. "To make you uncomfortable."

"Are you always so honest?"

"I don't find any reason to lie."

"What is your name?"

"That's the question you want to ask me?"

"I'm tired of calling you 'the suit' in my head," I reply.

"You could call me, sir."

I frown. *No way in hell am I going to call him that.*

"Rowan Wells."

"I've made my decision, Rowan."

He smiles. "I knew you wouldn't give me the respect to call me, Mr. Wells."

"Why would I? You drugged me and my friend, then threw us in a tower with no way of escape, and now are threatening to kill one of us. I don't think you've earned my respect."

"Touché."

I take a deep breath, before telling Rowan my decision. "Langston must live. I choose him."

Rowan raises his eyebrows. "You'll choose death in order to save him?"

"Yes, kill me. Do whatever you want with me, just ensure that Langston lives."

"I didn't know that such love could exist, but I was wrong."

I'm about to open my mouth to say I don't love Langston, and I have no doubt that he doesn't love me, but what's the use? It doesn't matter why I'm saving him, just that Rowan accepts my deal.

"Do we have a deal? I'll answer any questions you have, and you can ask Langston any questions you have of him. And after we are finished, you will let Langston go free."

He holds out his hand to me, and I reluctantly take it, revolting from his frosty touch. "We have a deal, Miss Dunn."

We shake, and I'm careful not to be the first to pull away. I don't want to show any weakness, even though my lack of food and water is beginning to get to me. My head is spinning, my sight is fuzzy, and my body feels lethargic.

"What now?" I ask.

"Now, we chat. After we are finished, I'll have a chat with Langston. And then I'll set him free, far away from here, so he doesn't attempt a rescue."

"Where do you want me to start?"

"By telling me what is on your half of the letter your father gave you."

I frown. "How do you know about the letter? And that it was split between the two of us?"

He shakes his head. "I'm the one asking the questions, Miss Dunn, not you. What did the letter say?"

I consider my options. I have to tell him some truths, but I don't intend to tell him everything. He'll believe what I have to say. Langston will be safe whether I tell the full truth or not.

"The letter said that there was a treasure that would change my life. It didn't specify what the treasure was, just that it exists. The letter told me not to search for it, that it could destroy me."

"Get to the specifics, Miss Dunn; stop stalling."

I roll my eyes. "I'm just telling you what the letter said. The letter also said that whoever goes after it has to be married. They need to be madly in love in order to seek the treasure." I leave out that only a Dunn is able to get the treasure. I don't want him changing his mind and deciding to keep me alive.

He frowns, and I look down at his bare ring finger.

"I take it you're not married?" I smirk.

"I'm not."

"Well, you better find a wife quick if you want to go after the treasure."

He stares at me like I could be that wife.

"You want me dead, remember? I can't be your wife."

He growls. "Continue."

"The letter says you can only find the treasure where the sea takes you."

"What does that mean?"

I shrug. "There is a reason I haven't figured out where the treasure is; I only have half the information."

"Why, if you care so dearly about Langston and vice versa, haven't you both shared all the information with each other?"

Because he's wrong about us. We don't actually care about each other.

"For the same reason you won't let us both live. Us both only having a piece of the puzzle has ensured our survival to this point."

He nods and then leans back on the couch, waiting slightly more patiently for me to continue. He almost looks bored with my tale.

"There was something about meeting a man in Egypt where he's hidden a clue. A partial password 862. And to follow the stars if you ever get lost."

Rowan looks at me suspiciously. "Was there anything else in your half of the letter?"

"No," I lie. Most of what I gave him was a lie, but it all rattled off my tongue with confidence. There is no way to tell if I made everything up or told the truth. That is until he speaks to Langston and none of my information fits with his.

"I'll go speak with Langston and then be back shortly," Rowan says, standing.

"How will you get him to speak to you?" I'm afraid he's planning on torturing him to get him to speak.

He grins at me. "By making the same deal with him."

"What?" I breathe.

"I'm sure he'll spill his guts to save you. Although, I suspect he'll be more truthful."

He stands and heads to the door, but I can't let him leave, not until I'm assured that he won't hurt or kill Langston.

I jump up, suddenly full of strength, and run to him.

"You made a deal with me! You can't hurt Langston." I grab his arm, trying to get him to stay and talk to me.

"You lied to me, Miss Dunn."

"I didn't," I plead.

"I don't believe you."

"Don't hurt him. You promised to let him go. Please."

He shakes his head. "I'll do what is necessary to get the information I seek."

I don't know what his words mean. *Have I been a fool for trusting him? Should I have told him the entire truth? Would that have ensured Langston survived, or was his plan all along to kill us both?*

"Don't worry, I still plan on keeping one of you alive; I just haven't decided who yet."

"Him—keep Langston alive."

"Maybe you should have told me the truth, and I would consider your plea."

He goes to open the door, and I grip his arm, trying to keep him with me. If he's with me, he can't hurt Langston.

"Let go," he orders.

"Promise me you won't hurt him, and I'll tell you the truth."

He pauses, as if considering my deal, but then I see his fist coming at my face.

I try to turn, but the impact hits me all the same. He knocks me hard in the jaw, forcing my feeble body to fall back to the floor.

Before I know what's going on, Rowan is gone. My tears fall immediately—not from my own pain, but from the fear of losing Langston. I failed in saving him, and I don't know what to do to fix it.

LANGSTON

"Is that everything?" he asks me, sitting in his suit like this is a business arrangement, and not like I've been drugged and tied up like an animal. I was only given a half dose this last time, so I don't feel as out of it as I did before, but that's why he added chains to my arms and legs.

I sit quietly, trying to remember anything else I can about my half of the letter.

"I believe so."

He nods. I'm not sure if this man believes me or not, but I've told him everything. Every word I said was the truth.

"Thank you for your honesty, Mr. Pearce."

I exhale an exhausted breath. I would do anything to save Liesel. Even if it makes me a terrible father, I've failed so many times to protect Liesel before.

I still have hope I'll be able to escape once Liesel is safely away, but if I can't, I know my kids will understand why I made this sacrifice. Enzo, Zeke, and Beckett will step in and make excellent father figures in my place. My children won't grow up without a father or with an evil one. Me staying alive isn't a requirement for them to grow up safely.

"You believe me?"

"I do."

"What happens next? Where will you set Liesel free?"

His eyes cut to me, and from the look in them, I've been lied to.

"Where. Are. You. Releasing. Liesel?"

He stands up.

I try to tackle him, but my restraints keep me in my chair.

"I wish I could say I'm a man of my word, but I'm not. You should have expected as much."

"Release her. I'll help you get the treasure. I'll do anything you want. Release her!"

He smirks. "Liesel made me a better offer."

My heart sinks. He's going to rape her, do unthinkable things to her body before he kills her. I can see it in the gleam in his eyes.

"Please," I beg.

"You two are the strangest couple I've ever met. I don't know how you can be married to another woman, when you so clearly love her."

I don't love her. I don't correct him; it's not worth the energy.

"Let her go."

He shakes his head. "I will keep my word to her. I'll let you go. Enjoy your freedom, Mr. Pearce. But know that she'll be dead long before you can save her. And if you return, I'll have no choice but to kill you, too. So for the sake of your children, I suggest you get on with your life and forget about her."

Forget about Liesel? Impossible.

The nameless man walks out the door, and I strain against my metal chains with everything inside of me.

"Hold still, and we'll get you out of here, man," one of the guards says, grabbing onto the restraints on my arms.

I continue to thrash like a great white shark on dry land. I have to escape. I have to get to Liesel.

"Sedate him," the head guard says to the other. "We can dump him far away from here, and we won't have to deal with him."

"But then he'll be dead weight, and I don't want to carry him."

I throw an elbow in one of the men's faces, hitting him in the nose and gushing blood.

"I'll do it. I don't want a broken nose like you," he chuckles to himself as he goes to grab another syringe.

No! If they sedate me, I won't be able to fight. I'll never be able to live with myself if they hurt Liesel.

I have to find a way to keep the drug from entering my system. My blood is boiling with rage and adrenaline by the time the squat, balding man returns. The other man's nose is still bleeding.

"I'm going to get some ice for my nose while the drug takes effect, then we can deal with him," the first guard says before walking out the door.

The man with the syringe approaches me from the back. I have to come up with a plan, something to stop the drug from taking over.

I continue to thrash as the man tries to grab ahold of me.

"Hold still," he says.

I don't. I jerk wildly as I feel him jab my shoulder. I feel him start to push the liquid into my muscle, and I pull away as he pushes in the liquid.

"There. Now you'll relax," the man says as he walks out of the room, leaving me tied to the chair.

I don't know if he pushed all of the drug into my shoulder or if I succeeded in spilling most down my back. I feel a coolness on my spine, and I hope it's some of the spilled liquid, but it's probably wishful thinking.

My eyelids grow heavy, confirming that at least some of the drug entered my system. I just hope it doesn't last. I hope that I can regain my strength before they move me from this castle. For now, I have to sleep.

No, I have to stay awake. I have to fight.

Think about Liesel. Think about what she could be going through. Think about her dead.

I feel sleepy and tired, but the pull of the drug never fully pulls me under.

When I hear footsteps approaching again, I pretend I'm asleep, so they think the drug worked. I force myself to slump in my chair, my eyes to close, and my breathing to still.

"He seems out," one of the men says.

I feel a finger poking me. I moan softly, but otherwise, don't move.

"Yep, looks good to go."

I hear and feel the unlocking of my chains. I want to make a run for it, but I have to be patient. I have to choose the exact right moment.

"Should we remove the restraints? He weighs a ton by himself; I don't want to have to carry anything I don't have to."

"We can remove the chains from his legs, but keep his wrists cuffed together in case he wakes up earlier than we expect."

I feel the chains being removed from my legs and my heart rate speeds. Luckily, these idiots don't notice the change in my pulse.

"I'll take his shoulders; you carry his legs."

"Which way are we taking him?"

"We'll take him out the back door and then pull the truck around to toss him in the back. Then drive him to the boat and dump him on the mainland somewhere."

I decide to wait until they carry me out of the house before I make my move. They will be exhausted from carrying me, and if I'm lucky, they will leave me alone while they get the truck. I just have to stay conscious until then, a slightly more difficult task while keeping my eyes closed. My body wants to fall asleep, while my heart and soul want to fight.

They lift me clumsily in the air, practically dragging me against the floor. I suspect I'll hit several bumps in the floor while they carry me and will have to force myself to not react.

My intuition proves correct.

My back is scraped all up and down from hitting the jagged stone floor. My shoulder feels ablaze from being dragged by the arms, but I never react.

Finally, I'm dropped onto softer ground. I hear a bird chirping, feel the warmth of the sun, and smell fresh-cut grass.

"I'll pull the truck around; you watch him."

I hear footsteps crunching on leaves as the guard walks away.

I wait a second longer, and then I attack. I stand and run at the remaining man. I wrap my chains around his neck and begin to choke him before he even realizes I'm awake. Within seconds, I drain the life from him, and he drops to the ground.

I find his gun and wait around the corner for his friend to return. When I spot him driving the truck up, I take aim and kill him with a single shot.

I don't know if there are cameras or other guards nearby who could be alerted, but I don't stick around to find out. I have one mission—find Liesel and get us both out of here.

The door that leads back to the house is unlocked, so I easily slip back inside. My wrists are still bound together, but there is enough space between them for me to use the gun without any trouble. But if a fight gets into hand to hand combat, I'm not sure how I'd fare with the chains and my drowsiness. My goal is to shoot any guards dead before a fight gets that far.

I don't know where Liesel is being kept. I don't know her condition or if everything the man in the suit said was a lie. I just know I have to get to her.

I come to a fork, where the hallway splits. The room I was kept in is on the right. I know instinctually to head to the left. Our captor would keep us at either ends of the castle to make it as hard as possible for us to reach each other.

There are several doors through the hallway. I want to burst through them all to see if Liesel is in each and every one of them, but I don't know who is on the other side of the door, and I won't risk getting captured again.

Instead, I'm stealth-like as I approach each door quickly but carefully. I place my ear against the thick doors. They may be thick, but they aren't modern. Thankfully, I can hear beyond the door into each room.

Two men are talking behind the first door, but neither of them mention Liesel after a few seconds.

I move on to the second door, and hear nothing—empty.

Finally, I make it to the third door where I hear sobs that wrap around my heart like prickly vines. Liesel is crying, and it breaks me.

I hold the gun carefully in my hand in case she's in the middle of being tortured. I'll kill every motherfucker who dares to touch her.

I pop the door open and aim around the room, expecting to take out the devil and his minions. Instead, all I see is Liesel.

I drop to my knees next to her. She hasn't looked up yet to realize that it's me.

"Please," she begs.

"Huntress," I say as soothingly as I can.

She lifts her head.

I gasp and immediately wish I could take my reaction back. But her face startles me—it's black, blue, and swollen. I don't know the extent of the rest of her injuries, but my imagination runs wild with horrid images of what the man in the suit did to her.

"Are you really here?" she whispers through her tears.

"Yes, I'm here."

She smiles as she falls against my chest. "You're here to save me?"

I nod with her head under the crook of my chin. My arms are useless to hold her like I want between how injured they are, the chains, and the gun I'm still gripping.

She thinks I'm her savior.

I will do whatever it takes to get her out of this castle, but I'm not her savior. I always fail at rescuing her until it's too late. This time is no different.

"You shouldn't have saved me," she whispers.

CHAPTER 22

LIESEL

You shouldn't have saved me.

Those words ring truer than any I've ever spoken. My head rests against his chest for a split second, but I'm terrified that Rowan or one of the guards is going to come back and kill Langston on the spot.

"We have to go," Langston says, ignoring my comment.

"Is there anything I can do about the chains?"

"No."

"Do you have a gun or weapon for me?"

"No, and even if I did, you wouldn't aim to kill."

He's right, but I could still do some damage.

He stares at me like something's wrong with me. "Do you want me to carry you?"

"Could you?" I raise an eyebrow.

"Yes," he growls.

"No, I don't need you to carry me."

He starts to walk toward the door he entered through, but I grab his hand, stopping him.

"This way," I nod in the direction of the other door. "It leads straight outside the castle."

He walks in front of me. "Stay behind me, Liesel. Do not jump in front of me, understand? Don't you dare try to take a bullet for me."

"Lead the way," is all I say. I won't make any promises.

He sighs and then pushes the door open as I grab onto his hips and duck down as we walk through the door, short hallway, and then out the front door.

"Where are all the guards?" I whisper.

"I killed a couple of them, but I'm not going to wait around to find the rest. Want to run through the forest or steal a car?"

Before I can answer, we hear voices approaching.

"Woods," I mouth at him.

He nods, and he backs me into the brush while he keeps his gun aimed in the direction of the castle, until we get to the thick of the forest where we can no longer be seen. Then, we start running.

Langston isn't as fast as me, I realize, which makes me try to study him as we run.

"Are you hurt?" I ask.

"Drugged."

I frown. "Are you going to pass out on me?"

"No, I only got a partial dose. I'll be fine soon, but it's best to keep my adrenaline up to help get the drug out of my system faster."

I nod, and we keep running. It's a bit freeing to be running through the woods with my childhood friend. Even though I'm barefoot and pantless, and we are running for our lives, it's still enjoyable. This is what I missed the most about Langston, being together like this.

He must feel it too, because he gives me a knowing smile before turning back around.

Suddenly, his smile drops, as do his feet. I stop and turn when I see what we are running toward—the edge of a cliff.

"What do we do?" I ask as we both look over the edge.

"We have two choices—run along the perimeter of the island and try to find a boat, or we jump."

"Jump? And where would we swim to?"

"Do you see that land?"

I nod.

"It looks like it's only a few miles from here."

I nod, understanding. It's an exhausting swim. I turn and look back. I won't go back to the castle, and I won't allow Langston to die at Rowan's command. We could circle the island, but it only gives the men more opportunity to find us. They won't suspect that we jumped into the water. And since no boats are missing, it will take longer for them to search for us across the channel.

Then I look at his hands. "You aren't going to be able to swim with those chains."

We both look over the edge, searching for options. There's some driftwood floating nearby.

"I have to try."

Langston has always been a fish in water. He's always belonged in the ocean. And I know if he were to die, he'd prefer the ocean swept him away.

"On the count of three," I say to gather strength.

"One," he says.

"Two," I say.

"Three," we both say as we leap.

I don't know how tall the cliff is, but the fall seems to go on forever. We hit the water, and I immediately start kicking as hard as I can toward the surface. I'm not afraid that I won't take another breath, but I need to make sure Langston makes it to the surface.

I breach the surface at the same time Langston does. We both smile wide.

"Here," Langston pushes a piece of wood in my direction.

I grab onto it, and then he grabs hold of another. We both turn ourselves in the direction of the closest piece of land and start kicking.

I don't think I breathe until we are at least halfway between the island and the far shore.

"Do we know what country we are in?" I ask as we swim.

"No, I didn't get much information out of the suit."

"The suit?"

"The man in charge."

"Oh, you mean Rowan Wells."

"He told you his name?"

"I demanded he tell me, and he did."

His eyes widen. "You are a better manipulator than I thought."

"I'll take that as a compliment."

Our kicking continues to get slower the longer we go. The water gets cooler as the sun begins to set. I don't know what I'm more afraid of—freezing to death in this water or drowning from exhaustion.

"Do you think there are sharks in this water?" I ask, trying to distract us with a different type of gloom.

"I'm sure there are."

I shiver, and he laughs at me.

"Don't tell me my kick-ass, warrior in a dress and heels, survived torture, huntress is afraid of sharks?"

"Everyone is afraid of sharks. Haven't you watched any horror movies? Sharks are one of the top killers."

He laughs, which makes me smile. I'm shocked I can still make him laugh.

"So, what's the plan when we make it to shore?" I ask.

"Find some shelter, ideally some food and warm clothes, and pray we find someone who will let us use a phone, computer, or something to contact Kai and Enzo without drawing too much attention to ourselves. Then we hide and hope Kai and Enzo find us before Rowan does."

I look out at how far we have left to go. I'm beginning to doubt I have the strength. "And if we're too tired to make it to shore tonight?"

"Don't talk like that. We're strong enough. Trust me, I won't let us drown."

"Then, start talking. I'm going to need a lot of distraction if I'm going to make it to shore without whining the whole way."

"I can provide a distraction," he flashes me a wicked grin with a wink, and I know his mind has gone to very dirty places.

I think I'm going to enjoy the rest of our swim.

CHAPTER 23

LANGSTON

I made a mistake. I should have insisted that we found a boat to take us across instead of swimming this length. We've been swimming half the day, and we still have a long way to go.

We are both exhausted and freezing.

Liesel is a trooper. She's barely complained, has been kicking harder than I have, and is usually further ahead of me in the ocean.

But from how my own body aches, I know she's struggling. And I know how much she hates the ocean—this is her own special kind of torture.

The drugs in my system finally wore off an hour ago, which only left a massive headache in their place. I'm dehydrated and my legs are cramping, but that's nothing compared to the burning fire in my shoulder as I grip the driftwood. I really need to have a doctor look at my shoulder. I suspect that I'm going to need surgery and rehab to ever use it again without pain, but that will have to wait.

It would be easier to stop and let the ocean take me, but there is no way I'm giving up—not on Liesel and not on my kids.

I try to think of something funny to distract us, but I can't come up with anything. I want to ask her about what happened back in the castle. *How did she get the suit to tell him his name? What deal did she make with him? Why did she make the deal?*

But conversations like that need to wait until we are on shore and face to face.

"What are you thinking about? Because the look on your face says you're undressing me with your eyes and thinking of dirty, filthy things you want to do to me," Liesel says.

I grin, glad to hear her interpretation. *She wants me dirty? I can be dirty.*

"Just trying to decide if I'd rather fuck you in the ocean or on the sand. Which would be hotter?"

She scrunches her nose. "Neither."

I laugh. "Because I disgust you?"

"No, I have no problem fucking a good looking man if there is little chance we are going to survive tomorrow. But the ocean is freezing, and the sand is messy."

"Would you consider the ocean if I warmed you up?"

"Maybe," she says.

"Or the sand if I promised you could be on top and I'd clean you off afterward?"

"Hmm," she purrs.

I grin but don't get too excited. We're just blabbing to distract ourselves. We aren't fucking—now or ever.

We don't talk for a while. We just focus on kicking and keeping our heads above water. The sun begins to set, and the cool water turns ice cold. Every part of me is numb. My head falls onto the driftwood, too hard to hold up. I can no longer see where we are going.

"Langston," Liesel whispers.

My eyes flutter open, and I realize I've practically been asleep while kicking.

"Look!"

I lift my head, taking almost all the strength I have left. But it's worth the effort—shore.

"We're going to make it," we both say at the same time with a renewed energy.

We kick harder, and luckily, the tide gives us a push as well until our feet hit sand. We stumble up to get out of the water, and then we crash onto the sandy beach, collapsing with heavy breaths.

"We made it. I can't believe we just did that," Liesel says.

I nod. I don't want her to think we are out of danger, but I don't want to worry her either. We both need to rest before we move on. We just can't rest as long as we need, or it will all be for nothing.

The moon is shining down on us, and for once, I think we finally did something right.

"We should get up and find a better place to rest for tonight," I say.

"Okay."

Liesel pushes herself up and then holds out her hand to me. I don't want to seem weak, but she's the physically stronger between the two of us right now. I take her hand, and she helps me up.

"Can you walk?" she asks, still gripping my hand.

I look down at where our hands meet. "I can with you by my side."

"Good, then let's go."

We start walking up the beach and into the nearby forest. I don't know where we are in the world, and I don't care. We just need to find some shelter for tonight and hope that Rowan doesn't find us. In the morning, it will be easier for us to escape once we've regained our strength.

"What are we looking for?" Liesel asks.

I stop suddenly. "That—that is what we are looking for."

A small cabin sits in the woods. There are no cars parked in the gravel drive and no lights on.

I pull my gun from where I fastened it to my waistband.

"You're not going to shoot an innocent person," Liesel commands.

"I'm not, but it could be a trap. Or if someone does live here, they might try to protect their property if they see me. I won't hurt them unless they work for Rowan."

"Okay," she says.

"Stay here, and let me check it out."

I know she wants to protest, but she stays put as I circle the cabin. It looks like someone's summer cabin, but from the chill in the air, it's no longer summer here. I peer in through several windows, and after not seeing any sign of anyone, I circle to the backdoor and kick it open.

I search through the dark but don't find any signs of people currently living here. I walk to the front and open the door.

"It's clear. Come in," I say.

Liesel walks inside the cabin, and I shut the door behind her. The lights are still off, but I can tell she's shivering. I want nothing more than to put my arms around her. The only problem is my hands are still cuffed.

"Is it safe to turn the lights on?" Liesel asks.

I nod. It would be best to keep the lights off, but right now, we need simple comforts like electricity.

Liesel finds the light switch, and the lights turn on, illuminating us both.

I look at Liesel. She's drenched; goosebumps stand out through the sand and mud stuck to her legs. The leather jacket she kept on to keep her warm is dripping water everywhere, and her hair is a matted mess of water and seaweed.

She looks at me the same way, with disgusted disbelief. I'm just as soaked. My jeans are stuck to me, and the handcuffs dug ugly red marks around my wrists.

"We need to figure out a way to get those cuffs off you; then we can figure out the rest."

"Let's look for something to pick the lock." I saw an ax to chop firewood in front of the shed out back, but I'd prefer to have the cuffs off, not just separated.

Liesel starts to head toward one of the bedrooms to look.

"Stay," I say, unable to get my words out fast enough.

She turns and stares at me with her mouth open and eyes narrowed. "Why? I thought I was supposed to help you look for something to pick the lock with."

"Yes, but don't leave my sight. I don't want to worry about you, and I'm the only one with a weapon."

She keeps staring at me confusedly.

"Please," I add.

She returns to my side, and we head to the kitchen first.

I find a knife. She finds a paperclip.

I hand the knife to her. "Keep this with you at all times."

She takes it reluctantly, and I take the paperclip from her. It takes me a minute to get the first lock to come free on my left wrist, but then the second pops open easily, and the chains drop to the floor.

"Here," Liesel says, putting a cool dish rag over my wrists to soothe the pain.

"Thank you." I clear my throat. "You should shower and see if you can find any clothes to warm you up. I'll keep look out here and see if I can find any food for us."

She nods and then heads to the bathroom in back of the house; I follow at a distance to keep her somewhat near. I hate letting her out of my sight at all, but she needs to shower, and I will listen carefully for any intruders.

The fridge is practically empty besides some expired ketchup and dressing bottles. The pantries have a few cans of beans and vegetables. I pull those out and find some frozen pizzas in the deep freezer.

I pop the pizzas in the oven just as Liesel comes back into the kitchen.

"That wasn't a very long shower," I say.

"I didn't want to be apart from you any longer than I had to."

I turn to look at her and grin.

"I like this look."

She holds out her arms, and a flannel shirt hangs down well past her hands. Black sweatpants start to drop from her hips, but she grabs them.

"It's all I could find. A man must live in this house alone. I can't wait to see you in flannel."

I want to kiss her, to hold her in my arms, but I'm still soaking wet and filthy. She's clean, and I don't want to ruin her new clothes.

"I put a couple of frozen pizzas in the oven, but there are a couple of cans of beans on the counter if you get hungry before they're done."

She nods and walks to the kitchen to peek in on the pizzas.

"Here." I hold out the gun to her. "Hold on to this until I get back from the shower."

She stares at it. "No, it's better off with you. I have my knife. If someone comes, you'll save me."

I frown, hating her comment, but knowing she's right. I go to the bathroom to shower and dress as quickly as possible. The task is hard because of how sore and dizzy I am, never mind that I can barely lift my right arm to shoulder height. But I make do and dress in a flannel shirt and khaki pants.

When I return to the kitchen and catch sight of Liesel pulling the pizza out of the oven, my heart beats again.

She smiles at me as she places the pizzas on plates and then carries them to the small kitchen table where she's already filled two large glasses of water.

I try not to completely collapse into the chair as to not worry Liesel, but the sound the chairs makes when I sit gives me away. Liesel frowns, but we don't speak of it. We both dig into the food and drink every drop of water.

We both keep our eyes on each other as we eat, trying to find answers to all our burning questions without actually asking them. I need to ask her what happened. I need to find out how broken she is, how much she hates me for not rescuing her sooner. But I'm enjoying the way she's batting her eyelashes at me, the way her skin is glowing after her shower, and how adorable she looks in oversized flannel.

But I can't get past the bruises on her face, though. I certainly can't face what other bruises and marks I may be missing beneath the flannel.

"I'm sorry," I start after we both have enough food in our bellies to have this talk.

"What do you have to be sorry about?"

"I'm sorry that I couldn't save you. I got there too late." I think of Rowan's face, how smug he was that she'd made him a better offer. I close my eyes as I relive that memory. My mind goes to him beating her, raping her, taking everything left of her—all because I couldn't fight off two men, some chains, and a drug fast enough.

"Langston." I feel her hand on mine, and I open my eyes to find her kneeling in front of me.

"What are you doing?" I stand up abruptly and pull her up until she's standing too.

"I'm trying to break through your horrid imagination."

"What do you mean?"

She touches my hand to her face. "This is the worst that happened to me. I wasn't beaten. I wasn't tortured. I wasn't raped."

My eyes dart side to side, trying to figure out if she's telling the truth or not. But all I find is an odd kindness staring back at me.

"You saved me before anything could happen."

"Thank god," I exhale sharply and painfully.

She shivers.

"Let's go sit on the couch. I'll start a fire, and we can tell each other everything that happened and make a plan to get out of here," I say.

She nods, and our hands interlock as I lead her to a spot on the couch. Luckily, there is already wood by the fireplace, so I don't have to go out into the cold so soon. I start the fire and then sit down next to Liesel.

"Tell me everything."

She stares at me with a blank expression. "I think you've pieced together most of it."

"You took a deal with Rowan?"

She nods.

"Who did you choose to go free?"

She lets go of my hand. "I chose you."

I frown. "And that would mean that he'd kill you?"

She nods.

"Why? Why would you save me when I've been nothing but horrible to you? I killed your fiancé and threatened to kill you! Your decision was easy; why would you save me?"

She bites her lip as she considers her next words. I think she's going to say something about not being able to take a father away from her kids. Or a joke answer about wanting to be the one to kill me myself. Or maybe she thought if I was free, I could come back and save her before Rowan killed her, which would have been risky.

"You would have never killed me," she says.

I frown, although, maybe she's right. Maybe I wouldn't have. I don't know.

"I couldn't choose my life over yours. And I know you made the same decision. You chose to keep me alive instead of saving yourself."

"Why?" I ask again, begging her to say the words I've wanted to hear her say since I was fifteen and first noticed her turning into a woman, no longer just my neighbor, closest friend, and later enemy. I've wanted her to say that we could be something more for so long.

She sighs as if she can't quite say the words she wants to say. Instead, she bemoans, "Why couldn't you have saved me before?"

That is what ultimately broke us—me not saving her. She can't forgive me for it, and I can't forgive myself.

Then, she leans forward, thrusting herself into my arms as she presses her lips against mine, expressing what she can't say with her kisses.

CHAPTER 24

LIESEL

I don't know why I kiss Langston. To keep myself from saying the words on the edge of my tongue. To keep from having to explain myself to him. Or just because I want something life-affirming after what we went through.

Whatever the reason, the kiss is exactly what we both need.

It fills my soul with warmth, kindness, and passion. His lips heat my body better than the fire ever could.

Langston tries to use his right arm to pull me closer, but he winces, forgetting how injured it is. He switches to his far less injured left hand to grab my hips. He's trying to move me closer to him, so I help him out by scooting my hips until I'm as close to I can be to him without climbing on top of him.

He pulls back. "Climb on my lap, huntress."

I can't deny either of us right now.

"Don't let me hurt you," I say as I straddle his lap.

He pushes my hips down, until I'm resting on top of him. "You could never hurt me."

Then he leans back on the couch, and my body falls on top of his until my lips are once again pressed against his. My tongue pushes in his mouth this time, unable to resist tasting all of him.

Our moans echo through the room, tuning out the crackle of the fire.

Langston's hands rest at my hips and mine on his chest as we both enjoy each other's bodies. Each kiss pushes me closer to something I've wanted but denied myself for too long.

Closer.

Closer.

Closer.

Until I'm bursting with my decision. And yet, I still deny myself, deny us.

I lean back; I need to stop kissing Langston. I need to think straight before I make this decision.

"Is something wrong?"

Everything—everything is wrong.

I can't ask the question I really want. But sitting on Langston's lap, feeling the way I do, I feel like I don't need him to answer to know what I want—something I never thought I'd ever get.

"I choose you," I say.

Langston stares into my eyes, not understanding that I'm on the brink of a decision that will change both of our lives.

I always thought I hated Langston. I thought he hated me.

He chose to marry another. And I said yes to a fiancé.

We have both made threats and mistakes that have destroyed the other's life.

But none of that matters.

We could die tonight, tomorrow, next week, and all I can think is that I want Langston. I want him despite all the pain and heartbreak —whether it makes me a cheater and whore. No matter if I'm wrong and we are still enemies. If Langston still threatens my life after this night. If my heart completely breaks. Nothing will matter, because I will have had tonight.

"And I choose you," he says, before kissing my bottom lip tenderly, and falling back again with a sigh. He thinks our night is done and we should snuggle off together in bed. He doesn't know what I'm thinking. He doesn't realize that our words are as good as an 'I love you.'

"Fuck me, Langston."

His mouth falls open, just an inch, and his pupils dilate. "I don't think I heard you right."

"You did."

"Why...I mean, are you sure?"

"Yes, I've wanted you since I was sixteen. I never thought it would happen. The amount of hate, heartache, and pain we've caused each other almost ensured we never would, but if I'm going to die, I'd rather die knowing whether you are the worst or best fuck of my life."

He smiles. "Definitely the best. But I've got you beat; I wanted this since I was fifteen."

He grabs the back of my neck and pulls me to his lips, kissing me hard and hungrily on every spot of my lips as his tongue dances with mine. I'm so turned on from kissing him that I'm afraid I'm going to explode the second he enters me.

But then he pulls away, and I'm afraid he's changed his mind.

"Why are you frowning?" he asks, as he runs his thumb across my bottom lip.

"I'm afraid you're going to remember you're married, that you have a life waiting for you, that you hate me and are going to stop this."

He shakes his head. "My marriage means nothing, but if you need me to file for divorce, I will." He searches my eyes before continuing. "And I've never wanted anything more. I never thought you'd say yes, so I've never asked. But you don't ever have to doubt how much I want this. It probably won't change anything between us..." He kisses my ear, running his tongue lazily around it.

I shiver.

Then he continues. "But then again, it could change everything."

I catch my breath as his words put any doubt behind me. Things may end badly, I may become jealous or angry, but I won't regret this.

"Tonight, we are on the same side, huntress. I'm going to enjoy exploring every part of your body. I know we should sleep, but if these are to be my last hours, I can't imagine a better way to spend my time."

I suspect we've been on the same side more than just tonight, but I don't say that.

"Fuck me, killer. Make me forget every man before you, and spoil me for any man after."

When I say the word after, he growls possessively like he can't stand the thought of anyone after him.

I grin—that's up to him. Things won't change as much as Langston might like. Sex doesn't change much. We are still two broken people, hurt by the world, who, in return, have hurt each other to prevent ourselves from suffering further pain. We are still too controlling, too temperamental. If we tried to take a run at a real relationship, we'd spend the whole time fighting and bickering. Neither of us would survive, but we can survive one night of hot sex.

He stands with me in his arms.

"Langston!" I squeal. "Put me down; you don't want to hurt your arm."

He tilts his head, and then he buries his head against my neck. "I'd rather lose my arm than not fuck you properly. Don't worry about my arm; all I feel is you."

He starts walking, holding me as if he has the strength of an ox, not like a man who has had his shoulder dislocated, was drugged, and then swam miles in open water while having his arms handcuffed together.

"And I want to fuck you in a proper bed for the first time. Then I plan on having you on every surface in this house," he growls.

He carries me effortlessly as his lips hungrily find mine. He doesn't flick the lights on as we enter the bedroom, which disappoints me. I need to see all of him when he fucks me.

"You have to stop pouting like that, huntress."

He winks at me as he lays me down on the bed. The room is pretty dark, so I can barely make out his shadow until a spark flickers. There's another fireplace in the bedroom, and now that he's started it, the room simmers with a romantic glow.

He moves around the room, lighting some candles on the night-stands to light the room enough where I can make Langston out clearly, but not so much that it ruins the effect. When he's finished, he walks back over to the bed and stands at the foot of the bed.

"You're going to have to trust me, huntress."

"What if I can't?"

"Then, I'll have to show you that you can."

He starts on the buttons of his flannel shirt, unbuttoning them slowly.

"My sexy lumberjack," I tease as I watch him strip at the foot of the bed.

He looks at me seriously, stone-faced. The tone shifts between us from playful to pensive.

He finishes the last button, removes his shirt and drops it on the floor. I've seen him shirtless plenty of times, we've lived together shirtless, but there's something different about seeing him this way and knowing what's going to come next.

I assume he's going to stop there and then work on undressing me, but he doesn't stop. He unbuttons his khaki pants and pushes them down his body, until he's standing naked in front of me.

My eyes immediately memorize everything about him. Every hard line, sharp edge, and roughness about his body. Every scar, mark, and bruise. My favorite part is the V that starts at his hip bones and guides my eyes to his long, thick, and veiny cock.

As soon as I see him standing naked before me while I'm still fully clothed, all my doubts vanish. My mouth waters, my eyes dilate, and my body tingles with anticipation.

He smiles softly at my reaction, knowing that such a small action gained a tiny bit of my trust. He didn't give me control, but he made himself vulnerable, which is a good start.

I tingle with anticipation and start unbuttoning my own shirt. He looks at me uncomfortably, holding back, but he lets me unbutton my own shirt. I need some control now in order to give up a little later, so he lets me have this moment.

The shirt falls open, and my bare breasts stare up at him. The bruise around my ribs has turned yellow and green and is barely visible beneath the glow of the fireplace, thank god.

His eyes grow, and his body tenses as he stares down at me. His hands are twitching to touch me, but he's letting me control this moment. I don't know how this is going to work between us—both battling to drive the sexual experience in the way we want.

I hook my thumbs into the waistband of my sweatpants and begin to move them down over my hips as I lay in front of Langston.

He bites his lips and fists his hands, rooting his feet into the ground to let me finish. But as I struggle to get the pants off my feet, he steps in.

He grabs my pants and yanks them off until I'm lying naked in front of him.

There's a part of me that wants him to become the alpha male inside him that he brings out when he's with other women. And then there's a part of me that wants his sweetness and obedience to my orders.

"Stop thinking so much," he whispers.

I rake my bottom lip through my teeth. "I'm trying, but I need you to promise me something first. Don't lie to me tonight. Not with your words and definitely not with your body. If there is one thing I need most of all, it's for us to be completely honest. If you hate fucking me, tell me."

He frowns. "First, it's not possible for me to hate fucking you. But I know what you mean—I won't lie, not to you, not now."

"I won't lie either."

He slowly inches himself over my body until his strong body is hovering over mine, not touching. I stare at his arms that must be aching.

"I won't lie, but I'm not going to be sweet and let you make the decisions. Your brain is on overdrive thinking too much right now." He takes my hand and kisses my palm. "Can you handle me taking control?"

A million sparks fly through my hand where he kisses me. "For now. I'll let you know when I want it back."

"You're something else."

"Kiss me," I say, bossing him around.

He leans down to kiss me but misses my lips purposefully and landing on the corner of my mouth.

I moan, needing him to kiss me properly. Needing him to press his body against mine. Needing so much and not sure if I'm going to get it tonight.

He takes his time kissing each corner of my mouth, then each side of my neck until I'm squirming beneath him. Only then does he kiss my lips. By then, any doubts or thoughts have disappeared.

His kisses are hungry and wild, not as controlled as I know he likes them to be—it seems he's letting go too.

Neither of us needs to be in control. We just need to let our bodies and souls take over.

Our eyes meet and seem to agree. His body presses down gently on top of mine. Our bodies fit perfectly, as if we were designed for each other.

His cock presses down on my lower stomach as his mouth reconnects with mine. His hand finds my breast as mine trails down his back. And then, as if we both decide at the exact same time, we flip. I'm on top; he's beneath me.

I claw at his chest and rub up against his cock, using him to get myself wetter before he enters me. His hands massage my breasts, flicking his thumbs across my sensitive nipples.

"You're drenched," Langston says with a smug smile.

I am—I'm so ready for him. I've been ready for him for years.

I lean down and kiss him as he bucks up against me.

Then, at the same time, we freeze.

"Condom?" I ask.

He frowns. "Any chance you think our cabin friend has one?"

I crawl up the bed, reluctantly letting go of Langston to dig into the drawer of the rugged-looking nightstand. I find cigarettes, a lighter, and a small bottle of rum, but no condoms.

I look around the room and see the door is open to the bathroom.

"Be right back," I run into the bathroom. I check every drawer and cabinet, but I find none.

I sigh, as I grip the counter.

"It's okay, I can just make you come," Langston says from the doorway. His eyes pour over me, drenching my pussy further. He looks at me like I'm the only woman in the world he's ever had eyes for.

"I could pull out?" he asks, as he steps behind me and wraps his arms around my waist.

I take a deep breath. I don't want to have our first and possibly only time together lack feeling him coming inside me.

I meet his eyes in the mirror. His eyes are soft, kind, and maybe even loving. Maybe I'm reading too much into his expression, but I know what I want.

"I trust you," I say.

He sucks in a breath when I touch his hand and slide his hand down my front so he can feel how wet I still am for him. Throughout my search, nothing changed; if anything, I want him more now than before.

"I'll pull—"

"No, I trust you. Take control. Fuck me like you want." If I get pregnant, we'll figure it out.

He fists my hair with one hand as he kisses me roughly down my neck and spine, while his other hand dips between my legs. He already knows how to work my body and clit, touching me with just enough pressure to make me weak in the knees.

"I've dreamed of this so many fucking nights...and as much as I would love to fuck you here and look into your eyes in the mirror as you come, I want you in a fucking bed our first time."

He flips me around until I fall into his body. I jump as he grabs my ass and hungrily kisses my body.

We walk into the bedroom and collapse on the bed together—full of sweat, wetness, and saliva. All of it turns me on more.

He settles between my legs at the same time he lifts my hands and binds them together in his fist above my head. He doesn't push inside me; he lowers his head to bite my nipple with his teeth.

I expect there to be a nervous anxiety as he takes control of my body, but it never comes.

I trust him.

"Tell me you want me. Tell me how dirty your thoughts are. Tell me you want my cock." I see the tiniest hint of concern in his eyes, not sure if I'm going to back out. He really needs this, as much or more than me.

I slide my hips down, just enough to envelope the tip of his cock, but that's all the power he gives me. He slams inside me, filling me completely.

I gasp at how he fills me.

He stills as soon as he's fully inside me and our eyes lock once again. His fill with tears. He leans down and kisses me so tenderly on the lips. "Are you okay? I meant to be gentle, but I can't control myself with you."

"I'm more than okay."

"Good, because being inside you is fucking incredible."

Together we decide wordlessly when to start moving. My hips rock at the same time his begin to thrust, which makes us both smile. He's still gripping my hands above my head as he thrusts inside.

I've never felt anything like it—not with Waylon, not with any man. With Langston, I don't want to fight him. And even though he has absolute control over my body, I feel like I have all the power. If I move my hips, he moves his. If I slow my breath, he speeds up until I'm panting again.

"This—this is..." he can't finish his words as he slams into me.

I arch, driving him as deeply as I can into my body. We're both close to coming. We are close to ending this chapter. Seconds before we come, Langston releases my hands.

"I trust you, too."

One more thrust, and he's filling me with his warm cum and screaming my name, which pushes me into an explosion of an orgasm of my own.

"There was no way I would have killed you, not even if my life depended on it," Langston says, still inside me as he rolls himself onto his back and me on top. "I could never hurt you, huntress. All I've ever wanted to do was protect you from the demons, me included."

He would have never killed me. We said we would only tell truths tonight, and I believe him. He could never hurt me.

That also means that when he killed Waylon, he knew exactly what he was doing somehow. It's time to spill more of the truth, so he'll stop beating himself up. But for now, I want to fuck him until the sun rises.

CHAPTER 25

LANGSTON

I have to leave Liesel to get us some food. So far, I've done well on keeping my promise of fucking her on every surface in this small cabin. I've fucked her twice in the bed, once in the bathroom, and once on the couch. But unfortunately, we need more fuel if we are going to continue.

I feel the need to make up for a lifetime of not having her in one night. We have no idea what tomorrow brings. *Could Rowan's men be outside right now, ready to kill us? And if we survive, how do we deal with our pasts?*

I scrounge up some bottles of water and start digging through the cans to see which we should choose, when I feel Liesel's hands wrap around my naked waist, and her front rubs up against my back.

Jesus, one-touch and I'm already hard again. My shoulder is going to be sore tomorrow. I could possibly be doing permanent damage to the nerves in my arm, but I don't care. There isn't one thing about tonight that I'll regret.

"I missed you," Liesel says.

I moan as she finds my cock with her fingers and slides me through her fist.

"I've been gone for less than two minutes."

"It was too long," she says.

I groan, and I know the food is going to have to wait. There is someone I'd much rather eat. I let her thrust her hand over me one more time, ensuring I'm hard before I turn around.

She squeals when I slam her down on the counter, and part of the cabinet door falls open. It isn't the first piece of furniture I've broken tonight. The bedframe broke right down the middle I fucked her so hard.

I spread her legs wide and then sweep my fingers over her opening. She's wet. She's been wet for me all night. I've seen her fuck Waylon all night, but this feels different. With him, she required to be in control. She tied him up, bossed him around, forced him to wear a condom.

Tonight, we are both just going with the flow. Doing everything we've ever dreamed of doing. Living for all the years we might not.

The second I find her wet, I brace her legs as I push inside, slamming her hard against the cabinet. We both like wild, passionate sex. The kind that breaks things and pushes our limits. The kind where we battle with our tongues, our touch, our thrusts.

She grabs my hair and yanks hard as I pound into her again. She tilts my head and takes over my mouth while I grab harder onto her thighs.

I don't know how we fit so well together. I was always afraid sex with Liesel was going to be impossible because of the damage we come from. But somehow, our roughness and insecurities fit together. I push and she pulls. When she yanks, I jerk. Like magnets, that if pushed together the wrong way repel each other, when we turned the correct way, we are pulled together by forces greater than ourselves.

She bites my lip as I grab hold of her ass and deepen my thrusts.

She growls.

I moan.

Until tears threaten her eyes.

I hurt her—fuck.

But it's too late to stop now. Our orgasms are crashing down on us in waves. Another chance that I could get her pregnant. I never asked if she's on the pill or another form of birth control that might still have some effect now. I didn't ask what day she is in her cycle. But I suspect because of the conditions we've been held in, combined with stress and lack of food, it's very unlikely that I'll get her pregnant. Not that I wouldn't welcome another child, but I don't want to complicate an already complicated situation.

I grab onto her hips as I fill her with more of my seed, and I feel her orgasm squeeze around me. Only once our orgasms have passed can I finally wipe away her tear.

"I'm sorry, was I too rough?"

She smiles through her tears. "No, I'm sorry. I haven't cried in years. You opened the floodgates, and now I cry about everything."

"Are these happy tears?"

"They're everything tears."

I run my hand through her wavy, blonde locks, and then I kiss her forehead. I don't know how I ever thought I could kill her, no matter what she did. Liesel Dunn doesn't deserve to die, and no matter what nickname she uses, I'll never be her killer.

"Now, we really must eat or drink something or we'll pass out," I say.

She pouts.

I laugh and turn around. "Climb on."

She laughs as she climbs onto my back and wraps her legs and arms around my naked body as I begin to open drawers to find a can opener.

"How are we going to get back tomorrow, do you think?" Liesel asks.

I haven't told her I found a satellite phone in one of the drawers. I'm not ready to be rescued yet. I'm afraid of what will happen when we return to the real world.

I finally got Liesel. I'm not ready to give her up. I don't know if I'll ever be.

"Together," I answer.

I don't know what will happen tomorrow, but we will arrive there together.

CHAPTER 26

LIESEL

"Enzo is coming to get us," Langston says, waking me.

I pull the covers up to my chin but don't wake up fully. I'm too happy in the mattress, even though I only slept for probably less than an hour last night and Langston had to sleep directly on the floor since we broke the frame.

Langston walks over and sits on my edge of the bed.

I frown—he's put boxer briefs back on, which means he's not going to fuck me again.

"I have coffee," he says, holding a red camping mug out to me.

I sigh but sit up and take the mug from him.

He smiles softly at me as his eyes drag down from my matted hair to my naked torso.

"Wait...Enzo is coming?"

"Yes, I found a satellite phone when I was looking for the coffee beans. I let you sleep for as long as I could, but we need to leave in five to meet him in a nearby field."

I sip the bitter coffee. We're leaving. I should be happy we are getting rescued. Rowan and his men won't be able to kill us, but I'm not happy. I've never been more unhappy.

"What's wrong? Is the coffee bad?"

I nod. "It's a bit stale."

"You can sleep on the helicopter, and we can get more caffeine when we get back to Miami."

I give him a measured smile. "I better get dressed."

His eyes dart away to give me privacy as I head to the bathroom. I purposely don't close the door as I shower quickly, hoping that Langston will join me, but after spending all of my five minutes in the shower, I get dressed, disappointed and lonely.

It seems our one night together is over. Our connection is all in the past now. The sex, lust, passion is all gone.

I run my hand through my hair, as I can't find a comb, when Langston finally pops his head in. "Ready?"

I nod and follow him out of the house. We are both wearing our lumberjack outfits again, but I couldn't find any shoes that fit me. All I have on my feet are thick socks, unlike Langston, who found real shoes. He moves much faster through the thick brush than I can. I keep stepping on thorns, and my soreness and foul mood aren't helping.

"Hop on," Langston says, crouching down in front of me.

"I can walk."

"I know, but I'm tired of listening to your grumbling, and we'll get out of here and to safety much faster if you get on my back."

I jump on his back with a thud.

He grunts but doesn't say anything else as he starts jogging with me on his back. I'm impressed he has the stamina after last night. I try to keep my thoughts on last night, but all I can think about going home means going to where his wife and kids live.

I'm a horrible, horrible person.

"We're almost there."

I hear the buzzing of the helicopter before we reach the clearing, and my heart flutters. I didn't realize that I was anxious about getting out of here until now. I almost died. Only now am I safe.

Enzo's helicopter comes into view, and Langston carries me on. We both settle into the back seat. Beckett sits up front next to Enzo.

"You two both okay? Any injuries we need to take care of right away?" Beckett shouts over the whirling blades.

"No, we're good. Just get us home," Langston answers.

We both grab a pair of headsets as the helicopter takes off.

"Press this button, and you will talk to me only." Langston points to a red button on the headset. "Use this button to talk to everyone." He points to a blue button.

I press the blue button. "Thank you both for saving us."

"We were worried sick. I'm glad you called; we had no idea where you went," Enzo says.

"A Mr. Rowan Wells had us. He was after the treasure," Langston says.

"We have a team out ready to take them out. He won't be a problem again," Enzo says.

Langston looks at me and pushes the button that allows only the two of us to speak to each other. "You should sleep." He holds out his arms, indicating that I can sleep on his lap if I want.

I yawn. I should sleep. But I want to get a few things straightened out first.

"What are we going to do when we get back?"

Langston fidgets with the cord connected to his headset. "I don't know exactly. What I do know is we need to start working together as far as the treasure goes. We can decide who gets it or how to split it later, but if we are going to be attacked constantly, we are stronger together."

I nod, agreeing. "So, where do we start?"

Langston stares at me a moment, considering his answer. "Peru."

"Peru?"

"That's all my side said. To start the search in Peru."

"Where exactly in Peru? Peru doesn't give us a whole lot to go off of."

"The only other clue was cut off. The letters 'tayt' and then the rest was smudged. I assume we start in Machu Pichu and go from there. It's the most famous place in all of Peru."

"No, it's Ollantaytambo. My half had the letters 'Ollan.' It's an Inca town in the Sacred City."

He nods excitedly. We just worked together to figure out where to start. We now have three of the clues from the paper. The city to start in. That others will be searching. And that to get the treasure, you must be married. Langston is. I'm not.

"I need to find someone to marry. That will double our odds of being able to get the treasure."

Langston shakes his head viciously. "No, you aren't getting married."

I roll my eyes. "You're not the boss of me. And you're married. I should be too. That's what's in the note."

"We'll discuss it later," Langston says, switching off his headset and placing it on the hook.

I sigh and take mine off. *One step forward, two steps back.*

I lean back and try to close my eyes to get some sleep, but there is no use. I'm infuriated with Langston. I keep my eyes closed, though, hoping I'll fall asleep eventually. Slumber never comes with Langston snoring next to me.

"Hello," I hear Enzo say faintly from the front. "Yes, I have them." I realize he must be taking a call from Kai.

I smile. I'm jealous of their relationship. It wasn't always easy for them, but it was always clear to everyone around them how right they were for each other, even when I was trying to steal Enzo away for myself.

"Yes, our plan worked."

My ears perk up at that. *Plan? What plan?*

"They were gossiping like two schoolgirls and batting eyelashes at each other. I think they are a bit grouchy from lack of sleep. But yes, Rowan said they were willing to die for one another, that they loved one another. They're planning on working together from now on."

I can't believe I'm hearing this. I open my eyes the tiniest of bits to look over at Langston, but he's still sound asleep.

It was a setup—all of it. They hired Rowan and his team to pretend to kidnap us so Langston and I would be forced to work out our problems.

I'm pissed. I can't believe they played us like that. Unfortunately, there is nothing I can do about it until we land.

♡

"We need to make a quick stop here to refuel; then we'll take you on to your house, Langston," Enzo says before he hops out. Beckett follows, and they both head inside a hangar.

I turn to Langston. "We were set up."

He yawns. "What are you talking about?"

"Rowan was hired by Enzo and all of your supposed friends to try and push us together."

He huffs. "You aren't serious."

"I am. I overheard Enzo talking to Kai on the phone while you were sleeping."

"You heard over the sound of the rotor blades while Enzo was talking into his headset?" He raises his eyebrows in disbelief.

"Yes."

"They would hire someone to kidnap us, torture us, and threaten to kill us—why?"

"Because they are sick of us fighting and playing games like the sex yacht. They thought if we went through a life-threatening ordeal together, it would bring us closer together."

It worked. We did.

For a second, I think Langston is going to believe me. Then he blinks rapidly and runs his hand through his hair. "That's crazy."

"Crazy as me pretending to kill your best friend?"

He narrows his eyes at me.

"Look!" I point into the small hanger that Enzo and Beckett entered. There is a man standing with them for only a second. A man in a suit with sharp-looking hair. He laughs with them then disappears down a hallway.

"That was Rowan," Langston growls.

"See! I told you they schemed against us."

"Well, let's have a little fun in return." He smirks.

I smile along with him. "What do you have in mind?"

Langston climbs into the front seat and pops a compartment open, pulling out a gun. He hands it to me and then pulls his own gun from his waistband. "Let's go get justice for our kidnapping."

My eyes widen. "We aren't really going to kill Rowan, are we?"

"No, but Enzo and Beckett will think we are going to."

I smile, liking this plan. "I just wish Kai, Siren, and Zeke were here to see us."

He thinks a moment. "I think I can arrange that."

I have no idea what he has planned, but I trust him.

Dammit, I trust him. I trust him with everything, even after our quarrel. No matter if their methods were fucked up, their plan worked. Langston and I are a lot closer now.

We walk casually out of the helicopter with our guns in hand. Enzo and Beckett aren't paying us any attention as we stroll to the back of the building. Langston pops a door open and holds his gun out. I follow him doing the same, even though I feel like my gun is for show more than anything else. We already know I won't kill anyone.

We sneak down the hallway before popping into a room where we find Rowan chatting with a pilot.

"Don't move," Langston says, aiming the gun at him.

Rowan freezes with terror in his eyes. "Now, calm down. We should talk about things."

"Talk about what? How you tortured and threatened to kill us? You're not walking out of here alive," I say.

Rowan's face turns pale.

"Mr. Black, will you come in here and explain things a moment?" Rowan shouts.

"You don't want Enzo. He'll kill you right away, while I plan on killing you slowly."

Enzo and Beckett round the corner. To their credit, they don't give anything away. They assess the situation and wait to see what we will do.

"Who is this man?" Enzo asks.

"The man who kidnapped and tortured us," I say.

Rowan's eyes dart to Enzo for help.

"Put your hands behind your back, Rowan," Langston says.

He complies.

"Here, tie him up with these, Liesel. And if you move an inch while she ties you up, I'll shoot you in the balls," Langston orders.

Rowan tenses but keeps his hands behind his back while I tie him up.

Langston trains his gun on his head as he grabs him by the arm and leads him out of the building.

"Not here, Langston. Let's get him back to headquarters, then we can take care of him," Enzo says. It's the first thing he says that gives him away. Enzo takes care of business wherever and whenever. He doesn't need to wait and do it back at headquarters.

Langston nods as he leads Rowan into the back of the helicopter. I hop in the front, and then Langston hops into the pilot's seat before Enzo and Beckett can make it to us. He starts the engine, and then we are taking off.

I should be thinking about how betrayed I was by people who used to be my friends, but all I can think about is how good Langston looks flying a helicopter.

Langston laughs, reading my face as Rowan moans like he's been shot or something behind us.

"Will you shut up?" I say.

"Don't kill me. Mr. Black was the one who hired me. It was all a game to try and get you two closer together. It was for your own good. I hardly touched you two. I gave you a couple of bruises and Langston a dislocated shoulder. I just did what Mr. Black told me to do," he quivers.

"We know," we both say with smug smiles.

"So, you aren't going to kill me?"

"No, but they don't know that. We'll let them think you are drowning in the middle of the ocean."

He laughs. "And where will you hide me?"

Langston winks at me. "In the middle of the fucking ocean." He presses a button, and the side door opens, then he flys the helicopter sideways until Rowan falls out the door and splashes down in the water.

A phone lights up in front of us, and Langston answers. "Yes?"

"Turn the fuck back around," Enzo says.

"Why would I do that?"

"The man you just kidnapped works for me. He's a good man. He has a daughter. Don't kill him."

"His blood is on your hands. You fucking set us up, had us

tortured, and thought it was for the best. I don't want to see your face, or you'll end up with a black eye and the inability to have more kids."

"Where is he?" Enzo huffs.

"The middle of the ocean, just like Liesel and I had to endure. Except I tied his hands behind his back instead of the front. You better hope he's a good swimmer." Then Langston hangs up.

"That was cruel."

"You disapprove?"

"No. It was cruel, but definitely deserved."

"You know we have more in common than just being good lays?"

I smile at the twinkle in his eye. Maybe there's a chance yet of one more fuck.

CHAPTER 27

LANGSTON

I put the helicopter down near my place on a field by the beach. I turn the engine off and then turn to Liesel. In a matter of minutes, we are going to have to deal with the real world.

Kai is going to call me to lecture me about hurting Rowan, even though the guy got a lot less than he deserved. A few minutes in the cool ocean water is nothing compared to what we dealt with at his hands. I don't care who hired him; he's still an asshole. We'll have to deal with Phoenix and possibly explain our relationship to my kids.

But we can put off the inevitable for a few more moments.

We attack each other at the exact same time, so quickly that Liesel still has her seatbelt on and gets pulled back as she grabs for my neck.

I laugh and unbuckle her before I pull her hard across the seat and onto my lap. I grab her neck and kiss her lips with everything I've been holding back since I woke her up with coffee this morning.

"I thought we were done. I thought you wanted nothing to do with me," she says hungrily between kisses.

"I'll never be done with you, huntress. Even if there comes a day when I can't kiss you like this, I'll never be done with you."

I hike her shirt up as my hands run over her smooth skin, trying to memorize everything.

No, I won't be so defeated. Why shouldn't we keep fucking? We are two consenting adults, who—

"Fucking heaven," I groan as Liesel's hands work their way down my pants.

She sucks on my bottom lip with a smirk to her eyes.

"Ever done it in a helicopter?" she squeals.

I shake my head.

After that, everything becomes frantic. Our hands, our mouths, our eyes. Mine work on her pants as hers work my mouth. Then she's unbuttoning my pants, while I'm pushing up her shirt.

I take her nipple in my mouth too roughly, but I love the sharp intake of breath. She retaliates by gripping my cock just a little too hard. But that's how it is between us—a wicked fight that leaves us both with more pleasure than we deserve.

At the same time, I grab her hips as she slides down on my cock.

"God, I've missed you."

"You had me less than five hours ago, and you can have me—"

"Langston?" Phoenix says.

Liesel freezes in my arms, trying to hide, run, anything to not be here right now. Meanwhile, my cock, and even a sliver of my heart, can't let her go.

I don't look at Phoenix. I look at Liesel. Phoenix I know how to deal with, but Liesel I have no idea.

"Give us a minute, Dunn," I say to Phoenix before realizing my mistake—Dunn is also Liesel's last name.

Liesel rips herself off of me, and I've never felt so bare.

She throws open the door and takes off before I even have my pants up.

I jump out of the helicopter after her, not sure what to do. When I hear Phoenix shouting after me, I don't stop.

I have to talk to Liesel.

But then I hear laughter that makes me stop—my kids.

CHAPTER 28

LIESEL

I run, not because I'm afraid of Phoenix. Not because I care what she has to say, but because of what Langston will say or do. I can't be here to witness him choosing her over me. I'm a strong woman, but I can't handle that.

I'll have to go back eventually and talk to him, but I won't until after he's greeted his wife.

His wife.

How could I be so stupid?

I sit down on the sand, staring out at the ocean. My flannel shirt and sweatpants are going to be too warm to sit out here in the sun too long, but I just need a little time to let my heart settle.

I hear Langston approaching a second later.

My heart spurs to life, happy that he is choosing me over her. *But maybe it's just to let me down first before he leaves me and grovels to her?*

"It's okay. You can go talk to her. Things can go back to how they were before. We will stop the fighting, stop trying to rip each other apart. We'll just find the treasure and stop people from coming after us. I'll go stay at Siren and Zeke's. I need to thank them for going along with my scheme and see if they were involved with Enzo and Kai's plan."

He sits down next to me as I ramble.

I guess we are doing this now.

"Tell me how you feel, Liesel. The truth."

"We don't have to keep telling the truth to each other. That was before; things are different now. I can lie to you."

"You won't."

"How do you know?"

"I just do."

I can't tell him how I feel because I don't even know. But I can offer him a bit of truth that has been eating at me—another problem we have to solve.

"I don't know how I feel or what you and I should do next. Date? Keep fucking? Become your mistress?"

He winces at the last one. "I would never ask you to be my mistress. Phoenix means nothing to me, not like Waylon meant to you."

My eyes meet his gaze. "Waylon didn't mean what you think he meant to me."

He frowns. "I saw you mourn his death. You fell apart. You cried for the first time in years. You arranged to fake my best friend's death to hurt me back. Don't tell me that Waylon meant nothing to you."

"Waylon was blackmailing me."

He tilts his head, and his eyes plead for that to be true, revealing a hint of his true feelings. Langston wants me for himself. He doesn't want me to have been taken by another man, even a dead man.

"He was blackmailing me—forcing me to play the part of his fiancée and eventually wife in order to find the whereabouts of my son. After Kai returned him to his adopted parents when I refused to see him, thinking he was better off with his adoptive parents, I changed my mind. I wanted to check up on him, but when I went to the adoptive parents' address, they were gone. I searched, but I couldn't find any sign of them.

"And then I met Waylon. He had the information I needed. Once we were properly married, he'd tell me what happened to my son."

"You didn't love Waylon?"

"No, I didn't love him. I thought he was a horrible man, but he was the only person who could tell me what happened to my son."

We hear the kids playing in the sand, then Phoenix's voice telling them not to go near the water.

"It seems you and I were always destined to be with others. You made a good choice in Phoenix. She seems like a loyal person and loving mother. I'm happy for you. Last night was nice, but it's time to go back to reality. You belong with Phoenix, and I belong—"

"We are fated to be together. That's how I've always felt, and you've always fought it. I don't know if we are still destined to be together, but I do know something that might change your mind."

"Honestly, Langston, I don't think I can be with any man right now. I need to focus on finding my son." *Besides, I already know my fate is to be alone.*

"I can help in that department."

"What do you mean?" my heart skips.

"I can help you find your son."

I shake my head. "I've already had everyone's help. No one could find him."

"That's because I didn't want them to know. I didn't want him found until I was ready to tell you."

"Langston, do you know where my son is?"

"Yes." He tilts his head toward his two kids playing in front of us. "He's right in front of you."

♡

THANK YOU SO MUCH FOR READING VICIOUS! LANGSTON & LIESEL'S story continues in ENDLESS: A Truth or Lies World Collection!
Only one of us can live. And I know who that person will be...

One-click ENDLESS now >

"AN ABSOLUTE MUST READ SERIES. LOVE THIS!"

ALSO BY ELLA MILES

LIES SERIES:

Lies We Share: A Prologue

Vicious Lies

Desperate Lies

Fated Lies

Cruel Lies

Dangerous Lies

Endless Lies

SINFUL TRUTHS:

Sinful Truth #1

Twisted Vow #2

Reckless Fall #3

Tangled Promise #4

Fallen Love #5

Broken Anchor #6

TRUTH OR LIES:

Taken by Lies #1

Betrayed by Truths #2

Trapped by Lies #3

Stolen by Truths #4

Possessed by Lies #5

Consumed by Truths #6

DIRTY SERIES:

Dirty Beginning

Dirty Obsession

Dirty Addiction

Dirty Revenge

Dirty: The Complete Series

ALIGNED SERIES:

Aligned: Volume 1 (Free Series Starter)

Aligned: Volume 2

Aligned: Volume 3

Aligned: Volume 4

Aligned: The Complete Series Boxset

UNFORGIVABLE SERIES:

Heart of a Thief

Heart of a Liar

Heart of a Prick

Unforgivable: The Complete Series Boxset

MAYBE, DEFINITELY SERIES:

Maybe Yes

Maybe Never

Maybe Always

Definitely Yes

Definitely No

Definitely Forever

STANDALONES:

Pretend I'm Yours

Finding Perfect

Savage Love

Too Much

Not Sorry

ABOUT THE AUTHOR

Ella Miles writes steamy romance, including everything from dark suspense romance that will leave you on the edge of your seat to contemporary romance that will leave you laughing out loud or crying. Most importantly, she wants you to feel everything her characters feel as you read.

Ella is currently living her own happily ever after near the Rocky Mountains with her high school sweetheart husband. Her heart is also taken by her goofy five year old black lab who is scared of everything, including her own shadow.

Ella is a USA Today Bestselling Author & Top 50 Bestselling Author.

Stalk Ella at:
www.ellamiles.com
ella@ellamiles.com